TALES OF
THE MONKS

TALES
OF THE MONKS

FROM THE

GESTA ROMANORUM

EDITED BY

MANUEL KOMROFF

TUDOR PUBLISHING COMPANY

NEW YORK

New Edition April, 1936

CONTENTS

CONTENTS

viii CONTENTS

CONTENTS

ix

PREFATORY NOTE

The Tales of the Monks or *Gesta Romanorum* were the most popular stories of the Middle Ages. These tales of feudal manners, eastern imagery, exploits of classical heroes, adventurous chivalry and mystical spiritual wonders stand at the fountain-head of European fiction. They were the source, directly or indirectly, of literature in Boccaccio, Chaucer, Shakespeare, Schiller, Rossetti and many lesser known writers.

Originally *The Tales of the Monks* were intended to serve as a manual for preachers. They were compiled mainly to illustrate moral and religious virtue. But the tales served more than one use. For the lazy monk they took the place of long and difficult religious works. They were also easier and safer to read than the classics. And besides all this they had a distant and colorful romantic air which allowed them to be concluded with an edifying and symbolic application. The age was one of great mystery and everything was supposed to contain a double or a hidden meaning. Acteon, the Greek hunter, torn to pieces by his hounds, became at this time a symbol of the persecution of Christ.

These wearisome and preaching applications, so remote from the essence of the tales, have been entirely omitted from the present edition, which was revised with the view of restoring these famous tales to the field of fiction from which they originated and where they rightly belong. These tales were not invented by the monks but were compiled by them, probably about the year 1340. They became quite fashionable before 1358 when Boccaccio was supposed to have completed his Decameron.

In the migrations of fiction every tale in this volume is important and each helps to illustrate the incorporation of eastern fable and Gothic traditions with the classical story.

A great many of these stories had their origin in the East. Some can be traced to Greek and Latin historical legends and a few to European folk-lore. A direct link may be established with the writings of Lucius Seneca, who lived in Cordova, Spain, and was well known in Rome during the Early Empire. Seneca prepared ten books of imaginary legal cases to be used in training Greek and Roman orators. Many of the romantic elements of Seneca's themes were later incorporated in *The Tales of the Monks*. As Seneca was born about 54 B. C. and died A. D. 39, it is certain that his themes, as well as those from the East, were without Christian applications.

Tales of great antiquity in the East were eagerly seized by the hordes who visited Palestine as pilgrims or soldiers. Eastern story-tellers related many of them in the bazaars and during long periods of idleness. They became a pleasant source of diversion and entertainment and being related many times over were not soon forgotten.

In this manner the stories of the East came to the monks of Europe. The compilation made by the monks has not only proved a source of inspiration for literary masters but it also stands as one of the most interesting and very earliest European collection of tales.

The task of bringing these tales back to the realm of fiction has made necessary several minor changes. These are mainly in the paragraphing and punctuation. Simple titles have also been proposed for each story; titles that are directly related to the narrative of the tale and not to the moral application found in the early editions. These liberties were taken only to make the tales more readable. The text, however, except for an occasional correction, has been kept in its original wording and retains its rare medieval flavor.

M. K.

THE TEXT

Of *The Tales of the Monks* over 165 hand-lettered manuscripts in both Latin and German have survived. With the invention of printing these tales at once went into many editions. The earliest English translation was published in a Black Letter edition between the years 1510 and 1515. This was revised by Richard Robinson who brought out as many as six editions during the years 1577–1601. Between the years 1648 and 1703 as many as eight impressions came forward as well as a new translation from the Latin by someone who signs himself "B. P."

The translation by the Rev. Charles Swan was printed in 1824 in two volumes. This translation was later revised by Wynnard Hooper and in 1877 printed in Bohn's famous library. This last text forms the basis for the present edition.

TALES OF THE MONKS

TALES OF THE MONKS FROM THE GESTA ROMANORUM

Tale 1

THE DAUGHTER OF A KING

POMPEY WAS A WISE AND POWERFUL KING. HE HAD AN
only daughter, remarkable for her beauty, of whom he was
extremely fond. He committed her to the custody of five
soldiers; and charged them, under the heaviest penalties, to
preserve her from every possible injury. The soldiers were on
guard night and day; and before the door of her bed-chamber they suspended a burning lamp, that the approach of an
intruder might be the more easily detected. And they kept
a dog, whose bark was loud and piercing, to rouse them from
sleep.

From all these circumstances, it would appear that every
precaution had been taken: but, unhappily, the lady panted
for the pleasures of the world. As she was one day looking
abroad, a certain duke passed by, who regarded her with im-
pure and improper feelings. Observing her beauty, and ascertaining that she was the reputed heir to the throne, he
became enamoured, and made her many promises to obtain
her consent; which she, hoping much from his words, gave,
and straightway slew the dog, put out the lamp, and rising
by night, fled with the duke.

In the morning, however, inquiries were set on foot. Now, there was at that time in the king's palace a champion of remarkable prowess, who ever did battle for justice in that realm. When he understood the contempt which the lady had exhibited towards her parent, he armed himself, and hastened after the fugitives. A battle speedily ensued, in which the champion triumphed, and decapitated the seducer on the spot. The lady he conveyed back to the palace; but being refused admittance to the presence of her father, thenceforward she passed her time in bitterly bewailing her misdeeds.

It happened that a wise person in the emperor's court heard of her repentance. On all occasions when his services were required, he had proved himself an active mediator between majesty and its offenders; and being now moved with compassion, he reconciled her to her indignant parent, and betrothed her to a powerful nobleman. After this she received many and diverse gifts from her father. In the first place he presented to her a tunic, which extended to the heel, composed of the finest and richest woof, having the following inscription:—"I have forgiven thee, see that thou add not to thy offence."

From the king also she received a golden coronet, bearing the legend, "Thy dignity is from me." The champion, who had conquered in her behalf, gave a ring, on which was engraved, "I have loved thee, learn thou to love."

The mediator also bestowed a ring, inscribed as follows, "What have I done? How much? Why?" Another ring was presented by the king's son; and there was engraved upon it, "Thou art noble, despise not thy nobility." Her own brother bestowed a similar gift, of which the motto ran thus:— "Approach; fear not—I am thy brother." Her husband likewise added a golden signet, which confirmed his wife in the inheritance of his goods, and bore this superscription, "Now thou art espoused, sin no more."

The lady received these various presents, and kept them as long as she lived. She succeeded in regaining the favour of those whose affections her former conduct had alienated, and closed her days in peace.

Tale 2

THE COMMAND OF DUTY

THE EMPEROR TITUS MADE A LAW, THAT WHOSOEVER PROvided not for his parents should be condemned to death. It happened that there were two brethren, descended from the same father. One of them had a son, who discovered his uncle in the greatest indigence; and immediately, in compliance with the law, but in opposition to the will of his father, administered to his wants. Thereupon the father expelled him from his house. Notwithstanding, he still maintained his poor uncle, and supplied him with every requisite. By and by, the uncle became rich and the father indigent.

Now, when the son beheld the altered circumstances of his parent, he liberally supported him also, to the great indignation of his uncle, who drove him from his house and said, "Formerly, when I was poor, thou gavest me support, in opposition to thy father; for which I constituted thee my heir, in the place of a son. But an ungrateful son ought not to obtain an inheritance; and rather than such, we should adopt a stranger. Therefore, since *thou* hast been ungrateful to thy father in maintaining me contrary to his command, thou shalt never possess my inheritance."

The son thus answered his uncle: "No one can be punished for executing what the law commands and compels. Now, the law of nature obliges children to assist their parents in necessity, and especially to honour them: therefore, I cannot justly be deprived of the inheritance."

Tale 3

NOT TWICE

A CERTAIN EMPEROR DECREED, THAT IF ANY WOMAN WERE taken in adultery, she should be cast headlong from a very high precipice. It chanced that a woman, convicted of the crime, was immediately conveyed to the place of punishment, and thrown down. But she received no injury in the fall. They therefore brought her back to the judgment-seat; and when the judge perceived that she was unharmed, he commanded that she should again be led to the precipice, and the sentence effectually executed.

The woman, however, addressing the judge, said, "My Lord, if you command this, you will act contrary to the law, which punishes not twice for the same fault. I have already been cast down as a convicted adultress, but God miraculously preserved me. Therefore, I ought not to be subjected to it again."

The judge answered, "Thou hast well said; go in peace:" and thus was the woman saved.

Tale 4

BETWEEN DEATH AND MARRIAGE

DURING THE REIGN OF CÆSAR A LAW WAS ENACTED, THAT if a man maltreated a woman, and overcame her by violence, it should remain with the aggrieved party, whether the person so offending should be put to death, or married to her, without a portion. Now, it fell out that a certain fellow violated two women upon the same night; the one of whom sought to put him to death, and the other to be married to him. The violator was apprehended and brought before the judge, to answer respecting the two women, according to law.

The first woman insisting upon her right, desired his death; while the second claimed him for her husband.

The first woman said, "It cannot be denied that the law ordains that I should obtain my wish."

The other replied, "In like manner the law raises its voice for me. But because my demand is of less importance, and more charitable, I doubt not but that sentence will be given in my favour."

Both women complained, and both required the enforcement of the law. When either side had been heard, the judge ordered that the second woman should obtain the man for her husband. And so it was done.

Tale 5

THE PRISONER AND THE KING'S DAUGHTER

THE SUBJECT OF A CERTAIN KING FELL INTO THE HANDS of pirates, and wrote to his father for ransom. But the father would not redeem him; so the youth wasted away in prison. Now, he who detained him in chains had a daughter of great beauty and virtue. She was at this time in her twentieth year, and frequently visited the young man with the hope of alleviating his griefs. But he was too disconsolate to hearken.

It one day fell out that, while the damsel was with him, the youth said to her, "Oh, that you would try to set me free, kind maiden!"

She replied, "But how am I to effect it? Thy father, thine own father, will not ransom thee; on what ground then should I, a stranger, attempt it? And suppose that I were induced to do so, I should incur the wrath of my parent, because thine denies the price of thy redemption. Nevertheless, on one condition thou shalt be liberated."

"Kind damsel," returned he, "impose what thou wilt; so that it be possible, I will accomplish it."

"Promise, then," said she, "to marry me, whenever an opportunity may occur."

"I promise," said the youth, joyfully, "and plight thee a faith that shall never be broken."

The girl straightway set him free from his bonds, without her father's knowledge, and fled with him to his own country.

When they arrived, the father of the youth welcomed him, and said, "Son, I am overjoyed at thy return; but who is the lady under thy escort?"

He replied, "It is the daughter of a king, to whom I am betrothed."

The father returned, "On pain of losing thy inheritance, I charge thee, marry her not."

"My father," exclaimed the youth, "what hast thou said? My obligations to her are greater than they are to you; for when imprisoned and fettered by my enemy, I implored you to ransom me; but you would not. Now, she not only released me from prison, but from deadly peril—and, therefore, I am resolved to marry her."

The father answered, "Son, I tell thee that thou canst not confide in her, and consequently ought not to espouse her. She deceived her own father, when she liberated thee from prison; for this did her father lose the price of thy ransom.

Therefore, I am of opinion that thou canst not confide in her, and consequently ought not to espouse her. Besides, there is another reason. It is true she liberated thee, but it was for the gratification of her passions, and in order to oblige thee to marry her. And, since an unworthy passion was the source of thy liberty, I think that she ought not to be thy wife."

When the lady heard such reasons assigned, she answered, "To your first objection, that I deceived my own parent, I reply that it is not true. He deceives who takes away or diminishes a certain good. But my father is so rich that he needs not any addition. When, therefore, I had maturely weighed this matter, I procured the young man's freedom. And if my father had received a ransom for him, he had been but little richer; while you would have been utterly impoverished. Now, in acting thus, I have served you, who refused the ransom, and have done no injury to my parent. As for your last objection, that an unworthy passion urged me to do this, I assert that it is false. Feelings of such a nature arise either from great personal beauty, or from wealth, or honours; or finally, from a robust appearance. None of which qualities your son possessed. For imprisonment had destroyed his beauty; and he had not sufficient wealth even to effect his liberation; while much anxiety had worn away his strength, and left him emaciated and sickly. Therefore, compassion rather persuaded me to free him."

When the father had heard this, he could object nothing more. So his son married the lady with very great pomp, and closed his life in peace.

Tale 6

THE OATH OF SELF-DESTRUCTION

A CERTAIN EMPEROR, NO LESS TYRANNICAL THAN POWERful, espoused a very beautiful girl, the daughter of a king.

After the ceremony was concluded, each solemnly vowed that the death of the one should be followed by the voluntary destruction of the other.

It happened once that the emperor went into a far country, and continued there a long time. Being desirous to prove the fidelity of his wife, he directed a messenger to inform her that he was dead. When this intelligence was communicated, she remembered the oath which had been administered, and precipitated herself from a lofty mountain, with an intention to die. But she received little injury, and in a short space was restored to health. Then once again she desired to throw herself from the mountain, and so die.

Her father understanding this, forbade obedience to the mandate and oath prescribed by her husband. Still, as she seemed anxious to comply with them, the father said, "Since you refuse assent to my request, depart at once from my presence."

But she replied, "I will not do that; and I will prove, by good reasons, my right to remain. When an oath is sworn, ought it not to be faithfully maintained? I have sworn to my husband that I would destroy myself, if I survived him: therefore, it is no crime to fulfil my vow, and I ought not to be driven from your palace. Moreover, no one should be punished for that which is commendable. Now, since man and woman are one flesh, according to the laws of God, it is commendable for a wife to perish with her husband. On which account, there was a law in India, that a wife after the decease of her lord should burn herself, as evidence of her grief and love; or else be deposited alive in his sepulchre. And therefore, I think that I do no wrong to kill myself for the love of my husband."

The father answered, "When you said that you were bound by an oath to act thus, you should have remembered that such an obligation is not binding, because its end is deprivation of life. An oath should always be consistent with reason; and therefore yours being unreasonable is of no force. As for the other argument, that it is praiseworthy in a wife to die with her husband, it avails you not. For although they are one in the body, united by carnal affections, yet they are two persons in soul, and are really and substantially different. Therefore, neither does this afford any resource."

When the lady heard these words, she could argue no further, but complied with the request of her parent. She refrained from soliciting destruction; but though apprized of her husband's existence soon after, she would not return to him.

Tale 7

TWO BROTHERS

WHEN DIOCLETIAN WAS EMPEROR, THERE WAS A CERTAIN noble soldier who had two sons, whom he entirely and truly loved. The younger of them married a harlot, without the knowledge of his father, and the infamy of this proceeding overwhelmed him with the greatest grief. He sternly banished him from his presence, and left him to the rebukes of conscience, and to the agonies of approaching want. A beautiful child was born to him, and he was reduced to great distress.

In this situation he despatched a messenger to his parent, to supplicate relief; and when his wretchedness was made known, it moved him to compassion, and he forgave him all. After their reconciliation, the son entrusted to his father's protection the child that the harlot bore him, and it was taken to his house and educated as his own.

But when the elder brother heard what had happened, he

was exceedingly wroth, and said to his father, "Thou art mad, and I will prove it by satisfactory reasons. He is mad who fosters and adopts a son by whom he has been grievously wronged. Now, my brother, whose son that child is, did you great injury when he espoused a harlot contrary to your will. Therefore, I am persuaded that you are mad—for you both protect the child, and are at peace with him."

Here the father answered, "Son, I am reconciled to thy brother, in consequence of his own contrition, and the urgent entreaties of his friends. Therefore, it becomes me to love my recovered son more than you; because you have often offended me, but never sought a reconciliation: and since you have not humbly acknowledged your transgressions, you are more ungrateful than your brother has been, whom you would have me banish from my house. You ought rather to rejoice that he is reconciled to me. But because you have exhibited so much ingratitude, you shall not receive the inheritance designed for you. It shall be given to your brother."

And so it was done.

Tale 8

THE ROBBER AND THE THREE STATUES

WHEN THE EMPEROR LEO REIGNED, HIS CHIEF PLEASURE consisted in seeing beautiful women. Wherefore he caused three images to be made, to which he dedicated a stately temple, and commanded all his subjects to worship them. The first image stretched out its hand over the people, and upon one of its fingers was placed a golden ring bearing the following legend: *"My finger is generous; behold this ring."* The second image had a golden beard, and on its brow was written, "*I have a beard: if any one be beardless, let him come to me, and I will give him one.*" The third image had a golden cloak and purple tunic, and on its breast appeared these words, in large golden characters, "*I fear no one.*" These three images were fabricated of stone.

Now, when they had been erected according to the command of the emperor, he ordained that whosoever conveyed away either the ring, or golden beard, or cloak, should be doomed to the most disgraceful death. It so chanced that a certain fellow entering the temple, perceived the ring upon the finger of the first image, which he immediately drew off. He then went to the second, and took away the golden beard. Last of all, he came to the third image, and when he had removed the cloak he departed from the temple.

The people, seeing their images despoiled, presently communicated the robbery to the emperor. The transgressor was summoned before him, and charged with pilfering from the images, contrary to the edict.

But he replied, "My lord, suffer me to speak. When I entered the temple, the first image extended towards me its finger with the golden ring—as if it had said, 'Here, take the ring.' Yet, not merely because the finger was held forth to me, would I have received it; but, by and by, I read the superscription, which said, 'My finger is *generous*—take the ring.' At once I understood that it was the statue's pleasure to bestow it upon me, and therefore I took it. Afterwards, I approached the second image with the golden beard; and I communed with my own heart, and said, 'The author of this statue never had such a beard, for I have seen him repeatedly; and the creature ought, beyond question, to be inferior to the Creator. Therefore, it is fitting and necessary to take away the beard.' But although he offered not the smallest opposition, yet I was unwilling to carry it off, until I distinctly perceived, 'I have a beard: if any one be beardless, let him come to me, and I will give him one.' I am beardless, as your Majesty may see, and therefore, for two especial reasons, took away the beard. The first was, that he should look more like his author, and not grow too proud of his golden beard. Secondly, that by these means I might protect my own bald pate. Again, I came to the third image, which bore a golden cloak. I took away the cloak, because, being of metal, in the winter time it is extremely cold; and the image itself is made of stone. Now, stone is naturally cold; and if it had retained the golden cloak it would have been adding cold to cold, which were a bad thing for the image. Also, if it had possessed this cloak in summer, it would have proved too heavy and warm for the season. However, I should not have borne it away even for these causes, if there had not been written upon the breast, 'I fear nobody.' For I discovered in that vaunt such intolerable arrogance, that I took away the cloak, merely to humble it."

"Fair sir," replied the emperor, "Does not the law say expressly that the images shall not be robbed, nor the ornaments upon them molested on any pretence? You have impudently taken away that which did not belong to you, and therefore I determine that you be instantly suspended on a gallows."

And so it was done.

Tale 9

THE EMPEROR AND HIS SON

ALEXANDER WAS A RENOWNED AND PRUDENT EMPEROR. He married the daughter of the King of Syria, and had by her a beautiful son. The boy grew, but coming to man's estate, he conspired against his father, and continually sought his death. This conduct surprised the emperor, and conversing with the empress, he said, "Fair wife, tell me, I pray thee, without reserve, hast thou ever forsaken me for another?"

"My lord," answered his wife, "what is the purport of your question?"

"Your son," said he, "seeks my life. It amazes me; and if he were mine he could not do it."

"Heaven can witness," returned the lady, "that I am innocent. He is truly your son, but to what end he pursues your destruction, I cannot surmise."

The emperor, satisfied on this point, spoke to his son with the utmost mildness. "My dear son," said he, "I am your father; by my means you came into the world, and will succeed me on the throne. Why then do you desire my death? I have ever loved and cared for you, and my possessions are not less yours than mine. Cease, I conjure you, from such an iniquitous pursuit; and curtail not the few brief hours that are assigned me."

Nevertheless the son disregarded his father's entreaties, and every succeeding day discovered fresh proofs of a hard and depraved heart; sometimes endeavouring to slay him in public, and sometimes resorting to secret assassination.

When the father became aware of this, he retired into a very secluded apartment, and took with him his son. Presenting a naked sword, he said, "Take this weapon, and now hesitate not to put a speedy end to the existence of thy parent; for it will be esteemed less shameful to be slain by my own son, quietly and in secret, than to be exposed to the uproar and observation of the people."

The son, struck with the enormity of what he purposed, cast aside the extended sword, and falling upon his knees, wept aloud. "Oh, my father," said he, "I have done thee wrong—open and notorious wrong, and am no more worthy to be called thy son. Yet forgive me, dearest father, and once again restore me to thy forfeited love. From henceforth I will be indeed thy son, and in all things execute thy pleasure."

When the overjoyed parent heard this, he fell upon his neck, and kissed him. "Oh, my beloved son, be faithful and affectionate, and thou shalt find a fond and indulgent father." He then clothed him in gorgeous apparel, and brought him to the banqueting-chamber, where he was sumptuously feasted with all the nobles of his empire.

The emperor lived a short time after this, and finished his career in peace.

Tale 10

THE RINGS OF MEMORY AND OBLIVION

THE EMPEROR VESPASIAN LIVED A LONG TIME WITHOUT children; but at last, by the counsel of certain wise men, he espoused a beautiful girl, brought to him from a distant country. He afterwards travelled with her into foreign lands, and there became father of a son.

In the course of time, he wished to revisit his own kingdom; but his wife obstinately refused to comply, and said, "If you leave me, I will kill myself."

The emperor, therefore, in this dilemma, constructed two rings; and upon the jewels with which they were richly ornamented, he engraved images possessing very singular virtues. One bore an effigy of Memory; and the other an effigy of Oblivion. They were placed upon the apex of each ring; and that which represented oblivion he bestowed upon his wife. The other he retained himself; and as their love had been, such was the power of the rings.

The wife presently forgot her husband, and the husband cared but little for the memory of his wife. Seeing, therefore, that his object was achieved, he departed joyfully to his own dominions, and never afterwards returned to the lady. So he ended his days in peace.

Tale 11

ALEXANDER AND THE GIRL OF POISON

ALEXANDER WAS A PRINCE OF GREAT POWER, AND A DISciple of Aristotle, who instructed him in every branch of learning. The Queen of the North having heard of his proficiency, nourished her daughter from the cradle upon a certain kind of deadly poison; and when she grew up, she was considered so beautiful, that the sight of her alone affected many with madness. The queen sent her to Alexander to espouse. He had no sooner beheld her, than he became violently enamoured, and with much eagerness desired to possess her; but Aristotle observing his weakness, said— "Do not touch her, for if you do, you will certainly perish. She has been nurtured upon the most deleterious food, which I will prove to you immediately. Here is a malefactor, who is already condemned to death. He shall be united to her, and you will soon see the truth of what I advance."

Accordingly the culprit was brought without delay to the girl; and scarcely had he touched her lips, before his whole frame was impregnated with poison, and he expired. Alexander, glad at his escape from such imminent destruction, bestowed all thanks on his instructor, and returned the girl to her mother.

Tale 12

THE UNQUENCHABLE THIRST

IN THE REIGN OF OTHO THERE WAS A CERTAIN SLIPPERY priest, who created much disturbance among his parishioners, and many were extremely scandalized. One of them, in particular, always absented himself from Mass, when it fell to the priest's turn to celebrate it.

Now, it happened on a festival day, during the time of Mass, that as this person was walking alone through a meadow, a sudden thirst came upon him; insomuch that he was persuaded, unless present relief could be obtained, he should die. In this extremity, continuing his walk, he discovered a rivulet of the purest water, of which he drank. But the more he drank, the more violent became his thirst.

Surprised at so unusual an occurrence, he said to himself, "I will find out the source of this rivulet, and there satisfy my thirst."

As he proceeded, an old man of majestic appearance met him, and said, "My friend, where are you going?"

The other answered, "I am oppressed by an excessive drought, surpassing even belief. I discovered a little stream of water, and drank of it plentifully; but the more I drank, the more I thirsted. So I am endeavouring to find its source, that I may drink there, and, if it be possible, deliver myself from the torment."

The old man pointed with his finger. "There," said he, "Is the springhead of the rivulet. But tell me, mine honest friend, why are you not at church, and with other good Christians hearing Mass?"

The man answered, "Truly, master, our priest leads such an execrable life, that I think it utterly impossible he should celebrate it so as to please God."

To which the old man returned, "Suppose what you say is true. Observe this fountain, from which so much excellent water issues, and from which you have lately drunk."

He looked in the direction pointed out, and beheld a putrid dog with its mouth wide open, and its teeth black and decayed, through which the whole fountain gushed in a surprising manner. The man regarded the stream with great terror and confusion of mind, ardently desirous of quenching his thirst, but apprehensive of poison from the fetid and loathsome carcase, with which, to all appearance, the water was imbued.

"Be not afraid," said the old man, regarding his repugnance, "Because thou hast already drank of the rivulet; drink again, it will not harm thee."

Encouraged by these assurances, and impelled by the intensity of his thirst, he partook of it once more, and instantly recovered from the drought. "Oh, master!" cried he, "Never man drank of such delicious water."

The old man answered, "See now; as this water, gushing through the mouth of a putrid dog, is neither polluted nor loses aught of its natural taste or colour, so is the celebration of Mass by a worthless minister. And therefore, though the vices of such men may displease and disgust, yet should you not forsake the duties of which they are the appointed organ."

Saying these words, the old man disappeared; and what the other had seen he communicated to his neighbours, and ever after punctually attended Mass. He brought this unstable and transitory life to a good end, and passed from that which is corruptible to inherit incorruption.

Tale 13

BLOOD ON THE QUEEN'S HAND

A CERTAIN EMPEROR WAS STRONGLY ATTACHED TO A BEAU-
tiful wife. In the first year of their marriage, she was delivered of a son, upon whom she doated with extravagant
fondness. When the child had completed its third year, the
king died; for whose death great lamentation was made
through the whole kingdom. The queen bewailed him bitterly; and, after his remains were deposited in the royal sepulchre, took up her residence in another part of the country,
accompanied by her son.

This child became the object of an affection so violent,
that no consideration could induce her to leave him; and
they invariably occupied the same bed, even till the boy had
attained his eighteenth year. Now, when the devil perceived
the irregular attachment of the mother, and the filial return
exhibited by the son, he insinuated black and unnatural
thoughts into their minds; and from time to time repeating
his detestable solicitations, finally overthrew them. The queen
became pregnant; and the unhappy son, filled with the deepest horror, and writhing beneath the most intolerable agony,
quitted the kingdom, and never was heard of again.

In due time the queen was delivered of a lovely female,
whom her eyes no sooner beheld, than—(mark, ye who
dream that one dereliction from virtue may be tried with
impunity—mark!) desperate at the remembrance of her
fearful crime, and apprehensive of detection, she snatched
up a knife that lay beside her, and plunged it into the infant's
breast. Not content with this exhibition of maternal inhu-

manity, she cut it directly across the throat, from whence the blood rapidly gushed forth, and falling upon the palm of her left hand, distinctly impressed four circular lines, which no human power could erase.

Terrified, not less at the singular consequence of her guilt than at the guilt itself, she carefully concealed this awful and mysterious evidence, and dedicated herself for life to the service of the blessed Virgin. Yet, though penitent for what she had done, and regularly every fifteenth morning duly confessed, she scrupulously avoided any disclosure relating to that horrid transaction. She distributed alms with the most unbounded liberality; and the people, experiencing her kindness and benevolence, evinced towards her the greatest respect and love.

It happened on a certain night, as her confessor knelt at his devotions, repeating five times aloud the "Ave Maria," that the blessed Virgin herself appeared to him, and said, "I am the Virgin Mary, and have an important communication to make to thee."

The confessor, full of joy, answered, "Oh, dear Lady, wherein can thy servant please thee?"

She replied, "The queen of this kingdom will confess herself to you; but there is one sin she has committed, which shame and horror will not permit her to disclose. On the morrow she will come to you; tell her from me, that her alms and her prayers have been accepted in the sight of my Son; I command her, therefore, to confess that crime which she secretly committed in her chamber—for, alas! she slew her daughter. I have entreated for her, and her sin is forgiven, if she will confess it. But if she yield no attention to your words, bid her lay aside the cover upon her left hand; and on her palm you will read the crime she refuses to acknowledge. If she deny this also, take it off by force."

When she had thus spoken, the blessed Virgin disappeared. In the morning, the queen with great humility was shrieved of all her sins—that one excepted. After she had uttered as much as she chose, the confessor said, "Madam, and dear daughter, people are very inquisitive to know for what strange reason you constantly wear that cover upon your left hand. Let me see it, I beseech you, that I may ascertain why it is concealed, and whether the concealment be pleasing to God."

The queen answered, "Sir, my hand is diseased, and therefore I cannot show it." Hearing this, the confessor caught hold of her arm, and notwithstanding her resistance, drew off the cover.

"Lady," said he, "Fear not; the blessed Virgin Mary loves you; and it is she who hath commanded me to do this."

When the hand was uncovered, there appeared four circles of blood. In the first circle there were four letters in the form of a C; in the second, four D's; in the third, four M's; and in the fourth, four R's. Upon the outward edge of the circles, in the manner of a seal, a blood-coloured writing was distinguishable, containing the legend beneath. First, of the letter C,—which was interpreted, *"Casu cecidisti carne cœcata."* [Blinded by the flesh thou hast fallen.] The letter D, *"Dœmoni dedisti dona donata."* [The gifts that were bestowed on thee thou hast given to the devil.] The letter M, *"Monstrat manifestè manus maculata."* [The stain upon thy hand discovers thee.] The letter R, *"Recedet rubigo, regina rogata."* [When the queen is interrogated the red marks will vanish.]

The lady beholding this, fell at the confessor's feet, and with many tears meekly related her dreadful offences. Then being entirely and truly penitent, she was absolved; and a very few days afterwards, slept the sleep of death. Her death was long lamented by the whole state.

Tale 14

OF THE SON WHO LIBERATED HIS FATHER

IN THE REIGN OF THE EMPEROR DOROTHEUS A DECREE was passed that children should support their parents. There was, at that time, in the kingdom, a certain soldier, who had espoused a very fair and virtuous woman, by whom he had a son. It happened that the soldier went upon a journey, was made prisoner, and very rigidly confined. Immediately he wrote to his wife and son for ransom.

The intelligence communicated great uneasiness to the former, who wept so bitterly that she became blind. Whereupon the son said to his mother, "I will hasten to my father, and release him from prison."

The mother answered, "Thou shalt not go; for thou art my only son—even the half of my soul, and it may happen to thee as it has done to him. Hadst thou rather ransom thy absent parent than protect her who is with thee, and presses thee in her affectionate arms? Is not the possession of one thing better than the expectation of two? Thou art my son as well as thy father's; and I am present, while he is absent. I conclude, therefore, that you ought by no means to forsake me to redeem your father."

The son very properly answered, "Although I am thy son, yet he is my father. He is abroad and surrounded by the merciless; but thou art at home, protected and cherished by loving friends. He is a captive, but thou art free—blind, indeed; but he perhaps sees not the light of heaven, and pours forth unheeded groans in the gloom of a loathsome dungeon oppressed with chains, with wounds, and misery. Therefore it is my determination to go to him and redeem him."

The son did so; and every one applauded and honoured him for the indefatigable industry with which he achieved his father's liberation.

Tale 15

THE LIFE OF SAINT ALEXIUS

IN THE REIGN OF ONE OF THE ROMAN EMPERORS LIVED A youth, named Alexius, the son of Eufemian, a noble Roman, at that time the chief ornament of the emperor's court. He was attended by a band of three thousand youths, girded with golden girdles, and habited in silken vestures. Eufemian was well known for his charity. He daily maintained three tables, to which the widow and the orphan were ever welcome. Their necessities were often supplied by his own person; and at the ninth hour, in company with other devout men, he sat down to dinner.

His wife, whose name was Abael, was as religious and charitable as himself. But there is ever some bitterness mixed up with the draught of human joy; and in the midst of so much splendour, the want of a successor was long a source of unavailing affliction. At length their prayers were heard; Heaven, in its benevolence, blessed them with a son, who was carefully instructed in all the polite learning of the period. Arriving at the age of manhood, he proved himself an acute and solid reasoner. But reason is no barrier against love; he became attached to a lady of the blood-royal, and was united to her.

On the very evening of their nuptials, when the clamour of the feast had subsided, the pious youth commenced a theological disquisition, and strove with much force and earnestness to impress his bride with the fear and love of God. When he had concluded, recommending her to preserve the same modesty of demeanour for which she had always been distinguished, he consigned to her care his gold ring, and the clasp of the sword-belt which usually begirt him.

"Take charge of these vanities," said he, "For I give them up; and as long as it shall please God, keep them in remembrance of me: may the Almighty guide us." He then provided a sum of money, and going down to the sea-coast, secretly embarked in a ship bound for Laodicea. From thence he proceeded to Edessa, a city of Syria. It was here that the image of our Lord Jesus Christ, wrought upon linen by supernatural hands, was preserved.

On reaching this place he distributed whatever he had brought with him to the poor; and putting on a worn and tattered garment, joined himself to a number of mendicants who sat in the porch of the temple dedicated to the Virgin Mary. He now constantly solicited alms; but of all that he received, only the smallest portion was retained—an unbounded charity leading him to bestow the residue upon his more needy, or more covetous brethren.

The father of Alexius, however, was overwhelmed with sorrow at the inexplicable departure of his son; and despatched his servants in pursuit of him to various parts of the world. These servants were very diligent in their inquiries; and it chanced that certain of them came to the city of Edessa, and were recognized by Alexius; but, pertinaciously concealing himself under the garb of want and misery, he passed unknown and unsuspected.

The men, little aware who was experiencing their bounty, conferred large alms upon the paupers amongst whom he sojourned; and his heart silently but gratefully acknowledged the benefaction: "I thank thee, O my God, that thou hast thought good to dispense thine alms by the hands of my own servants."

On this unsuccessful issue of their search, the messengers returned; and when the intelligence of their failure reached his mother, she shut herself up in a remote chamber, and there gave utterance to her griefs. She slept upon the ground, with sackcloth only for a covering; and solemnly vowed never to change her way of life until she recovered her lost son.

The bride said to her father-in-law, "Until I hear tidings from my sweet husband I will remain with you."

In the mean time, Alexius remained a beggar in the porch of St. Mary's church for the space of seventeen years; until at length the image of the Virgin which stood within the sacred edifice, said to the warden, "Cause that man of God to enter the sanctuary: for he is worthy of the kingdom of heaven, upon whom the spirit of God rests. His prayer ascends like incense to the throne of grace." But since the warden knew not of whom she spoke, she said once more, "It is the man who sits at the entrance of the porch." The warden then went out quickly, and brought him into the church.

Now, a circumstance of this extraordinary nature soon attracted remark; and the veneration with which they began to consider Alexius, approached almost to adoration. But he despised human glory, and entering a ship, set sail for Tarsus, in Cilicia; but the providence of God so ordered, that a violent tempest carried them into a Roman port.

Alexius, informed of this circumstance, said within himself, "I will hasten to my father's house; no one will know me, and it is better that I prove burthensome to him, than to another." As he proceeded, he met his father coming from the palace, surrounded by a large concourse of dependents, and immediately he shouted after him, "Servant of God, command a poor and desolate stranger to be conveyed into your house, and fed with the crumbs which fall from the table: so shall the Lord have pity on the wanderer you love."

The father, out of love to his son, gave him into the charge of his followers, and appropriated to him a room in his house. He supplied him with meat from his own table, and appointed one who was accustomed to attend upon himself to serve him. But Alexius discontinued not the fervency of his devotion, and macerated his body with fasts and other austerities. And though the pampered servants derided him, and frequently emptied their household utensils on his head, his patience was always invincible.

In this manner, for seventeen years under his own father's roof, his life was spent; but at last, perceiving by the spirit that his end approached, he procured ink and paper, and recorded the narrative of his life.

Now, on the succeeding Sunday, after the solemnization of Mass, a voice echoing like thunder among the mountains, was heard through the city. It said, "Come unto me, all ye that labour, and I will give you rest."

The people, terrified and awe-struck, fell upon their faces; when a second time the voice exclaimed, "Seek out a man of God to offer a prayer for the iniquity of Rome."

Search was accordingly made, but no such man could be found; and the same voice waxing louder, and breathing as it were with the mingled blast of ten thousand thousand trumpets, again spoke, "Search in the house of Eufemian."

Then the Emperors Arcadius and Honorius, in conjunction with the Pontiff Innocent, proceeded towards the house to which the words of the Invisible directed them, and as they approached, the servant who attended upon Alexius came running to his master, and cried, "What think you, my lord? Is not the mendicant stranger a man of exemplary life?" Eufemian, following up the suggestion, hastened to his chamber and found him extended upon the bed. Life had already passed, but his countenance retained a dazzling emanation of glory, like the countenance of a cherub in its own pure and beatified element.

A paper occupied the right hand, which Eufemian would have borne away, but he was unable to extricate it from the grasp of the dead man. Leaving him, therefore, he returned to the emperors and the pontiff, and related what he had seen. They were astonished, and entering the apartment exclaimed, "Sinners though we are, we direct the helm of State, and provide for the well-being of the pastoral government. Give us, then, the paper, that we may know what it contains."

Immediately the pontiff drew near, and put his hand upon the scroll which the deceased yet firmly grasped,—and he instantly relaxed his hold. It was read to the people; and when the father, Eufemian, heard its contents, he was paralyzed with grief. His strength deserted him, and he staggered and fell. Returning to himself a little, he rent his garment, plucked off the silver hairs of his head, and tore the venerable beard that swept his unhappy bosom. He even inflicted severe wounds upon himself, and falling upon the dead body, cried, "Alas! my son—my son! why hast thou laid up for me such deadly anguish? Why, for so many years, hast thou endured a bitterness which death itself cannot exceed? Wretched man that I am, he who should have been the guardian of my increasing infirmities, and the hope and the honour of my age, lies upon this miserable bed, and speaks not. Oh! where is consolation to be found?"

At this instant, like an enraged and wounded lioness breaking though the toils with which the hunters had encompassed her, the poor broken-hearted Abael, who had followed in the press, rushed desperately forward. Her garments were torn, and hanging about her in shreds; her hair dishevelled and flying; her eyes, wild and sparkling with the violence of emotion, were raised piteously to heaven. With that strength which frenzy sometimes supplies, she burst through the multitude who struggled to detain her; and approaching the body of her deceased child, said, or rather shrieked, in a heart-piercing accent, "I will pass; I will look upon my soul's only comfort. Did not this dried fountain suckle him? Have not these withered arms supported him? Hath he not slept—ah! not such sleep as this!—while I have watched him? Oh, my child!"

Saying this, she threw her emaciated form upon the unconscious object of her solicitude; and again giving vent to her sorrows, exclaimed, "My own dear boy! light of the dimmed eyes that will soon close upon all, since thou art gone—why hast thou wrought this? why wast thou so inhuman? Thou didst see our tears—thou didst hearken to our groans—yet camest not forward to abate them. The slaves scoffed at and injured thee, but thou wert patient—too, too patient." Again and again the unfortunate mother prostrated herself upon the body, clasping him in her arms, and passing her hand reverently over his seraphic features. Now, she impressed a kiss upon the cold cheek and eyelids which her tears had moistened—and now bending over him, muttered something in a low and inaudible voice.

Suddenly turning to the spectators, she said, "Weep, I pray ye, weep: ye who are regarding the agonies of a bereaved parent—have ye no tear to spare her? Abiding together for seventeen years, I knew him not! not him, my beloved and beautiful! They taunted him, and showered their unmanly blows upon his enduring head. Oh! who will again bring tears to my burning eyelids? Who—who will bear a part in my misery?"

The wife, whom Alexius had married and quitted on the evening of their nuptials, had been borne along by the congregating populace; but distress, until now, had held her silent. As Abael ceased, she sprung forward and cried, *"Thou,* miserable! what then am I? Woe is me! to-day I am desolate; to-day I am all a widow! Now, there is none for whom I may look—none whom I may yet expect, although he come not. Where shall mine eye see gladness? The glass of my joy is broken—shivered—shivered: my hope is extinct; and grief is all the portion of my widowhood."

The multitude, penetrated by the various calamities of which they were witnesses, sympathized with the sufferers, and wept aloud.

By command of the pontiff and the two emperors, the body was deposited on a sumptuous bier, and brought into the middle of the city. Proclamation was made that the man of God was discovered, whom they had before sought in vain; and every one crowded to the bier.

Now, if any infirm person touched the hallowed corpse, instantly he was strengthened. The blind received their sight; those who were possessed of devils were set free, and all the sick, be the disorder what it might, when they had once come in contact with the body, were made whole.

These miraculous effects attracted the attention of the emperors and the pontiff. They determined to support the bier; and when they had done so, they were sanctified by the holiness which proceeded from the corpse. They then scattered great abundance of gold and silver about the streets, that the people's natural cupidity might draw them aside, and the bier be carried forward to the church; but strange to say, careless of all else, they pressed yet the more vehemently to touch it.

At length, after great exertions, he was brought to the church of St. Boniface the Martyr; and there, for the space of seven days, they tarried, praising God.

They constructed a monument, glittering with gold and precious stones, and here, with the greatest reverence, placed the body of their Saint. Even from the very monument, so sweet an odour of sanctity broke forth, that it seemed to be entirely filled with the most fragrant aroma. He died about the year of our Lord three-hundred-and-twenty-eight.

Tale 16

ENGRAVED UPON AN ANCIENT TOMB

WE READ OF A CERTAIN ROMAN EMPEROR, WHO BUILT A magnificent palace. In digging the foundation, the workmen discovered a golden coffin, ornamented with three circlets, on which were inscibed, "I have expended—I have given— I have kept—I have possessed—I do possess—I have lost— I am punished. What I formerly expended, I have; what I gave away, I have."

The emperor, on seeing this, called to him the nobles of his empire, and said, "Go, and consider among ye what this inscription signifies."

The noblemen replied, "Sire, the meaning is, that an emperor, who reigned before your majesty, wished to leave an example for the imitation of his successors. He therefore wrote, 'I have expended,'—that is, my life; judging some, admonishing others, and governing to the best of my ability. 'I have given,'—that is, equipments to my soldiers, and supplies to the needy; to every one according to his desert. 'I have kept,'—that is, exact justice; showing mercy to the indigent, and yielding to the labourer his hire. 'I have possessed,'— that is, a generous and true heart; recompensing faithfully those who have done me service, and exhibiting at all times a kind and affable exterior. 'I do possess,'—that is, a hand to bestow, to protect, and to punish. 'I have lost,'—that is, my folly; I have lost the friendship of my foes, and the lascivious indulgences of the flesh. 'I am punished,'—that is, in hell; because I believed not in one eternal God, and put no faith in the redemption."

The emperor hearing this, ever after regulated himself and his subjects with greater wisdom, and finished his life in peace.

Tale 17

STORY OF THE SIX KINDS OF SERVICE

AN EMPEROR DECREED THAT WHOEVER WISHED TO SERVE him should obtain his wish, conditionally that he struck three times upon the palace gate, by which those within might understand that he wished to take service.

Now, there was a certain poor man in the Roman empire, called Guido; who, on hearing the mode by which admission to the emperor's service was to be attained, thus thought— "I am a poor fellow, of low descent; it is better for me to serve and acquire wealth than to live in independence and starve." So he proceeded to the palace, and according to the edict, gave three blows upon the gate.

The porter immediately opened it, and brought him in. He was introduced and made his obeisance to the emperor, who said, "What seek you, my friend?"

Guido replied, "I wish to serve your majesty."

"And for what office may you be fit?" returned the emperor.

"I can serve, with tolerable expertness, in six capacities," said Guido. "First, I can act as body-guard to the prince; I can make his bed, dress his food, and wash his feet. Secondly, I can watch when others sleep, and sleep when others watch.

Thirdly, I can drink good drink, and tell whether it be good or not. Fourthly, I can invite company to a festival for my master's honour. Fifthly, I can make a fire without the least smoke, which will warm all that approach it. Sixthly, I can teach people the way to the Holy Land, from whence they will return in excellent health."

"By my faith," said the emperor, "These are fine matters, and will be useful on many occasions. Thou shalt stay with me, and serve me first as body-guard. In each department thou shalt remain a full year."

Guido expressed himself content; and every night made ready the emperor's bed, washed the linen, and occasionally changed it. Then he lay down at the entrance of the chamber, armed at all points. He likewise provided a dog, whose barking might warn him of any danger. Once every week he washed the emperor's feet, and in all respects ministered so faithfully and manfully, that not the least fault was found with him. The emperor, therefore, was well pleased; and at the expiration of the year made him his steward, preparatory to the fulfilment of the second office, which was to watch. Then Guido commenced his operations; and during the whole summer collected a variety of stores, and watched with great assiduity the fittest opportunities. So that on the approach of winter, when others, who had wasted the proper season, began to labour and lay up, he took his ease, and thus completed the service of the second year.

When the emperor perceived his diligence and shrewdness, he called to him his chief butler, and said, "Friend, put into my cup some of the best wine, mingled with grape-juice and vinegar, and give it to Guido to taste; for that is his third ministry, namely, to taste good drink, and pronounce upon its qualities." The butler did as he was commanded.

When Guido had tasted, he said, "It was good; it is good; it will be good. That is, the grape-juice which is new will be good when it is older; the old wine is good, at present; and the vinegar was good formerly."

When the emperor saw that he had such a sound judgment of the beverage, he said, "Go now through town and country, and invite all my friends to a festival; for Christmas is at hand: herein shall consist your fourth ministry."

Guido instantly set out; but instead of executing the orders he had received, he invited none but the emperor's enemies; thus, on Christmas Eve, his court was filled with them.

When he observed this, he was exceedingly perturbed, and calling Guido to him, said, "How is this? Did you not say that you knew what men to ask to my table?"

He answered, "Surely, my lord."

"And said I not," returned the emperor, very much provoked, "Said I not that thou wert to invite my *friends?* How comes it that thou hast assembled only my enemies?"

"My lord," replied Guido, "suffer me to speak. At all seasons, and at all hours, your friends may visit you, and they are received with pleasure; but it is not so with your enemies. From which reflection I persuaded myself that a conciliating behaviour and a good dinner would convert your inveterate enemies into warm friends."

This was really the case; before the feast concluded they all became cordial partisans, and as long as they lived remained faithful to their sovereign. The emperor, therefore, was much delighted, and cried, "Blessed be God, my enemies are now my friends! Execute thy fifth ministry, and make both for them and me a fire that shall burn without smoke."

Guido replied, "It shall be done immediately," and he thus performed his promise. In the heat of summer, he dried a quantity of green wood in the sun: having done this, he made with it, in winter, a fire that blazed and sparkled, but threw out no smoke; so that the emperor and his friends warmed themselves without inconvenience. He was now directed to perform his last service, and promised great honours and wealth on completing it also, equally to the satisfaction of his master.

"My lord," said Guido, "Whoever would travel to the Holy Land must follow me to the seaside." Accordingly, proclamation being made, men, women, and children in immense crowds hastened after him. When they arrived at the appointed place, Guido said, "My friends, do you observe in the sea the same things which I do?"

They answered, "We know not that."

"Then," continued he, "Do you perceive in the midst of the waves an immense rock? Lift up your eyes and look."

They replied, "Master, we see it well enough, but do not understand why you ask."

"Know," said he, "That in this rock there is a sort of bird continually sitting on her nest, in which are seven eggs. While she is thus employed the sea is tranquil; but if she happen to quit her nest, storm and tempest immediately succeed; insomuch that they who would venture upon the ocean are certain to be cast away. On the other hand, as long as she sits upon the eggs, whoever goes to sea will go and return in safety."

"But," said they, "How shall we ascertain when the bird is on her nest, and when she is not?"

He replied, "She never quits her nest except on some particular emergency. For there is another bird, exceedingly hostile to her, and labouring day and night to defile her nest and break the eggs. Now, the bird of the nest, when she sees her eggs broken and her nest fouled, instantly flies away possessed with the greatest grief; then the sea rages, and the winds become very boisterous. At that time you ought especially to avoid putting out of port."

The people made answer, "But, master, what remedy is there for this? How shall we prevent the unfriendly bird from approaching the other's nest, and so pass safely over the waters?"

"There is nothing," returned Guido, "Which this unfriendly bird so much abhors as the blood of a lamb. Sprinkle, therefore, with this blood the inside and the outside of the nest, and as long as one single drop remains it will never approach it: the bird of the nest will sit; the sea will continue calm; and you will pass and repass with perfect safety."

When they had heard this, they took the blood of the lamb, and sprinkled it as he had said. They then passed securely to the Holy Land; and the emperor, seeing that Guido had fulfilled every ministry with wisdom, promoted him to a great military command, and bestowed on him immense riches.

Tale 18

THE PREDICTION OF THE STAG

A CERTAIN SOLDIER, CALLED JULIAN, UNWITTINGLY KILLED his parents. For being of noble birth, and addicted, as youth frequently is, to the sports of the field, a stag which he hotly pursued suddenly turned round and addressed him: "Thou who pursuest me so fiercely shalt be the destruction of thy parents."

These words greatly alarmed Julian, who feared their accomplishment even while he disavowed the probability. Leaving, therefore, his amusement, he went privately into a distant country, and enrolled himself in the bands of a certain chieftain. His conduct, as well in war as in peace, merited so highly from the prince he served, that he created him a knight, and gave him the widow of a castellan in marriage, with her castle as a dowry.

All this while, the parents of Julian bewailed the departure of their son, and diligently sought for him in all places. At length they arrived at the castle, and in Julian's absence were introduced to his wife, who asked them what they were. They communicated without reserve the occasion of their search, and their sorrow for an only child. Convinced by this explanation that they were her husband's parents—for he had often conversed with her about them, and detailed the strange occurrence which induced him to flee his country —she received them very kindly; and in consideration of the love she bore her husband, put them into her own bed, and commanded another to be prepared elsewhere for herself.

Now, early in the morning, the lady castellan went to her devotions. In the mean time Julian returning home, hastened, according to custom, to the chamber of his wife, imagining that she had not yet risen. Fearful of awaking her, he softly entered the apartment, and perceiving two persons in bed, instantly concluded that his wife was disloyal. Without a moment's pause, he unsheathed his sabre, and slew both.

Then he hurried from the chamber, and acidentally took the direction in which the church lay, and by which his wife had proceeded not long before. On the threshold of the sacred building he recognized her, and struck with the utmost amazement, inquired who they were that had taken possession of his bed. She replied that they were his parents; who, after long and wearisome search in pursuit of him, arrived at his castle the last evening.

The news was as a thunderbolt to Julian; and unable to contain himself he burst into an agony of tears. "Oh!" he exclaimed. "Lives there in the world so forlorn a wretch as I am? This accursed hand has murdered my parents, and fulfilled the horrible prediction which I have struggled to avoid. Dearest wife, pardon my fatal suspicions, and receive my last farewell; for never will I know rest, until I am satisfied that God has forgiven me."

His wife answered, "Wilt thou abandon me then, my beloved, and leave me alone and widowed? No—I have been the participator in thy happiness, and now will participate in thy grief."

Julian opposed not, and they departed together towards a large river, that flowed at no great distance, and where many had perished. In this place they built and endowed a hospital, where they abode in the truest contrition of heart. They always ferried over those who wished to cross the river, and received great numbers of poor people within the place.

Many years glided by, and, at last, on a very cold night, about the mid-hour, as Julian slept, overpowered with fatigue, a lamentable voice seemed to call his name, and beg him in dolorous accents to take the speaker across the river. He instantly got up, and found a man covered with the leprosy, perishing for very cold. He brought him into the house, and lighted a fire to warm him; but he could not be made warm. That he might omit no possible means of cherishing the leper, he carried him into his own bed, and endeavoured by the heat of his body to restore him.

After a while, he who seemed sick, and cold, and leprous, appeared enveloped in an immortal splendour: and waving his light wings, seemed ready to mount up into heaven.

Turning a look of the utmost benignity upon his wondering host, he said, "Julian, the Lord hath sent me to thee, to announce the acceptance of thy contrition. Before long both thou and thy partner will sleep in the Lord."

So saying, the angelic messenger disappeared. Julian and his wife, after a short time fully occupied in good works, died in peace.

Tale 19

OF THE QUARREL BETWEEN POMPEY AND CÆSAR

WE READ IN THE ROMAN ANNALS OF A PRINCE CALLED Pompey. He was united to the daughter of a nobleman, whose name was Cæsar. It was agreed between them to bring the whole world into subjection; and with this view Pompey gave instructions to his associate to possess himself of certain distant fortresses: for the latter being a young man, it became him to be most active.

In the mean while, Pompey, as the chief person of the commonwealth, endeavoured to guard it against the machinations of their enemies; and appointed a particular day for the return of Cæsar—in failure of which, he was to be deprived of his citizenship for ever.

Five years were allowed him; and Cæsar, assembling a large army marched rapidly into the country he was about to attack. But the inhabitants being warlike, he was unable to subdue them in the specified time. Caring, therefore, to offend Pompey less than to relinquish his conquests, he continued abroad considerably beyond the five years; and was consequently banished the empire.

When Cæsar had concluded the campaign he turned towards Rome, marching with his forces across a river, distinguished by the name of Rubicon. Here a phantom of immense stature standing in the middle of the water, opposed his passage. It said, "Cæsar, if your purpose be the welfare of the state—pass on; but if not, beware how you advance another step."

Cæsar replied, "I have long fought for, and am still prepared to undergo every hardship in defence of Rome; of which I take the gods whom I worship to be my witnesses."

As he said this, the phantom vanished. Cæsar then spurred his war-horse and crossed the river; but having effected his passage, he paused on the opposite bank:—"I have rashly promised peace," said he; "For in this case, I must relinquish my just right."

From that hour he pursued Pompey with the utmost virulence even to the death; and was himself slain afterwards by a band of conspirators.

Tale 20

THE PROPHECY

IN THE REIGN OF THE EMPEROR CONRAD, THERE LIVED A certain count, called Leopold, who for some cause, fearing the indignation of his master, fled with his wife into the woods, and concealed himself in a miserable hovel. By chance the emperor hunted there; and being carried away by the heat of the chase, lost himself in the woods, and was overtaken by nightfall. Wandering about in various directions, he came at length to the cottage where the count dwelt, and requested shelter.

Now, his hostess being at that time pregnant, and near the moment of her travail, prepared, though with some difficulty, a meal, and brought whatever he required. The same night she was delivered of a son. While the emperor slept, a voice broke upon his ear, which seemed to say, "Take, Take, Take."

He arose immediately, and with considerable alarm said to himself, "What can that voice mean? 'Take! Take! Take!' What am I to take?" He reflected upon the singularity of this for a short space, and then fell asleep.

But a second time the voice addressed him, crying out, "Restore, Restore, Restore."

He awoke in very great sorrow. "What is all this?" thought he. "First, I was to 'Take, Take, Take,' and there is nothing for me to take. Just now the same voice exclaimed, 'Restore, Restore, Restore,' and what can I restore when I have taken nothing?"

Unable to explain the mystery, he again slept; and the third time the voice spoke. "Fly, Fly, Fly," it said, "For a child is now born, who shall become thy son-in-law."

These words created great perplexity in the emperor; and getting up very early in the morning, he sought out two of his squires, and said, "Go and force away that child from its mother; cleave it in twain, and bring its heart to me."

The terrified squires obeyed, and snatched away the child as it hung at its mother's breast. But observing its very great beauty, they were moved to compassion, and placed it upon the branch of a tree, to rescue it from the wild beasts; and then killing a hare, they conveyed its heart to the emperor.

Soon after this, a duke travelling in the forest, passed by, and hearing the cry of an infant, searched about; and discovering it, placed it, unknown to any one, in the folds of his garment. Having no child himself, he conveyed it to his wife, bade her nourish it as their own, and gave it the name of Henry.

The boy grew up, handsome in person and extremely eloquent; so that he became a general favourite. Now, the emperor, remarking the extraordinary quickness of the youth, desired his foster-father to send him to court; where he resided a length of time. But the great estimation in which he was held by all ranks of people, caused the emperor to repent what he had done; and to fear lest he should aspire to the throne, or probably be the same child he had commanded his squires to destroy.

Wishing to secure himself from every possible turn of fortune, he wrote a letter with his own hand to the queen to the following purport: "I command you, on pain of death, as soon as this letter reaches you, to put the young man to death." When it was completed, he went by some accident into a church, and seating himself upon a bench, fell asleep. The letter had been enclosed in a purse, which hung loosely from his girdle; and a certain priest of the place, impelled by an ungovernable curiosity, opened the purse and read the purposed wickedness.

Filled with horror and indignation, he cunningly erased the passage commanding the youth's death, and wrote instead, "Give him our daughter in marriage." The writing was conveyed to the queen, who finding the emperor's signature, and the impression of the royal signet, called together the princes of the empire, and celebrated their nuptials with great pomp.

When this was communicated to the emperor he was greatly afflicted, but when he heard the whole chain of miraculous interposition from the two squires, the duke, and the priest, he saw that he must resign himself to the dispensations of God. And, therefore, sending for the young man, he confirmed his marriage, and appointed him heir to his kingdom.

Tale 21

HOW THE BANISHED KING WARNED HIS COUNTRY

JUSTIN RECORDS THAT THE LACEDÆMONIANS CONSPIRED against their king; and prevailing, banished him. It happened that a king of the Persians plotted the destruction of the same state, and prepared to besiege Lacedæmon with a large army.

The exile, though smarting beneath the wrongs accumulated on him by his own subjects, could not but have regard for the land of his nativity. Having ascertained, therefore, the hostile designs of the Persian monarch against the Lacedæmonians, he reflected by what means he might securely forewarn them of the impending danger. Accordingly, taking up his tablets, he communicated his discovery, and explained how they might best resist and defeat the invading armies.

When he had written, he enveloped the whole in wax, and finding a trustworthy messenger, despatched him to the chiefs of the state. On inspection of the tablets no writing could be distinguished; for the entire surface of the wax discovered not the slightest impression. This naturally gave rise to much discussion, and each delivered his opinion as to the intent and further disposal of the tablets. But the mystery none of them could unravel.

Now, it chanced that a sister of the Lacedæmonian king, undertanding their perplexity, requested permission to inspect them. Her desire was granted; she commenced a minute investigation, and assisted by that peculiar shrewdness which women frequently display in emergencies, raised the wax, and a portion of the writing became manifest. She had now a clue, and proceeding in her work, gradually removed the waxen covering and exhibited the legend at full. The nobles of the council, thus pre-monished, rejoiced exceedingly; took the necessary steps, and secured themselves against the menaced siege.

Tale 22

HOW THE EGYPTIANS DEIFIED ISIS AND SERAPIS

AUGUSTINE TELLS US THAT, WHEN THE EGYPTIANS FORmerly deified Isis and Serapis, they proceeded in this manner.

First, they made a law that whosoever declared them to be mortal, or so much as spoke of their birth, should be put to an ignominious death.

Then they erected two images; and that the aforesaid law should be strictly observed, they placed near them, in every temple dedicated to their honour, another of diminutive form, having a forefinger laid upon its lips,—to indicate that silence was indispensably required of those who entered their temples.

In this way they endeavoured to repress the promulgation of truth.

Tale 23

THE POISONED HEART

SAINT AUGUSTINE RELATES THAT AN ANCIENT CUSTOM formerly prevailed, in compliance with which emperors, after death, were laid upon a funeral pile and burnt; and their ashes deposited in a certain lofty place. But it happened that one of them died whose heart resisted the fury of fire.

This circumstance created the utmost astonishment, and all the rhetoricians, and other wise men of every province, were summoned to one place. The question was then proposed to them, and they thus answered: "The emperor died by poison, and through the influence of the latent venom his heart cannot be consumed."

When this was understood, they drew the heart from the fire, and covered it with the antidote *theriaque,* and immediately the poison was expelled. The heart, being returned to the flames, was soon reduced to ashes.

Tale 24

THE MAGICIAN AND THE ENCHANTED GARDEN

THERE WAS A CELEBRATED MAGICIAN, WHO HAD A VERY beautiful garden, in which grew flowers of the most fragrant smell and fruits of the most delicious flavour. In short, nothing on earth could exceed it. But he invariably refused admittance to all except to fools, or such as were his enemies.

When suffered to pass in, however, their wonder was extreme; and they straightway implored to be allowed to remain. But the magician would grant this boon to no one who did not give up his inheritance to him. The fools, of course, believing it to be Paradise, while they themselves were the chosen and happy possessors of the land, gave not another thought to the future. The consequence was that, one night, finding them asleep, the magician cut them off; and thus, through the instrumentality of a factitious Eden, perpetrated the foulest crimes.

Tale 25

THE STAFF AND SCRIP OF THE PILGRIM

A CERTAIN NOBLE LADY SUFFERED MANY INJURIES FROM A tyrannical king, who laid waste her domains. When the particulars of it were communicated to her, her tears flowed fast, and her heart was oppressed with bitterness.

It happened that a pilgrim visited her, and remained there

for some time. Observing the poverty to which she had been reduced, and feeling compassion for her distresses, he offered to make war in her defence, on condition that, if he fell in battle, his staff and scrip should be retained in her private chamber, as a memorial of his valour, and of her gratitude.

She faithfully promised compliance with his wishes; and the pilgrim, hastening to attack the tyrant, obtained a splendid victory. But, in the heat of the contest, he was himself mortally wounded. The lady, aware of this, did as she promised: the staff and scrip were suspended in her chamber.

Now, when it was known that she had recovered all her lost possessions, three kings made large preparations to address, and, as they hoped, incline her to become the wife of one of them. The lady, forewarned of the intended honour, adorned herself with great care, and walked forth to meet them.

They were received according to their dignity; and whilst they remained with her, she fell into some perplexity, and said to herself, "If these three kings enter my chamber, it will disgrace me to suffer the pilgrim's staff and scrip to remain there." She commanded them to be taken away; and thus forgot her vows, and plainly showed her ingratitude.

Tale 26

THE GARMENT OF THE ILLEGITIMATE SON

THERE WAS A QUEEN WHO DISHONOURED HERSELF WITH A servant, and bore him a son. This son, on arriving at maturity, practised every description of wickedness, and conducted himself with the greatest insolence toward the prince, his reputed father.

The prince, unable to account for such perversion of mind,

interrogated the mother as to the legitimacy of her child; and finding, by her reluctant confession, that he was not his son, though loth to deprive him of the kingdom, he ordained that his dress, for the time to come, should be of a different texture and colour. One side to be composed of the most ordinary materials, and the other of the most valuable; so that when he looked upon the baser portion, his pride might be abated, and the vicious tendencies, in which he had indulged, relinquished. On the other hand, when he surveyed the more gorgeous part, his hopes might be raised, and his spirit prompted to goodness.

By this judicious device, he became remarkable for humility, and ever after abandoned his dishonest life.

Tale 27

THE STEWARD WHO DISOBEYED HIS KING

A VERY RICH AND POWERFUL EMPEROR HAD AN ONLY daughter of uncommon beauty. She was consigned to the care of five soldiers, who were commanded to be constantly in arms; and every day a stated sum was paid them out of the king's treasury. This emperor had a steward whom he greatly favoured; and a valuable but ferocious dog, which it was necessary to confine with triple chains, since it killed all it could seize.

It happened that, as the emperor lay in bed, he formed a resolution to proceed to the Holy Land; and in the morning, when he arose, sent for the steward, and said, "I am about to undertake an expedition to Palestine; to your vigilance I commit my only daughter, with the soldiers of her guard. The dog, likewise, which I specially value, I entrust to your care; and, on pain of instant death, let there be no deficiency in attendance upon my daughter. You shall supply the soldiers with all that they require; but observe that the dog is securely chained, and fed sparingly, so that his ferocity may abate."

The steward approved of all the emperor's injunctions, and promised faithfully to comply with them; instead of which he acted in direct opposition. The dog was fed with the most unsuitable food, and not guarded as he ought to have been. He denied the necessaries of life to the lady, and robbed the soldiers of their pay, who, being needy and unemployed, roamed over the country in great distress. As for the poor girl, forsaken and destitute, she passed from her chamber into the courtyard of the hall which she occupied, and there wandered up and down in sorrow and tears.

Now, the dog, whose savage nature improper food had increased, burst by a sudden and violent movement from the bonds that enchained him, and tore her limb from limb. When this afflicting circumstance was known in the kingdom, it excited universal regret. And when the emperor heard of his daughter's death, he was deeply moved. The steward was summoned before him, and asked why the lady had been left unprovided for, the soldiers unpaid, and the dog improperly fed, contrary to his express command. But the man was unable to answer, and offered not the least excuse. The torturers, therefore, were called in; he was bound hand and foot, and thrown into a fiery furnace.

The emperor's decree gave satisfaction to the whole empire.

Tale 28

LITTLE DOG'S TEARS

IN THE KINGDOM OF A CERTAIN EMPRESS THERE LIVED A knight, who was happily espoused to a·noble, chaste, and

beautiful wife. It happened that he was called upon to take
a long journey, and previous to his departure he said to the
lady, "I leave you no guard but your own discretion; I believe it to be wholly sufficient." He then embarked with his
attendants. She meanwhile continued at her own mansion,
in the daily practice of every virtue.

A short period had elapsed, when the urgent entreaties of
a neighbour prevailed with her to appear at a festival; where,
amongst other guests, was a youth, upon whom the excellence and beauty of the lady made a deep impression. He
became violently enamoured of her, and despatched various
emissaries to declare his passion, and win her to approve his
suit. But the virtuous lady received his advances with the
utmost scorn. This untoward repulse greatly disconcerted
the youth, and his health declined. Nevertheless he visited
the lady oft, which availed him nothing; he was still despised.

It chanced that on one occasion he went sorrowfully
towards the church; and, upon the way, an old woman accosted him, who by pretended sanctity had long obtained an
undue share of reverence and regard. She demanded the cause
of the youth's apparent uneasiness.

"It will profit me nothing to tell thee," said he.

"But," replied the old woman, "as long as the sick man
hides his malady from the physician he cannot be cured.
Discover the wound, and it is not impossible but a remedy
may be found. With the aid of Heaven I will restore you to
health." Thus urged, the youth made known to her his love
for the lady.

"Is that all?" said the beldam. "Return to your home, I will
find a medicine that shall presently relieve you." Confiding
in her assurances, he went his way.

It seems she possessed a little dog, which she obliged to fast
for two successive days; on the third, she made bread of the

flour of mustard, and placed it before the pining animal. As soon as it had tasted the bread, the pungent bitterness caused the water to spring into its eyes, and the whole of that day tears flowed copiously from them. The old woman, accompanied by her dog, posted to the house of the lady whom the young man loved; and the opinion entertained of her sanctity secured her an honourable and gracious reception.

As they sat together, the lady noticed the weeping dog, and was curious to ascertain the cause. The crone told her not to inquire, for that it involved a calamity too dreadful to communicate. Such a remark, naturally enough, excited still more the curiosity of the fair questioner, and she earnestly pressed her to detail the story.

This was what the old hag wanted; she said, "That little dog was my daughter—too good and excellent for this world. She was beloved by a young man, who, thrown into despair by her cruelty, perished for her love. My daughter, as a punishment for her hard-hearted conduct, was suddenly changed into the little dog respecting which you inquire."

Saying these words, a few crocodile tears started into her eyes; and she continued, "Alas! How often does this mute memorial recall my lost daughter, once so beautiful and virtuous: now—oh, what is she now? Degraded from the state of humanity, she exists only to pine away in wretchedness, and waste her life in tears. She can receive no comfort; and they who would administer it can but weep for her distresses, which surely are without a parallel."

The lady, astonished and terrified at what she heard, secretly exclaimed—"Alas! I too am beloved; and he who loves me is in like manner at the point of death."

Then, instigated by her fears, told the whole circumstance to the old woman, who immediately answered, "Beautiful lady, do not disregard the anguish of this young man: look upon my unhappy daughter, and be warned in time. As she is, you may be."

"Oh!" returned the credulous lady, "My good mother, counsel me; what would you have me do? Not for worlds would I become as she is."

"Why, then," answered the treacherous old woman, "send directly for the youth, and give him the love he so eagerly desires."

The lady said, "May I entreat your holiness to fetch him; there might be some scandal circulated if another went."

"My dear daughter," said she, "I suffer with you, and will presently bring him hither."

She arose and returned with him; and thus the youth obtained his mistress. And so, through the old woman's means, the lady was led into adultery.

Tale 29

PUNISHMENT FOR CORRUPTION

AN EMPEROR ESTABLISHED A LAW THAT EVERY JUDGE CONvicted of corrupt administration of justice should undergo the severest penalties.

It happened that a certain judge, bribed by a large sum, gave a notoriously corrupt decision. This circumstance reaching the ears of the emperor, he commanded him to be flayed. The sentence was immediately executed, and the skin of the culprit nailed upon the seat of judgment, as an awful warning to others to avoid a similar offence.

The emperor afterwards bestowed the same dignity upon the son of the deceased judge, and on presenting the appointment, said, "Thou wilt sit, to administer justice, upon the skin of thy delinquent sire: should any one incite thee to do evil, remember his fate; look down upon thy father's skin, lest his fate befall thee."

Tale 30

THE THREE HONOURS

A CERTAIN KING DETERMINED ON THE OCCASION OF SOME victory to appoint three especial honours, and an equal number of disagreeable accompaniments. The first of the honours was that the people should meet the conqueror with acclamations and every other testimony of pleasure. The second, that all the captives, bound hand and foot, should attend the victor's chariot. The third honour was that, wrapped in the tunic of Jupiter, he should sit upon a triumphal car, drawn by four white horses, and be thus brought to the capital.

But lest these exalted rewards should swell the heart, and make the favourite of fortune forget his birth and mortal character, three causes of annoyance were attached to them. First, a slave sat on his right hand in the chariot—which served to hint that poverty and unmerited degradation were no bars to the subsequent attainment of the highest dignities. The second annoyance was that the slave should inflict upon him several severe blows, to abate the haughtiness which the applause of his countrymen might tend to excite—at the same time saying to him "Know thyself, and permit not thy exaltation to render thee proud. Look behind thee, and remember that thou art mortal." The third annoyance was this, that free licence was given, upon that day of triumph,

to utter the most galling reproaches, and the most cutting
sarcasms, against the victor while enjoying his triumph.

Tale 31

THE PHILOSOPHY OF DEATH

WE READ THAT AT THE DEATH OF ALEXANDER A GOLDEN
sepulchre was constructed, and that a number of philosophers
assembled round it.

One said—"Yesterday, Alexander made a treasure of gold;
and now gold makes a treasure of him."

Another observed—"Yesterday, the whole world was not
enough to quench his ambition; to-day, three or four ells
of cloth are more than sufficient."

A third said—"Yesterday, Alexander commanded the
people; to-day, the people command him."

Another said—"Yesterday, Alexander could enfranchise
thousands; to-day, he cannot avoid the spear of death."

Another remarked—"Yesterday, he pressed the earth; to-
day, it oppresses him."

"Yesterday," continued another, "all men feared Alexander; to-day, men count him as nothing."

Another said—"Yesterday, Alexander had a multitude of
friends; to-day, not one.

Still another said—"Yesterday, Alexander led on an army;
to-day, that army bears him to the grave."

Tale 32

A NOTE ON POISON

SENECA MENTIONS THAT IN POISONED BODIES, ON ACCOUNT
of the malignancy and coldness of the poison, no worm will

enter; but if the body be struck with lightning, in a few days it will be full of them.

Tale 33

A TREE FOR WIVES TO HANG UPON

VALERIUS TELLS US THAT A MAN NAMED PALETINUS ONE day burst into a flood of tears, and calling his son and his neighbours around him, said, "Alas! aslas! I have now growing in my garden a fatal tree, on which my first poor wife hung herself, then my second, and after that my third. Have I not therefore cause for the wretchedness I exhibit?"

"Truly," said one who was called Arrius, "I marvel that you should weep at such an unusual instance of good fortune! Give me, I pray you, two or three sprigs of that gentle tree, which I will divide with my neighbours, and thereby afford every man an opportunity of indulging the laudable wishes of his spouse."

Paletinus complied with his friend's request, and ever after found this remarkable tree the most productive part of his estate.

Tale 34

ARISTOTLE'S ADVICE TO ALEXANDER

WE READ THAT ALEXANDER THE GREAT WAS THE DISCIPLE of Aristotle, from whose instructions he derived the greatest advantage. Amongst other important matters, he inquired of his master what would profit himself, and at the same time be serviceable to others.

Aristotle answered, "My son, hear with attention; and if you retain my counsel, you will arrive at the greatest honours. There are seven distinct points to be regarded. First, that you do not overcharge the balance. Secondly, that you do not feed a fire with the sword. Thirdly, stress not at the crown; nor, Fourthly, eat the heart of a little bird. Fifthly, when you have once commenced a proper undertaking, never turn from it. Sixthly, walk not in the highroad; and, Seventhly, do not allow a prating swallow to possess your eaves."

The king carefully considered the meaning of these puzzling directions; and, observing them, experienced their utility in his subsequent life.

Tale 35

WITH THE BLOOD OF A LAMB

IN THE ROMAN ANNALS WE READ THAT IT WAS CUSTOMARY, when peace was established between noblemen who had been at variance, to ascend a lofty mountain, and take with them a lamb. This they sacrificed in pledge of complete reunion; thereby intimating, that as they then poured forth the blood of the lamb, so should his blood be poured forth, who infringed the smallest article of that solemn compact.

Tale 36

WHAT IS MAN?

WE ARE TOLD OF A CERTAIN KING WHO, BEYOND ALL OTHER things, wished to make himself acquainted with the nature of man. Now, in a remote part of his kingdom, there dewlt a famous philosopher, by whose great science many surprising mysteries were expounded. When the king heard of his celebrity, he despatched a messenger to him to command his immediate appearance at court.

The philosopher willingly complied with the king's wish. On his reaching the palace, the royal inquirer thus addressed him: "Master, I have heard much of your extraordinary wisdom, and profound research into natural phenomena. I would myself bear testimony to the truth of the general report. In the first place, tell me what is man?"

The philosopher answered, "Man is a wretched thing; this is his beginning, middle, and end. There is no truth so apparent; and therefore Job said, 'Man that is born of a woman is full of miseries.' Look upon him at his birth; he is poor and powerless. In the middle period of his life, you will find the world attacking him, narrowing his comforts, and contributing to the eternal reprobation of his soul. If you review the end, you will mark the earth opening to receive him! And then, O king! what becomes of the pomp of your regal establishment—of the pride of your worldly glory?"

"Master," said the king, "I will ask you four questions, which if you answer well and wisely, I will elevate you to wealth and honour. My first demand is, What is man? My second, What is he like? The third, Where is he? and the fourth, With whom is he associated?"

The philosopher replied, "At your first question, my lord, I cannot but laugh. You ask, 'What is man?' Why, what is he but the slave of death—the guest of the place he dwells in —a traveller hastily journeying to a distant land! He is a slave, because he is subject to the hand of the tomb; death fetters him, sweeps off from the scene even the memorials of his name, and causes his days to drop away, like the leaves in autumn. But according to his desert will he be rewarded or punished. Again, man is the 'guest of the place he dwells in,' for he lingers a few short hours, and then oblivion covers him as with a garment. He is also a 'a traveller journeying to a distant land.' He passes on, sleepless and watchful, with scarce a moment given him to snatch the means of subsistence, and discharge the relative duties of his station. Death hurries him away. How much, therefore, are we called upon to provide every requisite for the journey—that is, the virtues which beseem and support the Christian.

"To your second question, 'What is man like?' I answer that he resembles a sheet of ice, which the heat of noon certainly and rapidly dissolves. Thus man, mixed up of gross and elementary particles, by the fervour of his own infirmities, quickly falls into corruption. Moreover, he is like an apple hanging upon its parent stem. The exterior is fair, and promises a rich maturity—but there is a worm preying silently within; ere long it drops to the earth, perforated and rotten at the core. Whence, then, arises human pride?

"The third query is, 'Where is man?' I reply, in a state of war, for he has to contend against the world, the flesh, and the devil.

"Your fourth demand was, 'With whom is he associated?' With seven troublesome companions, which continually beset and torment him. These are, hunger, thirst, heat, cold, weariness, infirmity, and death. Arm, therefore, the soul against the devil, the world, and the flesh, whose wars are divers seductive temptations. Various preparations are needful for an effectual resistance. The flesh tempts us with voluptuousness; the world, by the gratifications of vanity; and the devil, by the suggestions of pride. If, then, the flesh tempt thee, remember that, though the day and the hour be unknown, it must soon return into its primitive dust; and, remember yet more, that eternal punishment awaits thy abandoning of virtue. So, in the second chapter of the Book of Wisdom, 'Our body shall become dust and ashes.' It follows that, after these passages of mortal life, oblivion shall be our portion—we and our deeds alike shall be forgotten. The recollection of this will often oppose a barrier to temptation, and prevent its clinging with fatal tenacity to the heart.

"If the vanity of the world allure thee, reflect upon its ingratitude, and thou wilt be little desirous of becoming bound to it. And though thou shouldst dedicate thy whole life to its service, it will permit thee to carry off nothing but thy sins. This may be exemplified by the fable of the partridge. A partridge, anxious for the safety of her young, on the approach of a sportsman ran before him, feigning herself wounded, in order to draw him from her nest. The sportsman, crediting this appearance, eagerly followed. But she lured him on, until he had entirely lost sight of the nest, and then rapidly flew away. Thus the sportsman, deceived by the bird's artifice, obtained only his labour for his pains.

"So it is with the world. The sportsman who approaches the nest is the good Christian, who acquires food and clothing by the sweat of his brow. The world calls, and holds out the temptation, which his frailty cannot resist. She tells him that if he follow her, he will attain the desire of his heart. Thus he is gradually removed from works of goodness, and follows the vanities of this world. Death comes and bears on his pale steed the deceived and miserable man, since he neither has those worldly goods he sought nor the fruit of good works. See how the world rewards its veterans! So, in the second chapter of James, 'The whole world is placed in evil; is composed of the pride of life,' &c.

"In the third place, if the devil tempt thee, remember Christ's sorrows and sufferings—a thought which pride cannot surely resist. 'Put on,' says the apostle, 'the whole armour of God, that ye may stand fast.' Solinus tells us, speaking of the wonders of the world, that Alexander had a certain horse which he called Bucephalus. When this animal was armed, and prepared for battle, he would permit no one but Alexander to mount; and if another attempted it, he presently threw him. But in the trappings of peace, he made no resistance, mount him who would.

"Thus a man, armed by the passion of our Lord, receives none into his heart but God; and if the temptations of the devil strive to sit there, they are cast violently down. Without this armour, it is open to every temptation. Let us then study to clothe ourselves with virtue, that we may at length come to the glory of God."

Tale 37

THE EAGLE AND THE SERPENT

PLINY MENTIONS THE STORY OF AN EAGLE THAT HAD BUILT her nest upon a lofty rock, whose young a kind of serpent called *Perna* attempted to destroy. But finding that they were beyond her reach, she stationed herself to windward and emitted a large quantity of poisonous matter, so as to infect the atmosphere and poison the young birds.

But the eagle, led by the unerring power of instinct, took this precaution. She fetched a peculiar sort of stone called agate which she deposited in that quarter of the nest which was against the wind; and the stone by virtue of certain occult properties which it possessed, prevented the malicious intentions of the serpent from taking effect.

Tale 38

A DOVE WARNS THE CITY

IN THE REIGN OF THE EMPEROR HENRY II., A CERTAIN CITY was besieged by its enemies. Before they had reached its walls a dove alighted in the city, around whose neck a letter was suspended, which bore the following inscription:—"The generation of dogs is at hand; it will prove a quarrelsome breed; procure aid, and defend yourselves resolutely against it."

Tale 39

FROM DISCORD TO PEACE

THE ROMAN ANNALS SAY, SUCH DISCORD EXISTED BETWEEN two brothers, that one of them maliciously laid waste the lands of the other.

The Emperor Julius having heard of this, determined to punish the offender capitally. The latter, therefore, understanding what was meditated, went to the brother whom he had injured, and besought forgiveness; at the same time requesting that he should screen him from the emperor's vengeance.

But they who were present at the interview rebuked him, and declared that he deserved punishment, not pardon. To which he from whom forgiveness was asked made the following reply: "That prince is not worthy of regard who in war assumes the gentleness of a lamb, but in peace puts on the ferocity of a lion. Although my brother should not incline towards me, yet will I endeavour to conciliate him. For the injury he did me is sufficiently avenged now that he is asking for pardon."

And thus he restored peace between the enraged emperor and his brother.

Tale 40

HOW THE KNIGHT TESTED HIS WIFE'S AFFECTIONS

MACROBIUS RELATES THAT A CERTAIN KNIGHT, IN CONSE-quence of something he had witnessed, suspected his wife of transferring her affections from himself to another. He interrogated her on the subject, but she firmly denied it. Not satisfied with her asseverations, the knight inquired for a cunning clerk; and having found such as he wanted, he proposed to him the question which disturbed his rest.

The clerk answered, "Unless I am permitted to see and converse with the lady, I cannot take upon me to decide."

"I pray you, then," said the knight, "dine with me to-day, and I will give you the opportunity you require."

Accordingly the clerk went to the knight's house to dinner. The meal being concluded, our clerk entered into conversation with the suspected lady, and spoke to her on various topics. This done, he took hold of her hand; and, as if accidentally, pressed his finger upon her pulse. Then, in a careless tone, adverting to the person whom she was presumed to love, her pulse immediately quickened to a surprising degree, and acquired a feverish heat.

By and by the clerk mentioned her husband, and spoke of him in much the same way as he had done of the other; when the motion of her pulse abated, and its heat was entirely lost. Whereby he plainly perceived that her affections were alienated; and, moreover, that they were placed upon the very person respecting whom she had been accused.

Thus, by the management of a learned clerk, the knight ascertained the truth of his suspicion.

Tale 41

DEATH OF THE ATHENIAN KING

COSDRAS, KING OF THE ATHENIANS, HAVING DECLARED WAR against the Dorians, assembled an army, and despatched messengers to the oracle of Apollo, to ascertain the fortune of the engagement. The god answered that, unless he himself fell by the sword of the enemy, he should not win the battle.

The Dorians, also, understanding the response of the oracle, strictly enjoined their soldiers to spare the life of Cosdras; but the king, disguising himself, cut his way into the heart of the hostile army. One of their soldiers seeing this, pierced him to the heart with a lance.

Thus, by the sacrifice of his own life, he rescued his people from the hands of their enemies, and his death was bewailed not less by the adverse host than by his own subjects.

Tale 42

A PROPHECY CONCERNING THE FALL OF ROME

VALERIUS RECORDS THAT HE ONCE SAW IN THE CITY OF Rome a very lofty column, on which were inscribed four letters, three times repeated—three P's, three S's, three R's, and three F's. When the letters had attracted attention, he exclaimed, "Woe, woe; I see confusion to the city."

The nobles, hearing what had been done, said to him, "Master, let us understand thy conceit."

He answered, "The meaning of the inscription is this: 'Pater patriæ perditur.' [The father of his country is lost.] 'Sapientia secum sustollitur.' [Wisdom has departed with him.] 'Ruunt reges Romæ.' [The kings of Rome perish.] 'Ferro, flamma, fame.' " [By the sword, by fire, by famine.]

The event afterwards fully approved the veracity of the prediction.

Tale 43

A LIFE FOR THE ABYSS

IN THE MIDDLE OF ROME THERE WAS ONCE AN IMMENSE chasm, which no human efforts could fill up. The gods being questioned relative to this extraordinary circumstance, made answer that, unless a man could be found who would voluntarily commit himself to the gulf, it would remain unclosed for ever.

Proclamations were sent forth, signifying that he who was willing to offer himself as sacrifice for the good of his country should appear—but not a man ventured to declare himself.

At length Marcus Curtius said, "If ye will permit me to live as I please during the space of one whole year, I will cheerfully surrender myself, at the end of it to the yawning chasm."

The Romans assented with joy, and Curtius indulged for that year in every wish of his heart. Then, mounting a noble steed, he rode furiously into the abyss, which immediately closed over him.

Tale 44

STORY OF THE FLEXIBLE GLASS

BEFORE TIBERIUS ASCENDED THE THRONE, HE WAS REMARK-
able for his wisdom. His eloquence was brilliant, and his
military operations invariably successful. But when he became emperor his nature seemed to have undergone a perfect
revolution. All martial enterprises were abandoned, and the
nation groaned beneath his relentless and cruel tyranny. He
put to death his own sons, and therefore it was not be be expected that he should spare those of others. The patricians
threatened, and the people cursed him. Formerly he had
been noted for temperance, but now he showed himself the
most intemperate of a dissolute age; insomuch that he obtained the surname of Bacchus.

It happened that a certain artificer fabricated a plate of
glass, which, being exhibited to the emperor, he attempted,
but ineffectually, to break it. It bent, however, beneath
his efforts, and the artificer, applying a hammer and work-
ing upon the glass as upon copper, presently restored it to
its original form.

Tiberius inquired by what art this was effected; and the
other replied that it was a secret not to be disclosed. Immediately he was ordered to the block, the emperor alleging that
if such an art should be practised, gold and silver would be
reckoned as nothing.

Tale 45

THE CONTEST BETWEEN THE FOUR BROTHERS

THERE WAS A WISE AND RICH KING WHO POSSESSED A BE-
loved, but not a loving wife. She had three illegitimate sons,

who proved ungrateful and rebellious to their reputed parent. In due time she brought forth another son, whose legitimacy was undisputed; and after arriving at a good old age, the king died, and was buried in the royal sepulchre of his fathers.

But the death of the old king caused great strife amongst his surviving sons, about the right of succession. All of them advanced a claim, and none would relinquish it to the other; the three first presuming upon their priority in birth, and the last upon his legitimacy. In this strait, they agreed to refer the absolute decision of their cause to a certain honourable knight of the late king.

When this person, therefore, heard their difference, he said, "Follow my advice, and it will greatly benefit you. Draw from its sepulchre the body of the deceased monarch; prepare, each of you, a bow and single shaft, and whosoever transfixes the heart of his father shall obtain the kingdom."

The counsel was approved, the body was taken from its repository and bound to a tree. The arrow of the first son wounded the king's right hand—on which, as if the contest were determined, they proclaimed him heir to the throne. But the second arrow went nearer, and entered the mouth; so that he, too, considered himself the undoubted lord of the kingdom. However, the third perforated the heart itself, and consequently imagined that his claim was fully decided, and his succession sure.

It now came to the turn of the fourth and last son to shoot, but he broke forth into a lamentable cry, and with eyes swimming in tears, said, "Oh! my poor father; have I then lived to see you the victim of an impious contest— thine own offspring lacerate thy unconscious clay?—Far, oh! far be it from me to strike thy venerated form, whether living or dead."

No sooner had he uttered these words, than the nobles of

the realm, together with the whole people, unanimously elected him to the throne; and depriving the three barbarous wretches of their rank and wealth expelled them for ever from the kingdom.

Tale 46

THE MAN WHO GATHERED MORE THAN HE COULD CARRY

JULIUS RELATES THAT IN THE MONTH OF MAY A CERTAIN man entered a grove, in which stood seven beautiful trees in leaf. The leaves so much attracted him, that he collected more than he had strength to carry. On this, three men came to his assistance, who led away both the man and the load beneath which he laboured.

As he went out he fell into a deep pit, and the extreme weight upon his shoulders forced him to the very bottom.

The same author also relates, in his history of animals, that if, after a crow has built her nest, you wish to hinder her from hatching her eggs, place between the bark and the tree a quantity of pounded glass; and as long as it remains in that situation, she will never bring off her young.

Tale 47

THE DANISH KING AND THE THREE MAGI

A DANISH KING HAD THE GREATEST REVERENCE FOR THE three Eastern Magi whom the star led to Jerusalem on the nativity of our blessed Lord; and he was usually in the habit of invoking them to his aid upon any dilemma. The pious king set out with a great company to Cologne, where the bodies of these sainted kings are preserved with great splendour, taking with him three golden crowns, constructed after a wonderful and royal fashion. Besides this, he distributed more than six thousand marks to the church and to the poor, thus leaving an example of faith to his people.

As he returned to his own dominions, he fell into deep sleep; and dreamt that he beheld the three kings bearing upon their heads the crowns he had lately presented, from whence issued a dazzling lustre. Each appeared to address him in turn.

The first and the elder of the three said, "My brother, thou hast happily arrived hither, and happily shalt thou return."

The next said, "Thou hast offered much, but more shalt thou carry back with thee."

The third said, "My brother, thou art faithful; therefore with us shalt thou conjointly reign in heaven at the end of twenty-three years."

Then the elder presented to him a box filled with gold— "Receive," said he, "a treasury of wisdom, by which thou wilt judge thy people with equity."

The second presented a box of myrrh, and said, "Receive the myrrh of prudence, which will bridle the deceitful workings of the flesh: for he best governs who is master of himself."

The third brought a box full of frankincense, saying, "Receive the frankincense of devotion and clemency; for thus shalt thou relieve and soothe the wretched. And as the dew moistens the herbage and promotes a large increase of fertility, so the clemency of a king lifts him to the stars."

The sleeping monarch, surprised at the distinctness and singularity of his vision, suddenly awoke, and found the boxes, with their rich contents, deposited by his side. Returning to his own kingdom, he devoutedly fulfilled the purport of his dream, and on the conclusion of the period foretold, he was worthy to possess an everlasting throne.

Tale 48

BY HIS OWN DEVICES

DIONYSIUS RECORDS THAT WHEN PERILLUS DESIRED TO BE-come a craftsman of Phalaris, a cruel and tyrannical king who depopulated the kingdom of Agrigentum, and was guilty of many dreadful excesses, he presented to him, already too well skilled in cruelty, a brazen bull, which he had just constructed. In one of its sides there was a secret door, by which those who were sentenced should enter and be burnt to death.

The idea was that the sounds produced by the agony of the sufferer confined within should resemble the roaring of a bull; and thus, while nothing human struck the ear, the mind should be unimpressed by a feeling of mercy.

The king highly applauded the invention, and said, "Friend, the value of thy industry is yet untried; more cruel even than the people account me, thou thyself shalt be the first victim."

Indeed, there is no law more just than that "the artificer of death should perish by his own devices," as Ovid has observed.

Tale 49

THE TREACHERY OF THE DUCHESS AND ITS REWARD

PAULUS, THE HISTORIAN OF THE LONGOBARDS, RELATES that Conan, king of the Hungarians, was besieging a castle in the town of Julius, called Sondat. Rosimila, the duchess of that place, had four sons and two daughters. When she perceived that Conan was a wonderfully handsome man, she sent him a secret message, saying, "If you will take me to wife I will surrender the castle to you."

The king acquiesced and the castle was given up; but the sons, indignant at the treacherous conduct of their mother, fled together. Conan, however, adhering to his promise, married the duchess on the following day.

But the next morning after the nuptials, he delivered her to twelve Hungarian soldiers, to be publicly abused and mocked; and on the third day, he commanded her to be stabbed, and transfixed from the throat downward, observing, "that a wife who betrayed her country to gratify her evil passions, ought to possess such a husband."

Tale 50

THE EMPEROR GIVES AN EYE FOR HIS SON

VALERIUS INFORMS US THAT THE EMPEROR ZELONGUS MADE a law by which, if any one abused a virgin, he should lose both his eyes. It happened that his only son trespassed in this manner with the daughter of a certain widow, who immediately hastened into the presence of the emperor, and spoke thus: "My lord, you have righteously decreed that he who defiles a virgin shall lose his sight. Your only son has dishonoured my daughter; command him to be punished."

These words greatly distressed the emperor, but he gave instant orders respecting the punishment of his son.

On this, two noblemen observed: "The young man is your only child, and heir to the throne; it were impious if for this he should lose his eyes."

The emperor answered, "Is it not evident to you that I myself ordained this very law? Disgraceful as the occasion is, it may break my heart, but not my resolution. My son has been the first to transgress the law, and therefore shall be the first to undergo the penalty."

"Sire," said the nobleman, "let us implore you, for the sake of Heaven, to forgive the errors of your child."

Somewhat subdued by the urgency of their entreaties, the emperor, after a moment's pause, said, "My friends, listen to me: my eyes are the eyes of my son; and his are in like manner mine. Pluck out, therefore, my right eye, and let him surrender his left; thus, the law will be satisfied."

The paternal affection of the emperor was indulged, and the whole kingdom extolled the prudence and justice of their prince.

Tale 51

WHY THE CORRUPT GOVERNORS WERE RETAINED

JOSEPHUS MENTIONS THAT TIBERIUS CÆSAR, WHEN ASKED why the corrupt governors of provinces remained so long in office, answered by a fable.

"I have seen," said he, "an infirm man covered with ulcers, grievously tormented by a swarm of flies. When I was going to drive them away for him with a flap, he said to me, 'The means by which you think to relieve me would, in effect, promote tenfold suffering. For by driving away the flies now saturated with my blood, I should afford an opportunity to those that were empty and hungry to supply their place. And who doubts that the biting of a hungry insect is not ten thousand times more painful than that of one completely gorged —unless the person attacked be stone, and not flesh.' "

Tale 52

THE PROMISE KEPT

VALERIUS RECORDS THAT FABIUS REDEEMED CERTAIN CAPtives by the promise of a sum of money; which when the senate refused to confirm, he sold all the property he possessed, and with the produce paid down the stipulated sum, caring less to be poor in lands than poor in honesty.

Tale 53

WHY THE OLD WOMAN PRAYED FOR THE KING

VALERIUS MAXIMUS STATES THAT, WHEN ALL THE SYRACUsans desired the death of Dionysius, king of Sicily, a single woman, of great age, every morning entreated the gods to continue his life beyond hers. Dionysius, surprised at this solitary exception, inquired the reason. She answered, "When I was a girl, and governed by a tyrant, I wished for his removal, and presently we obtained a worse instead. Having got rid of him, a worse still succeeded; and therefore, under the justifiable apprehension that your place may be filled up by yet a worse, I pray earnestly for your longer continuance."

Dionysius, hearing this, gave her no farther trouble.

Tale 54

THE GATE OF EMPEROR FREDERIC

THE EMPEROR FREDERIC II. CONSTRUCTED A CURIOUS MAR-
ble gate at the entrance of Capua. It stood above a fountain
of running water; and upon it the statues of the emperor
and two of his judges were sculptured.

In a half circle over the head of the right-hand judge was
inscribed as follows: "He who regards his own safety and innocence, let him enter here." Similarly over the head of the
left-hand judge appeared this scroll, "Banishment or imprisonment is the doom of the envious." In a semicircle over
the emperor's head was written, "Those whom I made miserable, I recompensed." In like manner, above the gate was
inscribed, "In Cæsar's reign I became the guardian of the
kingdom."

Tale 55

THE RETURN OF THE BANISHED WIFE

A CERTAIN GREAT KING HAD A HANDSOME SON, WHO PROVED
himself, on all occasions, wise, bold, and courteous. The same
king had four daughters also, whose names were Justice,
Truth, Mercy, and Peace. Now, the king, being very desirous
of procuring for his son a suitable partner, despatched a messenger in search of a beautiful virgin, to whom he should be
united. At last, the daughter of the King of Jerusalem was
selected, and married to the young prince, who was much
struck with the beauty of his bride.

At this time there was in the court a servant whom the king's son principally trusted, and to whom he had confided the care of one of his provinces. This man, in return for the benefits accumulated upon him, seduced the lady, and wasted the country over which he was placed. When the husband, therefore, knew of his wife's infidelity, he was overwhelmed with sorrow, and took from her every honour.

Thus she fell into extreme poverty; and, reduced to despair by the wretchedness of her condition, walked from place to place begging her bread, and wishing for death, that came not to her relief. But at length the husband, softened by her distress, sent messengers to recall her to his court.

"Come, lady," they said, "come in perfect safety. Thy lord wishes thy return; fear nothing."

Yet she refused, and exclaimed, "Tell my lord that I would willingly come to him, but I am unable to do so. If he asks why, say, in compliance with an imperious law. If a man marry, and his wife prove an adultress, he shall give her a bill of divorcement; but from that hour, she can be no longer his wife. To me such a writing has been given—for, alas! I am an adultress; therefore, it is impossible for me to return to my lord."

"But," replied the messengers, "our lord is greater than the law which he made himself: and since he is disposed to show mercy towards you, we repeat that you may properly comply with his wishes, secure from further punishment or reproach."

"How shall I know that?" said the lady; "if my beloved would assure me of it; if he would deign to come and kiss me with the kiss of his lip, then should I feel certain of favour."

When the messengers communicated to the prince what had passed between them and his afflicted wife, he called together the noblemen of his kingdom, and deliberated upon the measures it became him to adopt. After mature reflection, they determined that some man of experience and judgment should be sent to persuade her to return.

But they who answered this description refused to undertake the office; and the husband, in his extremity, despatched once more a messenger, whom he commissioned to speak thus: "What can I do for you? There is not a man in my dominions who will execute my wishes!"

These words increased the anguish of the unfortunate lady, and she wept bitterly. Her condition was related to the prince, and he earnestly besought his father to give him permission to bring back his wife, and to calm her sorrows.

The king acquiesced— "Go," said he, "go now in thy might, and reinstate her in the seat from which she has fallen." The messengers were then ordered to return and apprize her of the purposed visit.

But the prince's elder sister, that is to say, JUSTICE, understanding what was meditated, hastened to her father, and said, "My lord, thou art just. You decided rightly concerning that harlot. You properly sanctioned the writing of divorcement, whereby she could no longer be my brother's wife; therefore, to the law let her appeal. And if, in violation of justice, you act thus, be assured that I will no longer be accounted your daughter."

The second sister, who was called TRUTH, then said, "My father, she has spoken truly. You have adjudged this woman an adultress: if you permit her to return, you destroy the very essence of truth, and therefore I, too, will no more fulfil the offices of a daughter."

But the third sister, called MERCY, hearing what had been said by the other two, exclaimed, "Oh, my lord, I also am thy daughter; forgive the offence of this repentant woman. If thou wilt not, thou abandonest Mercy, and she will never again acknowledge thee her father."

The fourth sister, whose name was PEACE, terrified at the discord between her parent and sisters, desired to leave the country, and fled.

Justice and Truth, however, relinquished not their purpose; and, putting into their father's hands a naked sword, said, "My lord, we present to you the sword of Justice. Take it, and strike the harlot who has wronged our brother."

But Mercy, rushing forward, snatched the weapon from their grasp. "Enough, enough," cried she; "long have you reigned, and inclinations have been your only law. Now forbear; it is fit that my wishes should sometimes be listened to. Remember that I, too, am the daughter of the king."

To this Justice made answer, "Thou hast said well: we *have* reigned long; and long will we preserve our authority. But since there is this discord, call our brother, who is wise in all things; and let him judge between us."

The proposal was assented to. They showed him the grounds of their dispute, and explained how Justice and Truth obstinately demanded the infliction of the law, while Mercy sought a free forgiveness.

"My beloved sisters," said the prince, "I am little satisfied with the flight of my sister Peace, whom your apparent strife has banished. This ought not to be, and shall not. And as for my adulterous wife, I am prepared to undergo her punishment myself."

"If this be your determination," observed Justice, "we cannot oppose you, my brother."

Then turning towards Mercy, he said, "Use your endeavour to restore my wife. But should I receive her, and she again falls, do you design to renew your pleading?"

"Not," said the other, "unless she be truly penitent."

The prince then conducted back his sister Peace, and caused each of the others to embrace her, in turn. Concord being thus re-established, he hastened to his erring wife. She was received with every honour, and ended her days in peace.

Tale 56

THE ENVYING MERCHANT AND THE PRINCE

A CERTAIN PRINCE DERIVED GREAT PLEASURE FROM THE chase. It happened, on one occasion, that a merchant accidentally pursued the same path; and observing the beauty, affability, and splendour of the prince, he said in his heart, "Oh, ye heavenly powers! that man has received too many favours. He is handsome, bold, and graceful; and even his very retinue are equipped with splendour and comfort." Under the impression of such feelings, he addressed himself to one of the attendants. "My friend," said he, "tell me who your master is?"

"He is," replied the other, "the despotic lord of an extensive territory; his treasury is filled with silver and gold; and his slaves are exceedingly numerous."

"God has been bountiful to him," said the merchant; "he is more beautiful than any one I ever beheld; and he is as wise as any I have met with."

Now, the person with whom he conversed related to his master all that the merchant had said; and as the prince turned homeward about the hour of vespers, he besought the merchant to tarry there all night. The entreaty of a potentate is a command; and the merchant, therefore, though with some reluctance, returned to the city. When he had entered the palace, the great display of wealth, the number of beautiful halls, ornamented in every part with gold, surprised and delighted him. But supper-time approached, and the merchant, by express command of the prince, was seated next his wife.

This honour, and her beauty and gracious manner, so enraptured the poor tradesman, that he secretly exclaimed, "Oh, Heaven! the prince possesses everything that his heart wishes; he has a beautiful wife, fair daughters, and brave sons. His family establishment is too expensive." As he thus thought, the meat was placed before him; but what was his consternation to observe that it was deposited in the skull of a human being, and served from thence to the prince and his guests on silver dishes. Horror-struck at what he saw, the merchant said to himself, "Alas, I fear I shall lose my head in this place!"

In the mean time the lady of the mansion comforted him as much as she could. The night passed on, and he was shown into a bed-chamber hung round with large pots; and in one corner of the room several lights were burning. As soon as he had entered, the door was fastened without; and the merchant was left alone in the chamber. Casting his eyes around him, he distinguished in the corner where the light was, two dead men hanging by the arms from the ceiling. This shocking circumstance so agonized him, that he was incapable of enjoying repose.

In the morning he got up. "Alas!" cried he, "they will assuredly hang me by the side of these murdered wretches."

When the prince had risen, he commanded the merchant to be brought into his presence. "Friend," said he, "what portion of my family establishment best pleases you?"

The man answered, "I am well pleased with everything, my Lord, except that my food was served to me out of a human head—a sight so sickening that I could touch nothing. And when I would have slept, my repose was destroyed by the terrible objects which were exhibited to me. And therefore, for the love of God, allow me to depart."

"Friend," replied the prince, "the head out of which you were served and which stood exactly opposite to my wife—my beautiful but wicked wife!—is the head of a certain duke. I will tell you why it was there. He whom I have punished in so exemplary a manner, I perceived in the act of dishonouring my bed. Instantly prompted by an uncontrollable desire of vengeance, I separated his head from his body. To remind the woman of her shame, each day I command this memento to be placed before her, in the hope that her repentance and punishment may equal her crime. A son of the deceased duke slew two of my kindred, whose bodies you observed hanging in the chamber which had been appropriated to you. Every day I punctually visit their corpses, to keep alive the fury which ought to animate me to revenge their deaths. And recalling the adultery of my wife, and the miserable slaughter of my kindred, I feel that there is no joy reserved for me in this world. Now, then, go in peace, and in future judge not of the life of any man until you know more of its true nature."

The merchant gladly availed himself of the permission to depart; and returned with greater satisfaction to the toils of traffic.

Tale 57

THE CARPENTER AND THE EMPEROR

WHEN TITUS WAS EMPEROR OF ROME, HE MADE A DECREE that the birthday of his first-born son should be held sacred; and that whosoever violated it by any kind of labour should be put to death. This edict being promulgated, he called Virgil, the learned man, to him, and said, "Good friend, I have established a certain law, but as offences may frequently

be committed without being discovered by the ministers of
justice, I desire you to frame some curious piece of art, which
may reveal to me every transgressor of the law."

Virgil replied, "Sire, your will shall be accomplished."

He straightway constructed a magic statue, and caused it
to be erected in the midst of the city. By virtue of the secret
powers with which it was invested, it communicated to the
emperor whatever offences were committed in secret on that
day. And thus, by the accusation of the statue, an infinite
number of persons were convicted.

Now, there was a certain carpenter, called Focus, who
pursued his occupation every day alike. Once, as he lay in
bed, his thoughts turned upon the accusations of the statue,
and the multitudes which it had caused to perish. In the
morning he clothed himself, and proceeded to the statue,
which he addressed in the following manner: "O statue!
statue! because of thy informations, many of our citizens
have been apprehended and slain. I vow to my God, that, if
thou accusest me, I will break thy head." Having so said, he
returned home.

About the first hour, the emperor, as he was wont, despatched sundry messengers to the statue, to inquire if the
edict had been strictly complied with. After they had arrived, and delivered the emperor's pleasure, the statue exclaimed, "Friends, look up; what see ye written upon my
forehead?"

They looked, and beheld three sentences which ran thus:
"Times are altered. Men grow worse. He who speaks truth
will have his head broken."

"Go," said the statue, "declare to his majesty what you
have seen and read." The messengers obeyed, and detailed the
circumstances as they had happened.

The emperor, therefore, commanded his guard to arm, and
march to the place where the statue was erected; and he fur-

ther ordered that, if any one presumed to molest it, they should bind him hand and foot, and drag him into his presence.

The soldiers approached the statue and said, "Our emperor wills you to declare who have broken the law, and who they were that threatened you."

The statue made answer, "Seize Focus the carpenter! Every day he violates the law and, moreover, menaces me."

Immediately Focus was apprehended, and conducted to the emperor, who said, "Friend, what do I hear of thee? Why dost thou break my law?"

"My lord," answered Focus, "I cannot keep it! for I am obliged to obtain every day eight pennies, which, without incessant labour, I have not the means of acquiring."

"And why eight pennies?" said the emperor.

"Every day through the year," returned the carpenter, "I am bound to repay two pennies which I borrowed in my youth; two I lend; two I lose; and two I spend."

"You must make this more clear," said the emperor.

"My lord," he replied, "listen to me. I am bound, each day, to repay two pennies to my father; for, when I was a boy, my father expended upon me daily the like sum. Now he is poor, and needs my assistance, and therefore I return what I formerly borrowed. Two other pennies I lend to my son, who is pursuing his studies; in order that if by any chance, I should fall into poverty, he may restore the loan, just as I have done to his grandfather. Again, I lose two pennies every day on my wife; for she is contradictious, wilful, and passionate. Now, because of this disposition, I account whatsoever is given to her entirely lost. Lastly, two other pennies I expend upon myself in meat and drink. I cannot do with less; nor can I obtain them without unremitting labour. You now know the truth; and, I pray you, give a righteous judgment."

"Friend," said the emperor, "thou hast answered well. Go, and labour earnestly in thy calling."

Soon after this the emperor died, and Focus the carpenter, on account of his singular wisdom, was elected in his stead, by the unanimous choice of the whole nation. He governed as wisely as he had lived; and at his death, his picture, bearing on the head eight pennies, was placed among the effigies of the deceased emperors.

Tale 58

THREE TRUTHS

A CERTAIN KING, NAMED ASMODEUS, ESTABLISHED AN ORDI- nance, by which every malefactor taken and brought before the judge should, if he declared three truths, against which no exception could be taken, obtain his life and property. It chanced that a certain soldier transgressed the law and fled. He hid himself in a forest, and there committed many atrocities, despoiling and slaying whomsoever he could lay his hands upon.

When the judge of the district ascertained his haunt, he ordered the forest to be surrounded, and the soldier to be seized and brought bound to the seat of judgment.

"You know the law," said the judge.

"I do," returned the other: "if I declare three unquestion- able truths, I shall be free; but if not, I must die."

"True," replied the judge: "take then advantage of the law's clemency, or this very day you shall not taste food until you are hanged."

"Cause silence to be kept," said the soldier.

His wish being complied with, he proceeded in the following manner:—"The first truth is this: I protest before ye all, that from my youth up I have been a bad man."

The judge, hearing this, said to the bystanders, "He says true?"

They answered, "Else, he had not now been in this situation."

"Go on, then," said the judge; "what is the second truth?"

"I like not," exclaimed he, "the dangerous situation in which I stand."

"Certainly," said the judge, "we may credit thee. Now then for the third truth, and thou hast saved thy life."

"Why," he replied, "if I once get out of this confounded place, I will never willingly re-enter it."

"Amen," said the judge, "thy wit hath preserved thee; go in peace."

And thus he was saved.

Tale 59

HOW THE PROUD EMPEROR WAS HUMBLED

WHEN JOVINIAN WAS EMPEROR, HE POSSESSED VERY GREAT power; and as he lay in bed reflecting upon the extent of his dominions, his heart was elated to an extraordinary degree. "Is there," he impiously asked, "is there any other god than me?" Amid such thoughts he fell asleep.

In the morning he reviewed his troops, and said, "My friends, after breakfast we will hunt." Preparations being made accordingly, he set out with a large retinue. During the chase, the emperor felt such extreme oppression from the heat, that he believed his very existence depended upon a cold bath. As he anxiously looked around, he discovered a

sheet of water at no great distance. "Remain here," said he
to his guard, "until I have refreshed myself in yonder
stream."

Then spurring his steed, he rode hastily to the edge of the
water. Alighting, he divested himself of his apparel, and experienced the greatest pleasure from its invigorating freshness and coolness. But whilst he was thus employed, a person
similar to him in every respect—in countenance and gesture
—arrayed himself unperceived in the emperor's dress, and
then mounting his horse, rode off to the attendants. The resemblance to the sovereign was such, that no doubt was entertained of the reality; and when the sport was over command was issued for their return to the palace.

Jovinian, however, having quitted the water, sought in
every possible direction for his horse and clothes, and to his
utter astonishment could find neither. Vexed beyond measure
at the circumstance, for he was completely naked, and saw
no one near to assist him, he began to reflect upon what
course he should pursue. "Miserable man that I am," said
he, "to what a strait am I reduced! There is, I remember, a
knight residing close by, whom I have promoted to a military
post; I will go to him and command his attendance and service. I will then ride on to the palace and strictly investigate
the cause of this extraordinary conduct."

Jovinian proceeded, naked and ashamed, to the castle of
the aforesaid knight, and beat loudly at the gate. The porter
inquired the cause of the knocking. "Open the gate," said
the enraged emperor, "and you will see whom I am."

The gate was opened; and the porter, struck with the
strange appearance he exhibited, replied, "In the name of all
that is marvellous, what are you?"

"I am," said he, "Jovinian, your emperor; go to your lord,
and command him from me to supply the wants of his sovereign. I have lost both horse and clothes."

"Thou liest, infamous ribald!" shouted the porter; "just before thy approach, the Emperor Jovinian, accompanied by the officers of his household, entered the palace. My lord both went and returned with him; and but even now sat with him at meat. But because thou hast called thyself the emperor, my lord shall know of thy presumption."

The porter entered, and related what had passed. Jovinian was introduced, but the knight retained not the slightest recollection of his master, although the emperor remembered him.

"Who are you?" said the former, "and what is your name?"

"I am the Emperor Jovinian," rejoined he; "canst thou have forgotten me? At such a time I promoted thee to a military command."

"Why, thou most audacious scoundrel," said the knight, "darest thou call thyself the emperor? I rode with him myself to the palace, from whence I am this moment returned. But thy impudence shall not go without its reward. Flog him," said he, turning to his servants, "flog him soundly, and drive him away."

This sentence was immediately executed, and the poor emperor, bursting into a convulsion of tears, exclaimed, "Oh, my God, is it possible that one whom I have so much honoured and exalted should do this? Not content with pretending ignorance of my person, he orders these merciless villains to abuse me!"

He next thought within himself, "There is a certain duke, one of my privy councillors, to whom I will make known my calamity. At least, he will enable me to return decently to the palace." To him, therefore, Jovinian proceeded, and the gate was opened at his knock.

But the porter, beholding a naked man, exclaimed in the greatest amaze, "Friend, who are you, and why come you here in such a guise?"

He replied, "I am your emperor; I have accidentally lost my clothes and my horse, and I have come for succour to your lord. I beg you, therefore, to do me this errand to the duke." The porter, more and more astonished, entered the hall, and communicated the strange intelligence which he had received.

"Bring him in," said the duke. He was brought in, but neither did he recognize the person of the emperor.

"What art thou?" he asked.

"I am the emperor," replied Jovinian, "and I have promoted thee to riches and honour, since I made thee a duke and one of my councillors."

"Poor mad wretch," said the duke, "a short time since I returned from the palace, where I left the very emperor thou assumest to be. But since thou hast claimed such rank, thou shalt not escape unpunished. Carry him to prison, and feed him with bread and water."

The command was no sooner delivered than obeyed; and the following day his naked body was submitted to the lash, and he was again cast into the dungeon.

Thus afflicted, he gave himself up to the wretchedness of his undeserved condition. In the agony of his heart, he said, "What shall I do? Oh, what will be my destiny? I am loaded with the coarsest insolence, and exposed to the malicious observation of my people. It were better to hasten immediately to my palace, and there discover myself—my servants will know me; and even if they do not my wife will know me!" Escaping, therefore, from his confinement, he approached the palace and beat upon the gate.

"Who art thou?" said the porter.

"It is strange," replied the aggrieved emperor, "it is strange that thou shouldst not know me; thou, who hast served me so long!"

"Served *thee!*" returned the porter indignantly, "thou

liest abominably. I have served none but the emperor."

"Why," said the other, "thou knowest that I am he. Yet, though you disregard my words, go, I implore you, to the empress; communicate what I will tell thee, and by these signs bid her send the imperial robes, of which some rogue has deprived me. The signs I tell thee of are known to none but to ourselves."

"In verity," said the porter, "thou art mad: at this very moment my lord sits at table with the empress herself. Nevertheless, out of regard for thy singular merits, I will intimate thy declaration within; and rest assured, thou wilt presently find thyself most royally beaten."

The porter went accordingly, and related what he had heard. But the empress became very sorrowful, and said, "Oh, my Lord, what am I to think? The most hidden passages of our lives are revealed by an obscene fellow at the gate, and repeated to me by the porter, on the strength of which he declares himself the emperor and my espoused lord!"

When the fictitious monarch was apprized of this, he commanded him to be brought in. He had no sooner entered than a large dog, which couched upon the hearth, and had been much cherished by him, flew at his throat, and, but for timely prevention, would have killed him. A falcon, also, seated upon her perch, no sooner beheld him, than she broke her leather straps and flew out of the hall.

Then the pretended emperor, addressing those who stood about him, said, "My friends, hear what I will ask of yon ribald. Who are you? and what do you want?"

"These questions," said the suffering man, "are very strange. You know I am the emperor and master of this place."

The other, turning to the nobles who sat or stood at the table, continued, "Tell me, on your allegiance, which of us two is your lord and master?"

"Your majesty asks us an easy thing," replied they, "and need not to remind us of our allegiance. That obscene wretch we have never before seen. You alone are he, whom we have known from childhood; and we entreat that this fellow may be severely punished, as a warning to others how they give scope to their mad presumption."

Then turning to the empress, the usurper said, "Tell me, my lady, on the faith you have sworn, do you know this man who calls himself thy lord and emperor?"

She answered, "My lord, how can you ask such a question? Have I not known thee more than thirty years, and borne thee many children? Yet, at one thing I do admire. How can this fellow have acquired so intimate a knowledge of what has passed between us?"

The pretended emperor made no reply, but addressing the real one, said, "Friend, how darest thou to call thyself emperor? We sentence thee, for this unexampled impudence, to be drawn, without loss of time, at the tail of a horse. And if thou utterest the same words again, thou shalt be doomed to an ignominious death." He then commanded his guards to see the sentence put in force, but to preserve his life. The unfortunate emperor was now almost distracted; and urged by his despair, wished vehemently for death.

"Why was I born?" he exclaimed. "My friends shun me; and my wife and children will not acknowledge me. But there is my confessor, still. To him will I go; perhaps he will recollect me, because he has often received my confessions." He went accordingly, and knocked at the window of his cell.

"Who is there?" said the confessor.

"The emperor Jovinian," was the reply; "open the window, and I will speak to thee." The window was opened; but no sooner had he looked out than he closed it again in great haste.

"Depart from me," said he "accursed thing; thou art not the emperor, but the devil incarnate."

This completed the miseries of the persecuted man; and he tore his hair, and plucked up his beard by the roots. "Woe is me!" he cried, "for what strange doom am I reserved?"

At this crisis, the impious words which, in the arrogance of his heart, he had uttered, crossed his recollection. Immediately he beat again at the window of the confessor's cell, and exclaimed, "For the love of Him who was suspended from the cross, hear my confession with the window closed."

The recluse said, "I will do this with pleasure"; and then Jovinian acquainted him with every particular of his past life; and principally how he had lifted himself up against his Maker, saying that he believed there was no other god but himself.

The confession made, and absolution given, the recluse opened the window, and directly knew him. "Blessed be the most high God," said he, "now do I know thee. I have here a few garments: clothe thyself, and go to the palace. I trust that they also will recognize thee."

The emperor did as the confessor directed. The porter opened the gate, and made a low obeisance to him. "Dost thou know me?" said he.

"Very well, my lord!" replied the menial; "but I marvel that I did not observe you go out."

Entering the hall of his mansion, Jovinian was received by all with a profound reverence. The strange emperor was at that time in another apartment with the queen; and a certain knight came out of the chamber, looked narrowly at Jovinian, and returning to the supposed emperor, said, "My lord, there is one in the hall to whom everybody bends; he so much resembles you, that we know not which is the emperor."

Hearing this, the usurper said to the empress, "Go and see

if you know him." She went, and returned greatly surprised at what she saw.

"Oh, my lord," said she, "I declare to you that I know not whom to trust."

"Then," returned he, "I will go and convince you." When he had entered the hall, he took Jovinian by the hand and placed him near him. Addressing the assembly, he said, "By the oaths you have taken, declare which of us is your emperor."

The empress answered, "It is my duty to speak first; but Heaven is my witness that I am unable to determine which is he."

And so said all.

Then the feigned emperor spoke thus, "My friends, hearken! That man is your king and your lord. He exalted himself to the disparagement of his Maker; and God, therefore, scourged and hid him from your knowledge. I am the angel that watches over his soul, and I have guarded his kingdom while he was undergoing his penance. But his repentance removes the rod; he has now made ample satisfaction, and again let your obedience wait upon him. Commend yourselves to the protection of Heaven."

So saying, he disappeared. The emperor gave thanks to God, and lived happily, and finished his days in peace.

Tale 60

HOW THE KING'S DAUGHTER LOST THE RACE

A CERTAIN KING HAD AN ONLY DAUGHTER, REMARKABLE for the beauty and dignity of her person. She was called Rosamond; and, at the early age of ten years, she proved

so swift a runner, that she invariably attained the goal be-
for her competitor. The king caused it to be proclaimed that
whosoever should surpass his daughter in speed should marry
her, and succeed to the throne; but in the event of a failure
he should lose his head. And even with the heavy penalty
before them, numbers permitted themselves to be buoyed
up by the hope of success to attempt, and to perish in the
attempt.

But it happened that a poor man, called Abibas, inhabited
that country, who thus communed with himself: "I am very
poor, and of a base extraction; if I may overcome this lady
and marry her, not only shall I be promoted myself, but all
who are of my blood." But wiser than the rest, he took the
three following precautions. First, he framed a curious garland of roses, of which he had ascertained that the lady was
devotedly fond. Then, he procured a girdle of the finest silk,
from a conviction that most damsels were partial to this sort
of clothing. And, lastly, he bought a silken bag, in which he
deposited a golden ball bearing the following inscription:
"Whosoever plays with me shall never have enough of play."
These three things he placed in his bosom, and knocked at the
palace gate. The porter inquired his business; and he stated
his wish in the usual form.

It happened that the princess herself stood at a window
close by, and heard Abibas express his intention to run with
her. Observing that he was poor, and his attire threadbare
and rent, she despised him from her very heart, and said,
"Lo! what poor wretch is this with whom I have to contend?" However, she prepared to run; and everything being
in readiness, they commenced the race.

Abibas would have been left at a considerable distance;
but taking the garland of roses from its repository, he skilfully threw it down before her, on which the maiden stooped,

picked it up, and placed it on her head. Delighted with the odour and beauty of the flowers, she paused to examine it; and Abibas took advantage of her forgetfulness and advanced rapidly towards the goal.

This awoke her to a recollection of what was going forward, and crying aloud, "Never shall the daughter of a prince be united to this miserable clown," she threw the garland from her into a deep well, and rushed onward like a whirlwind. In a few moments she overtook the youth, and extending her hand, struck him upon the shoulder, exclaiming, "Stop, foolish thing; hopest thou to marry a princess?"

Just as she was on the point of passing him, he drew forth the silken girdle, and cast it at her feet. The temptation again proved too strong for her resolution, and she stooped to gather it. Overjoyed at the beauty of its texture, she must bind it round her waist; and whilst she did this, Abibas had recovered more ground than he had lost.

As soon as the fair racer perceived the consequences of her folly, she burst into a flood of tears, and rending the girdle asunder, hurried on.

Having again overtaken her adversary, she seized him by the arm, striking him smartly at the same time: "Fool, thou shalt not marry me"; and immediately she ran faster than before.

Abibas, when he saw this, waited until she was near the goal, and then threw at her feet the bag with the golden ball. It was impossible to forbear picking it up; and equally impossible not to open it and peep at its contents.

She did so; but reading the inscription, "Who plays with me shall never have enough of play," she played so much and so long, that Abibas came first to the goal and married her.

Tale 61

THE PHILOSOPHER AND HIS WIFE

THE EMPEROR CLAUDIUS HAD AN ONLY DAUGHTER WHO was incomparably beautiful. As he lay in bed, he reflected seriously upon the best mode of disposing of her. "If," thought he, "I should marry her to a rich fool, it will occasion her death. But if I bestow her upon a wise man, although he be poor, his own wit will procure him riches."

Now, it happened that there dwelt in the city a philosopher called Socrates, whom the king very greatly esteemed. This person was sent for, and thus addressed, "My good friend, I design to espouse you to my only daughter." Socrates, overjoyed at the proposal, expressed his gratitude as he best could. "But," continued the emperor, "take her with this condition: that if she die first, you shall not survive her." The philosopher assented; the nuptials were solemnized with great splendour, and for a length of time their happiness was uninterrupted.

But at last she sickened, and her death was hourly expected. This deeply afflicted Socrates, and he retired into a neighbouring forest and gave free course to his alarm. Whilst he was thus occupied, it chanced that King Alexander hunted in the same forest; and that a soldier of his guard discerned the philosopher, and rode up to him.

"Who art thou?" asked the soldier.

"I am," replied he, "the servant of my master; and he who is the servant of my master is the lord of thine."

"How?" cried the other, "there is not a greater person in the universe than he whom I serve. But since you are pleased to say otherwise, I will presently lead you to him;

and we will hear who thy lord is." Accordingly, he was brought before Alexander.

"Friend," said the king, "concerning whom dost thou say that his servant is my master?"

The philosopher answered, "My master is reason; *his* servant is the will. Now, dost thou not govern thy kingdom according to the dictates of thy will? Therefore, thy will is thy master. But the will is the servant of my master. So that what I said is true, and thou canst not disprove it."

Alexander, wondering at the man's wit, candidly answered in the affirmative, and ever after ruled both himself and his kingdom by the laws of reason.

Socrates, however, entered farther into the forest, and wept bitterly over the expected decease of his wife. In the midst of his distress he was accosted by an old man who inhabited that part of the wood.

"Master," said he, "why art thou afflicted?"

"Alas!" answered the other, "I have espoused the daughter of an emperor upon the condition that if she died I should die with her: she is now on the point of death, and my life therefore will certainly be required."

"What!" said the old man, "Grievest thou for this? Take my counsel, and thou shalt be safe enough. Thy wife is of royal descent; let her besmear her breast with some of her father's blood. Then, do thou search in the depths of this forest, where thou wilt find three herbs; of one of them make a beverage and administer it to her; the other two beat into a plaster, and apply it to the afflicted part. If my instructions are exactly attended to, she will be restored to perfect health."

Socrates did as he was directed; and his wife presently recovered. When the emperor knew how he had striven to find a remedy for his wife's disorder, he loaded him with riches and honours.

Tale 62

THE PORTRAIT OF THE BEAUTIFUL FLORENTINA

WHEN SALUS WAS EMPEROR, THERE LIVED A VERY BEAU-
tiful woman, whose name was Florentina. She was so remarkably handsome that three kings sought her love, by one
of whom she was abused. This occasioned a war between
them, and great numbers of men fell on both sides. But the
nobles, unwilling to see so much waste of blood, interfered,
and addressing the emperor, bade him observe that, unless a
stop were put to the virulent animosity which divided them
the whole kingdom would be annihilated.

The emperor, duly considering what had been said, directed letters, impressed with the royal signet, to be sent to
the fair occasion of the war; by which, without delay, she
was commanded to appear before him. A herald bore the
mandate, but before he could deliver it she died. The herald,
therefore, returned, and the emperor, very much regretting
that he had lost sight of so beautiful a woman, caused all the
best artists in the kingdom to be summoned into his presence.

When they were assembled, he spoke as follows: "My
friends, the reason that I have sent for you is this. There was
a very beautiful woman, named Florentina, for whose love
a great number of men have lost their lives. She died before
I had an opportunity of seeing her. Do ye go, therefore;
paint her to the life, as she was in all her beauty. Thus shall
I discover wherefore so many were sacrificed."

The artists answered, "Your majesty wishes a thing which
is very difficult to execute. Her beauty was so surpassing, that
not all the artists in the world, save one, would be able to do

her justice; and he hides himself amongst the mountains. But he alone can perfectly fulfil your desires."

On receiving this information, messengers were despatched in pursuit of him. He was soon found, and brought before the curious monarch, who commanded him to paint Florentina as she appeared when living; and if he did it, his reward should be royal.

"Your request is extremely difficult," said the painter; "nevertheless, cause all the beautiful women in your kingdom to come before me for an hour at least, and I will do as you desire." The emperor complied, and made them stand in his presence. From these the artist selected four, and permitted the rest to return home.

Then he commenced his labours. First, he laid on a coat of red colour; and whatever was exquisitely beautiful in the four women, *that* he copied in his painting. In this manner it received its completion; and when the emperor beheld it, he said, "Oh, Florentina, had you lived to eternity, you ought to have loved that painter who has represented you in so much beauty."

Tale 63

HOW THE KNIGHT WON THE EMPEROR'S DAUGHTER

THE EMPEROR VESPASIAN HAD A DAUGHTER CALLED AGLÄES whose loveliness was greater than that of all other women. It happened that as she stood opposite to him on a certain occasion, he considered her very attentively, and then addressed her as follows: "My beloved daughter, thy beauty merits a loftier title than thou hast yet received. I will change thy name; henceforward, be thou called the LADY OF COM-

FORT, in sign that whosoever looks upon thee in sorrow may depart in joy."

Now, the emperor possessed, near his palace, a delicious garden, in which he frequently walked. Proclamation was made that whosoever wished to marry his daughter should come to the palace, and remain in this garden the space of three or four days; when they quitted it, the ceremony should take place. Immense crowds were allured by the apparently easy terms of the notice; they entered the garden, but were never again seen. Not one of them returned.

But a certain knight, who dwelt in some remote country, hearing of the conditions by which the daughter of a great king might be espoused, came to the gate of the palace and demanded entrance. On being introduced to the emperor, he spoke thus: "I hear it commonly reported, my lord, that whoever enters your garden shall espouse your daughter. For this purpose I come."

"Enter, then," said the emperor; "on thy return thou shalt marry her."

"But," added the knight, "I solicit one boon of your majesty. Before I enter the garden, I would entreat an opportunity of conversing a short time with the lady."

"I have no objection to that," said the emperor.

She was called, and the knight accosted her in these words: "Fair damsel, thou hast been called the *Lady of Comfort,* because every one who enters thy presence sorrowful returns contented and happy. I, therefore, approach thee sad and desolate—give me the means to leave thee in happiness: many have entered the garden, but never any reappeared. If the same chance happen to me—alas! that I should have sought thee in marriage."

"I will tell thee the truth," said the lady, "and convert thy unhappiness into pleasure. In that garden there is an enormous lion, which devours every one who enters with the hope of marrying me. Arm thyself, therefore, from head to foot, and smear your armour with gum. As soon as you have entered the garden the lion will rush toward you; attack him manfully, and when you are weary, leave him. Then will he instantly seize you by the arm or leg; but in so doing, the gum will adhere to his teeth, and he will be unable to hurt you. As soon as you perceive this, unsheath your sword and separate his head from his body. Besides the ferocious animal I have described, there is another danger to be overcome. There is but one entrance, and so intricate are the labyrinths, that return is nearly impossible without assistance. But here also I will befriend you. Take this ball of thread, and attach one of the ends to the gate as you enter, and, retaining the line, pass into the garden. But, as you love your life, beware that you lose not the thread."

The knight exactly observed all these instructions. Having armed himself, he entered the garden; and the lion, with open mouth, rushed forward to devour him. He defended himself resolutely; and when his strength failed he leapt a few paces back. Then, as the lady had said, the lion seized upon the knight's arm; but, since his teeth were clogged with gum, he did him no injury, and the sword presently put an end to the combat.

Unhappily, however, while exulting over his victory, he let go the thread, and in great tribulation wandered about the garden for three days, diligently seeking the lost clue. Towards night he discovered it, and with no small joy hastened back to the gate. Then, loosening the thread, he bent his way to the presence of the emperor; and in due time the LADY OF COMFORT became his wife.

Tale 64

THE WISE VIRGIN

A CERTAIN KING WAS REMARKABLE FOR THREE QUALITIES. Firstly, he was stronger in body than all men; secondly, he was wiser; and lastly, more beautiful. He lived a long time unmarried; and his counsellors would persuade him to take a wife. "My friends," said he, "it is clear to you that I am rich and powerful enough; and therefore want not wealth. Go, then, through town and country, and seek me out a beautiful and wise virgin; and if ye can find such a one, however poor she may be, I will marry her."

The command was obeyed; they proceeded on their search, until at last they discovered a lady of royal extraction with the qualifications desired. But the king was not so easily satisfied, and determined to put her wisdom to the test.

He sent to the lady by a herald a piece of linen cloth, three inches square; and bade her contrive to make for him a shirt exactly fitted to his body. "Then," added he, "she shall be my wife."

The messenger thus commissioned, departed on his errand, and respectfully presented the cloth, with the request of the king.

"How can I comply with it," exclaimed the lady, "when the cloth is but three inches square? It is impossible to make a shirt of that; but bring me a vessel in which I may work, and I promise to make the shirt long enough for the body."

The messenger returned with the reply of the virgin, and the king immediately sent a sumptuous vessel, by means of which she extended the cloth to the required size, and completed the shirt. Whereupon the wise king married her.

Tale 65

THE FOUR DIRECTIONS

A KING ONCE UNDERTOOK A JOURNEY FROM ONE STATE TO another. After much travel, he came to a certain cross, which was covered with inscriptions. On one side was written, "Oh, king, if you ride this way, you yourself will find good entertainment, but your horse will get nothing to eat." On another part appeared as follows: "If you ride this road, your horse will be admirably attended to, but you will get nothing for yourself." Again, on a third place was inscribed: "If you walk this path, you will find entertainment both for yourself and horse; but before you depart, you will be miserably beaten." On a fourth part of the cross it was said: "If you walk this way, they will serve you deligently, but they will detain your horse, and oblige you to proceed the rest of your journey on foot."

When the king had read the inscriptions, he began to consider which of the evils he should choose. He determined at length upon the first; "For," said he, "I shall fare very well myself, though my horse starve; and the night will soon pass away."

On this, he struck the spurs into his horse; and arrived at the castle of a knight, who entreated him courteously, but gave his steed little or nothing. In the morning he rode on to his own palace, and related all that he had seen.

Tale 66

THE KNIGHT, THE LADY, AND HER KINGDOM

THERE ONCE LIVED A KING WHO HAD A BEAUTIFUL AND beloved daughter. After his death she succeeded to the

throne, but, being young and unprotected, a certain tyrannical duke came to her, and, by means of large promises,
won her to dishonour. When his iniquitous purpose was accomplished, the girl wept bitterly; and soon after the tyrant expelled her from the inheritance. Thus reduced from
the splendours of royalty to the lowest state of wretchedness, she solicited alms.

It happened that as she sat weeping by the wayside, a certain knight passed by, and observing her great beauty, became enamoured of her. "Fair lady," said he, "what are you?"

"I am," replied the weeping girl, "the only daughter of a
king; after whose death a tyrant seduced and abused me,
and then deprived me of my inheritance."

"Well," returned the knight, "are you willing to marry
me?"

"Oh, my lord!" exclaimed she, "I desire it beyond anything that could happen."

"Then pledge me your faith," said the knight; "promise
to receive no one for your husband but me, and I will make
war upon the tyrant, and reinstate you in your possessions.
But if I fall in the conflict, I entreat you to retain my bloody
arms under your care, in testimony of affection; that in case
any one hereafter shall desire your love, you may enter the
chamber in which the arms hang, and may thus be reminded
of the proof I have given of my attachment and devotion
to your service."

"I promise faithfully," returned she, "to comply with
your wishes: but, oh! may your life be safe!"

The knight therefore armed himself, and proceeded to
engage the tyrant, who had heard of his intention, and prepared for the attack. The knight, however, overcame him,
and cut off his head; but, receiving a mortal wound, he died
on the third day. The lady bewailed his death, and hung up

his bloody armour in her chamber. She visited it frequently, and washed it with bitter tears.

Many noblemen sought to espouse her, and made magnificent promises; but invariably before returning an answer she entered the chamber, and, surveying the bloody armour steadfastly, exclaimed, amid abundance of tears, "Oh, thou, who devotedst thyself to death for one so unworthy, and restoredst me my kingdom!—far be it from me to renounce my plighted faith."

Then returning to those who sought her love, she declared her resolution never to unite herself with another. When they heard this they departed; and thus she remained single to the end of her life.

Tale 67

THE WISE AND FOOLISH KNIGHTS

THE EMPEROR MAXIMIAN WAS RENOWNED FOR THE WISdom of his government. In his reign there lived two knights, the one wise and the other foolish, but who had a mutual regard for each other. "Let us make an agreement," said the wise knight, "which will be advantageous to both."

The other assented, and by the direction of his friend, proceeded to draw blood from his right arm. "I," said the latter, "will drink of thy blood, and thou of mine; so that neither in prosperity nor in adversity shall our covenant be broken, and whatsoever the one gains, shall be divided by the other." The foolish knight agreed; and they ratified the treaty by a draught of each other's blood.

After this they both dwelt in the same mansion.

Now, the lord of the country had two cities, one of which was built on the summit of a lofty mountain. Since all who went to it would possess great wealth, and remain there for life, the path to this city was narrow and stony, and about midway three knights with a large army were stationed. The custom was that whosoever passed should do battle, or lose his life, with everything that he possessed. In that city the emperor appointed a steward, who received without exception all who entered, and ministered to them according to their condition.

But the other city was built in a valley under the mountain, the way to which was perfectly level and pleasant. Three soldiers dwelt there, who cheerfully received whosoever came, and served them according to their pleasure. In this city also a steward was placed, but he ordered all who approached to be thrown into prison, and on the coming of the judge to be condemned.

The wise knight said to his companion, "My friend, let us go through the world as other knights are wont to do, and seek our fortune." His friend acquiesced; they set out upon their travels, and presently came to a place where two roads met. "See," said the wise knight, "here are two roads. The one leads to the noblest city in the world, and if we go thither, we shall obtain whatsoever our hearts desire. But the other path conducts to a city which is built in a valley; if we venture there, we shall be thrown into prison, and afterwards crucified. I advise, therefore, that we avoid this road, and pursue the other."

"My friend," replied the foolish knight, "I heard long ago of these two cities; but the way to that upon the mountain is very narrow and dangerous, because of the soldiers who attack those that enter; nay, they frequently rob and murder them. But the other way is open and broad; and the soldiers who are stationed there receive passengers with hos-

pitality, and supply them with all things necessary. This is
sufficiently manifest; I see it, and had rather believe my own
eyes than you."

"It is true," returned his companion, "one way is difficult
to walk along, but the other is infinitely worse at the end:
ignominy and crucifixion will certainly be our doom. But
fear you to walk the strait road, on account of a battle, or
because of robbers? you, who are a soldier, and therefore in
duty bound to fight valiantly! However, if you will go with
me the way I desire, I promise to precede you in the attack;
and be assured with your aid we shall overcome every ob-
stacle."

"I protest to you," said the other, "I will not go your way,
but will take mine own."

"Well," replied the wise knight, "since I have pledged
you my word, and drank your blood in token of fidelity, I
will proceed with you, though against my better judgment."
So they both went the same path.

The progress was extremely pleasant till they reached the
station of the three soldiers, who honourably and magnificently entertained them. And here the foolish knight said to
the wise one, "Friend, did I not tell thee how comfortable
this way would be found; in all which the other is deficient?"

"If the end be well," replied he, "all is well; but I do not
hope it."

With the three soldiers they tarried some time; insomuch
that the steward of the city, hearing that two knights, contrary to royal prohibition, were approaching, sent out troops
to apprehend them. The foolish knight he commanded to be
bound hand and foot, and thrown into a pit, but the other
he imprisoned.

Now, when the judge arrived, the malefactors were all
brought before him, and among the rest our two knights—
the wiser of whom thus spoke: "My lord, I complain of my

comrade, who is the occasion of my death. I declared to him the law of this city, and the danger to which we were exposed, but he would not listen to my words, nor abide by my counsels. 'I will trust my eyes,' said he, 'rather than you.' Now, because I had taken an oath never to forsake him in prosperity or in adversity, I accompanied him hither. But ought I therefore to die? Pronounce a just judgment."

Then the foolish knight addressed the judge: "He is himself the cause of my death. For every one knows that he is reckoned wise, and I am naturally a fool. Ought he then so lightly to have surrendered his wisdom to my folly? And had he not done so, I should have returned to go the way which he went, even for the solemn oath which I had sworn. And therefore, since he is wise, and I am foolish, he is the occasion of my death."

The judge, hearing this, spoke to both, but to the wise knight first: "Thou who art wise, since thou didst listen so heedlessly to his folly and followedst him, and thou, foolish man, since thou didst not credit his word, but acted out thine own folly, ye shall both be suspended on the cross this very day."

Thus it was done.

Tale 68

THE THREE CROWING COCKS

IN THE REIGN OF GORDIAN, THERE WAS A CERTAIN NOBLE soldier who had a fair but vicious wife. It happened that her husband having occasion to travel, the lady sent for her gallant. Now, one of her handmaids, it seems, was skilful in interpreting the song of birds; and in the court of the castle there were three cocks.

During the night, while the gallant was with his mistress, the first cock began to crow. The lady heard it, and said to her servant, "Dear friend, what says yonder cock?"

She replied, "That you are grossly injuring your husband."

"Then," said the lady, "kill that cock without delay." They did so; but soon after the second cock crew, and the lady repeated her question.

"Madam," said the handmaid, "he says 'My companion died for revealing the truth, and for the same cause, I am prepared to die.'"

"Kill him," cried the lady,—which they did.

After this, the third cock crew. "What says he?" asked she again.

"Hear, see, and say nothing, if you would live in peace."

"Oh, oh!" said the lady, "*don't* kill him."

And her orders were obeyed.

Tale 69

THE MAGIC SHIRT

THE EMPEROR GALLUS EMPLOYED A SINGULARLY SKILFUL carpenter in the erection of a magnificent palace. At that period, a certain knight lived who had a very beautiful daughter; and who, perceiving the extraordinary wisdom of the artificer, determined to give him the lady in marriage. Calling him, therefore, he said, "My good friend, ask of me what you will; so that it be possible, I will do it, provided you marry my daughter." The other assented, and the nuptial rites were celebrated accordingly.

Then the mother of the lady said to the carpenter, "My son, since you have become one of our family, I will bestow upon you a curious shirt. It possesses this singular property, that as long as you and your wife are faithful to each other, it will neither be rent, nor worn, nor stained. But if—which Heaven forbid!—either of you prove unfaithful instantly it will lose its virtue." The carpenter, very happy in what he heard, took the shirt, and returned great thanks for the gift.

A short while afterward, the carpenter being sent for to superintend the building of the emperor's palace, took with him the valuable present which he had received. He continued absent until the structure was complete; and numbers, observing how much he laboured, admired the freshness and spotless purity of his shirt.

Even the emperor condescended to notice it, and said to him, "My master, how is it that in despite of your laborious occupation, and the constant use of your shirt, it still preserves its colour and beauty?"

"You must know, my lord," said he, "that as long as my wife and I continue faithful to each other, my shirt retains its original whiteness and beauty; but if either of us forget our matrimonial vows, it will sully like any other cloth."

A soldier, overhearing this, thought within himself, "If I can I will make you wash your shirt." Wherefore, without giving any cause of suspicion to the carpenter, he secretly hastened to his house, and solicited his wife to dishonour.

She received him with an appearance of pleasure, and seemed to be entirely influenced by the same feelings. "But," added she, "in this place we are exposed to observation; come with me, and I will conduct you into a private chamber."

He followed her, and closing the door, she said, "Wait here awhile; I will return presently." Thus she did every day, all the time supplying him only with bread and water. Without regard to his urgency, she compelled him to endure this humiliating treatment; and before long, two other soldiers came to her from the emperor's court, with the same evil views. In like manner, she decoyed them into the chamber and fed them with bread and water.

The sudden disappearance, however, of the three soldiers gave rise to much inquiry; and the carpenter, on the completion of his labours, received the stipulated sum, and returned to his own home. His virtuous wife met him with joy, and looking upon the spotless shirt, exclaimed, "Blessed be God! our truth is made apparent—there is not a single stain upon the shirt."

To which he replied, "My beloved, during the progress of the building, three soldiers, one after another, came to ask questions about the shirt. I related the fact, and since that time nothing has been heard of them."

The lady smiled, and said, "The soldiers respecting whom you feel anxious thought me a fit subject for their improper solicitation, and came hither with the vilest intent. I decoyed them into a remote chamber, and have fed them with bread and water."

The carpenter, delighted with this proof of his wife's fidelity, spared their lives, and liberated them; and he and his wife lived happily for the rest of their lives.

Tale 70

THE THREE CONDITIONS

A CERTAIN KING HAD A BEAUTIFUL AND WISE DAUGHTER, whom he was desirous of marrying. But she had sworn never to unite herself to any but upon three conditions. First, he was to state accurately how many feet there were in the length, breadth, and depth of the four elements. Secondly, he

was to change the north wind. And thirdly, he was to carry
fire in his bosom without injury.

When the king, therefore, understood his daughter's resolution, he proclaimed it through the kingdom, and promised to give her in marriage to whomsoever performed the
conditions. Many endeavoured, but failed; until at length
a certain knight from foreign parts heard of the girl's oath.
He hastened to the palace, conveying with him a single attendant, and an extremely fiery horse.

On being admitted into the king's presence, he said, "I
am desirous of espousing your majesty's daughter, and I am
prepared to solve the questions which have been proposed."

The king assented, and the soldier, calling his servant, commanded him to lie upon the earth. And when he was thus laid,
his master measured his length from one extremity to the
other. When he had done this, he said to the king, "My lord,
your first question is resolved; I find in the four elements
scarcely seven feet."

"How?" replied the king. "What has this to do with the
four elements?"

"My lord," answered the soldier, "every man, as well as
every animal, is composed of the four elements."

"Amen," said the king, " you have proved this very satis-
factorily. Now then for the second condition, which is to
change the wind."

Immediately he caused his horse to be brought into the
area of the court, and there administered a potion, by which
the animal was made perfectly quiet. This done, he turned
his horse's head towards the east, and said, "Observe, my
lord, the wind is changed from north to east."

"How?" answered the king, "What is this to the wind?"

"Sire," returned the soldier, "is it not obvious to your
wisdom that the life of every animal consists in his breath,
which is air? As long as he raged fiercely, so long was he in

the north. But when I had given him the potion I turned him toward the east, so that he is ready to bear his burden."

"This also," said the king, "you have well proved; go on to the third."

"My lord," replied the soldier, "this, so please you, I will perform before all your court." Then, taking up a handful of burning coals, he deposited them in his bosom, without injury to his flesh.

"Truly," exclaimed the king, "you have done very well in these matters: but tell me, how happens it that you are unhurt by the fire."

"It was not," returned the soldier, "by any power of my own, but by virtue of a singular stone, which I always carry about with me. And whosoever possesses this stone is able to resist the hottest fire."

The king, satisfied that the conditions had been accurately complied with, gave orders for his marriage with the lady. He loaded him with riches and honours, and they both ended their days in the greatest happiness.

Tale 71

A LAME AND A BLIND MAN

A KING MADE A GREAT FEAST, AND DESPATCHED MESSENGERS with invitations, in which the guests were promised not only a magnificent entertainment, but considerable wealth. When the messengers had gone through town and country, executing everywhere the commands of their king, it happened that there dwelt in a certain city two men, of whom one was valiant and robustly made, but blind; while the other was lame and feeble, but his sight was excellent.

Said the blind man to the lame, "My friend, ours is a hard case; for it is spread far and near that the king gives a great feast, at which every man will receive not only abundance of food, but much wealth; and thou art lame, while I am blind; how then shall we get to the feast?"

"Take my counsel," replied the lame man, "and we will obtain a share both of the dinner and wealth."

"Verily," answered the other, "I will follow any counsel that may benefit me."

"Well, then," returned the lame man, "thou art stout of heart, and robust of body, and therefore thou shalt carry me on thy back who am lame and weak, and I will guide you, since I have good sight; by this means we shall reach the festival and secure the reward."

"Be it as thou hast said," replied he of the legs; "get upon my back immediately."

He did so; the lame man pointed the way, and the other carried him. They arrived at the feast, and received the same recompense as the rest.

Tale 72

OF THE KING WHO GAVE THE CROWN TO HIS SON

A CERTAIN KING HAD AN ONLY SON, WHOM HE ARDENTLY loved. When the boy arrived at man's estate, day after day he solicited his father to resign the kingdom, and deliver to himself the sovereign power.

"My dear son," said the king, "if I were satisfied that you would treat me honourably and kindly during the remainder of my life, I should have no objection to relinquish the throne to you."

The son answered, "My lord, I will bind myself by an oath, before all the noblemen of the empire, to do in every respect as a son ought to do. Be confident that I will show greater honour to you than to myself."

The old king trusted to his assurances, and resigned the supreme command. But no sooner was the son crowned, and seated on the throne of his ancestors, than his heart underwent a total change. For a few years he gave due honour to his indulgent parent, but after that entirely neglected him.

This unexpected and unmerited treatment naturally exasperated the old king, and he began to complain to the wise men of the empire that his son had broken the contract. They, therefore, having always loved the father, reproved the son for his ingratitude. But the new king spurned them from him with fury; imprisoned his father in a castle, and permitted not the smallest access to him. Here he often endured the extremity of hunger, and every other species of wretchedness.

It happened that the king himself once passed the night in the same castle; and the father sent to him the following message:—"Oh, my son, pity thy old father who gave up everything to thee. I suffer thirst and hunger; and deprived of all comfort—even of wine to cheer me in my infirmity—I draw out my life."

"I know not," said the king, "that there is wine in this castle." He was told that there were five casks reposited in that place, but that without his permission the steward refused to draw wine from them.

"Suffer me, my dear son," said the unhappy father, "suffer me at least to recruit my wasted form with the first of these casks." The son refused, alleging that it was new, and therefore not good for old men.

"Then," said the old man, "give me the second cask."

"I will not do that," answered the king, "because it is kept for my own drinking, and for the young noblemen who attend me."

"Yet you will surely permit me to take the third," continued his father. "No," replied the other; "it is very strong, and you are so weak and infirm that it would kill you."

"The fourth cask, then?" said he, "give me that."

"It is sour, and would do you much injury."

"But," urged the father, "there is a fifth, allow me to retain it."

"Oh," said the king, "it is nothing but dregs; the noblemen would charge me with having slain thee in case thou wert permitted to drink of it."

The poor father, hearing excuses like these, went away very sorrowful; but secretly wrote letters to the noblemen, declaring how he had been treated, and imploring them to relieve him from the misery he was compelled to endure.

His ill-usage excited their pity and indignation; they restored the father, and threw the son into prison, where he died.

Tale 73

MADE BLIND BUT WITH NO GAIN

A CERTAIN KING OF ROME DECREED THAT EVERY BLIND MAN should annually receive a hundred shillings. It happened that twenty-three associates came into the city and entered a tavern to drink. They remained there seven days, both eating and drinking; but when they would reckon with the tavern-keeper, they had not sufficient money to defray the expense of what they had consumed. "Friends," quoth the host, "here be wanting a hundred shillings. I tell you, of a certainty, ye go not hence till ye have paid the uttermost farthing."

This rather startled the revellers, who, turning to one another, exclaimed, "What shall we do? We cannot pay so large a sum."

At length one of them observed, "Listen to me; I will give you the best advice. The king of this country has decreed that whosoever is blind shall receive from his treasury one hundred shillings. Let us then cast lots, and upon whomsoever the lot falls, we will deprive him of sight, and send him to the king for the promised benevolence. Thus we shall depart in peace."

They all agreed that the counsel was excellent; and casting lots, the chance fell upon the contriver of the expedient; whose eyes they immediately put out. He was then led to the palace. Arriving at the gate, they knocked and were admitted by the porter, who inquired their business.

The blind man answered, "I am one entitled, from my deficiency of sight, to the benefit of the royal donation."

"Well," said the porter, "I will inform the steward." He went accordingly; but the wary steward first determined to examine his exterior before he delivered the money. He did so, and then asked what he wanted.

"A hundred shillings," replied he, "which the law gives to every blind man."

"My friend," said the steward, "if I am not greatly mistaken, I saw you yesterday in a tavern with both eyes perfect. You misinterpret the law. It relates to those who, by some natural infirmity, or by accident, become blind—and against which there was no defence. Such the law protects and relieves. But you voluntarily surrendered your eyes; you drank away your money in a tavern, and planned this deceit. Seek, therefore, consolation and relief in the same place, for you shall not get a halfpenny here."

The blind man then retired in great confusion from the palace.

Tale 74

THE GOLDEN APPLE AND THE FOOL

A KING HAD AN ONLY SON, WHOM HE TENDERLY LOVED. HE caused a golden apple to be made at an immense expense; and shortly after its fabrication he sickened. Finding his end approach, he called to him his son, and spoke after the following manner:—"My dear son, I shall not recover from the sickness under which I suffer, and on my blessing I charge you, travel through town and country, and take with you the golden apple which I caused to be made; find out the greatest fool, and deliver to him that apple from me."

The son faithfully promised to execute his parent's wish; and the king, turning himself toward the wall, resigned his spirit. A splendid funeral was prepared, and after the interment the son set out upon his travels, with the apple in his possession.

He traversed many countries and kingdoms, and found abundance of fools, but none whom he thought quite worthy of the apple. At last he entered a certain province, and approached its principal city. Observing the king, very magnificently attended, riding through the streets, he asked various questions respecting the person he saw, and especially of the institutions of the country. He was answered that, according to their custom, the throne was annually vacated; and that the late possessor, deprived of every honour, was driven into banishment, where he died in obscurity and poverty.

The traveller, hearing this account, exclaimed, "*This* is the man; I have found him whom I sought"; and immediately hastening to the palace, he bent his knee, and cried, "Hail, oh king! my deceased father bequeathed to you this golden apple in his last will."

The king received the gift and said, "My friend, how can this be? Your royal parent knew nothing of me, nor have I ever performed any service to him. Why, then, hath he left me so valuable a present?"

"The king, my lord," replied he, "bequeathed it not more to you than to another; but on his blessing, he charged me to bestow it upon the greatest fool that I could find. And I have now travelled through various kingdoms and countries, but nowhere have I discovered so exquisite a fool and madman. Therefore, according to my sire's command, I resign the apple to your most gracious majesty."

"But," said the king, "on what account do you take me for so great a fool?"

"I will tell you, my lord," returned the other. "You are king for one year; and then, doomed to poverty and exile, you perish most miserably. I declare to you, I do not believe that there is in the whole world such an instance of excessive folly. For would any but a fool choose so short a time of splendour for an end so calamitous?"

"Why," replied the king, "you are doubtless right; and therefore, while I yet reign, I will prepare for my future existence. I will send the greater portion of my wealth into a remote land, upon which I may live in comfort, when I am driven into exile."

He did so; and for a number of years enjoyed great prosperity, and ended his life in peace.

Tale 75

THE THREE WIDOWS

THERE FORMERLY LIVED A KING WHO HAD THREE FAIR daughters. He married them to three dukes; but, unhappily, all their husbands died in the space of one year. The king, being made acquainted with this circumstance, would have had his daughters marry again, and calling the first into his presence he said, "My dear daughter, your husband is dead; I will therefore unite you to another."

But she would by no means consent, and assigned for it this reason: "If I marry again, I should love my second husband equally with the first; perhaps more, or it might be less. This ought not to be; for my first husband possessed my earliest affection—my virgin troth. Therefore the second ought not to be loved so well. But I might love him more, and this would increase the evil; on the other hand, if I loved him less, there would exist only contention between us. So that I resolve never to be espoused again."

The king, satisfied with what he heard, called another of his daughters, and proposed the same thing to her as to her eldest sister. She replied, "My lord, I also decline this matter. For should I comply, it must be either for riches, or power, or beauty. Now, of riches I have quite enough; my friends are sufficiently numerous to defend me; and as for beauty, I do not believe there was so beautiful a person in the world as my late husband. Therefore, I too resolve upon a single state."

The king then applied to the third daughter, and she gave the following reasons for refusing his request:—"If," said she, "I marry, my husband must desire me either for my beauty or my wealth. Now, it cannot be for the former, because I am not beautiful; then, it must be for the latter, and true love never existed which was founded upon mercenary feelings. When wealth flies, love flies with it. Therefore, I would on no account marry again. Moreover, the Sacred Writings say that a husband and wife are one body but two souls; therefore, the body of my husband is my body, and the converse. Every day I visit the sepulchre of my deceased lord, and he is ever present to my mind. For all these causes, I determine to remain as I am."

The king, pleased with the virtuous resolutions of his daughters, solicited them no more.

Tale 76

THE WONDERFUL SKILL AND FRIENDSHIP OF THE
TWO PHYSICIANS

TWO PHYSICIANS ONCE RESIDED IN A CITY, WHO WERE ADmirably skilled in medicine; insomuch that all the sick who took their prescriptions were healed, and it thence became a question with the inhabitants which of them was the best. After a while, a dispute arose between them upon this point.

Said one, "My friend, why should discord or envy or anger separate us? Let us make the trial, and whosoever is inferior in skill shall serve the other."

"But how," replied his friend, "is this to be brought about?"

The first physician answered, "Hear me. I will pluck out your eyes, without doing you the smallest injury, and lay them before you on the table; and when you desire it, I will replace them as perfect and serviceable as they were before. If, in like manner, you can perform this, we will then be esteemed equal, and walk as brethren through the world. But, remember, he who fails in the attempt shall become the servant of the other."

"I am well pleased," returned his fellow, "to do as you say." Whereupon, he who made the proposition took out his instruments and extracted the eyes, besmearing the sockets and the outer part of the lids with a certain rich ointment.

"My dear friend," said he "what do you perceive?"

"Of a surety," cried the other, "I see nothing. I want the use of my eyes, but I feel no pain from their loss. I pray you, however, restore them to their places as you promised."

"Willingly," said his friend. He again touched the inner and outer part of the lids with the ointment, and then, with much precision, inserted the balls into their sockets. "How do you see now?" asked he.

"Excellently," returned the other, "nor do I feel the least pain."

"Well, then," continued the first, "it now remains for you to treat me in a similar manner."

"I am ready," said the latter. And accordingly taking the instruments, as the first had done, he smeared the upper and under parts of the eye with a peculiar ointment, drew out the eyes and placed them upon the table.

The patient felt no pain; but added, "I wish you would hasten to restore them."

The operator cheerfully complied; but as he prepared his implements, a crow entered by an open window, and seeing the eyes upon the table, snatched one of them up, and flew away with it.

The physician, vexed at what had happened, said to himself, "If I do not restore the eye to my companion, I must become his slave." At that moment a goat, browsing at no great distance, attracted his observation. Instantly he ran to it, drew out one of its eyes, and put it into the place of the lost orb.

"My dear friend," exclaimed the operator, "how do things appear to you?"

"Neither in extracting nor in replacing," he answered, "did I suffer the least pain; but—bless me!—one eye looks up to the trees!"

"Ah!" replied the first, "this is the very perfection of medicine. Neither of us is superior; henceforward we will be friends, as we are equals; and banish far off that spirit of contention which has destroyed our peace."

They lived from this time in the greatest amity.

Tale 77

THE FAIR AND UGLY DAUGHTERS OF A KING

A CERTAIN KING HAD TWO DAUGHTERS, ONE OF WHOM WAS extremely beautiful, and very much beloved. The other, however, was of a dark, unprepossessing complexion, and hated as much as her sister was esteemed. This difference in their appearance caused the king to give them characteristic names. He called the first Rosamunda, that is, the fragrant rose; and the second, Gratiaplena, or the full of grace.

A herald was commanded to proclaim that all men should come to him, and he would give his daughters to those who were worthy. But whoever got the beautiful girl to wife should have nothing but her beauty; and he who selected the dark girl should succeed him to the throne.

Multitudes flocked to the summons; but every one still clung to the fair lady, and not even the temptation of a kingdom could induce any one to espouse the other. Gratiaplena wept bitterly at her unhappy fate.

"My daughter," said the king, "why are you so grievously afflicted?"

"Oh, my father," returned she, "no one visits or speaks kindly to me; all pay their attention to my sister, and despise me."

"Why, my dear daughter," said the father, "do you not know that whosoever marries you will possess the crown?"

The lady dried her tears, and was marvellously comforted.

Not long after a king entered the royal palace, and, seeing the great beauty of Rosamunda, desired her in marriage. The king, her father, consented, and she was espoused with great joy. But the other daughter remained many years unbetrothed.

At last a certain poor nobleman, very wisely reflecting that though the girl was abominably ugly yet she was rich, determined to marry her. He therefore went to the king, and solicited his consent; who, glad enough at the proposal, cheerfully bestowed her upon him; and after his decease bequeathed him the kingdom.

Tale 78

THE WIDOW

THE BEAUTIFUL DAUGHTER OF A CERTAIN KING WAS BEtrothed to a noble duke, by whom she had very handsome children. The duke died, and was greatly bewailed by the whole state. After his death her friends earnestly solicited the lady to marry a second time, alleging that her youth and beauty required it.

But she answered, "I will never marry again. My departed lord was so good and kind; he loved me so truly, that I verily believe I shall not live much longer. And if it were possible that I could forget what he has been, where shall I find another? Admitting that I should marry, perhaps my second husband would also precede me to the grave? Why, then, my grief would be awakened the second time, and my afflictions be as heavy as before! Moreover, if he were a bad man, it would indeed be torture to remember him who was good, while one so inferior had succeeded him. I am therefore determined to remain as I am."

Tale 79

THE LITTLE DOGS AND THE ASS

THERE WAS A CERTAIN KING WHO HAD A SINGULAR PARtiality for little dogs that barked loudly; so much so, indeed, that they usually rested in his lap. Being long accustomed to eat and sleep in this situation, they would scarcely do either elsewhere; seeming to take great pleasure in looking at him, and putting their paws upon his neck; and thus the king got much amusement from their antics.

Now, it happened that an ass, who noticed this familiarity, thought to himself, "If I should sing and dance before the king, and put my feet round his neck, he would feed me also upon the greatest dainties, and suffer me to rest in his lap."

Accordingly, quitting his stable, he entered the hall, and running up to the king, raised his clumsy feet with difficulty around the royal neck. The servants, not understanding the ass's courteous intention, imagined that he was mad; and pulling him away, thrashed him soundly. He was then led back to the stable.

Tale 80

THE HERMIT AND THE ANGEL

THERE FORMERLY LIVED A HERMIT, WHO IN A REMOTE CAVE passed night and day in the service of God. At no great dis-

tance from his cell a shepherd tended his flock. It happened
that this person one day fell into a deep sleep, and in the mean
time a robber, perceiving his carelessness, carried off his
sheep.

When the keeper awoke and discovered the theft, he
began to swear in good set terms that he had lost his sheep;
and where they were conveyed was totally beyond his knowledge. Now, the lord of the flock, when he heard this, was
filled with rage, and commanded him to be put to death.

This gave great offence to the hermit before mentioned.
"Oh, Heaven," said he to himself, "seest thou this deed? the
innocent suffers for the guilty: why permittest thou such
things? If thus injustice triumph, why do I remain here?
I will again enter the world, and do as other men do."

With these feelings he quitted his hermitage, and returned
into the world; but God willed not that he should be lost.
An angel in the form of a man was commissioned to join him.
Accordingly, crossing the hermit's path, he thus accosted
him—"My friend, where are you going?"

"I go," said the other, "to the city before us."

"I will accompany you," replied the angel; "I am a messenger from heaven, and come to be the associate of your
way."

They walked on together towards the city. When they had
entered, they entreated for the love of God harbourage during the night at the house of a certain knight, who received
them with cheerfulness, and entertained them with much
magnificence. The knight had an only son lying in the cradle,
whom he exceedingly loved. After supper, their bed-chamber was sumptuously decorated; and the angel retired with
the hermit to rest. But about the middle of the night the
former got up and strangled the sleeping infant.

The hermit, horror-struck at what he witnessed, said within himself, "Never can this be an angel of God; the good

knight gave him everything that was necessary; he had but this poor innocent, and this strange companion of mine has strangled him." Yet he was afraid to reprove him.

In the morning both arose and went forward to another city, in which they were honourably entertained at the house of one of the inhabitants. This person possessed a superb golden cup which he highly valued; and which, during the night, the angel stole.

The hermit thought, "Verily, this is one of the lost angels; our host has treated us well, and yet he has robbed him." But still he held his peace, for his apprehension was extreme.

On the morrow they continued their journey; and as they walked they came to a certain river, over which a bridge was thrown; they ascended the bridge, and about mid-way a poor man met them.

"My friend," said the angel to him, "show us the way to yonder city."

The pilgrim turned, and pointed with his finger to the road they were to take; but as he turned, the angel seized him by the shoulders, and threw him into the stream below.

At this the terrors of the hermit were again aroused—"It is the devil," exclaimed he internally—"it is the devil, and no good angel! What evil had the poor man done that he should be drowned?" He would now have gladly departed alone; but was afraid to give utterance to the thoughts of his heart.

About the hour of vespers they reached a city, in which they again sought shelter for the night; but the master of the house to whom they applied sharply refused it.

"For the love of Heaven," said the angel, "afford us a shelter, lest we fall a prey to the wolves and other wild beasts."

The man pointed to a stye— "That," said he, "is inhabited by pigs; if it please you to lie there, you may—but to no other place will I admit you."

"If we can do no better," returned the angel, "we must accept your ungracious offer."

They did so; and in the morning the angel, calling their host, said, "My friend, I give you this cup"; and he presented to him the stolen goblet.

The hermit, more and more astonished at what he saw, said to himself, "Now I am certain this is the devil. The good man who received us with all kindness he despoiled, and gives the plunder to this fellow who refused us a lodging."

Turning to the angel, he exclaimed, "I will travel with you no longer. I commend you to God."

"Dear friend," answered the angel, "first hear me, and then go thy way. When thou wert in thy hermitage, the owner of the flock unjustly put to death his servant. True it is he died innocently, but he had formerly done deeds for which he deserved to die. God allowed him to be slain, to enable him to escape the future consequences of those former sins of which he had not repented. But the guilty man who stole the sheep will suffer eternally, while the owner of the flock will repair, by alms and good works, that which he ignorantly committed. As for the son of the hospitable knight, whom I strangled in the cradle, know that before the boy was born he performed numerous works of charity and mercy, but afterwards grew niggardly and covetous, in order to enrich the child, of which he was fond. This was the cause of its death; and now its distressed parent again is become a devout Christian. Then, for the cup which I took from him who received us so kindly, know that before the cup was made, there was not a more abstemious person in the world; but afterwards he took such pleasure in it, and drank from it so often, that he was intoxicated twice or thrice during the day. I took away the cup, and he has turned to his former sobriety. Again, I cast the pilgrim into the river; and know that he whom I drowned was a good Christian, but had he proceeded much further, he would have fallen into a mortal sin. Now he is saved, and reigns in celestial glory. Then, that I bestowed the cup upon the inhospitable citizen, know nothing is done without reason. He suffered us to occupy the swinehouse, and I gave him a valuable consideration. But *he* will hereafter reign in hell. Put a guard, therefore, on thy lips, and detract not from the Almighty. For He knoweth all things."

The hermit, hearing this, fell at the feet of the angel and entreated pardon. He returned to his hermitage, and became a good and pious Christian.

Tale 81

THE BIRTH, LIFE AND DEATH OF POPE GREGORY

THE EMPEROR MARCUS HAD AN ONLY SON AND DAUGHTER, to whom he was extremely attached. When he was much advanced in years, he was seized with a grievous sickness; and seeing his end approach, summoned into his presence the chief nobles of his empire. "My friends," said he, "know that this day my spirit will return to the God who gave it. All my concern resides in an only daughter, whom I have not yet bestowed in marriage. Therefore, do thou, my son and heir, upon my blessing, provide for her an honourable and befitting husband; and as long as thou livest, value her as thine own self." Saying these words, he turned toward the wall, and his spirit fled. The state made great lamentation, and interred him with much magnificence.

The young emperor commenced his reign with great wisdom, and in all that related to his sister strictly fulfilled his father's dying injunction. He seated her in the same chair with him at table, and assigned to her a separate couch in the same apartment that he occupied himself. Here began their unhappiness.

Tempted by the devil, he gave way to the most horrible desires; and finally, in spite of the pleading of the wretched girl, violated every law both human and divine. Her tears, if tears could have retrieved the ignominy, had been enough. She wept bitterly, and refused all comfort; although the emperor attempted to console her, and showed the excess of grief and love.

About the middle of the year, as they sat at table, the brother narrowly scrutinized his sister's looks. "My beloved sister," said he, "why dost thou change colour? the upper part of thine eyelids darken."

"No wonder," she returned, "for I bear the weight of thy most fearful wickedness."

Hearing this, the emperor felt his spirit sink within him, and turning round, wept very bitterly. "Perish," said he, "the evil day that I was born; what is to be done?"

"My brother," said the lady, "hear me; we are not, alas, the first who have grievously offended God. There is, as you well know, a certain ancient knight, one of the most approved counsellors of our late father; call him thither, and, under the seal of confession, let us tell him the whole sad story; he will give us counsel how we may make atonement to God, and avoid disgrace before the world."

The emperor assented—"But," said he, "let us study in the first place to be reconciled to God." They were then both confessed, and their sorrow was perfect as sincere.

Afterwards sending for the knight, they revealed amid a flood of tears their crime. "My lord," he replied, "since ye are reconciled to God, hear what I counsel. As well for your own sins, as for the sins of your father, hasten to the Holy Land; and before you embark call together the noblemen of the kingdom, and explain to them your intent. And because your sister is your only heir, charge them to be obedient to her. Then, turning to me, command that she be placed under my custody; and that, as I value my life, she be securely and happily lodged. I will so provide that her condition be kept secret, and every one remain ignorant of her fate—unless, indeed, my wife be made acquainted with it, in order to wait upon her in her necessity." "You counsel well," rejoined the king, "and I will do as you have said."

Immediately the noblemen were summoned, and preparations made for the emperor's departure to the Holy Land. His sister was conveyed to the knight's castle; and when his wife beheld her she inquired whom he had brought.

He answered, "The king's sister; but, wife, swear to me by all that thou holdest sacred, on penalty of thy life, never to communicate to a living soul that which I am about to impart."

She swore accordingly; and the knight then informed her of the situation of the lady, and his desire that no one might attend her but herself. The obedient spouse promised compliance, and the lady was privately introduced into the hall appointed for her residence. She was splendidly attended, and when the time of her confinement came on, she was safely delivered of a beautiful boy.

As soon as the knight understood this, he entreated permission to call in a priest for the purpose of performing the rite of baptism. But she positively refused, declaring that its shameful birth forbade her to interfere, since it would expose her to detection and disgrace.

"Your crime indeed is heavy," returned the knight, "but consider, should your child, therefore, perish immortally?"

"My vow is registered in heaven," said the lady; "I have sworn, nor will I add perjury to my faults. Moreover, I command you to prepare an empty cask."

The knight obeyed; and the lady, placing therein the cradle with the new-born boy, inscribed on small tablets the following words: "Know ye, to whomsoever chance may conduct this infant, that it is not baptized, because it is the unholy offspring of incestuous affection. For the love of God, then, cause it to be baptized. Under the child's head you will discover a quantity of gold, and with this let it be nursed. At the feet is an equal weight of silver, designed to assist him in the future process of study."

This done, she deposited the tablets by the infant's side, the gold at the head, and the silver at its feet; then, enveloping it in silk garments embroidered with gold, she enclosed it in the cask, and directed the knight to cast it forthwith into the sea—trusting that, by the overruling providence of God, it might be carried into a place of safety. The knight faithfully executed the lady's wishes; he threw the cask into the sea, and, standing upon the shore watched its progress, until it was at length lost to his sight.

As he returned to his castle, a king's messenger met him, whom he thus accosted: "Friend, whence come you?"

"From the Holy Land."

"Indeed! what rumours are abroad?"

"My lord the king is dead; and we have brought his corpse to one of his own castles."

Hearing this, the good knight could not refrain from tears. At that moment, his wife approached, and, learning the unwelcome tidings, joined her tears to his. But the knight, recovering somewhat of the dejection of spirit into which the intelligence had thrown him, said to his wife, "Weep not, I pray thee, lest our mistress should perceive it, and inquire the cause. It were better to keep silence on this unwelcome subject, until she be risen from her child-bed." Saying this, the knight entered the queen's apartment, followed by his wife. But the manifest sorrow on their countenances could not escape the penetration of the lady, and she eagerly asked the occasion.

"Dear lady, we are not sad," they said, "but rather joyful at your rapid recovery."

"That is not true," replied she; "I conjure you, conceal nothing, be it for good or evil."

"A messenger," answered the knight, "has just returned from the Holy Land, conveying intelligence of my lord, your brother."

"What does the messenger say? Let him be called hither." This was done; and the lady asked after the king.

"He is dead," said the messenger, "and we have brought the body to his own kingdom, to be buried according to the rites of his country."

The lady, possessed of this fatal intelligence, fell upon the ground; and the knight and his wife, participating in her extreme grief, cast themselves beside her. For a length of time, they all three continued in this attitude; and so intense was their sorrow, that neither sound nor sense appeared remaining.

The lady arose first; tore her hair, wounded her face, and exclaimed in a shrill voice, "Woe is me! May that day perish in which I was conceived! May that night be no more remembered in which so great a wretch was born. How vast is my iniquity! In me all things are fulfilled. My hope is broken, and my strength; he was my only brother—the half of my soul. What I shall do hereafter, alas! I know not."

The knight arose and said, "Dearest lady, listen to me. If you suffer yourself to be thus concerned, the whole kingdom will perish. You only are left; and you are the lawful heir. Should you destroy yourself, the nation will remain at the mercy of foreign powers. Arise, then, and direct the body to be brought hither, and honourably interred. Afterwards, we will debate concerning the prosperity of the kingdom."

Quieted, if not comforted, by the knight's words, she arose, and proceeded with a noble company to the castle, where her brother's body lay. It was placed upon a bier; and no sooner had the queen entered than she fell upon the corpse and kissed it, from the crown of his head, even to the soles of his feet. Now, the soldiers, perceiving the violent grief of their queen, drew her from the bier, and led her into the hall; and then, with great pomp, carried the body to its sepulchre.

A short period after this, a certain Duke of Burgundy sent messengers to demand the lady in marriage; but she declared her fixed determination never to marry.

Irritated at her refusal, the duke observed, "If she had married me, I should indeed have been king of the country; but since it is her pleasure to despise me, she who fills the throne shall enjoy little satisfaction." Whereupon he collected his troops, and devastated every place to which he marched. He perpetrated a vast amount of ill, and subdued all opposition. The queen, in this extremity, fled to a strongly fortified city, where there was a castle well appointed and defended; and here she continued many years.

Let us now return to the boy, who was thrown into the sea. The cask in which he was placed floated through many countries, until it reached, at length, a certain monastery, about the sixth festival.

On that day, the abbot of the monastery proceeded to the sea-shore, and said to his fishermen, "My friends, make ready to fish"; and whilst they were preparing their nets, the vessel was tossed by the motion of the waves upon the shore. The abbot observed it, and said to his servants, "See ye that cask? open it, and find out what is within."

They did so, and behold, it was a newly born boy covered with very rich clothing. No sooner had the child looked upon the abbot, than it smiled. The sight greatly concerned the worthy monk. "Oh, my God," said he, "how comes it that we find a child in this deplorable situation?"

Raising it with his own hands, he perceived the tablets under its side, which the mother had placed there; and when he had read them, he discovered that it was the offspring of an incestuous bed, and not yet baptized—and saw that this sacrament was implored, for the sake of Heaven; and that gold and silver were deposited for his food and education.

When he had read this, and observed that the cradle was ornamented with rich cloth, he saw that the boy was of noble blood. He immediately baptized and called him after his own name, Gregory. He then entrusted him to a fisherman to nurse, with the gold and silver found upon him.

The boy grew up universally beloved. In his seventh year the abbot provided for his studies, which he mastered in a surprising manner; insomuch that the monks were as fond of him as though he had been of their own order. In a short time he acquired more knowledge than them all.

It happened that one day, as he played at ball with the son of the fisherman, his presumed father, by chance he struck him with the ball. The lad wept bitterly, and running home, complained to his mother that he had been struck by his brother Gregory. Instantly the angry mother issued out of doors, and harshly reproved him, exclaiming, "Audacious little vagabond, why hast thou struck my son? Thou!—of whose origin and country we know nothing—how darest thou do this?"

"Dear mother," answered Gregory, "am I not your son? Why do you speak to me in this manner?"

"My son!" said the woman; "no, in good troth; neither do I know whose thou art. All I know is that thou wert one day discovered in a cask, and that the abbot delivered thee to me to bring up."

When the boy heard this he burst into tears, ran hastily to

the superior, and said, "Oh, my lord, I have been a long time with you, and I believed that I was the fisherman's son; but I learn that it is not so; consequently, I am ignorant who my parents are. If it please you, my lord, suffer me to become a soldier, for here I will not remain."

"My son," said the abbot, "think not of it. The monks all love you, and I doubt not, after my decease, will promote you to the abbacy."

"My good lord," answered Gregory, "I know not my parents, and I will not continue longer than I can help in this intolerable suspense."

The abbot, finding solicitation useless, entered the treasury and brought to him the tablets which he had found in the cradle. "My son," he said, "read this; and what you are will be clear to you."

When he had read, he fell to the earth, and exclaimed, "Alas! are such, then, my parents? I will hasten to the Holy Land, and do battle for the sins of the unhappy authors of my being; and there I will end my life. I entreat you, therefore, my lord, without delay to make me a knight."

The abbot complied, and when his departure was made known, the whole convent and neighbourhood were loud in their lamentation.

Straightway he agreed with certain sailors for his passage to the Holy Land, and embarked. But as they sailed the wind became contrary, and they were suddenly driven upon the coast of that country in which his mother's castle stood. What the state was, and who reigned there, the sailors knew not; but as Gregory entered the city a citizen met him, and said, "My lord, whither are you going?"

"To seek an inn," was the reply. On which the hospitable citizen led him to his own house, and entertained him magnificently.

As they sat at table Gregory inquired of his host what state it was, and who was the lord of it. "Sir," returned the other, "awhile ago we had a very powerful emperor, but he died in the Holy Land, and left his throne to his sister. The Duke of Burgundy would have married her, but she was pleased to refuse his offer. Whereupon he has forcibly made himself master of the whole kingdom, save a single city in which the queen resides."

"May I," returned the young knight, "declare with safety the secret wish of my heart?"

"With the greatest safety."

"I am," continued the other, "a soldier. If it please you, go to-morrow to the palace and obtain for me a communication with the steward, and if he will promise to remunerate me, I will fight for this year in behalf of the lady."

"I doubt not, my lord," answered the citizen, "but that he will acquiesce with willingness. To-morrow I will do as you desire."

He went accordingly, and declared the occasion of his coming. The steward, not a little exhilarated, immediately sent off a messenger for Gregory; and, on his arrival, presented him to the queen, who expressed herself well satisfied with her champion. She observed him closely, but had not the remotest suspicion that it was her son, for she thought him long since overwhelmed in the waves. The steward therefore, in the presence of his mistress, pledged that he should serve a full year.

On the morrow he prepared for war, and assembled a large host. So judicious were his movements that Gregory triumphed in every engagement, and penetrated to the very palace of the duke, whom he finally took and beheaded.

Gregory after this continued the war from day to day with constant success; and the fame of his great strength and skill was carried to all parts of the realm. Thus, before the completion of the year which he had pledged to serve, he had wrested the whole kingdom from the hands of their enemies.

Then he went to the steward, and said, "Good friend, you know in what state I found your affairs, and in what a good condition I leave them. I therefore beg you to give me my hire, for I intend to proceed to another country."

"My lord," said the steward, "you have merited much more than our agreement stipulated; let us hasten to the queen, and there conclude as to the recompense."

They went accordingly; and the steward thus spoke: "My dear lady, I would say something, which will be to your advantage. From the absence of a head, we have sustained many grievous afflictions. It were desirable, therefore, for you to take a husband, who is able to defend us from a return of the like troubles. Your kingdom is rich enough, so that I would not advise you to select a spouse for his wealth. And this being allowed, I know not where you could find one in every respect so suitable and beneficial to the state as my lord Gregory."

The lady, as we have seen before, rejected a second marriage; but overcome by the arguments and urgency of her steward, appointed a day on which, after mature deliberation, she would give an answer.

That day came; and in the presence of all the assembled nobles, she arose and spoke thus: "Since my lord Gregory has valiantly and effectually liberated both us and our kingdom from oppressive foes, I *will* receive him for my husband."

The audience rejoiced; and an early period was fixed for the celebration of their nuptials. They were then married with the approbation of the whole country—the son to his own mother. But both were ignorant of the relationship. They loved each other tenderly; it happened, however, that the lord Gregory on one particular occasion went out to hunt; and a handmaid of the queen said to her, "Dear lady, have you not offended my lord in something?"

"Surely not," returned she. "I believe that there is not in the whole world a married pair so mutually attached to each other as we are. But why do you ask?"

"Because," said the handmaid, "every day, when the table is laid, my lord enters his private chamber in great apparent pleasure; but when he returns it is with lamentation and wailing. After that he washes his face; but why all this is done, I do not comprehend."

On hearing this, the lady immediately entered the private chamber before alluded to, and narrowly inspected every closet and crevice. At length, she came to the place wherein the tablets, inscribed with the disgrace of his birth, and which he was wont to read day by day, were deposited; and then she wept most piteously. For they were the same which she had laid in the cradle; and which, when they now stood up before her, as it were, by magic, she remembered too well.

She opened them, and recognized her own handwriting. "Alas!" she exclaimed, "how has he obtained this dark testimony of my crime, if he be not my son?" And then bursting into a lamentable cry, "Woe is me, that I ever saw the light of heaven—would that I had died ere I was born."

The soldiers in the hall, hearing the clamour produced by the anguish and storm of her mind, ran into the chamber, and found her stretched upon the earth. They stood around her a considerable time before she was able to talk, and when at length she could speak, she said, "If ye desire me to live, hasten immediately for my lord."

The spectators hearing her wish, mounted their horses, and rode to the king. They explained to him the imminent danger of his wife; and he forthwith left the chase, returned to the castle, and entered the chamber where the queen lay.

When she saw him, she said, "Oh, my lord, command us

to be left alone; what I have to say is for your private ear."

The room was accordingly cleared; and the lady eagerly besought him to say of what family he was. "That is a singular question," replied he, "but know that I am a native of a distant country."

"Oh," returned the lady, "I solemnly vow to God that, unless you declare to me the whole truth, I am sure I shall quickly die."

"I tell you," he said, "I was poor—possessed of nothing but the arms with which I freed you and the kingdom from slavery."

"Only tell me," urged the lady, "from what country you came, and who are your parents; and unless you speak truly, I will never more touch food."

"You shall be satisfied," said the king. "I was brought up by an abbot from my earliest age; and from him I learnt that I was found cradled in a cask."

Here the queen showed him the tablets, and said, "Dost thou remember these?" He looked, and fell prostrate on the earth.

"My *son!*" cried she, "For thou art so; my only son and my husband, and my lord! Thou art the child of my brother and myself. Oh, my son, I deposited in the cask with thee these tablets. Woe is me! Why, O God, didst thou permit my birth, since I was born to be guilty of so much wickedness! Would that the eye which looks upon me might reduce me to ashes; would that I had passed from the womb to the grave!" Then striking her head against the wall, she cried, "Oh, thou Almighty Being, behold my son—my husband, and the son of my brother."

"I thought," replied Gregory, "to shun this danger, and I have fallen into the snares of the devil. Dismiss me, lady, to bewail my misery: woe! woe! my mother is my mistress—my wife! See how Satan hath encompassed me!"

When the mother perceived the agony of her child, she said, "Dear son, for the residue of my life, I will atone for our crimes by hardships and wanderings. Thou shalt govern the kingdom."

"Not so," returned he; "do you remain, my mother: you are wanted to rule the realm. I will roam about, until our sins are forgiven."

The same night he arose, broke his lance, and put on the dress of a pilgrim. He bade his mother farewell, and, with naked feet, walked till he reached the uttermost boundaries of the kingdom. Having entered a certain city, he sought out the house of a fisherman, with whom he requested permission to lodge. When the fisherman had considered him attentively, and observed the comeliness of his person and the grace of his form, he said, "Friend, you are no true pilgrim; this is evident from the elegance of your body."

"Well," answered the other, "though I be not a true pilgrim, yet, for the love of God, I beseech you to give me harbourage."

Now, the fisherman's wife, looking upon him, was moved with a devout feeling, and entreated that he might be sheltered. He entered therefore; but directed his bed to be made for him at the gate. Fish, with water and bread, were given to him. Amongst other things, the fisherman said, "Pilgrim, if you would become holy, go into some remote place."

"Sir," answered Gregory, "I would willingly follow your advice, but I know of no such place."

"On the morrow," returned he, "I will myself conduct you."

"May God reward you," said the pilgrim. The next morning the fisherman bade him rise, and hurried him so much that he left his tablets behind the gate where he had slept.

The fisherman, with his companion, embarked upon the sea, and sailing about sixteen miles came to a huge rock, hav-

ing chains at its feet, which, without a key, could not be unloosed. After the fisherman had undone them, he cast the
keys into the sea, and returned home. The pilgrim remained
in that place seventeen years, with every feeling of the most
perfect penitence.

About this period the pope died; and at the moment of
his decease, a voice from heaven cried out, "Search after a
man of God, called Gregory, and appoint him my vicar."

The electors, greatly rejoiced at what they heard, sent
messengers into different parts of the world to seek him.

At length, some of them lodged in the house of the fisherman; and as they sat at supper, one said, "My friend, we are
much harassed by journeys through town and country, in
pursuit of a holy man, called Gregory, whom, when we find,
we are to place in the pontificate."

The fisherman, then recollecting the pilgrim, answered, "It
is now seventeen years since a pilgrim named Gregory lodged
in this house. I conducted him to a certain rock in the midst
of the sea, and there I left him. But it is so long ago, that he
may be dead." It happened that on the same day, a number
of fishes were caught; and as he gutted one of them, he found
the keys which seventeen years before he had cast into the
sea. Immediately he shouted, "Oh, my friends, behold these
keys! I cast them into the sea; and I draw from this circumstance a good omen respecting the success of your labours."

The messengers were much pleased with the man's good
omen, and early in the morning desired him to bring them to
the rock.

He did so, and there finding Gregory, they said, "Man of
God, go up with us; by the command of the Omnipotent, go
up with us; for it is His will that thou shouldst be appointed
His vicar upon earth."

To which Gregory replied, "God's will be done"; and then
followed them from the rock.

As soon as he approached the city, the bells rang of their own accord, which the citizens hearing, said, "Blessed be the Most High, he cometh who shall be Christ's vicar," and hastened to meet him. Saint Gregory, thus appointed, conducted himself worthily in every respect; and multitudes from every part of the world came to ask his counsel and assistance.

Now, his mother, hearing of the remarkable sanctity of the reigning pope, thought that nowhere could she find help sooner than from so holy a man. But that he was her son and husband she knew not. Hastening, therefore, to Rome, she confessed herself to the vicar of God; nor was it till after confession that the pope recollected his unhappy mother.

He then spoke thus: "Dearest mother, and wife, and mistress, the devil dreamt of bringing us to hell; but, by the grace of God, we have evaded his toils."

At these words, she fell at his feet; and even for very joy, wept bitterly. But the pope raised her up, and tenderly embraced her.

He founded a monastery over which he made her abbess, and a short time afterwards, both yielded up their souls to God.

Tale 82

THE ADULTEROUS BIRD

A CERTAIN KNIGHT HAD A VERY BEAUTIFUL CASTLE, UPON which two storks built their nest. At the foot of this castle was a clear fountain, in which the storks were wont to bathe themselves. It happened that the female stork brought forth young, and the male flew about to procure food.

Now, while he was absent, the female admitted a gallant;

and before the return of the male went down to the fountain to wash herself, in order that the other might perceive no disorder in her appearance. But the knight, often observing this with wonder, closed up the fountain, that the stork might no longer wash or bathe herself.

In this dilemma, after meeting her lover, she was obliged to return to her nest; and when the male came and saw by various signs that she had been unfaithful, he flew away, and brought back with him a great multitude of storks, who put the adulterous bird to death, in the presence of the knight.

Tale 83

THE BOAR WITHOUT A HEART

WHEN TRAJAN REIGNED HE TOOK GREAT PLEASURE IN GARdens. Having constructed one of uncommon beauty, and planted in it trees of every kind, he appointed his cook as keeper with instructions to defend it faithfully. But by and by a wild boar broke into the garden, overturned the young trees, and rooted up the flowers.

The keeper, whose name was Jonathan, perceiving this, cut off the boar's left ear, and the animal with a loud noise departed. But another day, the same boar re-entered the garden and committed great depredations; upon which Jonathan cut off his right ear. But notwithstanding this, he entered a third time; and the keeper, on seeing this, cut off his tail—without which he departed, as formerly, making a tremendous uproar. However, he appeared on a fourth occasion, and committed the like injuries; when Jonathan, more and more incensed, caught up a lance and transfixed him upon the spot. He was then sent to the royal kitchen and prepared for the king's table.

Now Trajan, it seems, was especially partial to the heart of any animal, and the cook observing that the boar's heart was particularly fat and delicate, reserved it for his own tooth. When, therefore, the emperor's dinner was served up, the heart was inquired after; and the servants returned to the cook.

"Tell my lord," said the fellow, "that it had no heart; and if he disbelieves it, say that I will present convincing reasons for the defect."

The servants delivered the cook's message, and the astonished emperor exclaimed, "What do I hear? There is no animal without a heart! But since he offers to prove his assertion we will hear him."

The cook was sent for, and spoke thus, "My lord, listen to me. All thought proceeds from the heart. It follows, therefore, that if there be no thought, there is no heart. The boar, in the first instance, entered the garden and committed much injury. I seeing it, cut off his left ear. Now, if he had possessed a heart, he would have recollected the loss of so important a member. But he did not, for he entered a second time. Therefore, he had no heart. Besides, if he had had a heart, when I had cut off his right ear, he would have meditated on the matter; which he did not, for he came again and lost his tail. Moreover, having lost his ears and his tail, had he possessed even a particle of heart, he would have thought; but he did not think, for he entered a fourth time and was killed. For these several reasons I am confident that he had no heart."

The emperor, satisfied with what he heard, applauded the man's judgment. And thus he escaped.

Tale 84

THE LADY, THE KNIGHT, AND THE FALCON

IN THE REIGN OF POMPEY THERE LIVED A FAIR AND AMIABLE lady; and near to her residence dwelt a handsome and noble knight. He was in the habit of visiting her frequently, and was much beloved by her. The knight coming once to see her observed a falcon upon her wrist, which he greatly admired. "Dear lady," said he, "if you love me, give me that beautiful bird."

"I consent," returned she, "but on one condition; that you do not attach yourself so much to it as to rob me of your society."

"Far be such ingratitude from your servant," cried the knight; "I would not forsake you on whatever emergency. And believe me, this generosity binds me more than ever to love you."

The lady presented the falcon to him; and bidding her farewell, he returned to his own castle. But he derived so much satisfaction from the bird, that he forgot his promise to the lady, and thought but little of her, while every day he sported with the falcon.

She sent messengers to him, but it was of no use; he came not: and at last she wrote a very urgent letter entreating him, without the least delay, to hasten to her and bring the falcon along with him. He acquiesced; and the lady, after salutation, requested him to let her touch the bird. No sooner was it in her possession, than she wrenched its head from the body.

"Madam," said the knight, not a little grieved, "what have you done?"

To which the lady answered, "Be not offended, but rather rejoice at what I have done. That falcon was the occasion of your absence, and I killed him that I might enjoy your company as I was wont."

The knight, satisfied with the reason, became once more a regular visitant.

Tale 85

THE HARPER AND THE WHISTLER

WHEN TIBERIUS REIGNED HE WAS PASSIONATELY FOND OF music. It happened that, as he once pursued the chase, he was struck with the sound of a harp, whose sweetness so delighted him, that he turned his horse's head and rode to the place from which it issued. When he arrived there, he perceived a broad sheet of water, and near it a certain poor man seated on the ground, having a harp in his hand. From hence arose the melody; and the emperor was refreshed and exhilarated by the delicious tones the harp gave forth.

"My friend," said the king, "inform me how it is that your harp sounds so sweetly."

"My lord," answered the other, "for more than thirty years I have sat by this stream, and God has bestowed upon me such grace, that the moment I touch the chords of my harp, the very fishes, enchanted with the harmony, come even into my hand, and afford sustenance to my wife and family. But, unhappily for me, a certain whistler has arrived within these few days from another country; and he whistles so admirably, that the fishes forsake me and go over to him. Therefore, my lord, since you are powerful, and the ruler of this kingdom, give me some aid against this abominable whistler."

"My friend," returned the king, "I can help you only in one thing; but I hope this will be enough. I have in my hunting-bag a golden hook, which I will give you; fasten it on the top of a rod, and then strike your harp. The sound will inveigle the fishes and as soon as they approach, by the means of the hook draw them to land. If you follow my advice, the whistler will depart in great trouble."

The poor man did as he was directed; and before the fishes could arrive at the place where the whistler was stationed, the hook brought them to land. The whistler, perceiving himself outdone, retired in much tribulation.

Tale 86

OF THE CHILD BORN IN DARKNESS

A CERTAIN EMPEROR MADE A LAW BY WHICH, IF ANY WOMAN were taken in adultery, she should be condemned to perpetual imprisonment. It happened that a knight espoused a noble lady, to whom he was greatly attached. The knight having been called by some emergency into foreign parts, his wife fell under the sentence of the law. She was accordingly cast into a dungeon, and there brought forth a remarkably handsome boy.

The child grew, and was beloved by all who saw him. But the mother consumed her hours in groans and tears, nor experienced the smallest comfort. The boy, observing the continual lamentation of his mother, said to her, "For what reason, dearest mother, do you afflict yourself in this manner?"

"Oh, my son!" returned she, "I have much reason to weep. Above our heads is an intercourse with mankind; and there the sun shines in his splendour. Here we are kept in utter darkness, and light never blesses our sight."

"I am ignorant of all this," said the boy, "because I was born in prison. As long as I receive a sufficiency of meat and drink, I shall willingly remain here."

As they thus conversed, the emperor and his guards were standing near the door of the prison. One of them solicited his sovereign to liberate the mother and son; and he, feeling their distress, and in consideration of the entreaties of his attendants, set them at liberty, and absolved them from future punishment.

Tale 87

THE EMPEROR WHO FORGOT HIS DEBT

AN EMPEROR, ENGAGED IN MORTAL WAR, WAS IN IMMINENT peril of death. A zealous knight, perceiving his danger, placed himself between the emperor and his enemies, and thus saved him from destruction. But in the attempt the knight was grievously wounded, and not until after a tedious and dangerous illness, healed. The scars, however, remained, and gave occasion to many commendations upon the valour and loyalty which he had exhibited.

It happened that the same knight was in danger of being defrauded of his inheritance. He went, therefore, to the emperor, and entreated that he would assist him and give sentence in his favour.

"My good friend," replied the emperor, "I cannot attend to you at present; but I will appoint a judge who shall examine your case, and do you every justice."

"My lord," cried the other, "how can you say so?" And immediately tearing open his vesture, he exposed the scars left by his wounds. "See what I have borne for you—yet you will neither vindicate nor assist me! Is it not unjust that, after I have undergone so much, another should be deputed to judge and advocate my cause?"

The emperor, hearing this, instantly replied, "My friend, you say true; when I was in peril you, and not another, preserved me."

Then, ascending the tribunal, he gave judgment in his favour.

Tale 88

POISON FOR THE ENEMIES

IT IS RELATED OF A CERTAIN PRINCE THAT, WITH ALL HIS power, he could not subdue his enemies. At length he made use of the following stratagem. He feigned a flight, and resigned his castles, with the provisions they contained, into the hands of his foes.

Now, the castles were furnished with casks of wine poisoned with the seed of a certain herb; insomuch that whosoever drank of it immediately fell asleep. He knew that his opponents were hunger-starved and gluttonous; and that, overjoyed to find such excellent quarters, they would drink to excess, and fall into a death-like sleep.

They did so, and the prince returning put them all to death.

Tale 89

THE THREE RINGS

A CERTAIN KNIGHT HAD THREE SONS, AND ON HIS DEATH-bed he bequeathed the inheritance to his first-born; to the second, his treasury; and to the third, a very valuable ring, of more worth indeed than all he had left to the others. But the two former had also rings; and they were all apparently the same.

After their father's death the first son said, "I possess that precious ring of my father."

The second said, "You have it not—I have."

To this the third son answered, "That is not true. The elder of us hath the estate, the second the treasure, and therefore it is but just that I should have the most valuable ring."

The first son answered, "Let us prove, then, whose claims to it have the pre-eminence."

They agreed, and several sick men were made to resort to them for the purpose. The two first rings had no effect, but the last cured all their infirmities.

Tale 90

HOW THE INHERITANCE WAS DIVIDED

THERE WAS FORMERLY A KING, IN WHOSE REIGN A LAW WAS enacted that the elder brother should divide the inheritance, and then that the younger should have the choice; the reason of which was that they considered it a greater proof of discretion to apportion than to select, and the elder ought to be the wiser. There was also another law, which permitted a son by a slave woman to receive an inheritance as well as the lawfully begotten sons.

Now, there were two brothers, the one born of a handmaid, and the other of a free woman, between whom an estate was to be divided. The elder, therefore, divided it in this manner. On one side he placed the whole inheritance, and on the other his brother's mother.

The latter reflected that he ought to love his parent beyond all else; and consequently chose her, trusting to the kindness and liberality of his brother. But here he was deceived; for he would supply him with nothing. Upon which he hastened to the judge, and complained that his brother had excluded him from his inheritance.

The brother made answer that the matter rested not with him, since he who chose, not he who divides, is secure of his portion.

Tale 91

THE THREE LAZY SONS

THE EMPEROR PLINY HAD THREE SONS, TO WHOM HE WAS extremely indulgent. He wished to dispose of his kingdom, and calling the three into his presence, spoke thus: "The most slothful of you shall reign after my decease."

"Then," answered the elder, "the kingdom must be mine; for I am so lazy, that sitting once by the fire, I burnt my legs, because I was too indolent to withdraw them."

The second son observed, "The kingdom should properly be mine, for if I had a rope round my neck, and held a sword in my hand, my idleness is such, that I should not put forth my hand to cut the rope."

"But I," said the third son, "ought to be preferred to you both; for I outdo both in indolence. While I lay upon my bed, water dropped from above upon my eyes; and though, from the nature of the water, I was in danger of becoming blind, I neither could nor would turn my head ever so little to the right hand or to the left."

The emperor hearing this, bequeathed the kingdom to him, thinking him the laziest of the three.

Tale 92

STORY OF THE MALE AND FEMALE SERPENTS

A CERTAIN KING HAD A WIFE NAMED CORNELIA. IT HAP-pened that, under a wall in one of the king's castles, two serpents were discovered; one male, and the other female. The king, hearing of this, interrogated his learned men as to the signification; and they assured him that they were hidden there to predict the death of a man or woman. They further declared that if the male were killed, a man should die; if the female, a woman and a wife.

"If this be so," said the king, "kill the male serpent, and let the female live; for a man ought more willingly to die himself than permit the death of his wife." And he gave this reason for it: "If my wife live, she may bring forth many sons who may succeed to my throne; but if she should die, the kingdom would want an heir."

Tale 93

TWO SONS RETURN HOME

A CERTAIN POWERFUL LORD SENT HIS TWO SONS TO STUDY, that they might, by their own efforts, obtain a livelihood. After some time he sent letters to them, to command their return to their own country; and they returned accordingly.

One of the brothers rejoiced at this, and was received with equal pleasure. He was, moreover, put in possession of a fair inheritance. But the other was much distressed at his recall. When his mother ran out to meet him, she kissed him, and while doing so bit off his lips. His sister, also, following the mother's example, bit off his nose. His brother also put out his eyes; and the father, entering, caught him by the hair of his head and flayed him alive.

Tale 94

HOW A KING'S DAUGHTER BECAME A LEPER

A KING BEING DESIROUS OF VISITING FOREIGN COUNTRIES, and possessing an only daughter of great beauty, indeed infinitely brighter than the sun, knew not into whose custody he might fearlessly consign her. At last he put her under the charge of his secretary, for whom he had the greatest regard. He commanded him to take every precaution, and especially to guard against her drinking of a singular fountain which sprung up in that country. For it had the property, although of a most exquisite flavour, of infecting with leprosy whosoever tasted it.

The secretary, therefore, in order to restore her to her father as beautiful as when he departed, reflected much upon his precarious employment; remembering, at the same time, that if she were at all injured he should lose his office, and be unable to meet his master. For a while he watched his charge with extreme vigilance; but the lady having discovered the fountain, went so cunningly to work, that she drank of it, and was consequently infected with a loathsome disease.

The secretary perceiving this, was filled with the most

poignant grief, and carried her away to a desert region. There he found a hermit; and beating with his hands upon the door of his cell, related to him all that had happened, beseeching him to point out how she might be healed.

"Go," said the hermit, "to a mountain which I will show you. In that place you will discover a certain stone and a peculiar kind of rod. Take this rod, and strike the stone sharply, strongly, and boldly, until a moisture exudes from it. Anoint the lady with this liquid, and she will be presently restored to her original beauty."

The secretary strictly followed the hermit's injunctions, and the lady became as she was before.

Tale 95

HOW CONSTANTINE ASSISTED THE ROMANS

WE READ IN THE ROMAN ANNALS OF A CERTAIN TYRANT called Maxentius, who would have deprived the Romans of their paternal estates. Yielding to the cruelty of the tyrant, they fled to Constantine, king of Britain.

At length, when many were assembled at his court, the emigrants stirred up the British monarch to revenge them upon the tyrant. Moved by their entreaties, Constantine mounted his horse, overthrew the tyrant, and restored the exiles to their inheritance.

Tale 96

FORGIVENESS WHILE THE CANDLE BURNT

KING ALEXANDER PLACED A BURNING CANDLE IN HIS HALL, and sent heralds through the whole kingdom, who made the following proclamation:—"If there be any minor transgressor, and he will come boldly into his presence, while the candle burns, the king will forgive the forfeiture. And whosoever is in this predicament, and comes not before the expiration of the candle, he shall perish by an ignominious death."

Many of the populace, hearing the proclamation, came to the king and besought his mercy. The king received them kindly; but there were many who neglected to come, and the very moment in which the candle expired, they were apprehended and put to death.

Tale 97

THE WARNINGS TO JULIUS CÆSAR

WE READ IN THE ROMAN CHRONICLES THAT, ABOUT THE twenty-second year from the building of the city, the people erected in the Forum a marble column, and on the top of it placed an image of Julius Cæsar. Upon the head they inscribed his name, because it was erected in his honour.

The same Julius Cæsar received three signs which were to happen at his death, or just before he was to die. On the hundredth day preceding this event, the effigy in the Forum was struck by lightning, and the first letter of his name erased. The very night before his death, the windows of his bed-chamber burst open with such a tremendous noise, that he thought the whole building had been overturned. And on the same day that he died, when about to go into the Capitol, letters were given him, declaring the danger in which he stood.

If he had read them he would have been saved.

Tale 98

A CUSTOM OF THE ROMANS DURING SIEGE

THE ROMANS HAD AN ANCIENT CUSTOM, THAT WHEN THEY besieged a castle or city, they lighted a single candle of a certain length; and as long as it burnt, they were prepared to receive overtures of peace, however vile the proposer. But after it was consumed they exercised the severest justice upon their enemies, nor could any one then be redeemed even by the sacrifice of all he was worth.

Tale 99

THE KNIGHT, THE SERPENT AND THE TOAD

IN THE REIGN OF CÆSAR THERE LIVED A NOBLE AND VALiant knight, who once rode by a certain forest, and beheld a serpent engaging with a toad. The latter obtained the mastery; which when the knight saw, he assisted the serpent; and grievously wounding the toad, reduced it to seek safety in flight. But the conqueror was also affected by the toad's venom.

The knight turned homeward, and for a long time lay sick of his wound. At last he made his will and prepared himself for death. Now, as he reclined near the fire, utterly hopeless of life, the serpent which he had preserved entered the apartment. When the attendants beheld it, they said, "My lord, my lord, a serpent has entered the room!"

When the knight saw it, he recollected that it was the same

he had aided in its contest with the toad, and through which he was laid upon his bed incurable.

"Do not molest it," said the knight, "I do not believe that it will harm me."

The serpent glided towards him, and applying its tongue to the wound, sucked up the poison till its mouth was quite full; and then, hastening to the door, cast it out. It returned twice to the wound, and did as before, until the venom was exhausted.

The knight commanded milk to be given to the serpent, which it instantly drank; and no sooner had it done so, than the toad from which the wound had been received, entered, and again attacked the serpent, in revenge for its having healed the knight.

The latter seeing this, said to his servants, "Without doubt, my friends, this is the toad which I wounded in defence of that serpent, and from which I derive all my infirmity. If it conquer, it will attack me; therefore, as ye love your master, kill it incontinently."

The servants, obedient to the knight's command, slew it with swords and clubs; while the serpent, as if to praise and thank its defender, twined around his feet, and then departed. The knight completely recovered his health.

Tale 100

THE SON SAVES HIS MOTHER

WHEN DIOCLETIAN REIGNED, HE DECREED THAT WHATSO-ever woman committed adultery should be put to death. It happened that a certain knight married a girl and had a son by her. The child grew, and every one loved him.

After a while his father went out to battle, and, fighting manfully, was deprived of his right arm. In the mean time his wife lost her honour; and the husband, on his return, discovering the shame, ought, according to law, to have put her to death.

Calling his son, therefore, he said, "My dear boy, your mother has committed adultery, and by law should die by my hand; but I have lost my arm, and am unable to destroy her. I command you to do this."

The son answered, "The law enjoins children to honour their parents; and if I were to slay my own mother, I should act contrary to the law, and bring down her curse on myself. Therefore in this I cannot obey you."

So the woman was saved from death by her son.

Tale 101

PLENTY, JOY AND LIGHT

WE READ OF A CERTAIN MAN, NAMED GANTER, WHO WISHED that his pleasures might never end. He got up one morning, and walked until he came to a kingdom in which the prince was lately deceased. The noblemen observing that he was a bold man, chose him for their king. He was, of course, much elevated with the election. But at night, when the servants brought him into his chamber, he perceived at the head of the bed a very fierce lion; a dragon was at the foot; on the right side, a huge bear; and serpents and toads on the left.

"What is all this?" asked Ganter; "Am I to sleep in company with all these beasts?"

"Yes, my lord," was the reply; "for all the former kings have done so, and by these beasts have been devoured."

"That is all very fine," returned Ganter, "but as I feel no relish for either the bed or the beasts, I will not be your king."

He therefore went his way, and came into another kingdom, where, in like manner, he was called to the throne. At night he entered the bed-chamber, and beheld a very superb couch, full of sharp razors.

"What!" exclaimed he, "am I to sleep in this bed?"

"Even so, my lord," replied the attendants; "for in this bed all our kings have laid, and have perished."

"Why," said Ganter, "everything is excellent, except this bed; but because of this I will not be your sovereign."

In the morning he again departed, and travelled for three days alone. On the way he saw an old man sitting above a fountain. His hand contained a staff, and when our traveller approached, he said, "My dear Ganter, whence come you?"

"I come," he replied, "from foreign countries."

"And where are you going?"

"To seek three things which I cannot find."

"What are they?"

"The first," said Ganter, "is unfailing plenty; the second, joy without sorrow; and the third, light without darkness."

"Take this staff," said the old man, "and go thy way. Before you is a high mountain, and at its foot a ladder with six steps. Go up it, and when you have attained the sixth, you will be at the top of the mountain. There you will discover a magnificent palace; strike three times at the gate, and the porter will answer you. Show him the staff, and say, 'The master of the staff commands you to admit me.' When you have gained admittance, you will find the three things which you seek."

Ganter did as the old man desired, and the porter, seeing the staff, permitted him to enter. He found what he had sought, and much more; and there he continued during the residue of his life.

Tale 102

THE EVIL MAGICIAN AND THE MAGIC MIRROR

IN THE REIGN OF TITUS THERE LIVED A CERTAIN NOBLE AND devout knight, who had a beautiful wife; but she dishonoured herself, and persisted in her dishonour. The knight, therefore, was very sorrowful, and resolved to visit the Holy Land. In this determination he said to his wife, "My beloved, I go to the Holy Land, and leave you to the guidance of your own discretion."

No sooner had he embarked than the lady sent for a certain skilful magician, whom she loved; and he dwelt with her. It happened that, as they lay in bed, the lady observed, "If you would do one thing for me, I might become your wife."

"What is it," replied he, "that will please you, and which I can perform for you?"

"My husband is gone to the Holy Land, and loves me little; now, if by your art you could destroy him, all that I possess is yours."

"I acquiesce," said the clerk, "but on condition that you marry me."

To this the lady bound herself, and the magician fashioned an image under the similitude and name of the knight, and fixed it before him on the wall.

In the mean time, while the knight was passing through the main street of Rome, a wise master met him in the way, and observing him narrowly, said, "My friend, I have a secret to communicate."

"Well, master, what would you please to say?"

"This day you are one of death's children, unless you follow my advice. Your wife is a harlot, and contrives your death."

The knight, hearing what was said of his spouse, put confidence in the speaker, and said, "Good master, save my life, and I will amply recompense you."

"Willingly," answered the other, "if you will do as I shall tell you." The knight promised, and the master took him to a bath, undressed him, and desired him to bathe. Then putting into his hand a polished mirror, said, "Look attentively upon this, and you will see wonders." He did so, and the meanwhile the master read to him from a book. "What see you?" he asked.

"I see," said the knight, "a certain clerk in my house, with an image of wax which resembles me, and which he has fastened in the wall."

"Look again," continued the master; "what do you perceive now?"

"He takes a bow, and places in it a sharp arrow; and now he aims at the effigy."

"As you love your life, the moment you discern the arrow flying to its mark, place yourself in the bath, and remain there until I tell you to come out."

As soon, therefore, as the arrow quitted the string, he plunged his body into the water. This done, the master said, "Raise your head and look into the mirror. What do you perceive now?"

"The effigy is not struck, and the arrow is sticking by its side. The clerk appears much concerned."

"Look in the mirror once more," said the master, "and observe what he does."

"He now goes nearer to the image, and refixes the arrow in the string in order to strike it."

"As you value your life, do as before."

Again the knight plunged his body into the water as soon

as he saw by the mirror that the clerk was bending the bow; and then, at the command of the master, resuming his inspection of the mirror, said—"The clerk makes great lamentation, and says to my wife, 'If the third time I do not strike the effigy, I shall lose my life.' Now he approaches so near that I think he cannot miss it."

"Take care," said the master, "as soon as you see him bend the bow, immerse your body as I before told you." The knight watched attentively, and as soon as he saw the clerk draw back the bow to shoot, plunged below the water. "Rise quickly, and look into the mirror." When he had done so, he began to laugh. "My friend," said the master, "why do you laugh?"

"I observe," answered he, "very distinctly, that the clerk has missed the effigy, and that the arrow, rebounding, has entered his bowels and destroyed him. My wife makes a hole under my bed, and there he is buried."

"Rise, then, dress yourself, and pray to God."

The knight returned sincere thanks for his life, and, having performed his pilgrimage, journeyed toward his own home. His wife met and received him with much apparent pleasure.

He waited a few days, and then sending for her parents, said to them, "My dear friends, hear why I have desired your presence. This woman, your daughter and my wife, has committed adultery; and, what is worse, designed to murder me."

The lady denied the accusation with an oath. The knight then began to relate the whole story of the clerk's actions and end. "And," he continued, "if you do not credit this, come and see where the clerk is buried."

He then led them into the bed-chamber, and dragged the body from its hiding-place. The judge was called, and sentenced her to be burnt, and her ashes to be scattered in the air. The knight soon afterwards espoused a beautiful virgin, by whom he had many children; and with whom he finished his days in peace.

Tale 103

THE THREE MAXIMS

DOMITIAN WAS A VERY WISE AND JUST PRINCE, AND SUF-fered no offender to escape. It happened that as he once sat at table, a certain merchant knocked at the gate. The porter opened it, and asked what he pleased to want. "I have brought some useful things for sale," answered the merchant.

The porter introduced him; and he very humbly made salutation to the emperor. "My friend," said the latter, "what merchandise have you to dispose of?"

"Three maxims of special wisdom and excellence, my lord."

"And how much will you take for your maxims?"

"A thousand florins."

"And so," said the king, "if they are of no use to me, I lose my money?"

"My lord," answered the merchant, "if the maxims do not stand you in stead, I will return the money."

"Very well," said the emperor; "let us hear your maxims."

"The first, my lord, is this—'Whatever you do, do wisely, and think of the consequences.' The second is—'Never leave the highway for a byway.' And, thirdly, 'Never stay all night as a guest in that house where you find the master an old man, and his wife a young woman.' These three maxims, if you attend to them, will be extremely serviceable."

The emperor, being of the same opinion, ordered him to be paid a thousand florins; and so pleased was he with the first, that he commanded it to be inscribed in his court, in his bedchamber, and in every place where he was accustomed to walk; and even upon the tablecloths of the palace.

Now, the rigid justice of the emperor occasioned a conspiracy among a number of his subjects; and finding the means of accomplishing their purposes somewhat difficult, they engaged a barber, by large promises, to cut his throat as he shaved him. When the emperor, therefore, was to be shaved, the barber lathered his beard, and began to operate upon it; but casting his eyes over the towel which he had fastened round the royal neck, he perceived woven thereon—"Whatever you do, do wisely, and think of the consequences."

The inscription startled the barber, and he said to himself, "I am to-day hired to destroy this man; if I do it, my end will be violent; I shall be condemned to the most shameful death. Therefore, whatsoever I do, it is good to consider the end, as the writing testifies."

Those thoughts disturbed the worthy barber so much that his hand trembled, and the razor fell to the ground. The emperor seeing this, inquired the cause.

"Oh, my lord," said the barber, "have mercy upon me: I was hired this day to destroy you; but accidentally, or rather by the will of God, I read the inscription on the towel, 'Whatever you do, do wisely, and think of the consequences.' Whereby, considering that, of a surety, the consequence would be my own destruction, my hand trembled so much, that I lost all command over it."

"Well," thought the emperor, "this first maxim hath assuredly saved my life; in a good hour was it purchased. My friend," said he to the barber, "on condition that you be faithful hereafter, I pardon you."

The noblemen, who had conspired against the emperor, finding that their project had failed, consulted with one another what they were to do next.

"On such a day," said one, "he journeys to a particular city; we will hide ourselves in a bypath, through which he will pass, and so kill him."

The counsel was approved. The king, as had been expected, prepared to set out; and riding on till he came to the bypath, his knights said, "My lord, it will be better for you to go this way, than to pass along the broad road; it is considerably nearer."

The king pondered the matter within himself. "The second maxim," thought he, "warns me never to forsake the highway for a byway. I will adhere to that maxim." Then turning to his soldiers, "I shall not quit the public road; but you, if it please ye, may proceed by that path, and prepare for my approach."

Accordingly a number of them went; and the ambush, imagining that the king rode in their company, fell upon them and put the greater part to the sword. When the news reached the king, he secretly exclaimed, "My second maxim hath also saved my life."

Seeing, therefore, that by this piece of cunning they were unable to slay their lord, the conspirators again took counsel, and said among themselves, "On a certain day he will lodge in a particular house, where all the nobles lodge, because there is no other fit for his reception. Let us then agree with the master of that house and his wife, for a sum of money, and then kill the emperor as he lies in bed."

This was agreed to. But when the emperor had come into the city, and had been lodged in the house to which the conspirators referred, he commanded his host to be called into his presence. Observing that he was an old man, the emperor said, "Have you got a wife?"

"Yes, my lord."

"I wish to see her."

The lady came; and when it appeared that she was very young—not eighteen years of age—the king said hastily to his chamberlain, "Away, prepare me a bed in another house. I will remain here no longer."

"My lord," replied he, "be it as you please. But they have made everything ready for you; were it not better to lie where you are, for in the whole city there is not so commodious a place."

"I tell you," answered the emperor, "I will sleep elsewhere."

The chamberlain, therefore, removed; and the king went privately to another residence, saying to the soldiers about him, "Remain here, if you like; but join me early in the morning."

Now, while they slept, the old man and his wife arose, being bribed to kill the king in his sleep, and put to death all the soldiers who had remained.

In the morning the king arose and found his soldiers slain. "Oh," cried he, "if I had continued here, I should have been destroyed. So the third maxim hath also preserved me." But the old man and his wife, with the whole of their family, were crucified.

The emperor retained the three maxims in memory during life, and ended his days in peace.

Tale 104

THE GRATEFUL LION

THERE WAS A KNIGHT WHO DEVOTED MUCH OF HIS TIME to hunting. It happened one day, as he was pursuing this diversion, that he was met by a lame lion, who showed him his foot. The knight dismounted, and drew from it a sharp thorn; and then applied an unguent to the wound, which speedily healed it. A while after this, the king of the country hunted in the same wood, and caught that lion, and held him captive for many years.

Now, the knight having offended the king, fled from his anger to the very forest in which he had been accustomed to hunt. There he betook himself to plunder, and spoiled and slew a multitude of travellers. But the king's sufferance was exhausted; he sent out an army, captured, and condemned him to be delivered to a fasting lion.

The knight was accordingly thrown into a pit, and remained in terrified expectation of the hour when he should be devoured. But the lion, considering him attentively, and remembering his former friend, fawned upon him; and remained seven days with him destitute of food. When this reached the ears of the king, he was struck with wonder, and directed the knight to be taken from the pit.

"Friend," said he, "by what means have you been able to render the lion harmless?"

"As I once rode along the forest, my lord, that lion met me lame. I extracted from his foot a large thorn, and afterwards healed the wound, and therefore he has spared me."

"Well," returned the king, "since the lion has spared you, I will for this time ratify your pardon. Study to amend your life."

The knight gave thanks to the king, and ever afterwards conducted himself with all propriety. He lived to a good old age, and ended his days in peace.

Tale 105

STORY OF THE BELL OF JUSTICE

THE EMPEROR THEODOSIUS HAD THE MISFORTUNE TO LOSE his sight. He put up a bell in his palace; and the law was, that whoever had any suit to make should pull the string with his own hands. When the bell rang, a judge, appointed to this end, descended and administered justice.

It chanced that a serpent made her nest immediately under the bell-rope, and in due time brought forth young. When they were old enough, one day she conducted them forth to enjoy the fresh air beyond the city. Now, while the serpent was absent, a toad entered and occupied her nest. When, therefore the former returned with her young, she found the toad in possession, and instantly began an attack. But the latter baffled her attempts, and obstinately maintained his station.

The serpent, perceiving her inability to eject the intruder, coiled her tail around the bell-rope, and forcibly rang the bell; as though she had said, "Descend, judge, and give me justice; for the toad has wrongfully seized my nest."

The judge, hearing the bell, descended; but not seeing any one, returned. The serpent, finding her design fruitless, once more sounded the alarm. The judge again appeared, and upon this occasion, seeing the serpent attached to the bell-rope, and the toad in possession of her nest, declared the whole circumstance to the emperor.

"Go down, my lord," said the latter, "and not only drive away the toad, but kill him; let the serpent possess her right." All which was done.

On a subsequent day, as the king lay in his bed, the serpent entered the bed-chamber, carrying a precious stone in her mouth. The servants, perceiving this, informed the emperor, who gave directions that they should not harm it; "For," added he, "it will do me no injury."

The serpent, gliding along, ascended the bed, and approaching the emperor's eyes, let the stone fall upon them, and immediately left the room. No sooner, however, had the stone touched the eyes than their sight was completely restored.

Infinitely rejoiced at what had happened, the emperor made inquiry after the serpent, but it was not heard of again. He carefully treasured this invaluable stone, and ended his days in peace.

Tale 106

THREE TRAVELLERS WHO HAD ONE LOAF BETWEEN THEM

THERE WERE ONCE THREE FRIENDS, WHO AGREED TO MAKE a pilgrimage together. It happened that their provisions fell short, and having but one loaf between them, they were nearly famished. "Should this loaf," they said to each other, "be divided amongst us, there will not be enough for any one. Let us then take counsel together, and consider how the bread is to be disposed of."

"Suppose we sleep upon the way," replied one of them; "and whosoever hath the most wonderful dream shall possess the loaf?"

The other two acquiesced, and settled themselves to sleep. But he who gave the advice arose while they were sleeping and ate up the bread, not leaving a single crumb for his companions. When he had finished he awoke them. "Get up quickly," said he, "and tell us your dreams."

"My friends," answered the first, "I have had a very marvellous vision. A golden ladder reached up to heaven, by which angels ascended and descended. They took my soul from my body, and conveyed it to that blessed place, where I beheld the Holy Trinity, and where I experienced such an overflow of joy as eye hath not seen nor ear heard. This is my dream."

"And I," said the second, "beheld the devils with iron instruments, by which they dragged my soul from the body, and plunging it into hell flames, most grievously tormented me, saying, 'As long as God reigns in heaven this will be your portion.' "

"Now then," said the third, who had eaten the bread, "hear my dream. It appeared as if an angel came and addressed me in the following manner:—'My friend, would you see what is become of your companions?' I answered, 'Yes, Lord. We have but one loaf between us, and I fear that they have run off with it.' 'You are mistaken,' he rejoined, 'it lies beside us; follow me.' He immediately led me to the gate of heaven, and by his command I put in my head and saw you; and I thought that you were snatched up into heaven and sat upon a throne of gold, while rich wines and delicate meats stood around you. Then said the angel, 'Your companion, you see, has an abundance of good things, and dwells in all pleasures. There he will remain for ever; for he has entered the celestial kingdom, and cannot return. Come now where your other associate is placed.' I followed, and he led me to hell-gates, where I beheld you in torment, as you just now said. Yet they furnished you, even there, with bread and wine in abundance. I expressed my sorrow at seeing you in misery, and you replied, 'As long as God reigns in heaven here I must remain, for I have merited it. Do you then

rise up quickly and eat up all the bread, since you will see
neither me nor my companion again.' I complied with your
wishes, arose and ate the bread."

Tale 107

THE UNDERGROUND PALACE

THERE WAS AN IMAGE IN THE CITY OF ROME STANDING IN
an erect posture, with the dexter hand outstretched; and
upon the middle finger was written, "STRIKE HERE." The
image stood a long time in this manner, and no one understood what the inscription signified. It was much wondered
at, and commented on; but this was all, for they invariably
departed as wise as they came.

At last, a certain subtle clerk, hearing of the image, felt
anxious to see it; and when he had done so, he observed the
superscription, "STRIKE HERE." He noticed that when the
sun shone upon the image, the outstretched finger was dis-
cernible in the lengthened shadow. After a little consideration he took a spade, and where the shadow pointed, dug a
the depth of about three feet. This brought him to a number
of steps, which led into a subterranean cavity.

Not a little exhilarated with his discovery, the clerk pursued the adventure. Descending the steps, he entered the hall
of a magnificent palace, in which he perceived a king and
a queen and many nobles seated at table, and the hall itself
filled with men. They were all clothed in costly apparel, and
kept the most rigid silence. Looking about, he beheld in one
corner of the place a polished stone, called a carbuncle, by
the single aid of which the hall was lighted. In the opposite
corner stood a man armed with a bow and arrow, in the act

of taking aim at the precious stone. Upon his brow was inscribed, "I am what I am: my shaft is inevitable; least of all can yon luminous carbuncle escape its stroke."

The clerk, amazed at what he saw, entered the bed-chamber, and found a multitude of beautiful women arrayed in purple garments, but not a sound escaped them. From thence he proceeded to the stables, and observed a number of horses and asses in their stalls. He touched them, but they were nothing but stone. He visited all the various buildings of the palace, and whatsoever his heart desired was to be found there.

Returning to the hall, he thought of making good his retreat. "I have seen wonders to-day," said he to himself, "but nobody will credit the relation, unless I carry back with me some incontrovertible testimony." Casting his eyes upon the highest table he beheld a quantity of golden cups and beautiful knives, which he approached, and laid his hands upon one of each, designing to carry them away.

But no sooner had he placed them in his bosom, than the archer struck the carbuncle with the arrow, and shivered it into a thousand atoms. Instantly, the whole building was enveloped in thick darkness, and the clerk, in utter consternation, sought his way back. But being unable, in consequence of the darkness, to discover it, he perished in the greatest misery, amid the mysterious statues of the palace.

Tale 108

THE TWO FAITHFUL THIEVES

IN THE REIGN OF A CERTAIN EMPEROR, THERE WERE TWO thieves who bound themselves by an oath never to quit one another on any emergency, even though death were the alternative. They afterwards committed many robberies, and were, on some occasions, guilty of murder.

It happened that one of them, being caught in some theft, was imprisoned and placed in fetters. His companion, understanding what had chanced, hastened to him, and said, "My friend, by the engagement which we have formed, I beg you to tell me what I can do to serve you."

"It appears," answered the other, "that I must die, having been taken in the act for which I am sentenced. But I will show you how to oblige me. Obtain permission to remain in my place, while I hasten to arrange my affairs, and provide for my wife and children. Having done this, I will return in due time and liberate you."

"My friend," answered the first, "I will readily comply with your wishes." He went therefore to the judge, and spoke thus: "My lord, my friend has been thrown into prison, and condemned to death. It seems that there is no chance for him; let it please you, then, to permit him to return home to arrange the affairs of his family, and I, in the mean time, will become his surety, and remain in prison."

"On such a day," replied the judge, "he, with some others, will be executed; if, upon that day, he return not before a certain hour, look you to it; your death is inevitable."

"My lord," answered the man, "I am prepared for the worst."

"Let him go, then; I consent to your wishes." The judge ordered the substitute to be ironed, and placed in prison in the room of his friend, who immediately set out to his family.

So long, however, did he postpone his return, that the day of execution arrived, and his pledge was unredeemed. The latter, therefore, was brought, with many others, to the seat of judgment. "Where is your friend?" said the judge; "he has not arrived to make good his word."

"I hope the best, my lord," replied the other; "I do not think he will fail me."

Some time passed over, and still he came not; and the prisoner was at length conducted to the cross. "You must attribute your death to yourself," said the judge; "do not charge it upon me. You have rashly trusted to your friend, and he has deceived you."

"My lord," replied he, "defer the crucifixion but for a moment, and suffer me to play upon an instrument three times before my death."

"Play!" exclaimed the judge; "Of what nature is that playing?"

"I will shout, my lord."

"As you please."

Accordingly he began to call. He shouted loudly once, twice, and at the third shout he distinguished, at some distance, a man running toward them with surprising velocity, "My lord! my lord! there is a man coming; stay the execution—perhaps it is my friend, and I shall yet be liberated!"

The judge waited, and the person they looked for made his appearance. "I am the man you expect," he exclaimed. "I have arranged my affairs, and meanwhile my friend has been in peril of death for me; let him now freely depart, for I am ready to suffer death for my crimes."

The judge regarded him for a few moments with attention, and then said, "My friend, tell me whence it comes that you are so faithful to one another?"

"My lord," he replied, "from our youth up we have been friends, and ever pledged ourselves to be faithful. For this reason he put himself in my place till I had settled my affairs."

"Well," said the judge, "because of this remarkable instance of fidelity, I pardon you. Remain with me, and I will provide all things necessary for your well-being."

They returned thanks to the judge, and promised equal fidelity to him. He then received them to favour; and all praised the judge who showed them this mercy.

Tale 109

HOW THE WICKED CARPENTER LOST HIS GOLD

A CERTAIN CARPENTER RESIDING IN A CITY NEAR THE SEA, very covetous and very wicked, collected a large sum of money, and placed it in the trunk of a tree, which he placed by his fireside, that no one might have any suspicion that it held money.

It happened once that, while all his household slept, the sea overflowed its boundaries, broke down that side of the building where the log was situated, and carried it away. It floated many miles, and reached, at length, a city in which there lived a person who kept open house. Arising early in the morning, he perceived the trunk of a tree in the water, and brought it to land, thinking it was nothing but a bit of timber thrown away by some one. He was a liberal, kind-hearted man, and a great benefactor to the poor.

It one day chanced that he entertained some pilgrims in his house; and the weather being extremely cold, he cut up the log for firewood. When he had struck two or three blows with the axe, he heard a rattling sound; and cleaving it in twain, the gold pieces rolled out in every direction.

Greatly rejoiced at the discovery, he reposited them in a secure place, until he should ascertain who was the owner.

Now, the carpenter, bitterly lamenting the loss of his money, travelled from place to place in pursuit of it. He came, by accident, to the house of the hospitable man, who had found the trunk. He failed not to mention the object of his search; and the host understanding that the money was his, said to himself, "I will prove, if God will, that the money should be returned to him."

Accordingly, he made three cakes, the first of which he filled with earth; the second, with the bones of dead men; and in the third, he put a quantity of the gold which he had discovered in the trunk.

"Friend," said he, addressing the carpenter, "we will eat three cakes, composed of the best meat in the house. Choose which you will have."

The carpenter did as he was directed; he took the cakes and weighed them in his hand, one after another, and finding that with the earth weigh heaviest, he chose it. "And if I want more, my worthy host," added he, "I will have that," laying his hand upon the cake containing the bones. "You may keep the third cake yourself."

"I see clearly," murmured the host, "I see very clearly that God does not will the money to be restored to this wretched man."

Calling, therefore, the poor and infirm, the blind and the lame, and opening the cake of gold in the presence of the carpenter, to whom he spoke, "Thou miserable varlet, this is thine own gold. But thou hast preferred the cake of earth, and dead men's bones. I am persuaded, therefore, that God wills not that I return thee thy money"—without delay, he distributed the whole amongst the paupers, and drove the carpenter away in great tribulation.

Tale 110

THE MIRACULOUS ADVENTURES OF THE KNIGHT
PLACIDUS

IN THE REIGN OF TRAJAN THERE LIVED A KNIGHT NAMED
Placidus, who was commander-in-chief of the emperor's
armies. He was of a very merciful disposition, but a worshipper of idols. His wife also participated in the same feelings, and adhered to the same religious rites. They had two
sons, educated in all the magnificence of their age and station; and from the general kindness and goodness of their
hearts, they merited a revelation of the way of truth.

As he was one day following the chase, he discovered a herd
of deer, amongst which was one remarkable for the beauty
and magnitude of its form. Separating itself from the rest, it
plunged into the thicker part of the forest. While the hunters,
therefore, occupied themselves with the remainder of the
herd, Placidus gave his attention to the noble animal in
question, and followed the course it had taken with all the
swiftness in his power.

While he was giving all his strength to the pursuit, the stag
at length scaled a lofty precipice, and Placidus, approaching
as near to it as he could, considered by what means it might
be secured. But as he regarded it with fixed attention, there
appeared, impressed upon the centre of the brow, the form
of the cross, which glittered with greater splendour than a
meridian sun.

Upon this cross an image of Jesus Christ was suspended;
and as formerly happened to the ass of Balaam, utterance
was supplied to the stag, which thus addressed the hunter:
"Why dost thou persecute me, Placidus? For thy sake I as-

sumed the shape of this animal. I am Christ whom thou ignorantly worshippest. Thine alms have gone up before Me, and therefore I come, that as thou hast hunted this stag, so may I hunt thee."

Some indeed assert that the image, hanging between the deer's antlers, said these things.

However that may be, Placidus, filled with terror, fell from his horse; and in about an hour returning to himself, arose from the earth and said, "Declare what Thou sayest, that I may believe in Thee."

"I am Christ, O Placidus! I created heaven and earth; I caused the light to arise, and divided it from darkness. I appointed days, and seasons, and years. I formed man out of the dust of the earth; and I became incarnate for the salvation of mankind. I was crucified, and buried; and on the third day I rose again."

When Placidus heard this, he fell again upon the earth, and exclaimed, "I believe, O Lord, that Thou art He that made all things; and that Thou art He who bringest back the wanderer."

The Lord answered. "If thou believest this, go into the city and be baptized."

"Wouldst Thou, O Lord, that I impart what has befallen me to my wife and children, that they also may believe?"

"Do so; tell them that they also may be cleansed from their iniquities. And do you, on the morrow, return hither, where I will appear again, and show you more fully of the future."

Placidus, therefore, departed to his own home, and communicated all that had passed to his wife. But she, too, had had a revelation; and in like manner had been enjoined to believe in Christ, together with her children. So they hastened at midnight to the bishop of the city of Rome, where they were entertained and baptized with great joy.

Placidus was called Eustacius, and his wife Theosbyta;
the two sons, Theosbytus and Agapetus. In the morning
Eustacius, according to custom, went out to hunt, and coming with his attendants near the place, he dispersed them, as
if for the purpose of discovering the prey.

Immediately the vision of yesterday reappeared, and pros-
trating himself, he said, "I implore Thee, O Lord, to make
clear what Thou didst promise to Thy servant."

"Blessed art thou, Eustacius, because thou hast received
the vessel of My grace, and thereby overcome the devil. Now
hast thou trod him to dust who beguiled thee. Now will thy
fidelity appear; for the devil, whom thou hast deserted, is
arming himself against thee in a variety of ways. Much must
thou undergo ere thou possessest the crown of victory. Much
must thou suffer that thou mayst be humbled, and abandon
the deep-seated vanity of this world, and once more be raised
by spiritual wealth. Fail not, therefore, nor look back upon
thy former condition. Thou must demonstrate thyself another Job; but from the very depth of thy humiliation, I will
restore thee to the summit of earthly splen.'our. Choose,
then, whether thou wouldst prefer thy trials now, or at the
conclusion of life."

Eustacius replied, "If it become me, O Lord, to be exposed
to trials, let them presently approach; but do Thou uphold
me, and supply me with patient fortitude."

"Be bold, Eustacius; My grace shall support your souls."
Saying thus, the Lord ascended into heaven. After which
Eustacius returned home to his wife, and explained to her
what had been decreed.

In a few days a pestilence carried off the whole of their
men-servants and maid-servants; and before long the sheep,
horses, and cattle also perished. Robbers plundered their habitation, and despoiled them of every ornament; while he himself, together with his wife and sons, fled naked and in the

deepest distress. But devoutly they worshipped God; and, apprehensive of an Egyptian disease, went secretly away. Thus were they reduced to utter poverty.

The king and the senate, greatly afflicted with their general's calamities, sought for, but found not the slightest trace of him. In the mean time this unhappy family approached the sea; and finding a ship ready to sail, they embarked in it. The master of the vessel observing that the wife of Eustacius was very beautiful, determined to secure her; and when they had crossed the sea, demanded their passage money, which, as he anticipated, they did not possess. Notwithstanding the vehement and indignant protestations of Eustacius, he seized upon his wife; and, beckoning to the mariners, commanded them to cast the unfortunate husband headlong into the sea. Perceiving, therefore, that all opposition was useless, he took up his two children, and departed with much and heavy sorrow.

"Alas for me and for you!" he exclaimed, as he wept over his bereaved offspring; "Your poor mother is lost, and in a strange land, in the arms of a strange lord, must lament her fate."

Travelling along, he came to a river, the water of which ran so high that it appeared hazardous in an eminent degree to cross with both children at the same time. One, therefore, he placed carefully upon the bank, and then passed over with the other in his arms. This effected, he laid it upon the ground, and returned immediately for the remaining child. But in the midst of the river, accidentally glancing his eye back, he beheld a wolf hastily snatch up the child, and run with it into an adjoining wood. Despairing of saving it, he hastened to the other; but while he was yet at some distance, a huge lion approached the child he had left, and, seizing it, presently disappeared. To follow was useless, for he was in the middle of the water.

Giving himself up, therefore, to his desperate situation, he began to lament and to pluck away his hair; and would have cast himself into the stream had not Divine Providence preserved him.

Certain shepherds, however, observing the lion carrying off the child in his teeth, pursued him with dogs; and by the peculiar dispensation of Heaven it was dropped unhurt. As for the other, some ploughmen witnessing the adventure, shouted lustily after the wolf, and succeeded in liberating the poor victim from its jaws.

Now, it happened that both the shepherds and ploughmen resided in the same village, and brought up the children amongst them. But Eustacius knew nothing of this, and his affliction was so poignant that he was unable to control his complaints.

"Alas!" he would say, "once I flourished like a luxuriant tree, but now I am stripped of my leaves. Once I was encompassed with military ensigns and bands of armed men; now I am a single being in the universe: I have lost all my children, and everything that I possessed. Remember, O Lord, that thou saidst my trials should resemble Job's; behold, they exceed them. For, although he was destitute, he had a couch, however vile, to repose upon; I, alas! have nothing. He had compassionating friends, while I have savage beasts who have carried off my sons, for my friends. His wife remained, but mine is forcibly carried off. Assuage my anguish, O Lord! and place a bridle upon my lips, lest I utter foolishness, and be cast away from before Thy face."

With such words he gave free course to the fulness of his heart; and after much travel entered a village, where he abode. In this place he continued for fifteen years, and tended the lambs of the men of that place as their hired servant.

To return to the two boys. They were educated in the same neigbourhood, but had no knowledge that they were brothers. And as for the wife of Eustacius, she preserved her purity, and suffered not the infamous usage which circumstances led her to apprehend. After some time her persecutor died.

In the mean while the Roman emperor was beset by his enemies, and recollecting how valiantly Placidus had behaved himself in similar straits, his grief at the deplorable mutation of fortune was renewed. He despatched soldiers through various parts of the world in pursuit of them; and promised to the discoverer infinite rewards and honours.

It happened that some of the emissaries, being of those who had attended upon the person of Placidus, came into the country in which he laboured, and one of them he recognized by his gait. The sight of these men brought back to the exile's mind the situation of wealth and honour which he had once possessed; and being filled with fresh trouble at the recollection—"O Lord!" he exclaimed, "even as beyond expectation I have seen these people again, so let me be restored to my beloved wife. Of my children I speak not; for I know too well that they are devoured by wild beasts."

At that moment a voice whispered, "Be faithful, Eustacius, and thou wilt shortly recover thy lost honours, and again look upon thy wife and offspring."

Now, when the soldiers met Placidus, they knew not who he was; and accosting him, they asked if he were acquainted with any foreigner named Placidus, with his wife and two sons. He replied in the negative, but requested that they would tarry in his house. They consented; and he conducted them home, and waited on them. And here, as before, at the recollection of his former splendour, his tears flowed. Unable to contain himself, he went out of doors, and when he had washed his face he re-entered, and continued his service.

By and by the appearance of their ancient master underwent a more exact scrutiny; and one said to the other,

"Surely this man bears great resemblance to him we inquire after."

"Of a truth," answered his companion, "you say well. Let us examine if he possess a scar on his head, which he received in action."

They did so, and finding a scar which indicated a similar wound, they leaped up and embraced him, and inquired after his wife and sons. He related his adventures; and the neighbours, coming in, listened with wonder to the account delivered by the soldiers of his military achievements and former magnificence. Then, obeying the command of the emperor, they clothed him in sumptuous apparel.

On the fifteenth day they reached the imperial court; and the emperor, apprized of his coming, went out to meet him, and saluted him with great gladness. Eustacius related all that had befallen him; he was then invested with the command of the army, and restored to every office that he had held prior to his departure.

When the soldiers were numbered, they were found to be too few to meet the enemy. He therefore drew together from all parts the young men of the country; and it fell in the lot of the village where his own children were educated, to send two to the army; and these very youths were selected by the inhabitants as the best and bravest of their number. They appeared before the general; and their elegant manners, united to a singular propriety of conduct, won his esteem. He placed them in the front of his troops, and began his march against the enemy.

After the rout of the foe, he caused his army to halt for three days at a certain place, where, as it happened, his wife was living in poverty. Strange to say, the sons themselves, in the general distribution of the soldiers, were quartered with their own mother, but all the while ignorant with whom they were stationed,

About mid-day the lads, sitting together, related the various adventures to which their infancy had been subject; and the mother, who was at no great distance, became an attentive auditor.

"Of what I was, while a child," said the elder of the brothers, "I remember nothing, except that my beloved father was a leader of a company of soldiers; and that my mother, who was very beautiful, had two sons, of whom I was the elder. We accompanied our parents from the habitation in which we had constantly resided during the night, and embarking on board a vessel that immediately put to sea, sailed I know not whither. Our mother remained in the ship, but wherefore, I am also ignorant. In the mean time our father carried my brother and myself in his arms, and me he left upon the nearer bank of a river, until he had conveyed the younger of us across. But no sooner had he accomplished his design, and was returning to my assistance, than a wolf darted from a thicket and bore my brother off in his mouth. Before he could hasten back to his rescue, a lion seized upon me, and carried me into a neighbouring wood. Certain shepherds, however, delivered and educated me amongst them, as you know. What has become of my father and my brother, I know not."

The younger brother here burst into a flood of tears, and exclaimed, "Surely I have found my brother; for they who brought me up frequently declared that I was emancipated from the jaws of a wolf." Then did they exchange embraces and shed tears.

The mother, who listened, it may be well supposed, with intense interest to what was going forward, felt a strong conviction that they were her own children. She was silent, however; and the next day went to the commander of the forces, and entreated permission to go into her own country. "I am a Roman woman," said she, "and a stranger in these parts."

As she uttered these words, her eye fixed with an earnest

and anxious gaze upon the countenance of him she addressed. It was her husband, whom she now for the first time recollected; and she threw herself at his feet unable to contain her joy.

"My lord," cried the enraptured matron, "I entreat you to relate some circumstances of your past life; for, unless I greatly mistake, you are Placidus, the master of the soldiery, since known by the name of Eustacius, whom our blessed Saviour converted, and tried by such and such temptations: I am *his* wife, taken from him at sea by a vile wretch, but who acomplished not his atrocious purposes. I had two sons, called Agapetus and Theosbytus."

When Eustacius heard this, he looked at her earnestly, and saw that it was his wife. They embraced and wept; giving glory to God, who brings joy to the sorrowful.

The wife then observed, "My lord, what has become of our children?"

"Alas!" replied he, "they were carried off by wild beasts"; and he repeated the circumstance of their loss.

"Give thanks," said his wife, "give manifold thanks to the Lord; for as His Providence hath revealed our existence to each other, so will He give us back our beloved offspring."

"Did I not tell you," returned he, "that wild beasts had devoured them?"

"True; but yesternight, as I sat in the garden, I overheard two young men relate the occurrences of their childhood, and whom I believe to be our sons. Interrogate them, and they will tell you."

Messengers were immediately despatched for this purpose, and a few questions convinced Eustacius of the full completion of his happiness. They fell upon each other's necks and wept aloud. It was a joyful occasion; and the whole army rejoiced at their being found, and at the victory over the barbarians.

Previous to their return the Emperor Trajan died, and was succeeded by Adrian, more wicked even than his predecessor. However, he received the conquerer and his family with great magnificence, and sumptuously entertained them at his own table. But the day following the emperor would have proceeded to the temple of his idols to sacrifice, in consequence of the late victory; and desired his guests to accompany him.

"My lord," said Eustacius, "I worship the God of the Christians; and Him only do I serve, and propitiate with sacrifice."

The emperor, full of rage, placed him, with his whole family, in the arena, and let loose a ferocious lion upon them. But the lion, to the astonishment of all, held down his head before them, as if in reverence, and humbly went from them. On which the emperor ordered a brazen furnace to be heated, and into this his victims were cast alive; but with prayer and supplication they commended themselves to the mercy of God, and three days after, being taken out of the furnace in the presence of the emperor, so untouched were their dead bodies by the fire that not a hair of their heads was singed, nor had the fiery vapours in any way affected them.

The Christians buried their corpses in the most honourable manner, and over them constructed an oratory. They perished in the first year of Adrian, A. D. 120, in the calends of November; or, as some write, the 12th of the calends of October.

Tale III

THE WHITE COW AND HER GOLDEN HORNS

A CERTAIN NOBLEMAN HAD A WHITE COW, TO WHICH HE was extremely partial. He assigned two reasons for this. First, because she was spotlessly white; and next, because she gave abundance of rich milk. The estimation in which the nobleman regarded his beast increased so much, that he constructed golden horns for her, and thought for a long time how she might be best secured.

Now, there lived at that time a man called Argus, who was entirely faithful to his employer, and, moreover, possessed an hundred eyes. The nobleman despatched a messenger to Argus, to request his attendance without delay.

On his arrival, he said, "I commit to your custody my cow with golden horns; and if you guard it securely I will liberally remunerate you. But if you permit her horns to be stolen, you shall die the death."

Argus accordingly received the cow under his charge; and every day attended her to the pasture, and watched her with unremitting care. At night he drove her home. But there dwelt in these days a certain greedy knave called Mercury, whose skill in music was surpassing. He had a great desire to possess the animal so narrowly watched; and he went frequently to her keeper, in the hope of prevailing with him, by prayers or promises, to deliver the horns to him. But Argus fixed a shepherd's staff, which he held, firmly in the ground; and addressed it in the person of his master: "Thou, oh staff, art my master, and at night I shall return to your castle. You will question me about the cow and her horns; I answer, 'My lord, the cow has lost her horns; for a robber, coming while I slept, ran off with them.' Now, you reply, 'Rascal! had you not an hundred eyes? How was it that they were all asleep, while the robber stole the horns? This is a lie, and I will put you to death.' And if I say that I had sold it, I shall be equally exposed to the indignation of my lord."

"Get thee gone, then," answered Mercury: "thou shalt have nothing."

With this threat Mercury departed, and the next day re-

turned with a musical instrument. He then began to tell
Argus stories, and to sing to him; until at last two of his eyes
dropped asleep; then two more, and finally, the whole head
sunk into a deep slumber. Mercury perceiving this, decapitated him, and bore away the cow with her golden horns.

Tale 112

THE PHYSICIAN AND HIS STEPMOTHER

THE EMPEROR GORGONIUS HAD A BEAUTIFUL WIFE, WHO
was delivered of a son. The boy grew up a universal favourite; but on attaining his tenth year the mother died, and was
splendidly interred. By the advice of his counsellors, the emperor took another wife, who conceived a dislike for her step-
son, and did him many injuries.

When this was communicated to the king, being desirous
of gratifying his new spouse, he banished the young man
from the kingdom. Thus driven from his home, he turned
his attention to medicine, and became in the course of time
a great and perfect physician.

The emperor, hearing of his celebrity, was much pleased at
it; and happening a short time afterwards to fall sick, sent
letters to recall him. When the son understood his father's
pleasure, he made haste to comply with it, and by his skill
in medicine soon restored him to convalescence. The fame of
this cure spread through the whole kingdom.

Now, it chanced that his stepmother sickened even to
death, and physicians from every place were summoned to
attend her. They all, however, unanimously declared that
death was inevitable, and, full of grief at the intelligence, the
emperor desired his son to undertake the cure.

"No, my lord," said he, "I cannot comply with your wishes."

"If you deny me," returned the father, "I will again banish you from the kingdom."

"Then," he replied, "you will act with the greatest injustice. You acknowledged yourself my father, yet banished me from you through this very woman's suggestion. My absence occasioned your sickness and sorrow, and my presence produces a like effect upon the queen, my unkind stepmother; therefore I will not cure her, but will immediately depart."

"The queen," returned the father, "is afflicted with the same infirmity that I was, and which you so effectually dispelled; let me entreat you to preserve her also."

"My beloved father," answered he, "although she has the same infirmity, her complexion is different. When I entered the palace, the joy you felt at my return contributed to your speedy recovery; but the reverse happens to my stepmother. If I speak, she is full of grief; if I touch her, she is carried beyond herself. Now, nothing is more beneficial to the sick than compliance with their wishes. She cannot bear my presence, and why should you wish it?"

By these excuses the son evaded the matter, and his stepmother died.

Tale 113

THE TOURNAMENT

THE EMPEROR ADONIAS WAS EXCEEDINGLY RICH, AND DElighted in tournaments and in tilting. He once held a tournament, and caused it to be proclaimed that the conqueror should obtain a magnificent reward.

This caused a great assemblage of the princes and peers of the kingdom; and the emperor ordained that the knights should be divided, so many on one side and so many on the other. But they who first entered the field were to dispose their shields and arms in order in a certain place; and further, whosoever of the adverse party would touch the shield of another with his lance, immediately he whose shield was touched, being previously armed by a maiden selected for the purpose, should descend to the contest, and if he proved victorious, should be crowned with a kingly crown, and eat meat at the royal table.

Now, a certain knight, having diligently inspected the shields of his antagonists, was wonderfully taken with one bearing three apples; and that shield he touched. Instantly the owner of it armed and met his opponent, and after a short conflict, cut off the challenger's head, and received the promised recompense.

Tale 114

THE WOODCUTTER AND THE DRAGON

IN THE REIGN OF A CERTAIN KING THERE LIVED A POOR MAN who was accustomed to go every day to a neighbouring forest to cut wood for sale. On one occasion, as he went with an ass, the thickness of the underwood caused him to lose his footing, and he fell unawares into a pit, from which he was unable to deliver himself.

In this pit lay a horrible dragon, whose scaly length completely encompassed it. The higher part was occupied by a number of serpents; as also the bottom; half way down was a round stone, which the serpents daily ascended and licked. After that the dragon licked it.

The poor man wondered at what he saw, and deliberated upon the meaning. "I have already remained here many days," thought he, "without sustenance; and unless I can obtain food, without doubt I must perish. I will do, therefore, as the serpents and dragon do."

Acordingly, he went up to the stone and began to lick it, when, to his astonishment, he found that it partook of every delicious flavour that imagination could devise, and was as much invigorated as if he had eaten all the food in the world. A few days after, a dreadful thunderstorm burst overhead; insomuch that the serpents left their retreat one after another; and when they had departed, the dragon which lay at the bottom of the well raised itself above, and would have flown away; but the poor man, observing this, caught hold of it by the tail, and by these means succeeded in escaping from the pit.

The dragon carried him a considerable distance, and dropped him in the same wood; but, ignorant of his situation, he was unable to find the way out. A company of merchants, however, happening to travel through that forest, showed him the path he wanted.

Very happy at his marvellous deliverance, he returned to his own city, and published what had occurred; but his death followed immediately afterwards.

Tale 115

THE VIRGINS AND THE ELEPHANT

A CERTAIN EMPEROR POSSESSED A FOREST, IN WHICH WAS AN elephant whom no one dare approach. This caused his majesty no little surprise, and calling together his nobles and wise men, he asked them what was the nature of this elephant.

They replied that he mightily approved pure and modest virgins. Thereupon, the emperor wished to despatch two beautiful and virtuous maids, who were likewise skilled in music, if any such were to be found in his kingdom.

At last, his emissaries discovered two who were honest and fair enough, and causing them to be stripped, one of them was required to carry a basin, and the other a sword. They entered the forest, and began to sing; and the elephant, attracted by the sound, soon approached.

In the mean time the virgins continued their song, till the elephant fondled them, and by and by fell asleep in the lap of one of the maids.

The other, perceiving this, slew him with the sword she had carried, while her companion filled the bowl with blood. Thus they returned to the king; and when he heard of their success, he rejoiced exceedingly, and ordered a very beautiful purple, and many other curious matters, to be made of the blood.

Tale 116

THE QUEEN OBLIGED TO LOVE HER STEPSON

KING PEPIN MARRIED A VERY BEAUTIFUL GIRL, BY WHOM HE had a son; but the mother died in her confinement. He therefore espoused another, and she also brought forth a son, whom he sent with the elder-born to be educated in another country.

Now, they so much resembled one another, that it was impossible to distinguish them; and when, after a length of time, the anxiety of the living mother to behold her son occasioned their return, although the one was younger by perhaps a year, he was as tall as his brother, which indeed frequently happens. But the resemblance to each other was so strong, that the mother knew not her own child. She earnestly entreated the king to determine her doubts, but he refused compliance with her wishes.

This occasioned a flood of tears; and the king, feeling distressed at her trouble, said, "Weep not; that is your son," and pointed to him who was born of the first wife.

This deception comforted the queen; and without delay she studiously sought to supply all his wants, to the neglect of him who was really her offspring.

The king, seeing this, asked, "Why do you deceive yourself? One of these two is your son, but which you have yet to learn."

"To what end is this?" answered she; "Tell me which is he?"

"No," said the king; "certainly not, and for this reason. If I tell you the truth, you will love one and neglect the other. I desire you, therefore, to attend equally to both, and when they have arrived at man's estate, I will show you which is which; then your happiness will be perfect."

The queen complied with her husband's will; she conducted herself with the strictest impartiality, until they had attained to manhood. On discovering her own child, she gave free course to her joy. Thus her days glided on, and ended in peace.

Tale 117

INGRATITUDE

THE EMPEROR FREDERIC DECREED THAT, IF ANY FEMALE were violated, whosoever freed her from the hand of the oppressor should have her for his wife if he wished. Now, it happened that a certain vile wretch caught up a young girl, and dragging her into a forest, there abused her. She shrieked violently; and a noble knight, riding by some chance in the same forest, heard her cries, and spurred on his horse to her assistance. He inquired the occasion of the clamour.

"Oh, my lord," said the damsel, "for the love of God, succour me. This villain has abused me, and threatened me with destruction."

"My lord," answered the fellow, "she is my wife, whom I have taken in adultery, and I therefore menaced her with death."

"Do not believe it, my lord," said the girl. "I never was his wife, nor have I been other than a maid, until treacherously maltreated by this ruffian. Help me, then, I implore you."

"I perceive plainly," said the knight, "that this wretch has oppressed you, and I will therefore free you from his hands."

"You will do this at your peril," answered the other; "I will defend my right to the last."

Saying which, he prepared himself for a contest. After a desperate struggle, the knight obtained the victory, but was dangerously wounded. He then said to the lady, "Are you pleased to espouse me?"

"Willingly," returned she; "I wish it from my heart, and here pledge my faith."

This done, the knight said, "You shall reside in my castle for a few days; and in the mean time I will go to my parents, and provide everything requisite for our union. After that, I will return and espouse you with great splendour."

"I am ready to obey you in all things," answered the lady; and the knight, having placed her as he had said, bade her farewell.

But while he was absent, an oppressive lord of that country went to the castle, where the girl was placed, and

knocked at the gate. She denied him admission; and he had
then recourse to magnificent promises. He declared himself
ready to espouse her honourably; and she, lending too credulous an ear to what was said, at last opened the gate. He went
in, and remained with her during the night.

In about a month's space, the knight returned to his castle. He knocked, but no one replied to him. Filled with the
greatest bitterness of heart, he said, "Oh, dear girl, recall
how I saved thy life, and the faith which you solemnly
pledged me. Speak, dear girl, and let me behold thy face."

The lady, hearing this, opened the window, and said,
"Look, you ass! what does it please ye to want?"

"I marvel," replied he, "at thy ingratitude. I received several dangerous wounds in defending thee; and if thou art incredulous, I will show them."

Saying this, he loosed his robe, and discovered the scars.
"Do not," added he, "be ungrateful; open the gate, that I
may receive you as my beloved wife." But she made no answer, and turned away.

The knight complained to the judge, and alleged the services he had rendered her. He displayed the wounds taken in
her behalf, and claimed her in recompense as his wife. The
judge, therefore, sent for the seducer, and said, "Hast thou
withheld the woman whom the knight's bravery freed from
uncourteous usage?"

"I have, my lord."

"And, according to law, she voluntarily became his wife?
How, then, darest thou affect the wife of another? First, you
entered his castle during his absence; next, you violated his
bed; lastly, for a long time you have kept his wife from him:
what have you to answer?"

He was silent; and the judge, turning to the woman, said,
"Girl! by the law of the land, you are doubly the wife of this
knight. First, because he freed you from a violator; and sec-

ondly, because you contracted yourself to him. Why hast thou opened the gate of thy husband's castle to another than he?"

She, also, was unable to answer; and the judge condemned both to be crucified. This was done accordingly, and much praise was given to the judge for the sentence he had pronounced.

Tale 118

TEN CHESTS FILLED WITH STONES

A CERTAIN KNIGHT, WHO HAD MADE A TEMPORARY RESIdence in Egypt, was desirous of laying up a sum of money which he possessed in that country. He inquired, therefore, for some person in whom he might repose confidence; and a certain old man being pointed out, he went and delivered to him ten talents. He then prepared for a pilgrimage.

His business completed, he returned, and demanded the amount of what he had deposited. But his agent, proving a rogue, asserted that he had never seen him; and, totally regardless of the knight's supplications and conciliatory language, bade him with much insolence to trouble him no further.

The knight, exceedingly disturbed at such unexpected usage, having accidentally met an old woman equipped in the garb of a devotee, and supported by a staff, removed a number of stones which stood in the way, and which might have cut her feet. Observing the despondency of the knight's demeanour, and at the same time suspecting that he was a foreigner, she entreated him to come near, and questioned him upon the cause of his solicitude. He gave her a full account of it, and the old woman counselled him what he should do.

"Bring me," said she, "to a man of your own country whom we may trust." He did so, and she directed him to fabricate ten chests, painted outwardly with curious devices and rich colours, bound with iron, and fastened with silver locks, but filled up with stones. All this was done, and the woman then bade the knight send them by ten porters to the warehouse of the rascally factor. "Let them come one after another, in order; and as soon as the first man has entered, do you boldly demand your money. I trust you will find it restored to you."

Accordingly, they proceeded to the factor's house, and the old woman addressed him as follows:—"My master, this stranger," pointing to the artificer of the chests, "lodges with me, and wishes to return to his native land. But first he would deposit his wealth, which is contained in ten chests, under the safeguard of some honourable and faithful person. And because I have heard this character of you, I should be unwilling to let any one else have the care of them."

As she spoke, a porter entered with the first che t; and at the same instant the knight appeared, to require his money. The knavish factor, fearing that if he disputed the right of the last, he should lose the golden harvest which the custody of ten such apparently valuable chests promised, came up to him in a soothing tone, and said, "My friend, where have you been? Receive, I pray you, the money which you laid up with me."

The knight was not slow in complying, and gave great thanks to God, and the old woman, for the sums he had almost despaired of. "Master," said she to the factor, "I and my man will go and make inquiry about the other chests, and hasten back immediately. Expect us; and take care of that which we have brought."

Thus, by the assistance of the devotee, the knight recovered his property.

Tale 119

THE UNGRATEFUL STEWARD

IN THE REIGN OF A CERTAIN KING THERE LIVED A PROUD AND oppressive steward. Now, near the royal palace was a forest well stocked with game; and by the direction of this person various pits were dug there, and covered with leaves, for the purpose of trapping the beasts.

It happened that the steward himself went into this forest, and with much exaltation of heart exclaimed internally, "Lives there a being in the empire more powerful than I am?"

This braggart thought was scarcely formed, ere he rode upon one of his own pitfalls, and immediately disappeared. In the pit, the same day had been taken a lion, a monkey, and a serpent. Terrified at the situation into which fate had thrown him, he cried out lustily, and his noise awoke a poor man called Guido, who had come with his ass into that forest to procure firewood, by the sale of which he got his bread. Hastening to the mouth of the pit, he was promised great wealth if he would extricate the steward from his perilous situation.

"My friend," answered Guido, "I have no means of obtaining a livelihood except by the faggots which I collect; if I neglect this for a single day, I shall be thrown into the greatest difficulties."

The steward repeated his promises of enriching him; and Guido went back to the city, and returned with a long cord, which he let down into the pit, and bade the steward bind it round his waist. But before he could apply it to the intended purpose, the lion leaped forward, and seizing upon the cord, was drawn up in his stead. Immediately, exhibiting great signs of pleasure, the beast ran off into the wood.

The rope again descended, and the monkey, having noticed the success of the lion, vaulted above the man's head, and shaking the cord, was in like manner set at liberty, and hurried off to his haunts. A third time the cord was let down, and the serpent, twining around it, was drawn up, gave signs of gratitude, and escaped.

"Oh, my good friend," said the steward, "the beasts are gone, now draw me up quickly, I pray you."

Guido complied, and afterwards succeeded in drawing up his horse, which the steward instantly mounted and rode back to the palace. Guido returned home; and his wife observing that he had come without wood, was very dejected, and inquired the cause. He related what had occurred, and the riches he was to receive for his service. The wife's countenance brightened.

Early in the morning her husband went to the palace. But the steward denied all knowledge of him, and ordered him to be whipped for his presumption. The porter executed the directions, and beat him so severely that he left him half dead.

As soon as Guido's wife understood this, she saddled their ass, and brought him home in a very infirm state. The sickness which ensued consumed the whole of their little property; but as soon as he had recovered, he returned to his usual occupation in the wood. Whilst he was thus employed, he beheld afar off ten asses laden with packs, and a lion following close on them, pursuing the path which led towards Guido. On looking narrowly at this beast, he remembered that it was the same which he had freed from its imprisonment in the pit. The lion signified with his foot that he should take the loaded asses, and go home. This Guido did, and the lion followed.

On arriving at his own door, the noble beast fawned upon him, and wagging his tail as if in triumph, ran back to the woods. Guido caused proclamation to be made in different churches, that if any asses had been lost, the owners should come to him; but no one appearing to demand them, he opened the packages, and, to his great joy, discovered them full of money.

On the second day Guido returned to the forest, but forgot an iron instrument to cleave the wood. He looked up, and beheld the monkey whose liberation he had effected; and the animal, by help of teeth and nails, accomplished his desires. Guido then loaded his asses and went home.

The next day he renewed his visit to the forest; and sitting down to prepare his instrument, discerned the serpent, whose escape he had aided, carrying in its mouth a stone of three colours; on one side white, on another black, and on the third red. It opened its mouth and let the stone fall into Guido's lap. Having done this, it departed.

Guido took the stone to a skilful worker, who had no sooner inspected it than he knew its virtues, and would willingly have paid him an hundred florins for it. But Guido refused; and by means of that singular stone obtained great wealth, and was promoted to a military command.

The emperor having heard of the extraordinary qualities which it possessed, desired to see it. Guido went accordingly; and the emperor was so struck with its uncommon beauty, that he wished to purchase it at any rate; and threatened, if Guido refused compliance, to banish him from the kingdom.

"My lord," answered he, "I will sell the stone; but let me say one thing—if the price be not given, it shall be presently restored to me." He demanded three hundred florins, and then, taking it from a small coffer, put it into the emperor's hands. Full of admiration, he exclaimed, "Tell me where you procured this beautful stone."

This he did; and narrated from the beginning the steward's accident and subsequent ingratitude. He told how severely he had been injured by his command; and the benefits he had received from the lion, the monkey, and serpent.

Much moved at the recital, the emperor sent for the steward and said, "What is this I hear of thee?"

He was unable to reply. "O wretch!" continued the emperor—"monster of ingratitude! Guido liberated thee from the most imminent danger, and for this thou hast nearly destroyed him. Dost thou see how even irrational things have rendered him good for the service he performed? But thou hast returned evil for good. Therefore I deprive thee of thy dignity, which I will bestow upon Guido; and I further sentence you to be suspended on a cross."

This decree infinitely pleased the noblemen of the empire: and Guido, full of honours and years, ended his days in peace.

Tale 120

HOW THE PRINCE RECOVERED HIS MAGIC TREASURES

KING DARIUS WAS A CAUTIOUS PRINCE, AND HAD THREE SONS, whom he much loved. On his deathbed he bequeathed the kingdom to his first-born; to the second, all his own personal acquisitions; and to the third a golden ring, a necklace, and a piece of valuable cloth.

The ring had the power to render any one who bore it on his finger beloved; and, moreover, obtained for him whatsoever he sought. The necklace enabled the person who wore it upon his breast to accomplish his heart's desire; and the cloth had such virtue, that whosoever sat upon it and thought where he would be carried, there he instantly found himself. These three gifts the king conferred upon the younger son, for the purpose of aiding his studies; but the mother retained them until he was of a proper age. Soon after the bequests, the old monarch gave up the ghost, and was magnificently buried.

The two elder sons then took possession of their legacies, and the mother of the younger delivered to him the ring, with the caution that he should beware of the artifices of women, or he would otherwise lose the ring. Jonathan, for that was his name, took the ring, and went zealously to his studies, in which he made himself a proficient. But walking on a certain day through the street, he observed a very beautiful woman, with whom he was so much struck, that he took her to him. He continued, however, to use the ring, and found favour with every one, insomuch that whatever he desired he had.

Now, the lady was greatly surprised that he lived so splendidly, having no possessions; and once, when he was in particularly good spirits, tenderly embraced him, and protested that there was not a creature under the sun whom she loved so much as she did him. He ought therefore, she thought, to tell her by what means he supported his magnificence.

He, suspecting nothing, explained the virtues of the ring; and she begged that he would be careful of so invaluable a treasure.

"But," added she, "in your daily intercourse with men you may lose it: place it in my custody, I beseech you."

Overcome by her entreaties, he gave up the ring; and when his necessities came upon him, she asserted loudly that thieves had carried it off. He lamented bitterly that now he had not any means of subsistence; and, hastening to his mother, stated how he had lost his ring.

"My son," said she, "I forewarned you of what would happen, but you have paid no attention to my advice. Here is the necklace; preserve it more carefully. If it be lost, you will for ever want a thing of the greatest honour and profit."

Jonathan took the necklace, and returned to his studies. At the gate of the city his mistress met him, and received him with the appearance of great joy. He remained with her, wearing the necklace upon his breast; and whatever he thought, he possessed. As before, he lived so gloriously that the lady wondered, well knowing that he had neither gold nor silver. She guessed, therefore, that he carried another talisman; and cunningly drew from him the history of the wonder-working necklace.

"Why," said the lady, "do you always take it with you? You may think in one moment more than can be made use of in a year. Let me keep it."

"No," replied he, "you will lose the necklace, as you lost the ring; and thus I shall receive the greatest possible injury."

"O my lord," replied she, "I have learnt, by having had the custody of the ring, how to secure the necklace; and I assure you no one can possibly get it from me." The silly youth confided in her words, and delivered the necklace.

Now, when all he possessed was expended, he sought his talisman; and she, as before, solemnly protested that it had been stolen. This threw Jonathan into the greater distress. "Am I mad," cried he, "that after the loss of my ring I should give up the necklace?"

Immediately hastening to his mother, he related to her the whole circumstance. Not a little afflicted, she said, "Oh, my dear child, why didst thou place confidence in the woman? People will believe thee a fool; but be wise, for I have nothing more for you than the valuable cloth which your father left: and if you lose that, it will be quite useless returning to me."

Jonathan received the cloth and again went to his studies. The harlot seemed very joyful; and he, spreading out the cloth, said, "My dear girl, my father bequeathed me this beautiful cloth; sit down upon it by my side."

She complied, and Jonathan secretly wished that they were in a desert place, out of the reach of man. The wish took effect; they were carried into a forest on the utmost boundary of the world, where there was not a trace of humanity. The lady wept bitterly, but Jonathan paid no regard to her tears. He solemnly vowed to Heaven that he would leave her a prey to the wild beasts unless she restored his ring and necklace; and this she promised to do. Presently, yielding to her request, the foolish Jonathon disclosed the power of the cloth; and, in a little time being weary, placed his head in her lap and slept. In the interim, she contrived to draw away that part of the cloth upon which he reposed, and sitting upon it alone, wished herself where she had been in the morning. The cloth immediately executed her wishes, and left Jonathan slumbering in the forest.

When he awoke, and found his cloth and his mistress departed, he burst into an agony of tears. Where to bend his steps he knew not; but arising, and fortifying himself with the sign of the cross, he walked along a certain path, until he reached a deep river, over which he must pass. But he found it so bitter and hot, that it even separated the flesh from the bones.

Full of grief, he conveyed away a small quantity of that water, and when he had proceeded a little further, felt hungry. A tree upon which hung the most tempting fruit invited him to partake; he did so, and immediately became a leper. He gathered also a little of the fruit, and conveyed it with him. After travelling for some time, he arrived at another stream, of which the virtue was such, that it restored the flesh to his feet; and eating of a second tree, he was cleansed from his leprosy. Some of that fruit he likewise took along with him.

Walking in this manner day after day, he came at length to a castle, where he was met by two men, who inquired what he was. "I am a physician," answered he.

"This is lucky," said the other; "the king of this country is a leper, and if you are able to cure him of his leprosy, vast rewards will be assigned you."

He promised to try his skill; and they led him forward to the king. The result was fortunate; he supplied him with the fruit of the second tree, and the leprosy left him; and washing the flesh with the water, it was completely restored. Being rewarded most bountifully, he embarked on board a vessel for his native city.

There he circulated a report that a great physician was arrived; and the lady who had cheated him of the talismans, being sick unto death, immediately sent for him. Jonathan was so much disguised that she retained no recollection of him, but he very well remembered her. As soon as he arrived, he declared that medicine would avail nothing, unless she first confessed her sins; and if she had defrauded any one, it must be restored. The lady, reduced to the very verge of the grave, in a low voice acknowledged that she had cheated Jonathan of the ring, necklace, and cloth; and had left him in a desert place to be devoured by wild beasts. When she had said this, the pretended physician exclaimed, "Tell me, lady, where these talismans are?"

"In that chest," answered she; and delivered up the keys, by which he obtained possession of his treasures. Jonathan then gave her of the fruit which produced leprosy; and, after she had eaten, of the water which separated the flesh from the bones. The consequence was that she was excruciated with agony, and shortly died.

Jonathan hastened to his mother, and the whole kingdom rejoiced at his return. He told by what means God had freed him from such various dangers; and, having lived many years, ended his days in peace.

Tale 121

THE OLD AND THE YOUNG KNIGHT

THERE FORMERLY LIVED A KING WHO HAD TWO KNIGHTS resident in one city. One of them was old, the other young. The old knight was rich, and had married a youthful damsel on account of her exquisite beauty. The young knight was poor, and espoused an old woman in consequence of her immense wealth.

It happened that the young knight walked by the castle of the elder, and in a window his wife sat, and sang deliciously. The youth was much taken with her, and said in his heart, "It would be ten thousand times better if that sweet girl were united to me, and her old doting husband possessed of my infirm wife." From that hour he conceived a violent affection for her, and made her many valuable presents.

The lady entertained a similar feeling, and, whenever she could, permitted him to visit her. She endeavoured also to secure him for her husband in the event of the old man's death.

Now, near the window of the castle which the old knight occupied, there grew a fig-tree, on which a nightingale stationed herself every evening, and uttered the most ravishing harmony. This circumstance drew the lady thither; and it became a custom with her to remain at the window a long time, to listen to the song of the nightingale. When her husband, good man! noticed this extreme watchfulness, he said,

"My dear, what is the reason that you get up every night with so much regularity?"

"A nightingale," answered she, "sings upon the fig-tree, opposite my window; and her song is so delightful that I cannot resist the pleasure of listening to it."

The old knight hearing this, arose early in the morning, and, armed with bow and arrow, hastened to the fig-tree. He shot the nightingale, and taking out the heart, presented it to his wife.

The lady wept exceedingly, and said, "Sweet bird, *thou* didst but what became thee. I alone am the occasion of thy death." Immediately she despatched a messenger to the youthful knight, to inform him of her husband's cruelty.

The intelligence grieved him to the heart's core, and he exclaimed internally, "If this cruel old wretch only knew how much his wife and I are attached to each other, he would treat me even more vilely!"

This reflection determined him; he cased himself in a double coat of mail, and entering the castle, slew the aged knight. Soon after this, his old wife dying, he married the young widow of the old knight. They lived many years, and ended their days in peace.

Tale 122

HOW THE LADY HELPS HER LOVER ESCAPE

A CERTAIN KNIGHT WENT TO GATHER GRAPES IN HIS VINE-yard. His wife, imagining that he would be absent for a longer time than he actually was, sent hastily for her gallant. While they were together the knight returned; for it seems, while plucking down a bunch of grapes, he had struck out an eye, and came home in great agony. The lady, hearing his knock at the gate, was much perturbed, and immediately concealed her lover.

The knight entering, complained of his wounded eye, and directed a bed to be prepared, that he might lie down. But the wife, fearing lest the gallant, who was hidden in the chamber, should be detected, said, "Why would you go to bed? Tell me what has happened."

He told her. "My dear lord," cried she, "permit me to strengthen the uninjured eye by medicinal applications, or the diseased part may communicate with the sound, and thereby both be irremediably injured."

The knight made no objection, and his wife spreading a large plaster so as completely to obstruct his sight, beckoned to her gallant, who escaped.

Satisfied with her successful stratagem, the lady observed to the husband, "There, dear! now I feel satisfied that your sound eye will take no injury. Go into your bed, and sleep."

Tale 123

HOLDING THE SHEET BEFORE THE HUSBAND

A SOLDIER, GOING INTO A FAR COUNTRY, ENTRUSTED HIS wife to the care of her mother. But some time after her husband's departure the wife fell in love with a young man, and communicated her wishes to the mother. She approved of the connection, and without delay sent for the object of her daughter's criminal attachment. But while they feasted, the soldier unexpectedly returned and beat at his gate.

The wife, in great tremor concealed the lover in her bed, and then opened the door for her husband. Being weary with travel, he commanded his bed to be got ready; and the wife, more and more disturbed, knew not what she should do.

The mother observing her daughter's perplexity, said, "Before you go, my child, let us show your husband the fair sheet which we have made."

Then standing up, she gave one corner of the sheet to her daughter and held the other herself, extending it before him so as to favour the departure of the lover, who took the hint and escaped.

When he had got clearly off, "Now," said the mother, "spread the sheet upon the bed with your own hands—we have done our parts in weaving it."

Tale 124

HOW THE KNIGHT OBTAINED HIS PARDON

A CERTAIN NOBLE KNIGHT HAD GRIEVOUSLY OFFENDED A king whose vassal he was. He sent messengers to the monarch to intercede for him, and they obtained his pardon, but on condition that he should enter the senate-house on foot and on horseback at the same time; that is, half walking, half riding. Moreover, he was to bring with him his most attached friend, the best joculator or jester, and his most deadly foe.

The knight, exceedingly distressed, reflected how these strange conditions were to be fulfilled. One night, as he exercised the hospitality of his mansion towards a pilgrim, he said privately to his wife, "I know those pilgrims often carry considerable sums of money along with them. If you think fit, let us kill this fellow, and get possession of his money."

"You say well," returned the lady; and when all were

asleep, at an early hour in the morning, the knight arose, and
awaking the pilgrim, bade him begone. He then slaughtered
a calf, cut it into small pieces, and placed its mutilated body
in a sack. Arousing his wife, he gave her the sack to hide in a
corner of the house, observing, "I have only deposited the
head, legs and arms in the sack; the body is interred in our
stable." He then showed her a little money, as if he had taken
it from the murdered pilgrim.

Now, when the day approached on which he was bound
to appear before his liege lord, he took upon his right hand a
dog, and on his left his wife and unweaned child. As they
drew near the royal castle he put one leg over the back of
the dog, as if he were riding, while with the other he walked;
and thus, as a pedestrian and equestrian, he entered the palace.

When the king observed his cunning, he was greatly surprised. "But," said the judge, "where is your most attached
friend?" Instantly unsheathing his sword, he severely
wounded the dog, which fled howling away.

The knight then called to him and the dog returned.
"Here," said he, "here is the most faithful of all friends."

"True," answered the king. "Where is your jester?"

"Here also," replied the knight, pointing to his infant:
"I never have so much pleasure as in the disportings of this
child."

"Well," continued the king. "Where is your worst enemy?"
Turning toward his wife, he struck her a violent blow, and
exclaimed, "Impudent harlot, how darest thou look wantonly
upon the king?"

The wife, furious at the injustice of the attack, shrieked
violently. "Cursed homicide," said she, "why dost thou smite
me? Dost thou forget that, in thine own house, thou per-
petratedst the most atrocious murder, and didst kill a pilgrim
for the sake of a little gold?"

Again the knight beat her. "Wretch!" said he. "Why dost thou not fear to disgrace thy child?"

To which she fiercely replied, "Come with me, and I will discover to you where the head and arms of the murdered pilgrim have been deposited in a sack; the body he has buried in the stable."

Search was accordingly made; and digging where the wife directed, they were astonished to find manifest tokens of a calf's flesh. The attending nobles, recognizing in this the wit of the man, greatly extolled him; and he was ever after exceedingly valued and honoured by his feudal lord.

Tale 125

THE SECRET BLACK CROW

THERE WERE TWO BROTHERS, OF WHOM ONE WAS A LAY-man and the other a parson. The former had often heard his brother declare that there never was a woman who could keep a secret. He had a mind to put this maxim to the test in the person of his own wife, and one night he addressed her in the following manner: "My dear wife, I have a secret to communicate to you, if I were certain that you would reveal it to nobody. Should you divulge it, it would cause me the greatest uneasiness and vexation."

"My lord," answered his wife, "fear not; we are one body, and your advantage is mine. In like manner, your injury must deeply affect me."

"Well, then," said he, "know that, my bowels being oppressed to an extraordinary degree, I fell very sick. My dear wife, what will you think? I actually voided a huge black crow, which instantly took wing, and left me in the greatest trepidation and confusion of mind."

"Is it possible?" asked the innocent lady; "but, husband, why should this trouble you? You ought rather to rejoice that you are freed from such a pestilent tenant."

Here the conversation closed; in the morning, the wife hurried off to the house of a neighbour. "My best friend," said she, "may I tell you a secret?"

"As safely as to your own soul," answered the fair auditor.

"Why," replied the other, "a marvellous thing has happened to my poor husband. Being last night extremely sick, he voided two prodigious black crows, feathers and all, which immediately flew away. I am much concerned."

The other promised very faithfully—and immediately told her neighbour that three black crows had taken this most alarming flight. The next edition of the story made it four; and in this way it spread, until it was very credibly reported that sixty black crows had been evacuated by one unfortunate varlet.

But the joke had gone further than he dreamt of; he became much disturbed, and assembling his busy neighbours, explained to them that having wished to prove whether or not his wife could keep a secret, he had made such a communication.

Soon after this, his wife dying, he ended his days in a cloister, where he learnt three letters: of which one was black; the second, red; and the third, white.

Tale 126

THE SECRET OF THE ROMAN SENATE

MACROBIUS STATES THAT A ROMAN YOUTH, NAMED PAPIRIUS, was once present with his father in the senate at a time when a very important matter was debated, which, on pain of death, was to be kept secret. When the lad returned home, his mother asked him what it was that was guarded under so heavy a penalty. He replied that it was unlawful to reveal it. The mother, little satisfied with the boy's reply, entreated, promised, threatened, and even scourged him, in the hope of extorting a communication. But he remained inflexible; and at last, willing to satisfy her, and yet retain his secret, said, "The council met upon this matter; whether it were more beneficial to the state that one man should have many wives, or one woman many husbands."

The mother no sooner heard this, than away she posted to divide the important secret with other Roman dames. And on the following day, assembling a large body, they went without hesitation to the senators, earnestly requesting that one woman might be married to two men, rather than two women to one man.

The senators, astonished at the shameless frenzy of a sex naturally modest, deliberated upon the best remedy. The boy Papirius, finding this, related to them the circumstance which had occasioned the uproar; and they, bestowing great commendation on his ingenuity, passed a decree that he should be present at their consultations whenever he would.

Tale 127

THE JUSTICE OF PROVIDENCE

A CERTAIN TYRANNICAL AND CRUEL KNIGHT RETAINED IN his service a very faithful servant. One day, when he had been to the market, he returned with this servant through a grove, and by the way lost thirty silver marks. As soon as he discovered the loss, he questioned his servant about it. The man solemnly denied all knowledge of the matter, and he spoke truth. But when the money was not to be found, he amputated the servant's foot, and leaving him in that place, rode home.

A hermit, hearing the groans and exclamations of the man, went speedily to his assistance. He confessed to him; and being satisfied of his innocence, conveyed him upon his shoulders to his hermitage. Then entering the oratory, he dared to reproach the All-just with want of justice, inasmuch as he had permitted an innocent man to lose his foot. For a length of time he continued in tears, and prayers, and reproaches; until at last an angel of the Lord appeared to him, and said, "Hast thou not read in the Psalms, 'God is a just judge, strong and patient'?"

"Often," answered the hermit meekly, "have I read and believed it from my heart; but to-day I have erred. That wretched man, whose foot has been amputated, perhaps under the veil of confession deceived me."

"Tax not the Lord with injustice," said the angel; "His way is truth, and His judgments equitable. Recollect how often thou hast read, 'The decrees of God are unfathomable.' Know that he who lost his foot, lost it for a former crime. With the same foot he maliciously spurned his mother, and cast her from a chariot, for which he has never done worthy penance. The knight, his master, was desirous of purchasing a war-horse, to collect more wealth, to the destruction of his soul; and therefore, by the just sentence of God, the money was lost. Now hear; there is a very poor man with his wife and little ones, who daily supplicate Heaven, and perform every religious exercise. He found the money, when otherwise he would have starved, and therewith procured for himself and family the necessaries of life, entrusting a portion to his confessor to distribute to the poor. But first he diligently endeavoured to find out the right owner. Not accomplishing this, the poor man applied it to its proper use. Place, then, a bridle upon thy thoughts; and no more upbraid the righteous Disposer of all things, as thou but lately didst. For He is true, and strong, and patient."

Tale 128

HOW THE JUDGE DISCOVERED THE TRUTH

IN THE REIGN OF THE EMPEROR MAXIMIAN THERE WERE two knights, of whom one feared God and loved justice, while the other was covetous and rich, and more studious of pleasing the world than his Maker. Adjoining this person's lands, the just knight had a piece of ground, which his greedy neighbour ardently desired to possess. He offered large sums for it; but being denied, he was filled with vexation.

It happened, however, that the just knight died; on hearing which, the other forged an instrument purporting to be written by the deceased knight. It stated that the land in question had been sold for a specified sum a short time previous to his death; and three men were hired to attest it. Having, by some means, obtained access to the dead knight, he introduced the witnesses; and finding his signet in the hall where he lay, took it, and, fixing it upon the thumb of the deceased, sealed the paper with the usual formalities. "You are witnessess of this deed?" said he to the men who accompanied him.

"We are," answered they; and then making good their retreat, the knight seized upon the land.

The son of the deceased complained grievously of this injustice. "Why have you taken possession of my land?" asked he.

"It was sold to me by your father."

"Impossible," cried the other; "my father many times refused to sell it; and that he afterwards did so, I will never believe."

They both went before the judge; and the covetous knight triumphantly produced the forged instrument, bearing the impression of the deceased's signet-ring, and brought forward the false witnesses to the sealing.

After examining it, the son said, "I know that this is my father's signet, but I know also that he never disposed of the land. How you obtained the signet and these witnesses, I am ignorant."

The judge, after some deliberation, took each of the witnesses aside in turn; and separately examined them, together with the knight. He asked the eldest if he knew the Lord's Prayer, and made him repeat it from beginning to end. He did this accurately, and was then placed apart. When the second witness appeared, the judge said, "My friend, your companion has told me facts as true as the Lord's Prayer; therefore, unless you inform me what I demand, you shall instantly hang upon a cross."

The fellow, imagining that his comrade had revealed the fraud, confessed how they had obtained the seal to the document. When the communication was made, he placed him apart; and sending for the third, spoke to him as to the other, and threatened him with the like penalty, unless he declared the fact. This man, therefore, corroborated his companion's account, and was then stationed by himself.

The old knight was then called; and the judge, putting on a stern aspect, spoke thus: "Wretched man! thy avarice hath blinded thee. Tell me how the deceased knight sold you the land." The culprit, not divining that the truth had been discovered, boldly persevered in the account he had before given.

"Foolish man!" answered the judge, "thy own witnesses

accuse thee. Didst thou not place the signet on the dead man's thumb, and sign the paper?"

When the knight found that his forgery was revealed, he fell prostrate upon the earth, and entreated mercy.

"Such mercy as thou meritest, thou shalt have," said the judge: "bear them away, and drag them at the tails of horses to the cross, upon which let them be immediately suspended."

The noblemen of the kingdom applauded the sentence, not less than the ingenuity of the investigation. The property of the unjust knight was conferred upon the son of him whom he had wished to wrong; the young man gave thanks to the king, and possessed his inheritance in peace.

Tale 129

THE TEST OF FRIENDSHIP

A CERTAIN KING HAD AN ONLY SON, WHOM HE MUCH LOVED. The young man was desirous of seeing the world and making friends for himself, and obtained his father's permission to this end. After an absence of seven years, he returned, and his father, overjoyed at his arrival, asked what friends he had acquired. "Three," said the son; "the first of whom I love more than myself; the second, equally with myself; and the third, little or nothing."

"You say well," returned the father; "but it is a good thing to prove them before you stand in need of their assistance. Therefore kill a pig, put it into a sack, and go at night to the house of him whom you love best, and say that you have accidentally killed a man, and if the body should be found you will be condemned to death. Entreat him, if he ever loved you, to give his assistance in this extremity."

The son did so; and the friend answered, "Since you have rashly destroyed a man, you must pay the penalty: for if the body were found in my house I should very likely be crucified. Now, because you were my friend, I will go with you to the cross, and bestow upon you three or four ells of cloth, to wrap your body in when you are dead."

The youth, hearing this, went in much indignation to the second of his friends, and related the same story. He received him like the first, and said, "Do you believe me mad, that I should expose myself to such peril? But, since I have called you my friend, I will accompany you to the cross, and console you as much as possible upon the way."

The prince then went to the third, and said, "I am ashamed to address you, for I have never benefited you in any way: but, alas! I have accidentally slain a man, and must hide the body or perish."

"My friend," answered the other, "I will readily do what you wish, and take the crime on myself; and, should it be necessary, I will be crucified for your sake."

This man, therefore, proved that he was his friend.

Tale 130

OF BRAVERY, WISDOM AND LOVE

THERE WAS A KING WHO PROMOTED A POOR MAN TO GREAT wealth, and committed to him the custody of one of his castles. Thus elevated, he became proud to an excess, and conspired against the king, and surrendered his castle into the hands of the enemy. This conduct gave the king great concern; and he deliberated upon the best means of regaining what he had lost. But he was told that this could not be done but by the possession of three things, namely; bravery, wisdom, and the love of his subjects.

Now, there were at that time in the kingdom three knights, of whom the first was the bravest of all men; the second, the wisest; and the third, the most attached to the king. These knights were severally sent with large armies to besiege the castle.

The bravest knight conducted his troops through a forest, in which the king's enemies awaited him; but while he was performing deeds of valour, an arrow from a cross-bow struck him in the groin, and he died of the wound.

In the mean time the wise knight brought up his forces and began to speak of right and law, hoping by these means to draw them to surrender the castle. But while he spoke, an arrow penetrated between the lungs and the stomach, and killed him.

The third knight perceiving the death of his comrades, entered the forest, and spoke so eloquently to the insurgents, that they listened gladly, and at last permitted him to enter the castle. And he so ordered matters that the opposing armies joined with him, and gave him entire possession; so that he planted his standard on the top.

When the king understood how prudently he had obtained the disputed fortress, he promoted him to great honours.

Tale 131

OF A KING WHO GAVE TO ALL

A KING ISSUED A PROCLAMATION THAT WHOSOEVER WOULD come to him should obtain all they asked. The noble and the rich desired dukedoms, or counties, or knighthood; and some, treasures of silver and gold. But whatsoever they desired they had. Then came the poor and the simple, and solicited a like boon.

"Ye come tardily," said the king; "the noble and the rich have already been, and have carried away all I possess." This reply troubled them exceedingly; and the king, moved with a feeling of pity, said, "My friends, though I have given away all my temporal possessions, I have still the sovereign power; for no one required this. I appoint ye, therefore, to be their judges and masters."

When this came to the ears of the rich, they were extremely disturbed, and said to the king, "My lord, we are greatly troubled at your appointing these poor wretches our rulers; it were better for us to die, than admit such servitude."

"Sirs," answered the king, "I do you no wrong; whatever you asked I gave; insomuch that nothing remains to me but the supreme power. Nevertheless, I will give you counsel. Whosoever of you has enough to support life, let him bestow the excess upon these poor people. They will then live honestly and comfortably, and upon these conditions I will resume the sovereignty and keep it, while you avoid the servitude ye apprehend."

And thus it was done.

Tale 132

HOW THREE PHYSICIANS GOT RID OF THEIR RIVAL

THERE ONCE LIVED IN THE SAME CITY FOUR PHYSICIANS, well skilled in medicine. The youngest of them, however, excelled the other three; insomuch that the sick went only to him. This excited the envy of the rest, and talking together upon this subject they said, "How shall we get rid of that troublesome fellow? everybody runs to him, and our gains are a mere trifle."

"Why," said one, "you know he goes every week on a visit to the duke, about three leagues off, and he will pay a visit there to-morrow. Now, I will go a league beyond the city, and there await his coming. You shall be stationed at the second league, and our fellow here at the third. And when he has advanced the first league, I will meet him and make the sign of the cross before him. Both of you must do the like. He will then ask the reason of this, and we will answer, 'Because you are a leper'; and his fear will certainly occasion it; 'for,' says Hippocrates, 'he who fears leprosy will through fear become a leper.' Thus diseased, no one will approach him."

And so it was done.

Tale 133

THE TWO FIGHTING GREYHOUNDS

A KING HAD TWO GREYHOUNDS, WHOM HE KEPT ALTER-nately chained up. As long as they were thus fastened they mutually loved and fawned upon each other, but no sooner were they unloosed than they exhibited the most deadly signs of mutual hostility. The king was much concerned at this; because when he would have coursed with them, and for that purpose set them at liberty, they fought so fiercely that he was unable to follow his sport.

This led him to consult some learned man, who recommended that the first of the dogs should be encountered by a strong and savage wolf; and then the second should be encouraged to the attack when his companion was in danger of being defeated. For when the first saw how the other aided him, they would in future be friends.

This was accordingly done; and as the strength of the first dog failed, the second was let loose, who, after a severe struggle, killed the wolf.

From this time, bound or unbound, they lived together in the most perfect friendship.

Tale 134

THE HERO REWARDED BY DEATH

SENECA RELATES THAT THERE WAS A LAW IN SOME CITY, by which a knight was obliged to be buried in armour; and further, that it was ordained if any one deprived the dead man of this armour, he should be put to death.

It happened that a certain city was besieged by a tyrannical despot, who, planting ambushes and pitfalls around the city, destroyed an indefinite number of the inhabitants. Fear made them incapable of longer resistance; and, while thus situated, a noble and valiant knight entered the city, and compassionated the distresses of the despairing citizens. They humbly petitioned him to undertake their defence, and free them from the imminent peril in which they stood.

"My friends," replied he, "this cannot be done except by a strong hand; and you perceive I am unarmed. It is in vain, therefore, to expect that I should go out to fight."

"My lord," observed one of the citizens, "but a few days since a knight was buried in this sepulchre, clad in most admirable armour; take it, and save our city."

The knight assented, received the arms of the deceased, and, encountering the enemy, put them to flight. He then restored the arms to their original tomb. But certain men, envious of the fame which he acquired by the exploit, accused him before the judge of having despoiled the dead of his armour contrary to law.

"My lord," answered he, "of two evils, the greater is to be avoided. Now, I could not defend your city without armour: and having taken that of the deceased, I returned it when the urgency had ceased. A thief would not have acted in this manner; he would have kept the arms, which I did not, and therefore merit rather recompense than charges of such a nature. Besides, if a house be on fire in the midst of a city, would it not be better that that single dwelling should be, without delay, completely destroyed, before other houses catch fire and the whole city is burnt to the ground? Apply this in my case. Was it not more beneficial that I should preserve your town by borrowing the armour than, by not borrowing, endanger all your lives?"

"Away with him, away with him," shouted they who were jealous and envious of his fame; "he deserves death; away with him!"

The judge could not resist their urgent petition, and condemned him to death. The sentence was accordingly executed, and the whole state lamented him with unfeigned regret.

Tale 135

LUCRETIA

AUGUSTINE RELATES, IN HIS WORK, *De Civitate Dei*, THAT Lucretia, a noble Roman lady, was the wife of Calatinus. The latter invited to his castle Sextus, the son of the Emperor Tarquinius, who became violently enamoured of his beautiful wife.

Selecting a seasonable opportunity, when both Calatinus and the emperor had departed from Rome, he returned to the above-mentioned castle, and slept there. During the night, not as a friend but foe, he secretly entered the bed-chamber of Lucretia, and putting one hand upon her breast, while he held a drawn sword in the other, said, "Comply with my wishes, or I will kill you."

But she resolutely repelled him; and Sextus, enraged, assured her that he would stab a slave and place him in her bed, so that the world should believe her guilty of the most low-lived and flagrant wickedness.

At last Sextus, accomplishing his villainy, went away; and the lady, full of the deepest grief, despatched letters to her father and husband, to her brothers, to the emperor, together with the governor; and when they were all present she spoke thus: "Not as a friend, but as a foe, Sextus entered my house. Calatinus, your bed has known the garments of a stranger; but though my body is violated, my mind is innocent. Acquit me of crime, and I will provide my own punishment." At these words, snatching a sword which she had hidden beneath her robe, she plunged it into her breast.

The assembled friends, taking up the weapon, swore by the blood of the injured Lucretia to drive the family of the Tarquins from Rome. And they did so.

As for Sextus, the author of this tragedy, he was miserably slaughtered not long after.

Tale 136

THE FOOLISH THIEF

A THIEF WENT ONE NIGHT TO THE HOUSE OF A RICH MAN, and scaling the roof, peeped through a hole to examine if any part of the family were yet stirring. The master of the house, suspecting something, said secretly to his wife, "Ask me in a loud voice how I acquired the property I possess, and do not stop until I bid you."

The woman complied, and began, "My dear husband, pray tell me, since you never were a merchant, how you obtained all the wealth which you have now collected."

"Foolish woman," answered her husband, "do not ask such questions." But she persisted in her inquiries; and at length, as if overcome by her urgency, he said, "Keep what I am going to tell you a secret, and your curiosity shall be gratified."

"Oh, trust me."

"Well, then, you must know that I was a thief, and obtained what I now enjoy by nightly robberies."

"It is strange," said the wife, "that you were never taken."

"Why," replied he, "my master, who was a skilful clerk, taught me a particular word, which, when I ascended the tops of people's houses, I pronounced seven times, and then got down into the house by the rays of the moon and took what I wanted, and then in like manner ascended again without danger and departed."

"Tell me, I beg you," returned the lady, "what that powerful word was."

"Hear, then; but never mention it again, or we shall lose all our property."

"Be sure of that," said the lady; "it shall never be repeated."

"It was—is there no one within hearing?—the mighty word was 'SAXLEM.'"

The lady, apparently quite satisfied, fell asleep; and her husband feigned it. He snored lustily, and the thief above, who had heard their conversation with much pleasure, attempting to take hold of a moon-ray and repeating the charm seven times, relaxed the hold both of hands and feet, and let himself drop through the skylight. He fell with a loud thud, and in the fall dislocated his leg and arm, and lay half dead upon the floor. The owner of the mansion, hearing the noise, and well knowing the reason, though he pretended ignorance, asked what was the matter.

"Oh!" groaned the suffering thief, "the words of your tale have deceived me."

The man captured him, and had him suspended on a cross in the morning.

Tale 137

THE BANISHED EMPEROR RETURNS

IN THE CHRONICLES OF EUSEBIUS WE READ OF AN EMPEROR who governed the Roman people with the greatest equity, sparing none, whether rich or poor; but measuring the punishment according to the extent of the crime. The self-interested senators, however, deposed him, and obliged him to flee in poverty from the kingdom. Immediately he fled to Constantine, and, entering into a close compact with him, on all occasions conducted himself so boldly and prudently, that he succeeded him to the sovereignty of the empire.

Then assembling an army, he besieged the city of Rome; and, when the Romans were unable to escape, but were always captured by him, the people sent out to him their senators, and young men and women, with their feet bare, who prostrated themselves before him, and humbly requested the forgiveness which he refused to grant.

At length they despatched his parents, who were resident in the city, alone upon this embassy. His mother wept and entreated; conjuring him by the breasts which he had sucked, to spare the place of his nativity.

Unable to resist the force of natural affection, he pardoned on her account their offences. He then marched into the city, and was honourably entertained.

Tale 138

HOW PEACE CAME FOR FATHER AND SON

A CERTAIN KING, NAMED MEDRUS, HAD AN ONLY SON, whom he constituted his heir. The son was ungrateful to his father, who punished him by immediate disinherison. The son, thus circumstanced, fled to the King of the Persians, the rival and enemy of his parent. He stated that he was ready to serve him to the death; and declared himself ready to make war upon the author of his being.

War was accordingly declared, and they fought together for some time with equal fortune. It happened that Medrus the king was grievously wounded, and the blood flowed very copiously. No sooner had his son perceived this, and reflected on it, than he straightway hurried to his father's side, and attacking the troops of the Persian monarch, put them to flight.

After this, of course, the compact was made void; and the son, returning to his father, meekly sought forgiveness, and obtained it. Thus, peace being established, he was again constituted his father's heir.

Tale 139

OF A REPTILE WHICH SLEW BY A LOOK

ALEXANDER THE GREAT WAS LORD OF THE WHOLE WORLD. He once collected a large army, and besieged a certain city, around which many knights and others were killed without any visible wound. Much surprised at this, he called together his philosophers, and said, "My masters, how is this? My soldiers die, and there is no apparent wound!"

"No wonder," replied they; "on the walls of a city is a reptile, whose look infects your soldiers, and they die of the pestilence it creates."

"And what remedy is there for this?" asked the king.

"Place a mirror in an elevated situation between the army and the wall where the reptile is; and no sooner shall he behold it, than his own look, reflected in the mirror, will return upon himself, and kill him."

And so it was done.

Tale 140

HOW EMPEROR HERACLIUS ADMINISTERED JUSTICE

THE EMPEROR HERACLIUS, AMONGST MANY OTHER VIRTUES, was remarkable for his inflexible justice. It happened that a certain man accused a knight of the murder of another knight, in this form;—"They two went out, in company with another, to war; but no battle was fought. He, however, returned without his companion; and, therefore, we believe that he murdered him."

The king appeared satisfied with the inference, and commanded the prisoner to be executed. But as they approached the place of execution, they beheld the lost knight advancing towards them, alive and well. The judge, enraged at this interruption of the sentence, said to the accused, "I order you to be put to death, because you are already condemned." Then turning to the accuser, "And you also, because you are

the cause of his death." "And you, too," addressing the restored knight—"because you were sent to kill a knight, and
you did not."

Tale 141

THE SUBTLE SERPENT

IN THE REIGN OF THE EMPEROR FULGENTIUS, A CERTAIN
knight named Zedechias, married a very beautiful but im-
prudent wife. In a certain chamber of their mansion a serpent dwelt.

Now, the knight's passionate inclination for tournaments
and jousting brought him to extreme poverty; he grieved
immoderately, and, like one who was desperate, walked backward and forward, ignorant of what he should do.

The serpent, beholding his misery, like the ass of Balaam,
was on that occasion miraculously gifted with a voice, and
said to the knight, "Why do you lament? Take my advice,
and you shall not repent it. Supply me every day with a certain quantity of sweet milk, and I will enrich you."

This promise pleased the knight, and he faithfully followed
the instructions of his subtle friend. The consequence was
that he had a beautiful son, and became exceedingly wealthy.

But it happened that his wife one day said to him, "My
lord, I am sure that serpent has great riches hidden in the
chamber where he dwells. Let us kill him and get possession
of the whole."

The advice pleased the knight, and at the request of his
wife he took a hammer and a vessel of milk, to destroy the
serpent. Allured by the milk, it put its head out of the hole,
as it had been accustomed; and the knight lifted the hammer
to strike it. The serpent, observing his intention, suddenly

drew back its head; and the blow fell upon the vessel. No sooner had he done this, than his offspring died, and he lost everything that he formerly possessed.

The wife, grieved by their common loss, said to him, "Alas! I have ill counselled you; but go now to the hole of the serpent, and humbly acknowledge your offence. Perhaps you may find grace."

The knight complied, and standing before the dwelling-place of the serpent, shed many tears, and entreated that he might once more be made rich.

"I see," answered the serpent, "I see now that you are a fool, and will always be a fool. For how can I forget that blow of the hammer which you designed for me, for which reason I slew your son and took away your wealth? There can be no real peace between us."

The knight, full of sorrow, replied thus: "I promise the most unshaken fidelity, and will never think the slightest injury, provided I may this once obtain your grace."

"My friend," said the serpent, "it is the nature of my species to be subtle and venomous. Let what I have said suffice. The blow offered at my head is fresh upon my recollection; get you gone before you receive an injury."

The knight departed in great affliction, saying to his wife, "Fool that I was to take thy counsel!" But ever afterwards they lived in the greatest poverty.

Tale 142

THE TRAITOR'S DOGS AND NETS IN THE KING'S FOREST

A CERTAIN POWERFUL KING PLANTED A FOREST, AND SURrounded it with a wall. He stocked it with various animals, in which he took infinite pleasure. It happened that one being

discovered meditating traitorous designs, his property was
confiscated, and himself banished from the land. This person, therefore, provided various kinds of dogs and nets, and
went privately into the royal forest to take and destroy the
animals which it contained.

The names of his dogs were Richer, Emuleym, Hanegiff,
Baudyn, Crismel, Egofyn, Beamis, and Renelen. By means of
these dogs and the nets he destroyed every animal in the
forest.

The king was greatly enraged at this circumstance, and
said to his son, "My dear son, arm yourself; call out the
troops, and slay this traitor, or drive him from the kingdom."

The youth answered, "I am ready to comply with your
wishes; but as I have heard that he is a man of great power,
it would be advisable to conceal myself for a certain time,
in company with a beautiful girl, whose wisdom surpasses
that of all others. I will converse with her, and then prepare
myself for battle."

The father replied, "Go to the castle Varioch; there you
will find a girl of inimitable prudence. By her means, you
may send a defiance to our enemy, and I will then promote
her to many honours."

This heard, the son entered the castle secretly, and was
received by the lady with great joy. He remained there some
time, and then departed, armed with the power of his father,
against the traitorous despoiler of the royal forest. In the
end he overthrew him, cut off his head, and returned in
triumph to the king's palace.

Tale 143

WHY THE KING IS SAD

A KING MADE A LAW, BY WHICH WHOSOEVER WAS SUDDENLY
to be put to death in the morning, before sunrise should be

saluted with songs and trumpets, and, arrayed in black garments, should receive judgment.

This king made a great feast, and invited all the nobles of his kingdom, who appeared accordingly. The most skilful musicians were assembled, and there was much sweet melody. But the sovereign was discontented and out of humour; his countenance expressed intense sorrow, and sighs and groans ascended from his heart. The courtiers were all amazed, but none had the courage to inquire the cause of his sadness. At last they requested the king's brother to ask the cause of his sorrow; he made known to him the surprise of his guests, and entreated that he might understand the occasion of his grief.

"Go home now," answered the king; "to-morrow you shall know." This was done.

Early in the morning the king directed the trumpets to sound before his brother's house, and the guards to bring him to the court. The brother, greatly alarmed at the sounding of the trumpets, arose, and put on sable vesture. When he came before the king, the latter commanded a deep pit to be dug, and a rotten chair with four decayed feet to be slightly suspended over it. In this chair he made his brother sit; above his head he caused a sword to hang, attached to a single silk thread; and four men, each armed with a extremely sharp sword, to stand near him; one before and one behind, a third on the right hand, and the fourth on the left. When they were thus placed, the king said, "The moment I give the word, strike him to the heart."

Trumpets and all other kind of musical instruments were brought, and a table, covered with various dishes, was set before him. "My dear brother," said the king, "what is the occasion of your sorrow? Here are the greatest delicacies—the most enrapturing harmony; why do you not rejoice?"

"How can I rejoice?" answered he. "In the morning trumpets sounded for my death; and I am now placed upon a fragile chair; if I move ever so little it will fall to pieces, and I shall fall into the pit and never come out again. If I raise my head, the weapon above will penetrate to my brain. Besides this, the four torturers around stand ready to kill me at your bidding. These things considered, were I lord of the universe, I could not rejoice."

"Now, then," answered the king, "I will reply to your question of yesterday. I am on my throne, as you on that frail chair. For my body is its emblem, supported by four decayed feet, that is, by the four elements. The pit below me is hell; above my head is the sword of divine justice, ready to take life from my body. Before me is the sword of death, which spares none, and comes when it is not expected; behind, a sword—that is, my sins, ready to accuse me at the tribunal of God. The weapon on the right hand is the devil; and that on the left is the worms which after death shall gnaw my body. And, considering all these circumstances, how can I rejoice? If you to-day feared me, who am mortal, how much more ought I to dread my Creator? Go, dearest brother, and be careful that you do not again ask such questions."

The brother rose from his unpleasant seat, and rendering thanks to the king for his life, firmly resolved to amend himself. All who were present commended the ingenuity of the royal answer.

Tale 144

FOUR PHILOSOPHERS EXPLAIN THE WORLD

IN THE REIGN OF A CERTAIN KING THERE HAPPENED A SUD-den and remarkable change, as from good to evil, from truth to falsehood, from strength to weakness, from justice to injustice. This fickleness excited the king's wonder; and inquiring the cause of four of the wisest philosophers, they went, after much deliberation, to the four gates of the city, and each inscribed thereon three causes.

The first wrote—"Power is justice; therefore the land is without law. Day is night; therefore there is no pathway through the land. The warrior flees from the battle; therefore the kingdom has no honour."

The second wrote—"One is two; therefore the kingdom is without truth. The friend is an enemy; therefore the kingdom is without faith. Evil is good; therefore the kingdom is without devotion."

The third wrote—"Reason is united with licentiousness; therefore the kingdom is without name. A thief is set on high; therefore the kingdom is without wealth. The dove would become an eagle; therefore there is no prudence in the land."

The fourth wrote—"The will is a counsellor; therefore the kingdom is ill ordered. Money gives sentence; therefore the kingdom is badly governed. God is dead; therefore the whole kingdom is full of sinners."

Tale 145

HOW SOCRATES DISCOVERED THE DRAGONS

ALBERTUS RELATES THAT IN THE TIME OF PHILIP THERE was a pathway lying between two mountains of Armenia, which had long been unused. For the air of that country was so poisonous, that whosoever breathed it died. The king, therefore, was desirous of ascertaining the cause of the evil, but no one could discover it.

At length Socrates was sent for, who requested him to build a mansion equal in loftiness with the mountains. This was done; and the philosopher then constructed a mirror of steel, with a perfectly pure and polished surface, so that from every part the appearance of the mountains was reflected in it.

Entering the edifice, Socrates beheld two dragons, one upon the mountain and the other in the valley, which simultaneously opened their mouths and drew in the air. As he looked, a youth on horseback, ignorant of the danger, wished to pass that way; suddenly he fell from his horse and died.

Socrates went without delay to the king, and declared what he had seen. The dragons were afterwards taken by a cunning trick, and instantly slain. Thus the path over these mountains became safe and easy to all who passed by.

Tale 146

THE PIRATE BECOMES PRINCE

AUGUSTINE TELLS US IN HIS BOOK, *De Civitate Dei*, THAT Diomedes, in a pirate's galley, for a long time infested the sea, plundering and sinking many ships. Being captured by command of Alexander, before whom he was brought, the king inquired how he dared to molest the seas.

"How darest thou," replied he, "molest the earth? Because I am master only of a single galley, I am termed a robber; but you, who oppress the world with huge armies, are called a king and a conqueror. Would my fortune change, I might become better; and were you more unlucky, you too would have so much the worse name."

"I will change thy fortune," said Alexander, "lest Fortune should be blamed by thy malignity."

Thus he became rich; and from a robber was made a prince and a dispenser of justice.

Tale 147

THE POISONED FOUNTAIN

THE ENEMIES OF A CERTAIN KING WISHED TO SLAY HIM, AND since he was powerful they resolved to destroy him by poison. Some of them came to the city where he abode, arrayed in humble garments.

Now, there was a fountain of water, from which the king frequently drank, and they impregnated it with the poison. The king, ignorant of their treason, drank according to custom, and died.

Tale 148

HOW AMON WAS SAVED BY A DOLPHIN

AULUS GELLIUS SAYS OF AMON, WHO WAS EXTREMELY RICH, that when he wished to pass from one kingdom to another, he hired a ship. The sailors designed to kill him for his wealth; but he obtained from them, that first he should sing in honour of the dolphins, which are said to be much delighted with the songs of men.

When, therefore, he was cast overboard, a dolphin caught him up, and carried him to land; and while the sailors believed him drowned, he was accusing them to the king, by whom they were condemned to death.

Tale 149

A MURDERER'S NAME

VALERIUS RECORDS THAT A CERTAIN NOBLEMAN INQUIRED of a philosopher how he might perpetuate his name. He answered that if he should kill an illustrious personage, his name would be eternally remembered.

Hearing this, he slew Philip, the father of Alexander the Great. But he afterwards came to a miserable end.

Tale 150

HOW WATER IS DRAWN WITH THE AID OF MUSIC

PLINY SAYS THAT THERE IS A CERTAIN LAND IN WHICH neither dew nor rain falls. Consequently, there is a general aridness; but in this country there is a single fountain, from which, when people would draw water, they are accustomed to approach with all kinds of musical instruments, and so march around it for a length of time.

The melody which they thus produce causes the water to rise to the mouth of the spring, and makes it flow forth in great abundance, so that all men are able to obtain as much as they will.

Tale 151

OF THE EVILS OF LEPROSY

IN THE KINGDOM OF A CERTAIN PRINCE THERE WERE TWO knights, one of whom was avaricious, and the other envious.

The former had a beautiful wife, whom every one admired and loved. But the spouse of the latter was ugly and disagreeable. Now, the envious knight had a piece of land adjoining the estate of his covetous neighbour, of which the last exceedingly desired possession. He made him many offers, but the envious person invariably refused to sell his inheritance for silver or gold.

At last, in the envy of his soul, he meditated how to destroy the beauty of the wife of the covetous knight, and offered him the land on condition of enjoying his wife for one night. The covetous wretch immediately assented; and bade his wife submit herself to his will.

This diabolical contract adjusted, the envious knight instantly infected himself with the leprosy, and communicated the disease to the lady, for which he assigned the following reason. He said that, being filled with envy at the beauty and grace which he observed in his neighbour's wife, while his own was so deformed and hateful, he had resolved to remove the disparity. The lady wept exceedingly; and related to her husband what had happened. This troubled him, but he bethought himself of a remedy.

"As yet," said he, "no symptoms of the disorder are perceptible. At a short distance from hence, there is a great city, and in it a university. Go there; stand in the public way, and entice every passenger to you. By this means, you will free yourself from the distemper."

The lady did as she was directed; and the emperor's son, passing by, fell violently in love with her. Afraid to infect a person so near the throne, she resisted his advances, and informed him that she was a leper. This, however, altered not the feelings of the young man; and accordingly the leprosy of the woman adhered to him.

Ashamed of what had befallen, and at the same time fearful of discovery, he went to his mistress, and abode with her.

This circumstance she stated to her husband, and he, much troubled, set his bed-chamber in order, and there the prince dwelt in the strictest seclusion, attended upon only by the lady. Here he continued seven years.

It chanced in the seventh year that there was an intolerable heat, and the leprous man had a vessel of wine standing by his side, designed to refresh his exhausted spirits. At this moment a serpent came out of the garden, and, after bathing itself in the vessel, lay down at the bottom. The prince, awaking from sleep, under the influence of an excessive drought, took up the vessel and drank; and, without knowing it, swallowed the serpent. The creature, finding itself thus unexpectedly imprisoned, began to gnaw his bowels so grievously as to put the leper to inconceivable anguish. The lady gave him much sympathy; and, indeed, for three days, he was an object of pity. On the fourth, however, an emetic being administered, he vomited, and cast up, together with the inward disease, the serpent which had tormented him.

Immediately the pain ceased; and by little and little the leprosy left him. In seven days his flesh was as free from the disorder as the flesh of a child; and the lady, much delighted, clothed him in sumptuous apparel, and presented him a beautiful war-horse, on which he returned to the emperor.

He was received with all honour, and after his father's death ascended the throne, and ended his days in peace.

Tale 152

WARNING THE ENEMY

A PRINCE, NAMED CLEONITUS, WISHING TO GIVE INSTRUCtions to certain of his subjects who were besieged by an enemy, ordered a soldier to go to the place attacked. In order to insult the invaders, he directed an inscription, skilfully fastened upon some arrows, to be prepared, and shot amongst the hostile armies.

It ran thus: "Have hope in the Lord, and be faithful; Cleonitus comes in person to raise the siege."

Tale 153

THE ADVENTURES OF APOLLONIUS, PRINCE OF TYRE

ANTIOCHUS, THE KING OF ANTIOCH, FROM WHOM THE CITY takes its name, had a daughter of such uncommon beauty that when she came of marriageable years, she was sought after with the greatest eagerness. But on whom to bestow her was a source of much anxiety to the king; and, from frequently contemplating the exquisite loveliness of her face, the delicacy of her form, and the excellence of her disposition, he began to love her with more than a father's love.

He burned with an unhallowed flame, and would have excited a similar feeling in his daughter. She, however, courageously persevered in the path of duty, until at length violence accomplished what persuasion had in vain struggled to effect. Thus situated, she gave a loose to her tears, and wept in an agony of the bitterest sorrow. At this moment her nurse entered, and asked the occasion of her uneasiness; she replied, "Alas, my beloved nurse, two noble names have just perished."

"Dear lady," returned the other, "why do you say so?" She told her. "And what accursed demon has been busy?" asked the nurse.

"Where," replied the lady, "where is my father? I have no

father; in me that sacred name has perished. But death is a remedy for all, and I will die."

The nurse, alarmed at what she heard, soothed her into a less desperate mood, and engaged her word not to seek so fearful a relief.

In the mean time the impious parent, assuming the garb of hypocrisy, exhibited to the citizens the fair example of an honest life. In secret he rejoiced at the success of his iniquity, and reflected upon the best means of freeing his unhappy daughter from the numerous suitors who honourably desired her hand. To effect this, he devised a new scheme of wickedness. He proposed certain questions, and annexed to them a condition, by which whosoever furnished an appropriate answer should espouse the lady; but failing, should be instantly decapitated. A multitude of crowned heads from every quarter, attracted by her unmatchable beauty, presented themselves; but they were all put to death. For, if any one chanced to develop the horrid secret, he was slain equally with him who failed, in order to prevent its being divulged. Then the head of the victim blackened upon the gate. The suitors, therefore, naturally grew less; for, perceiving so many ghastly countenances peering above them, their courage quailed, and they returned hastily to their several homes.

Now, all this was done that he who had produced this scene of wickedness might continue in uninterrupted possession. After a short time, the young prince of Tyre, named Apollonius, well-lettered and rich, sailing along the coast, disembarked and entered Antioch.

Approaching the royal presence, he said, "Hail, oh king! I seek thy daughter in marriage."

The king unwillingly heard him communicate his wishes, and fixing an earnest look upon the young man, said, "Dost thou know the conditions?"

"I do," answered he boldly, "and find ample confirmation at your gates."

The king, enraged at his firmness, returned, "Hear, then, the question—'I am transported with wickedness; I live upon my mother's flesh. I seek my brother, and find him not in the offspring of my mother.'"

The youth received the question, and went from the presence of the king; and after duly considering the matter, by the good providence of God, discovered a solution. He immediately returned, and addressing the incestuous wretch, said, "Thou hast proposed a question, oh king! attend my answer. Thou hast said, '*I am transported with wickedness*,' and thou hast not lied; look into thy heart. '*I live upon my mother's flesh*,'—look upon thy daughter."

The king, hearing this solution of the riddle, and fearing the discovery of his vices, regarded him with a wrathful eye.

"Young man," said he, "thou art far from the truth, and deservest death; but I will yet allow thee the space of thirty days. Recollect thyself. In the mean while, return to thy own country; if thou findest a solution to the enigma, thou shalt marry my daughter; if not, thou shalt die."

The youth, much disturbed, called his company together, and hastening on board his own vessel, immediately set sail.

No sooner had he departed, than the king sent for his steward, whose name was Taliarchus, and spoke to him in this manner: "Taliarchus, you are the most faithful repository of my secrets; you know, therefore, that Apollonius of Tyre has found out my riddle. Pursue him instantly to Tyre, and destroy him either with the sword or with poison. When you return, you shall receive a liberal recompense."

Taliarchus, arming himself, and providing a sum of money, sailed into the country of the young man.

When Apollonius reached his own home, he opened his coffers, and searched a variety of books upon the subject in question, but he still adhered to the same idea. "Unless I am much deceived," said he to himself, "King Antiochus entertains an impious love for his daughter." And continuing his reflections, he went on, "What art thou about, Apollonius? Thou hast resolved his problem, and still he has not given thee his daughter. Therefore, God will not have thee die."

Commanding his ships to be got ready, and laden with a hundred thousand measures of corn, and a great weight of gold and silver, with many changes of garments, he hastily embarked during the night, in company with a few faithful followers. They put to sea immediately; and much wonder and regret arose the next day among the citizens respecting him. For he was greatly beloved amongst them; and such was their sorrow, that the barbers, for a length of time, lost all their occupation; public spectacles were forbidden; the baths were closed, and no one entered either the temples or tabernacles.

While these things were going on, Taliarchus, who had been despatched by Antiochus to destroy the prince, observing every house shut up, and the signs of general mourning, asked a boy the occasion of it. "Sir," replied he, "are you ignorant of this matter, that you ask me? Understand, then, that Apollonius, prince of this country, having returned from a visit to King Antiochus, is nowhere to be found." Much rejoiced at what he heard, Taliarchus returned to his vessel, and sailed back again to his own country. Presenting himself to the king, he exclaimed, "Be happy, my lord; Apollonius, through dread of you, is not to be found anywhere."

"He has fled," returned the king; "but long he shall not escape me." And he immediately put forth an edict to this effect: "Whosoever brings before me the traitor Apollonius shall receive fifty talents of gold; but whosoever presents me with his head shall be rewarded with a hundred."

This tempting proposal stimulated not only his enemies, but his pretended friends, to follow him, and many dedicated their time and activity to the pursuit. They traversed sea and land, near and remote countries, but he fortunately escaped their search. The malicious king fitted out a navy for the same purpose, and commanded them to proceed with the utmost diligence in their employment.

Apollonius, however, arrived safely at Tharsus, and walking along the shore, he was recognized by a certain slave of his own household, called Elinatus, who happened that very hour to have reached it. Approaching, he made obeisance to the prince, and Apollonius, recognizing him, returned his salute as great men are wont to do; for he thought him contemptible.

The old man, indignant at his reception, again saluted him, "Hail, King Apollonius! Return my salute, and despise not poverty, if it be ornamented by honest deeds. Did you know what I know, you would be cautious."

"May it please you to tell me what you know?" answered the prince.

"You are denounced," returned the other.

"And who shall dare denounce a prince in his own land?"

"Antiochus has done it."

"Antiochus! For what cause?"

"Because you sought to be what the father of his daughter is."

"And what is the price of my capture?"

"He who shall take you alive is to receive fifty talents of gold; but for your head he will have a hundred. And therefore I caution you to be upon your guard."

Saying this, Elinatus went his way. Apollonius recalled him, and gave him the hundred talents of gold which had been set upon his head.

"Take," said he, "so much of my poverty; thou hast merited it; cut off my head, and gratify the malicious king. You possess the sum, and still you are innocent. I engage you, therefore, of my own free will, to do so great a pleasure to him who seeks my destruction."

"My lord," answered the old man, "far be it from me to take away your life for hire; the friendship of good men is of more value, and cannot be bought." Then, returning thanks to the prince for his munificence, he departed. But as Apollonius tarried on the shore, he perceived a person named Stranguilio approaching him with a sorrowful aspect, and every now and then uttering a deep lament.

"Hail, Stranguilio!" said the prince.

"Hail, my lord the king!" was his reply. "You appear concerned; tell me what occasions it?"

"To say truth," returned Apollonius, "it is because I have required the daughter of a king in marriage. Can I conceal myself in your country?"

"My lord," answered Stranguilio, "our city is extremely poor, and cannot sustain your attendants, in consequence of a grievous famine which has wasted the land. Our citizens are hopeless and helpless; and death, with all its accompanying horrors, is before our eyes."

"Give thanks to God," replied Apollonius, "who hath driven me a fugitive to your shores. If you will conceal my flight, I will present to you a hundred thousand measures of corn."

Full of joy, Stranguilio prostrated himself at the feet of the prince, and exclaimed, "My lord, if you will assist our starving city we will not only conceal your flight, but, if necessary, unsheath our swords in your defence."

Apollonius, therefore, hastened into the forum, and ascending the tribunal, spoke thus to the assembled population: "Men of Tharsus, understanding that an afflicting dearth of provisions troubles you, I, Apollonius, proffer aid. I believe that you will not forget the benefit I render you, but conceal my flight from those who unjustly pursue me. Ye know what the malice of Antiochus aims at, and by what providence I am brought hither to relieve you in this terrible emergency. I present to you a hundred thousand measures of corn at the price I gave for it in my own country—that is, at eight pieces for each measure."

The citizens, delighted at what they heard, gave thanks to God, and immediately prepared the corn for use.

But Apollonius, not forgetting the dignity of a king in the traffic of a merchant, returned the purchase-money to the state; and the people, struck with wonder at this unexpected instance of generosity, erected in the forum a chariot drawn by four horses, running side by side. In the car was a statue, representing Apollonius with his right hand rubbing the corn from the ear. His left foot trampled upon it; and on the pediment they placed the following inscription:—APOLLONIUS, PRINCE OF TYRE, BY A GIFT TO THE CITY OF THARSUS, PRESERVED ITS INHABITANTS FROM A CRUEL DEATH."

A few days afterwards, by the advice of Stranguilio and his wife Dionysias, the prince determined to sail for Pentapolis, a city of the Tyrrheni, where he might remain in greater tranquillity and comfort. They brought him, therefore, with much ceremony to the sea-shore; and then bidding his hosts farewell, he embarked. For three days and nights he sailed with favourable winds; but after losing sight of the Tharsian coast, they veered round, and blew from the north with great violence. The rain fell in heavy showers, mixed with hail; and the ship was carried away by the fury of the storm. Dark clouds brooded over them; and the blast, still increasing, threatened them with immediate death. The crew, imagining all was lost, caught hold of planks, and committed themselves to the mercy of the waves.

In the extreme darkness that followed, all perished. But

Apollonius, riding on a plank, was cast upon the Pentapolitan shore; on which, after leaving the water, he stood thoughtfully, and fixing his eyes upon the ocean, now in a calm, exclaimed, "Oh, ye faithless waves! better had I fallen into the hands of that savage king!—to whom shall I now go? What country shall I seek? Who will afford succour to an unknown and helpless stranger?"

As he spoke this, he beheld a young man coming towards him. He was a robust, hard-favoured fisherman, clad in a coarse frock. Apollonius, driven by his distresses, humbly besought this man's assistance, even with tears starting from his eyes. "Pity me," said he, "whosoever thou art; pity a man stripped of all by shipwreck—one to whom better days have been familiar, and who is descended from no ignoble family. But that you may know whom you succour, understand that I am a prince of Tyre, and that my name is Apollonius. Save, then, my life, I entreat you."

The fisherman, compassionating his sufferings, brought him to his own roof, and placed such as he had before him. And that there might be no deficiency in the charitable part he was acting, he divided his cloak, and gave one-half to the stranger; "Take," said the benevolent man, "take what I can give, and go into the city; there, perhaps, you will find one with more power to serve you than I am. If you are unsuccessful in your search, return hither to me. What poverty can provide you shall share. Yet should you hereafter be restored to your throne, do not forget or despise the coarse threadbare cloak of the poor fisherman."

"Fear not," said Apollonius; "should I prove ungrateful may I be shipwrecked again, nor find in my extremity a man like yourself." As he spoke, the fisherman pointed out the way to the city gates, which Apollonius shortly entered.

Whilst he reflected upon the path he should pursue, he

beheld a naked boy running along the street, having his head anointed with oil, and bound with a napkin.

The youth cried lustily, "Hear, hear, pilgrims or slaves; whosoever would be washed, let him haste to the gymnasium."

Apollonius, according to the proclamation, entered the bath, and pulling off his cloak, made use of the water. Whilst he was doing this, he cast his eyes around to discover some one of an equality with himself; and at last Altistrates, king of all that country, entered with a troop of his attendants. The king played with them at tennis; and Apollonius running forward, caught up the ball, and striking it with inconceivable skill and rapidity, returned it to the royal player. The king, motioning to his servants, said, "Give up your sport, give up your sport; for I suspect this youth is as good a player as I am."

Apollonius, flattered by this praise, approached the king, and catching up an unguent, with a dexterous hand anointed the king's body. Then, having gratefully administered a bath, he departed.

After he was gone, "I swear to you," said his majesty to his surrounding friends, "that I have never bathed so agreeably as I have done to-day by the kindness of a youth whom I do not know. Go," added he, to one of the attendants, "go, and inquire who he is." He followed accordingly, and beheld him equipped in the mean cloak received from the fisherman. Returning to the king, he said, "The youth is one who has suffered shipwreck."

"How do you know!" replied he.

"The man said nothing," answered the servant, "but his dress pointed out his circumstances."

"Go quickly," returned the king, "and say that I entreat him to sup with me."

Apollonius was content, and accompanied the servant back. The latter, approaching the sovereign, stated the return of the shipwrecked person, but that, ashamed of his mean habit, he was unwilling to enter. The king instantly gave command that he should be clothed in honourable apparel, and introduced to the supper-room.

Apollonius therefore entered the royal drawing-room, and was placed opposite to the king. Dinner was brought, and then supper. He feasted not, however, with the feasters, but continually cast his eye upon the gold and silver ornaments of the table, and wept.

One of the guests, observing this, said to the king, "He envies your regal magnificence, unless I am deceived."

"You suspect unhappily," answered he; "he does not envy me, but laments somewhat that he has lost." Then, turning to Apollonius, with a smiling countenance he said, "Young man, feast with us to-day, and hope that God has better things in store for you."

As he thus endeavoured to raise the drooping spirits of the youth, his daughter, a beautiful girl, entered, and first kissed her father, and then those who were his guests.

When she had gone through this ceremony, she returned to the king, and said, "My dear father, who is that young man reclining opposite to you in the place of honour, and whose grief appears so excessive?"

"Sweet daughter," answered he, "that is a shipwrecked youth, who pleased me to-day in the gymnasium; therefore I invited him to supper; but who he is I know not. If you wish to ascertain this, ask him—it becomes you to know all things; and perhaps, when you are made acquainted with his sorrows, you may compassionate and relieve them."

The girl, happy in the permission, approached the young man, and said, "Good friend, kindness proves nobility; if it be not troublesome, tell me your name and fortunes."

"Would you inquire my name?" replied he; "I lost it in the sea; or my nobility? I left it in Tyre."

"Speak intelligibly," said the girl; and Apollonius then related his name and adventures.

When he had made an end he wept, and the king perceiving his tears, said to his daughter, "My dear child, you did ill to inquire the name and occurrences of the young man's life. You have renewed his past griefs. But since he has revealed the truth, it is right that you should show the liberty you enjoy as queen."

The lady complied with the wishes of her father, and looking upon the youth exclaimed, "You are our knight, Apollonius! Put away your afflictions, and my father will make you rich." Apollonius thanked her with modesty and lamentation.

Then said the king, "Bring hither your lyre, and add song to the banquet." She commanded the instrument to be brought, and began to touch it with infinite sweetness. Applause followed the performance.

"There never was," said the courtiers, "a better or a sweeter song."

Apollonius alone was silent, and his want of politeness drew from the king a remark. "You do an unhandsome thing. Everybody else extols my daughter's musical skill; why then do you only discommend it?"

"Most gracious king," replied he, "permit me to say what I think. Your daughter comes near to musical pre-eminence, but has not yet attained it. Command, therefore, a lyre to be given me, and you shall then know what you are now ignorant of."

"I perceive," observed the king, "that you are universally learned," and directed a lyre to be presented to him. Apollonius retired for a few moments, and decorated his head; then, re-entering the dining-room, he took the instrument, and struck it so gracefully and delightfully that they unanimously agreed that it was the harmony not of Apollonius, but of Apollo.

The guests positively asserted that they never heard or saw anything better; and the daughter, regarding the youth with fixed attention, grew suddenly and violently enamoured. "Oh, my father," cried she, "let me reward him as I think fit."

The king assented; and she, looking tenderly upon the youth, said, "Sir Apollonius, receive out of my royal father's munificence two hundred talents of gold and four hundred pounds of silver, a rich garment, twenty men-servants, and ten handmaids"; then, turning to the attendants present, she continued, "Bring what I have promised." Her commands were obeyed; and the guests then rising, received permission to depart.

When they were gone, Apollonius also arose, and said, "Excellent king, pitier of the distressed! and you, O queen, lover of study and friend of philosophy, fare ye well."

Then addressing the servants bestowed upon him, he commanded them to bear away the presents he had received to an hostelry; but the girl, who became apprehensive of losing her lover, looked sorrowfully at her parent, and said, "Best king and father, does it please you that Apollonius, whom we have so lately enriched, should leave us? The goods we have given him will be purloined by wicked men." The king admitted this, and assigned him apartments in the palace, where he lived in great honour.

But the lady's affection so much increased, that it deprived her of all rest; and in the morning she hastened to the bedside of her father. Surprised at the early visit, he inquired what had roused her at so unusual an hour. "I have been unable to sleep," answered the lady; "and I wish you to permit me to receive instructions in music from the young stranger."

The king, pleased with his daughter's zeal for improvement, cheerfully assented, and commanded the youth to be brought into his presence. "Apollonius," said he, "my daughter is extremely desirous of learning your science; if you will instruct her, I will reward you abundantly."

"My lord," he answered, "I am ready to comply with your wishes"; and, accordingly, the girl was placed under his tuition. But her love preyed upon her health, and she visibly declined. Physicians were called in, and they had recourse to the usual expedients; but the diagnostics led them to no certain conclusion.

In a few days three young noblemen, who had long desired to espouse the lady, presented themselves before the king, and besought his favour. "You have often promised us," said they, "that one or the other should marry your daughter. We are rich, and of noble lineage: choose, then, which of us shall be your son-in-law."

"You come," replied the king, "at an unseasonable time. My daughter is unable to follow her usual pursuits, and for this reason languishes on her bed. But that I may not appear to you unnecessarily to protract your uncertainty, write each of you your names, and the settlement you will make her. She shall examine them, and choose between ye."

The suitors complied, and gave the writings to the king, who read, and sealed, and then despatched Apollonius with them to the lady. As soon as she beheld him whom she loved, she exclaimed, "Sir, how is it that you enter my chamber alone?" He presented the writings which her father had sent, and, having opened them, she read the names and proposals of the three suitors. Casting them aside, she said to Apollonius, "Sir, are you not sorry that I must be married?"

"No," returned he; "whatever is for your honour is pleasant to me."

"Ah! master, master," continued the girl; "but if you

loved me, you would grieve." She wrote back her answer, sealed, and delivered it to Apollonius to carry to the king. It ran in these words: "Royal sir and father, since you have permitted me to write my wishes, I do write them. I will espouse him who was shipwrecked."

The king read, but not knowing which of them had been in this predicament, he said to the contending parties, "Which of you has been shipwrecked?"

One, whose name was Ardonius, replied, "I have, my lord."

"What!" cried another, "diseases confound thee; mayst thou be neither safe nor sound. I know perfectly well that thou hast never been beyond the gates of the city; where, then, wert thou shipwrecked?"

When the king could not discover the shipwrecked suitor, he turned to Apollonius, and said, "Take thou the tablets and read; perhaps they will be more intelligible to you than they are to me." He took them, and running his eye over the contents, perceived that he was the person designed, and that the lady loved him. He blushed. "Dost thou discover this shipwrecked person, Apollonius?" asked the king. He blushed still deeper, and made a brief reply.

Now, in this the wisdom of Apollonius may be perceived, since, as it is in *Ecclesiastes*: "There is no wisdom in many words." And in *Peter*: "Christ hath left you an example to be diligently followed, who never sinned, neither was deceit found in His mouth." The same, also, the Psalmist declares: "As He said, so it was done"; wherefore He was to be called a true Israelite, in whom there was no guile. And *John*: "Therefore let us imitate Him in not cursing, nor rendering malediction for malediction, but reserve the tongue for blessing." Thus shall it become the pen of a ready writer—that is, of the Holy Spirit, suddenly pouring forth its gifts; according as it is said, "Suddenly a noise was heard in heaven." *Peter*: "He who would see happy days, let him refrain his tongue from evil, and his lips that they speak no guile"; that is, man ought not to murmur within himself nor act outward evil; so shall he enjoy quietness in this life, and in the future, eternal rest. For the first prevents the outbreaking of reproachful words to the injury of his neighbours; and it is the beginning of eternal peace. So the Psalmist: "I will sleep and repose in peace." For as the tongue of a good and quiet man is directed by the power of God; so the tongue of a malicious person is ministered unto by evil spirits. As it is written, "In our garden grows a whitethorn, upon which the birds rest." By this garden we should understand the mouth, surrounded by a double hedge—to wit, the teeth and the lips—for no other cause than that we may place a guard upon the mouth, and speak nothing but what is in praise of God. The thorn in the garden is the tongue itself, so called from its likeness; because, as the material thorn pricks *Saint Matthew;* "Twining a crown of thorns, they placed it upon His head, and the blood flowed down His blessed body in consequence of the puncture of the thorns," thus the thorn, that is, the tongue, pierces a man—one while by taking away his good sense; at another, by falsehood; and then, again, by discovering the evil that there is in any person: all which ought carefully to be shunned. But the birds resting upon the thorn are the devils, who incline man to vice, so that he becomes their servant. Therefore they will exclaim, in the last day, "Cast this man to us, O righteous judge! for since he would not be thine in all virtue, he is ours in all malice." Let every one of us keep in his tongue, which Cato declares to be the first virtue.

But to return to our story. When the king became aware of his daughter's inclination, he said to the three lovers, "In due time I will communicate with you." They bade him farewell and departed. But the king hastened to his daughter.

"Whom," said he, "wouldst thou choose for thy husband?"

She prostrated herself before him with tears, and answered, "Dear father, I desire to marry the shipwrecked Apollonius."

His child's tears softened the parent's heart; he raised her up, and said, "My sweet child, think only of thy happiness; since he is thy choice, he shall be mine. I will appoint the day of your nuptials immediately."

The following morning, he sent messengers to the neighbouring cities to invite the nobles. When they arrived, he said, "My lords, my daughter would marry her master. I desire you, therefore, to be merry, for my child will be united to a wise man." Saying this, he fixed the period of their spousals.

Now, it happened, after she became pregnant, that she walked with her husband, Prince Apollonius, by the seashore, and a fine ship riding at anchor in the distance, the latter perceived that it was of his own country. Turning to the master of the vessel, he said, "Whence are you?"

"From Tyre," replied the man.

"You speak of my own land, my friend."

"Indeed! and are you a Tyrian?"

"As you have said."

"Do you know," continued the master, "a prince of that country, called Apollonius? I seek him; and whenever you happen to see him, bid him rejoice. King Antiochus and his daughter, at the very same instant, were blasted with lightning. The kingdom has fallen to Apollonius."

Full of pleasure at the unexpected intelligence he had received, the prince said to his wife, "Will you acquiesce in my setting out to obtain the throne?" The lady instantly burst into tears.

"Oh, my lord," said she, "the journey is long, and yet you would leave me! If, however, it is necessary that you should go, we will go together."

Instantly hastening to her father, she communicated the happy news which had just been heard, that Antiochus and his daughter, by the just judgment of an offended God, had been struck with lightning, and his wealth and diadem reserved for her husband. And lastly, she entreated his permission to accompany him. The old king, much exhilarated with the intelligence, was easily prevailed upon to assent; and ships were accordingly prepared for their conveyance. They were laden with everything necessary for the voyage; and a nurse, called Ligoridis, was embarked, and a midwife, in anticipation of the young queen's parturition. Her father accompanied them to the shore, and with an affectionate kiss of each, took his leave.

When they had been at sea some days, there arose a fearful tempest; and the lady, brought by this circumstance into premature labour, to all appearance perished. The moaning and tears of her family almost equalled the storm; and Apollonius, alarmed at the outcry, ran into the apartment, and beheld his lovely wife like an inhabitant of the grave. He tore his garments from his breast, and cast himself with tears and groans upon her inanimate body.

"Dear wife!" he exclaimed, "daughter of the great Altistrates, how shall I console thy unhappy parent?"

Here the pilot, interrupting him, observed, "Sir, it will prejudice the ship to retain the dead body on board; command that it be cast into the sea."

"Wretch that you are," returned Apollonius, "would you wish me to hurl this form into the waves, that succoured me shipwrecked and in poverty?"

Then calling his attendants, he directed them to prepare a coffin, and smear the lid with bitumen. He also commanded that a leaden scroll should be placed in it, and the body, arrayed in regal habiliments, and crowned, was then deposited in the coffin. He kissed her cold lips, and wept bitterly. Afterwards giving strict charge respecting the new-born infant, he committed all that remained of his wife to the sea.

On the third day the chest was driven by the waves to the shores of Ephesus, not far from the residence of a physician, called Cerimon, who happened at that hour to be walking with certain of his pupils upon the sands. Observing the chest deserted by the waters, he commanded his servants to secure it with all speed, and convey it to his house; this done, he opened it, and discovered a beautiful girl, attired in royal apparel.

Her uncommon loveliness struck all the spectators with astonishment; for she was as a sunbeam of beauty, in which nature had created everything pure and perfect, and failed in nothing but in denying her the attribute of immortality. Her hair glittered like the snow, beneath which a brow of milky whiteness, smooth and unwrinkled as a plain, peacefully rested. Her eyes resembled the changeableness, not the prodigality, of two luminous orbs; for their gaze was directed by an unshaken modesty which indicated a constant and enduring mind. Her eyebrows were naturally and excellently placed; and her shapely nose, describing a straight line, rose centrically upon the face. It possessed neither too much length nor too little. Her neck was whiter than the solar rays, and ornamented with precious stones; while her countenance, full of unspeakable joy, communicated happiness to all who looked on her. She was exquisitely formed; and the most critical investigation could not discover more or less than there ought to be. Her beautiful arms, like the branches of some fair tree, descended from her well-turned breast; to which, delicately chiselled fingers, not outshone by the lightning, were attached. In short, she was outwardly a perfect model, —flashing through which, the divine spark of soul her Creator had implanted might be gloriously distinguished. Works of power ought to accord with each other: and hence all corporal beauty originates in the soul's loveliness. It has even been said, that mental excellence, however various, adapts the mass of matter to itself.

Be this as it may, the most perfect adaptation of soul and body existed in this lady, now discovered by Cerimon. "Fair girl," said he, "how camest thou so utterly forsaken?" The money, which had been placed beneath her head, now attracted his attention, and then the scroll of lead presented itself.

"Let us examine what it contains."

He opened it accordingly, and read as follows: "Whosoever thou art that findest this chest, I entreat thy acceptance of ten pieces of gold; the other ten expend, I pray thee, on a funeral. For the corpse it shrouds hath left tears and sorrows enough to the authors of her being. If thou dost neglect my request, I invoke upon thee curses against the day of judgment, and devote thy body to death, unhonoured and uninhumed."

When the physician had read, he directed his servants to comply with the mourner's injunction. "And I solemnly vow," added he, "to expend more than his sorrow requires."

Immediately he bade them prepare a funeral pile. When this was done, and everything laid in order, a pupil of the physician, a young man, but possessing the wisdom of old age, came to look upon the lady. As he considered her fair form attentively, already laid upon the pile, his preceptor said to him, "You come opportunely; I have expected you this hour. Get a vial of precious ointment, and, in honour of this bright creature, pour it upon the funeral pile."

The youth obeyed, approached the body, and drawing the garments from her breast, poured out the ointment. But accidentally passing his hand over her heart, he fancied that it beat. The youth was electrified. He touched the veins, and searched if any breath issued from the nostrils. He pressed his lips to hers; and he thought he felt life struggling with death. Calling hastily to the servants, he bade them place torches at each corner of the bier. When they had done this, the blood, which had been coagulated, presently liquefied; and the young man, attentive to the change, exclaimed to his master, "She lives! she lives! You scarcely credit me; come and see."

As he spoke, he bore the lady to his own chamber. Then heating oil upon his breast, he steeped in it a piece of wool, and laid it upon her body. By these means, the congealed blood being dissolved, the spirit again penetrated to the marrows. Thus, the veins being cleared, her eyes opened, and respiration returned.

"What are you?" said she. "Touch me not otherwise than I ought to be touched; for I am the daughter and the wife of a king."

Full of rapture at the sound of her voice, the young man hurried into his master's room, and related what had occurred.

"I approve your skill," returned he, "I magnify your art, and wonder at your prudence. Mark the results of learning, and be not ungrateful to science. Receive now thy reward; for the lady brought much wealth with her."

Cerimon then directed food and clothes to be conveyed to her, and administered the best restoratives. A few days after her recovery, she declared her birth and misfortunes; and the good physician, commiserating her situation, adopted her as his daughter. With tears she solicited permission to reside among the vestals of Diana; and he placed her with certain female attendants in the magnificent temple of the goddess.

In the mean while Apollonius, guided by the good providence of God, arrived at Tharsus, and disembarking, sought the mansion of Stranguilio and Dionysias. After mutual greetings, he narrated his adventures. "Wretched as I am in the death of a beloved wife, I have yet cause for joy in the existence of this infant. To you I will entrust her; for never, since his offspring has perished, will I again revisit the old Altistrates. But educate my girl with your own daughter Philomatia; and call her after your city, by the name of Tharsia. I would, moreover, pray you to take charge of her nurse, Ligoridis." With such words, he gave the child up to them, accompanied by large presents of gold and silver, and valuable raiment.

He then took an oath that he would neither cut his beard, or hair, or nails, until his daughter were bestowed in marriage. Grieving at the rashness of the vow, Stranguilio took the infant, and promised to educate it with the utmost care; and Apollonius, satisfied with the assurance, went on board his vessel, and sailed to other countries.

While these things were transacting, Tharsia attained her fifth year, and commenced a course of liberal studies with the young Philomatia, her companion. When she was fourteen, returning from school, she found her nurse, Ligoridis, taken with a sudden indisposition, and seating herself near the old woman, kindly inquired the cause. "My dear daughter," replied she, "hear my words, and treasure them in your heart. Whom do you believe to be your father and mother, and which is your native country?"

"Tharsus," returned she, "is the place of my nativity; my father, Stranguilio, and my mother, Dionysias."

The nurse groaned, and said, "My daughter, listen to me; I will tell you to whom you owe your birth, in order that, when I am dead, you may have some guide for your future actions. Your father is called Apollonius; and your mother's name is Lucina, the daughter of King Altistrates. She died the moment you were born! and Apollonius, adorning her with regal vesture, cast the chest which contained her into the sea. Twenty sestertia of gold were placed beneath her head, and whosoever discovered it was entreated to give her burial. The ship in which your unhappy father sailed, tossed to and fro by the winds which formed your cradle, at last put into this port, where we were hospitably received by Stranguilio and Dionysias, to whom your sire also recommended me. He then made a vow never to clip his beard, or hair, or nails, until you were married. Now, I advise that if after my death, your present friends would do you an injury, hasten into the forum, and there you will find a statue of your father. Cling to it, and state yourself the daughter of him whose statue that is. The citizens, mindful of the benefits received from him, will avenge your wrong."

"My dear nurse," answered Tharsia, "you tell me strange things, of which, till now, I was ignorant."

After some future discourse, Ligoridis gave up the ghost. Tharsia attended her obsequies, and lamented her a full year.

After this, she returned to her studies in the schools. Her custom was, on returning, never to eat until she had been to the monument erected in honour of her nurse. She carried with her a flask of wine, and there tarried, invoking the name of her beloved and lamented parents. Whilst she was thus employed, Dionysias, with her daughter Philomatia, passed through the forum; and the citizens, who had caught a glimpse of Tharsia's form, exclaimed, "Happy father of the lovely Tharsia; but as for her companion, she is a shame and a disgrace."

The mother, hearing her daughter vilified, while the stranger was commended, turned away in a madness of fury. She retired to solitary communication with herself. "For fourteen years," muttered she, "the father has neglected his daughter; he has sent no letters, and certainly he is dead. The nurse is also dead, and there is no one to oppose me. I will kill her, and deck my own girl with her ornaments." As she thus thought, her steward, named Theophilus, entered. She called him, and promising a vast reward, desired him to put Tharsia to death.

"What hath the maid done?" asked he.

"She hath done the very worst things; you ought not therefore to deny me. Do what I command you; if you do it not, you will bring evil on yourself."

"Tell me, lady, how is it to be done?"

"Her custom is," replied Dionysias, "on coming from the schools, not to take food until she has entered her nurse's monument; arm yourself with a dagger, seize her by the hair of the head, and there stab her. Then throw her body into the sea, and come to me; I will give you your liberty, with a large reward."

The steward, taking the weapon, went with much sorrow to the monument. "Alas!" said he, "shall I not deserve liberty except by the sacrifice of a virgin's life?"

He entered the monument, where Tharsia, after her occupation in the schools, had as usual retired; the flask of wine was in her hand. The steward attacked the poor girl, and, seizing her by the hair, threw her upon the ground. But as he was on the point of striking, Tharsia cried out, "Oh, Theophilus! what crime have I committed against you, or against any other, that I should die?"

"You are innocent," answered he, "of everything, save possessing a sum of money and certain royal ornaments left you by your father."

"Oh, sir!" said the forsaken orphan, "if I have no hope, yet suffer me to supplicate my Maker before I die."

"Do so," answered the steward, "and God knows that it is upon compulsion that I slay thee."

Now, while the girl was engaged in prayer, certain pirates rushed into the monument, expecting to carry off a booty; and observing a young maid prostrated, and a man standing over her in the act to destroy her, they shouted out, "Stop, barbarian! that is our prey, not your victory."

Theophilus, full of terror, fled hastily from the monument and hid himself by the shore.

The pirates carried off the maid to sea; and the steward, returning to his mistress, assured her that he had obeyed her commands. "I advise you," said he, "to put on a mourning garment, which I also will do, and shed tears for her death. This will deceive the citizens, to whom we will say that she was taken off by a sickness."

When Stranguilio heard what had been done, his grief was sincere and violent. "I will clothe myself in deep mourning," cried he, "for I too am involved in this fearful enormity. Alas! what can I do? Her father freed our city from a lingering death. Through our means he suffered shipwreck; he lost his property, and underwent the extreme of poverty. Yet we return him evil for good! He entrusted his daughter to our care, and a savage lioness hath devoured her! Blind wretch that I was! Innocent, I grieve. I am bound to a base and venomous serpent." Lifting up his eyes to heaven, he continued, "O God, thou knowest that I am free from the blood of this girl—require her of Dionysias." Then fixing a stern look upon his wife, "Enemy of God, and disgrace of man, thou hast destroyed the daughter of a king."

Dionysias made much apparent lamentation: she put her household into mourning, and wept bitterly before the citizens. "My good friends," said she, "the hope of our eyes, the beloved Tharsia, is gone—she is dead. Our tears shall bedew the statue which we have raised to her memory." The people then hastened to the place where her form, moulded in brass, had been erected, in gratitude for the benefits conferred upon that city by her father.

The pirates transported the maid to Machilena, where she was placed among other slaves for sale. A most wretched

and debauched pimp, hearing of her perfections, endeavoured to buy her. But Athanagoras, prince of that city, observing her lofty bearing, her beautiful countenance, and
wise conduct, offered ten golden sestertia.

"I will give twenty," said the pimp.

"And I, thirty."

"Forty!"

"Fifty!" called Athanagoras.

"Eighty!"

"Ninety!"

"I will give a hundred sestertia in ready money; if any
one offer more, I will give ten gold sestertia above."

"Why should I contend any farther with this pimp,"
thought Athanagoras. "I may purchase a dozen for
the price she will cost him. Let him have her; and by
and by I will enter covertly his dwelling and solicit her
love."

Tharsia was conducted by the pimp to a house of ill fame,
in an apartment of which there was a golden Priapus, richly
ornamented with gems.

"Girl! worship that image," said the wretch.

"I may not worship any such thing. Oh, my lord! are
you not a Lapsatenarian."

"Why?"

"Because the Lapsateni worship Priapus."

"Know you not, wretched girl, that you have entered the
house of a greedy pimp?"

Casting herself at his feet, she exclaimed, "Oh, sir! do not
dishonour me; be not guilty of such a flagrant outrage."

"Are you ignorant that, with a pimp and the torturer,
neither prayers nor tears are available?"

He sent for the overseer of the women, and desired him
to array Tharsia in the most splendid apparel, and proclaim
around the city the price of her dishonour. The overseer

did as he was ordered; and on the third day a crowd of people arrived, preceded by the pimp with music.

But Athanagoras came first in a mask, and Tharsia, looking despairingly upon him, threw herself at his feet. "Pity me, my lord; pity me, for the love of Heaven. By that Heaven I adjure you to save me from dishonour. Hear my story; and knowing from whom I sprung, respect my descent and defend my innocence."

She then detailed the whole fortunes of her life; and Athanagoras, confused and penitent, exclaimed, "Alas! and I too have a daughter, whom fate may in like manner afflict. In your misfortunes I may apprehend hers. Here are twenty gold pieces; it is more than your barbarous master exacts from you. Relate your narrative to the next comers, and it will insure your freedom."

Full of gratitude for the generous treatment she experienced, Tharsia returned him thanks, but entreated that her story might not be communicated to others. "To none but my own daughter," said he, "for it will be replete with moral advantage." So saying, and shedding some tears over her fallen estate, he departed. As he went out he met a friend, who stopped him and asked how the girl had behaved. "None better," returned the prince; "but she is very sorrowful."

The youth entered, and she closed the door as on the former occasion. "How much has the prince given you?" asked he. "Forty pieces," answered the girl.

"Here, then; take the whole pound of gold." Tharsia took the present, but falling at his feet, explained her situation. Aporiatus—for that was the young man's name— answered, "Rise, lady; we are men. All of us are subject to misfortunes."

He went out, and observing Athanagoras laughing, said to him, "You are a fine fellow! Have you nobody to pledge in tears but me?" Afraid that these words should betray the matter, they gave another turn to the discourse, and awaited the coming of some other person.

Great numbers appeared, but they all returned in tears, having given her sums of money. Tharsia having obtained the sum which the pimp had fixed as the price of her dishonour, presented it to him.

"Take care," said the monster, "that you bring me whatever money is presented to you." But the next day, understanding that she yet preserved her honour, his rage knew no bounds; and he immediately commissioned the overseer of the women to complete the iniquity. When he appeared the poor girl's tears flowed in profusion.

"Pity me, sir," she said, falling at his feet; "my misfortunes have created the compassion of others, and surely you will not alone spurn my request. I am the daughter of a king; do not dishonour me."

"This pimp," replied he, "is avaricious; I know not what I can do."

"Sir," answered Tharsia, "I have been educated in liberal pursuits. I understand music; if, therefore, you will lead me to the forum, you shall hear my performance. Propose questions to the people, and I will expound them; I have no doubt but I shall receive money enough."

"Well," said the fellow, "I will do as you would have me."

Proclamation being made, the people crowded to the forum; and her eloquence and beauty impressed them all. Whatever question they proposed, she lucidly answered; and by these means drew much wealth from the curious citizens. Athanagoras, also, watched over her with much anxiety—with little less, indeed, than he showed to his only child. He recommended her to the care of the overseer, and bought him to his interest by valuable presents.

Let us now return to Apollonius. After a lapse of fourteen years, he again made his appearance at the house of Stran-

guilio and Dioysias, in the city of Tharsus; no sooner had
the former beheld him, and he strode about like a madman.
"Woman," said he, addressing his wife, "what wilt thou do
now? Thou hast said that Apollonius was shipwrecked and
dead. Behold, he seeks his daughter; what answer shall we
make?"

"Foolish man," returned she, "let us resume our mourning, and have recourse to tears. He will believe that his child
died a natural death." As she said this, Apollonius entered.

Observing their funeral habiliments, he asked, "Do you
grieve at my return? Those tears, I fear, are not for yourselves, but for me."

"Alas!" replied the woman, "I would to Heaven that another, and not me or my husband, had to detail to you what
I must say. Your daughter Tharsia is suddenly dead!" Apollonius trembled through every limb, and then stood fixed as
a statue.

"Oh, woman, if my daughter be really as you describe,
have her money and her clothes also perished?"

"Some part of both," replied Dionysias, "is of course expended; but that you may not hesitate to give faith to our
assurances, we will produce testimony in our behalf. The
citizens, mindful of your munificence, have raised a brazen
monument to her memory, which your own eyes may see."
Apollonius, thus imposed upon, said to his servants, "Go
ye to the ship; I will visit the grave of my unhappy child."
There he read the inscription, as we have detailed above,
and then, as if imprecating a curse upon his own eyes, he
exclaimed in a paroxysm of mental agony, "Hateful, cruel
sources of perception, do ye now refuse tears to the memory
of my lamented girl." With expressions like these, he hastened to his ship, and entreated his servants to cast him
into the sea.

They set sail for Tyre, and for a time the breezes blew

prosperously; but changing, they were driven considerably out of their course. Guided by the good providence of God, they entered the port of Machilena, where his daughter still abode. The pilot and the rest of the crew shouted loudly on their approach to land, and Apollonius sent to inquire the cause.

"My lord," answered the pilot, "the people of Machilena are engaged in celebrating a birthday."

Apollonius groaned, "All can keep their birthdays except me. But it is enough that I am miserable; I give my attendants ten pieces of gold, and let them enjoy the festival. And whosoever presumes to utter my name, or rejoice in my hearing, command that his legs be immediately broken."

The steward took the necessary sums, and having purchased supplies, returned to the ship. Now, the bark which contained Apollonius being more honourable than the rest, the feast was celebrated there more sumptuously. It happened that Athanagoras, who was enamoured of the fair Tharsia, walked upon the sea-shore near the king's ship. "Friends," said he to those who accompanied him, "that vessel pleases me."

The sailors with which she was manned, hearing him applaud their vessel, invited him on board. He went accordingly; and laying down ten gold pieces upon the table, observed, "You have not invited me for nothing." They thanked him; and, in answer to certain questions he had put, informed the prince that their lord was in great affliction, and wished to die; they added, that he had lost a wife and daughter in a foreign country.

"I will give you two pieces of gold," said Athanagoras to Ardalius, one of the servants, "if you will go and say to him that the prince of this city desires a conference."

"Two gold pieces," answered the person he spoke to, "will not repair my broken legs. I pray you send another;

for he has determined thus to punish any one who approaches him."

"He made this law for you," returned the prince, "but not, I think, for me; I will descend myself; tell me his name." They told him—Apollonius.

"Apollonius" said he to himself; "so Tharsia calls her father."

He hastened into his presence, and beheld a forlorn and desolate person. His beard was of great length, and his head in the wildest disorder.

In a low, subdued tone of voice, he said, "Hail, Apollonius!" Apollonius, supposing it to be one of his own people, fixed on him a furious look, but, seeing an honourable and handsome man, remained silent. "You are doubtless surprised," said the prince, "at my intrusion. I am called Athanagoras, and am prince of this city. Observing your fleet riding at anchor from the shore, I was attracted by it; and amongst other things, being struck with the superior structure of this vessel, your sailors invited me on board. I inquired for their lord, and they answered that he was overwhelmed with grief. I have therefore ventured hither, in the hope of administering comfort to you, and drawing you once more into the light of joy. I pray God that it may prove so."

Apollonius raised his head. "Whosoever you are, go in peace. I am unworthy to appear at the banquet; and I do not desire to live."

Perplexed, yet anxious to console the unhappy king, Athanagoras returned upon deck; and despatched a messenger to the pimp, to require the immediate presence of Tharsia, whose musical skill and eloquence, he thought, could not but produce some effect.

She came, and received instructions from the prince. "If you succeed," said he, "in softening this royal person's affliction, I will present to you thirty gold sestertia, and as many of silver; moreover, for thirty days, redeem you from the power of your master." The girl accordingly prepared herself for the task.

Approaching the mourner, "Heaven keep you," said she, in a low plaintive voice, "and make you happy; a virgin that hath preserved her honour amid her misfortunes salutes you." She then sang to an instrument, with such a sweet and ravishing melody, that Apollonius was enchanted. Her song related to the fortunes she had experienced, and was to the following effect:—That she fell into the hands of dishonest people, who sought to traffic with her virtue; but that she passed innocent through all her trials. "Thus," continued she, "the rose is protected by its thorns. They who bore me off beat down the sword of the smiter. I preserved my virtue when attacked by my brutal owner. The wounds of the mind linger, and tears fail. In me behold the only offspring of a royal house. Contain your tears, and limit your anxiety. Look up to heaven, and raise your thoughts above. The Creator and Supporter of mankind is God; nor will He permit the tears of His virtuous servants to be shed in vain."

As she concluded, Apollonius fixed his eyes upon the girl, and groaned deeply. "Wretched man that I am," said he, "how long shall I struggle with my sorrows? But I am grateful for your attentions; and if again permitted to rejoice in the zenith of my power, your memory will support me. You say you are royally descended?—who are your parents? But begone; here are a hundred gold pieces; take them, and speak to me no more. I am consumed with new afflictions."

The girl received his donation, and would have left the ship; but Athanagoras stopped her. "Whither are you going?" said he; "you have as yet done no good; is your heart so pitiless that you can suffer a man to destroy himself, without striving to prevent it?"

"I have done everything that I could," answered Tharsia: "he gave me a hundred gold pieces, and desired me to depart."

"I will give you two hundred pieces if you will return the money to him, and say, 'My lord, I seek your safety, not your money.' "

Tharsia complied, and seating herself near to the king, said, "If you are determined to continue in the squalid state to which you have accustomed yourself, give me leave to reason with you. I will propose a question; if you can answer it, I will depart; if not, I will return your present and go."

"Keep what I have given; I will not deny your request. For though my evils admit of no cure, yet I determine to hearken to you. Put your question, then, and depart."

"Hear me; there is a house in a certain part of the world which bounds and rebounds, but it is closed against mankind. This house loudly echoes, but its inhabitant is ever silent; and both—the house and the inhabitant—move forward together. Now, if you are a king, as you assert, you should be wiser than I am. Solve the riddle."

"To prove to you that I am no impostor," said Apollonius, "I will reply. The house which bounds and rebounds and echoes is the wave; the mute inhabitant is a fish, which glides along with its residence."

Tharsia continued, "I am borne rapidly along by the tall daughter of the grove, which equally encloses an innumerable company. I glide over various paths, and leave no footsteps." "When I have answered your questions," said Apollonius, "I will show you much that you know not. Yet I am astonished that one so young should be endowed with wit so keen and penetrating. The tree enclosing a host, and passing through various ways without a trace, is a ship."

"A person passes through circumferences and temples without injury. There is a great heat in the centre which no one removes. The house is not uncovered, but it suits a naked inhabitant. If you would allay pain, you must enter into fire."

"I would enter, then, into a bath, where fire is introduced by means of round tables. The covered house suits a naked inhabitant; and he who is naked in this situation will perspire."

When she had said these and similar things, the girl threw herself before Apollonius, and drawing aside his hands, embraced him.

"Hear," said she, "the voice of your supplicant; regard a virgin's prayers. It is wicked in men of so much wisdom to destroy themselves. If you lament your lost wife, the mercy of God can restore her to you; if your deceased child, you may yet find her. You ought to live and be glad."

Apollonius, irritated at the girl's pertinacity, arose and pushed her from him with his foot. She fell and cut her cheek, from which the blood copiously flowed.

Terrified at the wound she had received, she burst into tears, and exclaimed, "O thou eternal Architect of the heavens! look upon my afflictions. Born amid the waves and storms of the ocean, my mother perished in giving life to her daughter. Denied rest even in the grave, she was deposited in a chest, with twenty gold sestertia, and thrown into the sea. But I, unhappy, was delivered by my remaining parent to Stranguilio and Dionysias, with the ornaments befitting a royal extraction. I was by them devoted to death; but whilst I invoked the assistance of God, a number of pirates rushed in and the murderer fled. I was brought hither; in His own good time God will restore me to my father Apollonius."

Here she concluded, and the royal mourner, struck with her relation, shouted with a loud voice, "Merciful God! Thou who lookest over heaven and earth, and revealest that which is hidden, blessed be Thy holy name." Saying this, he fell into the arms of his daughter. Tenderly he embraced her, and wept aloud for joy. "My best and only child," said he; "half of my own soul! I shall not die for thy loss. I have found thee, and I wish to live."

Exalting his voice yet more, "Run hither, my servants, my friends! all of ye; my misery is at an end. I have found what I had lost—my child, my only daughter!" Hearing his exclamations, the attendants ran in, and with them the prince Athanagoras. They discovered the enraptured king weeping upon his daughter's neck.

"See, see," said he, "this is she whom I lamented. Half of my soul! now will I live."

Participating in their master's happiness, they all wept.

Apollonius now divested himself of his mourning dress, and attired himself in regal habiliments. "Oh, my lord," said his followers, "how much your daughter resembles you! Were there no other guide, that would indicate her birth."

The delighted girl overwhelmed her recovered parent with kisses. "Blessed be God," cried she, "who has been so gracious to me, and given me to see, and live, and die with you." Then, entering into a more detailed account of her adventures, she related what she had endured from the wretched pimp, and how the Almighty had protected her.

Athanagoras, fearing lest another might demand her in marriage, threw himself at the king's feet, and modestly intimating how instrumental he had been in promoting their happy reunion, besought him to bestow his child upon him. "I cannot deny you," returned Apollonius, "for you have alleviated my sorrows, and been the means of my present and future happiness. Take her. But deeply shall that rascal feel my vengeance."

Athanagoras immediately returned to the city, and convoked an assembly of the people. "Let not our city perish," said he, addressing them, "for the crimes of one impious wretch. Know that King Apollonius, the father of the beautiful Tharsia, has arrived. Behold where his navy rides. He threatens us with instant destruction, unless the scoundrel who would have prostituted his daughter be given up to him." Scarcely had he spoken when the whole population, men and women, hurried off to implore the king's clemency.

"I advise you," said Athanagoras, "to take the wretch with you." Seizing the abominable man, they tied his hands to his back, and carried him along to the presence of offended majesty. Apollonius, clad in royal robes, his hair shorn, and crowned, ascended the tribunal with his daughter. The citizens stood round, in expectation of his address.

"Men of Machilena," said he, "to-day I have recovered my daughter, whom that villainous pimp would have corrupted. Neither pity, nor prayers, nor gold could prevail with him to desist from his atrocious purposes. Do ye, therefore, avenge my daughter."

The people, with one voice, answered, "Let him be burnt alive, and his wealth given to the lady." Instantly the wretch was brought forward and burnt.

"I give you your liberty," said Tharsia to the overseer, "because, by your kindness and the kindness of the citizens, I remained unsullied. I also present to you two hundred gold sestertia." Turning to the other girls, she added, "Be free, and forget your past habits."

Apollonius, again addressing the people, returned them thanks for their kindness to him and his daughter, and bestowed on them a donation of five hundredweight of gold. Shouts and applause followed; and they immediately set about erecting a statue to their benefactor in the midst of the city. Upon the base was the following inscription:—

TO APOLLONIUS, OF TYRE, THE PRESERVER OF OUR STATE; AND TO THE MOST HOLY THARSIA, HIS VIRGIN DAUGHTER.

A few days after the lady was espoused to Athanagoras, amid the universal joy of the city.

Intending to sail with his daughetr, and son-in-law, and followers to his own country by way of Tharsus, an angel advised him in a dream to make for Ephesus, and there, entering the temple with his daughter and her husband, relate in a loud voice all the varied turns of fortune to which he had been subject from his earliest youth.

Accordingly, he sailed for Ephesus. Leaving his ship, he sought out the temple to which his long-lost wife had retired. When his wife heard that a certain king had come to the temple with his daughter, she arrayed herself in regal ornaments, and entered with an honourable escort. The surrounding multitude was much struck with her beauty and modesty, and said there never was so lovely a virgin.

Apollonius, however, knew her not; but such was her splendour that he and his companions fell at her feet, almost fancying her to be Diana, the goddess.

He placed on the shrine precious gifts, and then, as the angel had ordained, he commenced his history. "I was born," said he, "a king. I am of Tyre, and my name is Apollonius. I solved the riddle of the impious Antiochus, who sought to slay me as the detector of his wickedness. I fled, and, by the kindness of King Altistrates, was espoused to his daughter. On the death of Antiochus, I hastened with my wife to ascend his throne; but she died on the passage, after giving birth to this my daughter. I deposited her in a chest, with twenty gold sestertia, and committed her to the waves. I placed my daughter under the care of those whose subsequent conduct was base and villainous, and I departed to the higher parts of Egypt. After fourteen years I returned to see my daughter. They told me she was dead; and crediting it, I endured the deepest anguish of mind. But my child was at length restored to me."

As he ended, the daughter of Altistrates sprung towards him, and would have clasped him in her arms. He repelled her with indignation, not supposing that it was his wife.

"Oh, my lord!" cried she, weeping, "better half of my soul! why do you use me thus? I am thy wife, the daughter of King Altistrates; and thou art of Tyre; thou art Apollonius, my husband and lord. Thou wert the beloved one who instructed me. Thou wert the shipwrecked man whom I loved with pure and fond regard."

Apollonius, awakening at the mention of these well-known circumstances, recollected his long-lost lady. He fell upon her neck, and wept for joy. "Blessed be the Most High, who hath restored me my wife and daughter."

"But where," said she, "is our daughter?" Presenting Tharsia, he replied, "Behold her." They kissed each other tenderly; and the news of this happy meeting was soon noised abroad through the whole city.

Apollonius again embarked for his own country. Arriving at Antioch, he was crowned, and then hastening to Tyre, he appointed Athanagoras and his daughter to the rule of this place. Afterwards assembling a large army, he sat down before Tharsus, and commanded Stranguilio and Dionysias to be seized and brought before him.

Addressing the Tharsians, he inquired, "Did I ever do an injury to any one of you?"

"No, my lord," answered they; "we are ready to die for you. This statue bears record how you preserved us from death."

"Citizens," returned Apollonius, "I entrusted my daughter to Stranguilio and his wife; they would not restore her."

"Oh, my lord," cried the unhappy woman, "thou hast read her fate inscribed on the monument."

The king directed his daughter to come forward; and Tharsia, reproaching her, said, "Hail! woman! Tharsia greets thee; Tharsia returned from the grave." Dionysias trembled; and the citizens wondered and rejoiced. Tharsia then called the steward. "Theophilus, dost thou know me? Answer distinctly, who employed thee to murder me?"

"My lady Dionysias."

The citizens, hearing this, dragged both the husband and wife out of the city and stoned them. They would have killed Theophilus also, but Tharsia, interposing, freed him from death. "Unless he had given me time to pray," she said, "I should not now have been defending him."

Apollonius tarried here three months, and gave large gifts to the city. Thence sailing to Pentapolis, the old King Altistrates received them with delight. He lived with his son, and daughter, and grandchild a whole year in happiness. After that he died, full of years, bequeathing the kingdom to his son and daughter.

As Apollonius walked one day upon the sea-shore, he recollected the kind-hearted fisherman who succoured him after his shipwreck, and he ordered him to be seized and brought to the palace. The poor fisherman, perceiving himself under the escort of a guard of soldiers, expected nothing less than death. He was conducted into the presence of the king, who said, "This is my friend, who helped me after my shipwreck, and showed me the way to the city"; and he gave him to understand that he was Apollonius of Tyre.

He then commanded his attendants to give him two hundred sestertia, with men-servants and maid-servants. Nor did his kindness stop here—he made him one of his personal attendants, and retained him as long as he lived. Elinatus, who declared to him the intentions of Antiochus, fell at his feet, and said, "My lord, remember thy servant Elinatus." Apollonius, extending his hand, raised him up, and enriched him. Soon after this a son was born, whom he appointed king in the room of his grandfather, Altistrates.

Apollonius lived with his wife eighty-four years; and ruled the kingdoms of Antioch and Tyre in peace and happiness. He wrote two volumes of his adventures, one of which he laid up in the temple of the Ephesians, and the other in his own library. After death, he went into everlasting life. To which may God, of His infinite mercy, lead us all.

Tale 154

THE HOLY CITY OF EDESSA

GERVASE RELATES THAT IN THE CITY OF EDESSA, IN CONSEquence of the presence of Christ's holy image, no heretic could reside—no pagan, no worshipper of idols, no Jew.

Neither could the barbarians invade that place; but if an hostile army appeared, any innocent child, standing before the gates of the city, read an epistle; and the same day on which the epistle was read, the barbarians were either appeased, or, becoming womanish, fled.

Tale 155

THE PHANTOM KNIGHT OF WANDLESBURY

THERE IS IN ENGLAND, AS GERVASE TELLS US, ON THE BORders of the episcopal see of Ely, a castle called Cathubica; a little below which is a place distinguished by the appellation of Wandlesbury, because, as they say, the Vandals, having laid waste the country, and cruelly slaughtered the Christians, here pitched their camp. Around a small hillock, where their tents were pitched, was a circular space of level ground, enclosed by ramparts, to which but one entrance presented itself.

Upon this plain, as it is commonly reported, on the authority of remote traditions, during the hush of night, while the moon shone, if any knight called aloud, "Let my adversary appear," he was immediately met by another, who started up from the opposite quarter, ready armed and mounted for combat.

The encounter invariably ended in the overthrow of one party. Concerning this tradition, I have an actual occurrence to tell, which was well known to many, and which I have heard both from the inhabitants of the place and others.

There was once in Great Britain a knight, whose name was Albert, strong in arms, and adorned with every virtue. It was his fortune to enter the above-mentioned castle, where he was hospitably received. At night, after supper, as is usual in great families during the winter, the household assembled round the hearth, and occupied the hour in relating divers tales.

At last, they discoursed of the wonderful occurrence before alluded to; and our knight, not satisfied with the report, determined to prove the truth of what he had heard, before he implicitly trusted it. Accompanied, therefore, by a squire of noble blood, he hastened to the spot, armed in a coat of mail. He ascended the mount, and then, dismissing his attendant, entered the plain. He shouted, and an antagonist, armed at all points, met him in an instant. What followed?

Extending their shields, and directing their lances at each other, the steeds were driven to the encounter and both the knights shaken by the clash. Their lances broke, but from the slipperiness of the armour, the blow did not take effect. Albert, however, so resolutely pressed his adversary, that he fell; and rising immediately, beheld Albert making a prize of his horse. On which, seizing the broken lance, he cast it in the manner of a missile, and cruelly wounded Albert in the thigh. Our knight, overjoyed at his victory, either felt not the blow, or disregarded it; and his adversary suddenly disappeared.

He, therefore, led away the captured horse, and consigned him to the charge of his squire. He was overlarge, light of step, and of a beautiful shape. When Albert returned, the household crowded around him, struck with the greatest wonder at the event, and rejoicing at the overthrow of the hostile knight, while they lauded the bravery of the magnanimous victor.

When, however, he put off his breeches, one of them was filled with clotted blood. The family were alarmed at the appearance of the wound; and the servants were aroused and despatched here and there. Such of them as had been asleep, admiration now induced to watch.

As a testimony of conquest, the horse, held by the bridle, was exposed to public inspection. His eyes were fierce, and he arched his neck proudly; his hair was a lustrous jet, and he bore a war-saddle on his back. The cock had already begun to crow, when the animal, foaming, curveting, snorting, and furiously striking the ground with his feet, broke the bonds that held him and escaped. He was immediately pursued, but disappeared in an instant.

The knight retained a perpetual memento of that severe wound; for every year, upon the night of that encounter, it broke out afresh. Some time after that, he crossed the seas and fell, valiantly fighting against the pagans.

Tale 156

HOW ULYSSES DISCOVERED ACHILLES

OVID, SPEAKING OF THE TROJAN WAR, RELATES THAT WHEN Helen was carried off by Paris, it was predicted that the city of Troy would not be captured without the death of Achilles. His mother, hearing this, placed him, in the dress of a female, amongst the ladies of the court of a certain king.

Ulysses, suspecting the stratagem, loaded a ship with a variety of wares; and besides the trinkets of women, took with him a splendid suit of armour. Arriving at the castle in which Achilles dwelt among the girls, he exposed his goods for sale. The disguised hero, delighted with the warlike implements upon which he gazed, seized a lance, and gallantly brandished it. The secret was thus manifested, and Ulysses conducted him to Troy.

The Greeks prevailed; and after his decease, and the capture of the city, the hostages of the adverse side were set at liberty.

Tale 157

FROM ONE PENNY TO FIVE

THERE WAS AN EMPEROR WHOSE PORTER WAS REMARKABLY wise. He earnestly besought his master that he might have the custody of a city for a single month, and receive, by way of tax, one penny from every crook-backed, one-eyed, scabby, leprous, or ruptured person. The emperor admitted his request, and confirmed the gift under his own seal.

Accordingly, the porter was installed in his office; and as the people entered the city, he took note of their defects, and charged them a penny, in conformity with the grant.

It happened that a hunchbacked fellow one day entered, and the porter made his demand. Hunchback protested that he would pay nothing. The porter immediately laid hands upon him, and accidentally raising his cap, discovered that he was one-eyed also. He demanded two pennies forthwith. The other still more vehemently opposed, and would have fled; but the porter catching hold of his head, the cap came off, and disclosed a bald scabby surface.

Whereupon he required three pennies. Hunchback, very much enraged, persisted in his refusal, and began to struggle with the determined porter. This produced an exposure of his arms, by which it became manifest that he was leprous. The fourth penny was therefore laid claim to; and the scuffle continuing, revealed a rupture, which entitled him to a fifth.

Thus, a fellow unjustly refusing to pay a rightful demand of one penny was necessitated, much against his inclination, to pay five.

Tale 158

THE TOMB OF AN ANCIENT GIANT

THERE WAS ONCE DISCOVERED AT ROME AN UNCORRUPTED body, taller than the wall of the city, on which the following words were inscribed:—"Pallas, the son of Evander, whom the lance of a crooked soldier slew, is interred here."

A candle burned at his head, which neither water nor wind could extinguish, until air was admitted through a hole made with the point of a needle beneath the flame. The wound of which this giant had died was four feet and a half long. Having been killed after the overthrow of Troy, he had remained in his tomb two thousand two hundred and forty years.

Tale 159

NOAH THE DISCOVERER OF WINE

JOSEPHUS, IN HIS WORK ON "THE CAUSES OF NATURAL Things," says that Noah discovered the wild vine, and because it was bitter, he took the blood of four animals, namely, of a lion, of a lamb, a pig, and a monkey. This mixture he united with earth, and made a kind of manure, which he deposited at the roots of the tree.

Thus the blood sweetened the fruit, with which he afterwards intoxicated himself, and, lying naked, was laughed at by his younger son. Assembling his children, he declared to them by what means he had produced this effect.

Tale 160

THE LADY WHO FLEW AWAY

IT OFTEN HAPPENS THAT THE DEVILS TRANSFORM THEMselves into angels of light, in order to foster in human hearts whatever is fiendish. In proof of which, a most remarkable instance is recorded.

When Valentine filled the espiscopal see of Arles, there stood on the outskirts of the diocese a castle, the lady of

which invariably quitted church before the celebration of
mass, for she could not bear to look on the consecration of
our Lord's body. This peculiarity gave her husband much
uneasiness, and he determined to ascertain the reason of
so singular a proceeding.

On a certain day, the gospel being ended, she was about to
retire, when, after much violent struggling, she was forcibly
detained by her husband and his attendants. The priest then
continued the service, and at the instant that he proceeded
to consecration, the lady, borne along by a diabolical spirit,
flew away, carrying along with her a portion of the chapel,
and was seen no more in those regions; and part of the very
tower is yet standing, in testimony of the truth of the above
relation.

Tale 161

THE GOLDEN DRINKING HORN

IN THE KINGDOM OF ENGLAND THERE IS A HILLOCK IN THE
midst of a thick wood, about the height of a man. Here
knights and other followers of the chase were accustomed to
ascend, when they suffered from heat and thirst, and sought
eagerly for relief.

From the nature of the place, and the circumstances of
their occupation, each ascended the hill alone; and each, as
if addressing some other, would say, "I thirst." Immediately,
beyond expectation, there started from the side one with a
cheerful countenance and an outstretched hand, bearing a
large horn ornamented with gold and precious stones, such
as we are still in the habit of using instead of a cup, and
full of the most exquisite, but unknown, beverage. This he

presented to the thirsty person; and no sooner had he drank, than the heat and lassitude abated. One would not then have thought that he had been engaged in labour, but that he was desirous of commencing an arduous employment.

After the liquor had been taken, the attendant presented a clean napkin to wipe the mouth. His ministry completed, he disappeared, without awaiting recompense, or permitting inquiry. He did this daily, and, aged as he seemed to be, his pace was singularly rapid. At last, a certain knight went to these parts for the purpose of hunting; and a draught being demanded, and the horn brought, instead of restoring it to the industrious rogue as custom and urbanity required, he retained it for his own use. But the knight's feudal lord, ascertaining the truth of this matter, condemned the plunderer; and presented the horn to Henry the Elder, king of England, lest he himself should be held a partaker in the crime.

Tale 162

THE DEVIL'S CASTLE

GERVASE OF TILBURY RELATES TO OTTO, THE ROMAN EMperor, a very remarkable occurrence, but at the same time full of excellent advice, and affording a reason for caution to the reckless.

There was in the bishopric of Girona, in Catalonia, a very high mountain, whose ascent was extremely arduous, and, except in one place, inaccessible. On the summit was an unfathomable lake of black water. Here also stood, as it is reported, a palace of demons, with a large gate continually closed; but the palace itself, as well as its inhabitants, existed in invisibility. If any one cast a stone or other hard substance into this lake, the demons exhibited their anger by furious storms.

In one part of the mountain was perpetual snow and ice; here there was abundance of crystal, and the sun never was seen. At its foot flowed a river, whose sands were of gold; and the precious metal thus obtained was named by the vulgar its *cloak*. The mountain itself, and the parts adjacent, furnished silver; and its unexhaustible fertility was not the least surprising of its peculiarities.

Not far from hence lived a certain farmer, who one day being much occupied with domestic matters, and troubled exceedingly by the incessant squalling of his little girl, at length, after the manner of people when angry, wished his infant at the devil. This evil desire was scarcely uttered, ere the girl was seized by an invisible hand, and carried off.

Seven years afterwards, a person journeying at the foot of the mountain near the farmer's dwelling, distinguished a man hurrying along at a rapid rate, and uttering in the most doleful tones, "Alas! for me, a wretched man! what shall I do to get rid of this huge load?"

The traveller stopped to inquire the occasion; and was told that, for the space of seven years last past, he had been committed to the custody of the demons upon that mountain, who daily made use of him as a chariot, in consequence of an unwary exclamation to that effect. The traveller, startled at an assertion so extraordinary, and a little incredulous, was informed that his neighbour had suffered in a similar degree; for that, having hastily committed his daughter to their power, they had instantly borne her off. He added that the demons, weary of instructing the girl, would willingly restore her, provided the father presented himself on the mountain and there receive her.

The traveller, thunder-struck at this communication,

doubted whether he should conceal things so incredible, or relate what he had heard. He determined, at last, to declare the girl's situation to her father; and hastening, accordingly, found him still bewailing the lengthened absence of his daughter. Ascertaining the cause, he went on to state what he had heard from the man whom the devils used as a chariot: "Therefore," said he, "I recommend you, attesting the Divine name, to demand of these devils the return of your daughter."

Amazed at what was imparted to him, the father deliberated upon the best method of proceeding and finally pursued the counsel of the traveller. Ascending the mountain, he passed forward to the lake, and commanded the demons to restore the girl whom his folly had committed to them. Suddenly a violent blast swept by him, and a girl of lofty stature stood in his presence. Her eyes were wild and wandering, and her bones and sinews were scarcely covered with skin. Her horrible countenance disclosed no sign of sensibility; and, ignorant of all language, she scarcely could be acknowledged for a human being.

The father, wondering at her strange appearance, and doubtful whether she should be taken to his own home or not, ran to the bishop of Girona, and, with a sorrowful aspect, detailed what had befallen him; at the same time requesting his advice. The bishop, as a religious man, and one entrusted with a charge of so much importance, narrated every circumstance respecting the girl to his diocese. He warned them against rashly committing their fortunes to the power of demons, and showed that our adversary the devil, as a raging lion, goeth about seeking whom he may devour; that he will slay those who are given to him, and hold them in eternal bonds, and torment and afflict those devoted to him for a time.

The man who was used by the devils as a chariot, remained

a long time in this miserable situation; but his subsequent faith and discretion emancipated him. He stated that near the above-mentioned place there was an extensive subterranean palace, whose entrance was by a single gate, enveloped in the thickest darkness. Through this portal the devils, who had been on embassies to various parts of the world, returned, and communicated to their fellows what they had done. No one could tell of what the palace was constructed, save themselves, and those who passed under their yoke to eternal damnation.

From all which, my beloved, we may gather the dangers we are exposed to, and how cautious we should be of invoking the devil to our assistance, as well as of committing our family to his power. Let us guard our hearts, and beware that he catch not up the sinful soul, and plunge it into the lake of everlasting misery; where there is snow and ice unthawed—crystal, that reflects the awakened and agonized conscience, perpetually burning with immortal fire.

Tale 163

VERSES FROM THE DEVIL

ALEXANDER HAD AN ONLY SON, CALLED CELESTINUS, WHOM he loved with the utmost tenderness. He desired to have him well instructed, and sending for a certain philosopher, said, "Sir, instruct my son, and I will bountifully remunerate you."

The philosopher acquiesced, and took the boy home with him. He diligently performed his duty; and it happened that one day, entering a meadow with his pupil, they perceived a horse lying on the ground, grievously affected with the mange. Near the animal two sheep were tied together, which busily cropped the grass that grew in abundance around them. It so chanced that the sheep were on each side of the horse, and the cord with which they were bound passed over his back and, chafing the sores, galled him exceedingly.

Disturbed by this circumstance, he got up; but the cord, then loaded with the weight of the sheep, afflicted him more and more; and, filled with fury, he began to run off at a great speed, dragging along the unfortunate sheep. And in equal proportion to their resistance was the augmentation of the horse's suffering. For the cord, having worn itself into a hollow, sunk, at every struggle, yet deeper into the wound.

Adjoining the meadow was the house of a miller, toward which the horse, impelled by the anguish of his wound, galloped, and entered, with the sheep hanging as we have said. The house was then unoccupied; but there was a fire burning upon the hearth, and the quadruped, plunging and striking with his hoofs, so scattered the fire that the flame caught hold of the building, and reduced it to ashes, together with the horse and the sheep.

"Young man," said the philosopher to his pupil, "you have perceived the beginning, the middle, and the completion of this incident; make me some correct verses upon it, and show me who is responsible for the burning of the house. Unless you do this, I assure you I will punish you severely."

Celestinus, during the absence of his master, applied himself diligently to study, but he was unable to execute his task. This much troubled him; and the devil met him in the likeness of a man, and said, "My son, what has made you so sorrowful?"

"Never mind; it is no use telling you."

"You know not that; tell me, and I will help you."

"I am charged," said the boy, "under a heavy punishment,

to make some verses about a scabby horse and two sheep, and I don't know how."

"Young man, I am the devil in a human form, and the best poet that ever lived; care nothing about your master, but promise to serve me faithfully, and I will compose such pleasant verses for you that they shall excel those of your pedagogue himself."

Celestinus gave his word to serve him faithfully if he fulfilled his engagement. The devil then produced the following verses:—

> Bound by a thong, that passed along
>   A horse's mangy hide,
> Two sheep there lay, as we should say,
>   One upon either side.
>
> The steed uprose, and upward goes
>   Each sheep with dangling breech;
> Borne by the horse's rapid course,
>   The miller's hut they reach.
>
> Scattering the fire with reckless ire,
>   The rafters caught the flame;
> And bleating breed and scabby steed
>   Were roasted in the same.
>
> Now had that wight, that miller hight,
>   Vouchsafed his house to keep:
> Ere he returned it had not burned,
>   Nor burned his horse and sheep.

The boy, made happy by the present, returned home.

"My child," asked the master, "have you stolen your verses, or made them?"

"I made them, sir."

He then read what we have given above; and the master,

struck with the greatest astonishment at their uncommon beauty, exclaimed, "My dear boy, tell me if any one made these for you?"

"No, sir; no one did."

"Unless you tell me the truth, I will flog you till the blood run."

The lad, fearful of what might follow, declared all that had occurred, and how he had bound himself to the devil. The master, grieved at the communication, induced the youth to confess himself and renounce this fearful confederacy.

When this was done he became a holy man, and, after a well-spent life, gave up his soul to God.

Tale 164

HOW SAINT PETER SAW THE FIVE PERVERSE MEN

WE READ IN A CERTAIN BOOK OF A CONVERSATION BETWEEN Jesus Christ and Saint Peter. "I saw," said the latter, "five men whom I thought madmen. The first ate the sand of the sea so greedily, that it slipped through his jaws on either side of his mouth. Another I observed standing upon a pit full of sulphur and pitch, of which the smell was intolerable; yet he strove earnestly to inhale it. The third lay upon a burning furnace, whose heat was not enough; he endeavoured to catch the sparks emitted from the furnace that he might eat them. A fourth sat upon a steeple of the temple in order to catch the wind. For this purpose he held his mouth open. The fifth devoured whatsoever of his own members he could get into his mouth, and laughed incessantly at every other man. Many beheld these five men, and much wondered why they did these things."

Tale 165

THE SINNERS

WE READ IN THE LIVES OF THE FATHERS, THAT AN ANGEL showed to a certain holy man three men labouring under triple stupidity. The first made a faggot of wood, and because it was too heavy for him to carry he added to it more wood, hoping by such means to make it light. The second drew water with great labour from a very deep well with a sieve, which he incessantly filled. The third carried a beam in his chariot; and wishing to enter his house, whereof the gate was so narrow and low that it would not admit him, he violently whipped his horse, until they both fell together into a deep well.

Having shown this to the holy man, the angel said, "What think you of these three men?"

"That they are three fools," answered he.

"Understand, however," returned the angel, "that they represent the sinners of this world. The first describes that kind of men who, from day to day, add new sins to the old, because they cannot bear the weight of those which they already have. The second man represents those who do good, but do it sinfully, and therefore it is of no benefit. And the third person is he who would enter the kingdom of heaven with all his worldly vanities, but is cast down into hell.

Tale 166

THE GAME OF CHESS

SCHACARIUM [BOARD] HAS SIXTY-FOUR SQUARES, DIVIDED by eight, as husband and wife, bridegroom and bride, clergy and lay, rich and poor. Six men are used at this game. The first is ROCHUS [rook] and it is of two kinds, white and black. The white is placed on the right hand, and the black upon the left. The reason of which is, that when all the SCHACI are fixed in their places, the noble, as well as the vulgar pieces, have certain goals towards which they must proceed.

The ROCHI alone, when they are enclosed, have no power of proceeding unless a way shall be cleared for them either by the higher or lower men. The ROCHUS moves directly across, and never to the corners, whether in going or returning; and if he moves laterally from the other side, and take some piece, he becomes a thief.

The second piece is ALPHINUS [bishop] which passes over three points. For in its proper place, that which is black is fixed to the right of the king, with the white on his left; and they are not called white and black with respect to their colour, but to their situation. Because the black piece, proceeding toward the right, that is, into the black and void space, is stationed before the HUSBANDMAN. But the left, by its own powers, moves two points, the one towards the white space on the right; and the other, towards the white and void space on the left.

Thus also of the third piece to the third square, by preserving its proper situation on the board; so that if it be black, to black and the contrary—proceeding in an angular direction.

The third kind is of Knights, of whom the right is white, and the left black. The white, when on his own square, has three moves—one towards the right in the black place before the HUSBANDMAN; the other in the black and void space before the WOOL-CARDER; the third, towards the left, in the place of a MERCHANT. When this piece is fixed near the king, it may move six squares, and when in the middle, eight. It is the same with the left. When the black is opposite to the king, and the white also opposite, they move together; one is placed before the queen, as the left; the other, before the king, as the right.

The fourth kind is of the inferior pieces [pawns], which have one and the same move. For from the square on which they are placed they may proceed to the third, and there, as in security, remain within reach of the king. But when they go out of the king's move, they are content with one square, and proceed in a direct line. Yet they never return in this manner, but secure by their progress those honours which belong by their position to the nobles. If they should be assisted by the knights and other noble pieces, and arrive at the line of squares where the adversary's nobles are posted, they acquire, by their valour, a power conferred by grace on the queen. But it should be observed that if the inferior pieces, going on the right, find any noble or vulgar adversary, and this in an angle, they may take or kill him on the right or the left; but the inferior piece never moves out of the straight line, to the right or left, unless he has obtained power of the queen.

The fifth piece in the play of the SCHACI is called the Queen. Her move is from white to black, and she is placed near the king; if she quit his side, she is captured. When she has moved from the black square in which she was first placed, she can go only from square to square, and this angularly, whether she go forward or return; whether she take, or is taken. But if it be asked why the queen is exposed to war, when the condition of a female is frail and unwarlike, we reply, when husbands go out to battle, it is customary for their women and wives, and the rest of their family, to live in the camp. And though they do not use a bow, and encumber men more by their whims than they destroy the foe by their valour, yet the queen is intended for the king's help. Therefore, that she may evince her affection, she accompanies him to battle.

The sixth kind of pieces used in this game are the Kings. The king shows above all the rest what is the nature of motion and progression. For since he may reside in the fourth square with the white, though he himself be black, he hath the Knight on the right hand in a white space, but the ALPHINUS and the ROCHUS in the black. In the left he holds opposite places. But though the king has more power and dignity than all the other pieces, it does not become him to move far from his throne; and therefore he begins his move from his own white square, like the ROCHI, from right and left. Yet he cannot be placed on the left in the black space, near the situation of the ROCHUS on the white; but he may go into the white space near the aforesaid ROCHUS in the corner square, where the guards of the city are fixed; and there he hath in such move the nature of the knight. But he takes these two moves in place of the queen.*

Tale 167

THE ARCHER AND THE NIGHTINGALE

AN ARCHER, CATCHING A LITTLE BIRD CALLED A NIGHTINgale, was about to put her to death. But, being gifted with language, she said to him, "What will it gain you to kill me? I cannot satisfy your appetite. Let me go, and I will give you three rules, from which you will derive great benefit, if you follow them accurately."

Astonished at hearing the bird speak, he promised her liberty on the conditions that she had stated.

"Hear, then," said she: "never attempt impossibilities; secondly, do not lament an irrecoverable loss; thirdly, do not

---

* This description of the ancient rules of chess is very obscure and in many points not accurate.

credit things that are incredible. If you keep these three maxims with wisdom, they will infinitely profit you."

The man, faithful to his promise, let the bird escape. Winging her flight through the air, she commenced a most exquisite song; and having finished, said to the archer, "Thou art a silly fellow, and hast to-day lost a great treasure. There is in my bowels a pearl bigger than the egg of an ostrich."

Full of vexation at her escape, he immediately spread his nets and endeavoured to take her a second time; but she eluded his art. "Come into my house, sweet bird!" said he, "and I will show thee every kindness. I will feed thee with my own hands, and permit thee to fly abroad at pleasure."

The nightingale answered, "Now I am certain thou art a fool, and payest no regard to the counsel I gave thee: 'Regret not what is irrecoverable.' Thou canst not take me again, yet thou hast spread thy snares for that purpose. Moreover, thou believest that my bowels contain a pearl larger than the egg of an ostrich, when I myself am nothing near that size! Thou art a fool; and a fool thou wilt always remain."

With this consolatory assurance she flew away. The man returned sorrowfully to his own house, but never again obtained a sight of the nightingale.

Tale 168

THE BLACK PIT AND A DROP OF HONEY

BARLAAM SAYS THAT A SINNER IS LIKE A MAN WHO, BEING afraid of a unicorn, stepped backward into a deep pit. But when he had fallen he laid hold of the branch of a tree, and drew himself up.

Looking below, he espied at the foot of the tree by which

he had ascended a very black well, and a horrible dragon encompassing it. The dragon appeared to expect his fall with extended jaws. Now, the tree was constantly being gnawed by two mice, of which one was white and the other black, and the man felt it shake. There were also four white vipers at its foot, which filled the whole pit with their pestilential breath.

Lifting up his eyes, the man beheld honey dropping from a bough of the tree; and, wholly forgetful of his danger, he gave himself up to the fatal sweetness.

A friend, stretching out to him a ladder, would have raised him entirely out; but, overcome by the allurement, he clung to the tree, which fell, and cast him into the jaws of the dragon. The monster immediately descending to the lowest pit, there devoured him. He thus died a miserable death.

Tale 169

THE TWELVE LAWS

TROGUS POMPEIUS RELATES OF LIGURIUS, A NOBLE KNIGHT, that he induced the inhabitants of the state to make oath that they would faithfully preserve certain just and wholesome, though rather severe laws, until he returned with an answer from the oracle of Apollo, whom he feigned to have made them.

He then went to Crete, and there abode in voluntary exile. But when he was dead, the citizens brought back his bones, imagining that they were then freed from the obligation of their oath.

These laws were twelve in number. The first insisted on obedience to their princes, and enjoined princes to watch over the well-being of their subjects, and to repress wickedness. The second law commanded economy, and considered war better provided for by sobriety than drunkenness. The third law ordained rewards to be proportioned to merit. The fourth laid down that silver and gold were the vilest of all things. The fifth divided the administration of government; empowering kings to make war, magistrates to give judgment, and the senate to try offenders. It also conferred upon the people permission to elect their rulers. The sixth law apportioned lands, and settled disputed claims respecting patrimony, so that no one could become more powerful than another. The seventh enjoined all feasts to be held in public, lest one person should be the cause of luxury to another; the eighth, that young men should have but one habit during the year; the ninth, that poor lads should be employed in the fields, and not in the forum, by which their first years should be spent in hard labour, not in idleness. The tenth law exacted that virgins be married without dowry; the eleventh, that wives be not chosen for money; and the twelfth, that the greatest honour should not be assigned to the greatest wealth, but to priority in years.

And whatever law Ligurius established, he himself observed beyond all others.

Tale 170

SAINT BERNARD AND THE GAMBLER

A CERTAIN GAMBLER MET SAINT BERNARD ON HORSEBACK. "Father," said he, "I will play with you, and stake my soul against your horse."

Immediately Saint Bernard dismounted, and said, "If you

throw more points than I, you shall have my horse; but if
not, I will take possession of your soul."

The gambler acceded; and taking up the dice, threw seventeen points. Thinking himself sure of the victory, he laid
hold of the bridle of Saint Bernard's steed.

"My son," said the holy man, "there are more points than
that in three dice." Accordingly, he threw eighteen points,
one more than the gambler; who forthwith put himself
under the guidance of the saint. After a life of great sanctity,
he came to a happy end, and passed into the joy of his Lord.

Tale 171

THE FRIENDSHIP OF TWO KNIGHTS

PETER ALPHONSUS RELATES A STORY OF TWO KNIGHTS, OF
whom one dwelt in Egypt and the other in Bagdad. Messengers often passed between them; and whatever there was
curious in the land of Egypt, the knight of that country
sent to his friend, and he, in like manner, sent back an equiva-
lent. Thus much kindness was manifested on both sides. But
neither had ever seen the other.

As the knight of Bagdad once lay upon his bed, he held
the following soliloquy:—"My correspondent in Egypt has
discovered much friendship for me; but I have never yet
seen him: I will go and pay him a visit." Accordingly, he
hired a ship and went into Egypt; and his friend, hearing
of his arrival, met him by the way, and received him with
much pleasure. Now, the knight had a very beautiful girl
in his house, with whom the knight of Bagdad was so smitten,
that he fell sick and pined away.

"My friend," said the other, "what is the matter with you?"

"My heart," returned his comrade, "has fixed itself upon one of the women of your household, and unless I may espouse her I shall die."

Upon this, all the household, save the individual in question, were summoned before him: and having surveyed them, he exclaimed, "I care little or nothing for these. But there is one other whom I have not seen; and her my soul loveth." At last this girl was shown to him. He protested that it was to her alone that he must owe his life.

"Sir," said his friend, "I brought this girl up with the intention of making her my wife; and I shall obtain much wealth with her. Nevertheless, so strong is my affection for you, that I give her to you with all the riches which should have fallen to my share."

The sick knight, overjoyed at his good fortune, received the lady and the money, and returned with her to Bagdad.

After a while the knight of Egypt became so extremely poor that he possessed no habitation. "I had better," thought he, "go to my friend of Bagdad, to him whom I enriched, and inform him of my wants." He did so; and reached Bagdad a while after sunset. "It is night," said he to himself; "if I go now to my friend's house, he will not know me, for I am so poorly dressed. I, who once used to have a large household about me, am now desolate and destitute. To-night, therefore, I will rest, and on the morrow will go to his mansion."

Happening to look toward a burial-ground, he observed the gates of a church thrown open, and here he determined to remain for the night. But while he was endeavouring to compose himself to sleep in a court of that place, there entered two men, who engaged in battle; and one was slain. The murderer instantly fled to the burial-ground, and escaped on the other side. By and by an extraordinary clamour penetrated through the whole city.

"Where is the murderer? Where is the traitor?" was the general cry.

"I am he," said our knight; "take me to crucifixion."

They laid hands on him and led him away to prison. Early the next morning the city bell rang, and the judge sentenced him to be crucified. Amongst those who followed to witness his execution was the knight whom he had befriended; and the former, seeing him led towards the cross, knew him at once.

"What!" cried he, "shall he be crucified, and I alive?" Shouting, therefore, with a loud voice, he said, "My friends! destroy not an innocent man. I am the murderer, and not he."

Satisfied with his declaration, they immediately seized him and brought both to the cross. When they were near the place of execution, the real murderer, who happened to be present, thought thus, "I will not permit innocent blood to be shed. The vengeance of God will sooner or later overtake me, and it is better to suffer a short pain in this world than subject myself to everlasting torments in the next." Then lifting up his voice, "My friends! for God's sake, slay not the guiltless. The dead man was killed without premeditation, and without the knowledge of either of these men. I only am the murderer; let these men go."

The crowd, hearing what he said, instantly apprehended and brought him with no little amazement to the judge. The judge, seeing the reputed criminals along with them, asked with surprise why they had returned. They related what had occurred; and the judge, adressing the first knight, said, "Friend, why did you confess yourself the murderer?"

"My lord," answered he, "I will tell you without deceit. In my own land I was rich; and everything that I desired I had. But I lost all this; and possessing neither house nor home, I was ashamed, and sought in this confession to obtain a remedy. I am willing to die; and for Heaven's love command me to be put to death."

The judge then turning to the knight of Bagdad—"And you, my friend! why did you avow yourself the murderer?"

"My lord," replied he, "this knight bestowed upon me a wife, whom he had previously educated for himself, with an infinite store of wealth. When, therefore, I perceived my old and valued friend reduced to such an extremity, and saw him led rudely to the cross, I proclaimed myself the murderer. For his love I would willingly perish."

"Now then," said the judge to the real murderer, "what have you to say for yourself?"

"I have told the truth," answered he. "It would have been a heavy crime, indeed, had I permitted two innocent men to perish by my fault, and I therefore prefer to undergo the penalty here, than to be punished at some other time, or perhaps in hell."

"Well," returned the judge, "since you have declared the truth and saved the lives of the innocent, study to amend your future life; for this time I pardon you—go in peace."

The people unanimously applauded the decision of the judge in acquitting the guilty person, whose magnanimity had rescued two innocent persons from death.

Tale 172

THE KNIGHT GUY OF WARWICK

IN THE REIGN OF A CERTAIN KING OF ENGLAND, THERE were two knights, one of whom was called Guido, and the other Tyrius. The former engaged in many wars, and always triumphed. He was enamoured of a beautiful girl of noble family, but whom he could not prevail upon to marry him, until he had encountered many enemies for her sake.

At last, at the conclusion of a particular exploit, he gained her consent, and married her with great splendour. On the third night succeeding their nuptials, about cock-crowing, he arose from his bed to look upon the sky; and amongst the most lustrous stars he clearly distinguished our Lord Jesus Christ, who said, "Guido, Guido! you have fought much and valiantly for the love of a woman; it is now time that you should encounter my enemies with equal resolution." Having so said, our Lord vanished.

Guido, therefore, perceiving that it was His pleasure to send him to the Holy Land, to avenge Him upon the infidels, returned to his wife. "I go to the Holy Land; should Providence bless us with a child, attend carefully to its education until my return."

The lady, startled at these words, sprung up from the bed as one distracted, and catching a dagger, which was placed at the head of the couch, cried out, "Oh, my lord, I have always loved you, and looked forward with anxiety to our marriage, even when you were in battle, and spreading your fame over all the world; and will you now leave me? First will I stab myself with this dagger."

Guido arose, and took away the weapon. "My beloved," said he, "your words alarm me. I have vowed to God that I will visit the Holy Land. The best opportunity is the present, before old age come upon me. Be not disturbed; I will soon return."

Somewhat comforted with this assurance, she presented to him a ring. "Take this ring, and as often as you look upon it in your pilgrimage, think of me. I will await with patience your return."

The knight bade her farewell, and departed in company with Tyrius. As for the lady, she gave herself up to her sorrows for many days, and would not be consoled. In due time she brought forth a son of extreme beauty, and tenderly watched over his infant years.

Guido and Tyrius, in the mean while, passed through many countries, and heard at last that the kingdom of Dacia had been subdued by the infidels. "My friend," said Guido to his associate, "do you enter this kingdom; and since the king of it is a Christian, assist him with all your power. I will proceed to the Holy Land; and when I have combated against the foes of Christ, I will return to you, and we will joyfully retrace our steps to England."

"Whatever pleases you," replied his friend, "shall please me. I will enter this kingdom; and if you live, come to me. We will return together to our country."

Guido promised; and exchanging kisses, they separated with much regret. The one proceeded to the Holy Land, and the other to Dacia. Guido fought many battles against the Saracens, and was victorious in all; so that his fame flew to the ends of the earth. Tyrius, in like manner, proved fortunate in war, and drove the infidels from the Dacian territory. The king loved and honoured him above all others, and conferred on him great riches.

But there was at that time a savage nobleman, called Plebeus, in whose heart the prosperity of Tyrius excited an inordinate degree of hate and envy. He accused him to the king of treason, and malevolently insinuated that he designed to make himself master of the kingdom. The king credited the assertion, and ungratefully robbed Tyrius of all the honours which his bounty had conferred. Tyrius, therefore, was reduced to extreme want, and had scarcely the common sustenance of life.

Thus desolate, he gave free course to his griefs; and exclaimed in great tribulation, "Wretch that I am! what will become of me?"

While he was taking a solitary walk in sorrow, Guido, journeying alone in the habit of a pilgrim, met him by the way, and knew him, but was not recognized by his friend. He, however, presently remembered Tyrius, and retaining his disguise, approached him, and said, "My friend, from whence are you?"

"From foreign parts," answered Tyrius, "but I have now been many years in this country. I had once a companion in arms, who proceeded to the Holy Land; but if he be alive or dead I know not, nor what have been his fortunes."

"For the love of thy companion, then," said Guido, "suffer me to rest my head upon your lap, and sleep a little, for I am very weary." He assented, and Guido fell asleep.

Now, while he slept, his mouth stood open; and as Tyrius looked, he discovered a white weasel pass out of it, and run towards a neighbouring mountain, which it entered. After remaining there a short space, it returned, and again ran down the sleeper's throat.

Guido straightway awoke, and said, "My friend, I have had a wonderful dream! I thought a weasel went out of my mouth, and entered yon mountain, and after that returned."

"Sir," answered Tyrius, "what you have seen in a dream I beheld with my own eyes. But what that weasel did in the mountain, I am altogether ignorant."

"Let us go and look," observed the other; "perhaps we may find something useful."

Accordingly, they entered the place which the weasel had been seen to enter, and found there a dead dragon filled with gold. There was a sword also, of peculiar polish, and inscribed as follows: "BY MEANS OF THIS SWORD, GUIDO SHALL OVERCOME THE ADVERSARY OF TYRIUS."

Rejoiced at the discovery, the disguised pilgrim said, "My

friend, the treasure is thine, but the sword I will take into my own possession."

"My lord," he answered, "I do not deserve so much gold; why should you bestow it upon me?"

"Raise your eyes," said Guido. "I am your friend!"

Hearing this, he looked at him more narrowly; and when he recollected his heroic associate, he fell upon the earth for joy, and wept exceedingly. "It is enough; I have lived enough, now that I have seen you."

"Rise," returned Guido, "rise quickly; you ought to rejoice rather than weep at my coming. I will combat your enemy, and we will proceed honourably to England. But tell no one who I am."

Tyrius arose, fell upon his neck, and kissed him. He then collected the gold, and hastened to his home; but Guido knocked at the gate of the king's palace. The porter inquired the cause, and he informed him that he was a pilgrim newly arrived from the Holy Land. He was immediately admitted, and presented to the king, at whose side sat the nobleman who had deprived Tyrius of his honours and wealth. "Is the Holy Land at peace?" inquired the monarch.

"Peace is now firmly established," replied Guido, "and many have been converted to Christianity."

"Did you see an English knight there, called Guido, who has fought so many battles?"

"I have seen him often, my lord, and have eaten with him."

"Is any mention made of the Christian kings?"

"Yes, my lord; and of you also. It is said that the Saracens and other infidels had taken possession of your kingdom, and that from their hands you were delivered by the valour of a noble knight, named Tyrius, afterwards promoted to great honour and riches. It is likewise said that you unjustly deprived this same Tyrius of what you had conferred, at the malevolent instigation of a knight called Plebeus."

"False pilgrim!" said Plebeus, "since thou presumest to utter these lies, hast thou courage enough to defend them? If so, I offer thee battle. That very Tyrius would have dethroned the king. He was a traitor, and therefore lost his honours."

"My lord, since he has been pleased to say that I am a false pilgrim, and that Tyrius is a traitor, I demand the combat. I will prove upon his body that he lies."

"I am well pleased with your determination: nay, I entreat you not to desist," answered the king.

"Furnish me with arms, then, my lord."

"Whatever you want shall be got ready for you."

The king then appointed a day of battle; and fearing lest the pilgrim Guido should in the mean time fall by treachery, he called to him his daughter, a virgin, and said, "As you love the life of that pilgrim, watch over him, and let him want for nothing."

In compliance, therefore, with her father's wish, she brought him into her own chamber, bathed him, and supplied him with every requisite.

On the day of battle Plebeus armed himself, and standing at the gate, exclaimed, "Where is that false pilgrim? Why does he tarry?"

Guido, hearing what was said, put on his armour, and hastened to the lists. They fought so fiercely, that Plebeus would have died had he not drank. Addressing his antagonist, he said, "Good pilgrim, let me have one draught of water."

"I consent," answered Guido, "provided you faithfully promise to use the same courtesy to me, should I require it."

"I promise," replied the other. Having quenched his thirst, he rushed on Guido, and they continued the battle with redoubled animosity. By and by, however, Guido himself thirsted, and required the same courtesy to be shown him as he had exhibited.

"I vow to Heaven," answered his enemy, "that you shall taste nothing, except by the strong hand."

At this ungrateful return, Guido, defending himself as well as he could, approached the water, leaped in, and drank as much as he wished. Then springing out, he rushed upon the treacherous Plebeus like a raging lion, who at last sought refuge in flight.

The king, observing what passed, caused them to be separated, and to rest for that night, that in the morning they might be ready to renew the contest. The pilgrim then reentered his chamber, and received from the king's daughter all the kindness it was in her power to display. She bound up his wounds, prepared supper, and placed him upon a strong wooden bed. Wearied with the exertions of the day, he fell asleep.

Now, Plebeus had seven sons, all strong men. He sent for them, and spoke thus: "My dear children, I give you to understand that, unless this pilgrim be destroyed to-night, I may reckon myself among the dead to-morrow. I never looked upon a braver man."

"My dear father," said one, "we will presently get rid of him."

About midnight, therefore, they entered the girl's chamber, where the pilgrim slept, and beneath which the sea flowed. They said to one another, "If we destroy him in bed, we are no better than dead men; let us toss him, bed and all, into the sea. It will be thought that he has fled."

This scheme was approved; and accordingly they took up the sleeping warrior, and hurled him into the waves. He slept on, however, without perceiving what had happened. The same night a fisherman, following his occupation, heard the fall of the bed, and by the light of the moon saw him floating upon the water. Much surprised, he called out, "In the name of God, who are you? Speak, that I may render assistance, before the waves swallow you up."

Guido, awoke by the clamour, arose, and perceiving the sky and stars above, and the ocean beneath, wondered where he was. "Good friend," said he to the fisherman, "assist me and I will amply reward you. I am the pilgrim who fought in the lists; but how I got hither, I have no conception."

The man, hearing this, took him into his vessel, and conveyed him to his house, where he rested till the morning.

The sons of Plebeus, in the mean while, related what they thought the end of the pilgrim and bade their parent discard his fear. The latter, much exhilarated, arose, and armed himself; and going to the gate of the palace, called out, "Bring forth that pilgrim, that I may complete my revenge."

The king commanded his daughter to awake and prepare him for battle. Accordingly, she went into his room, but he was not to be found. She wept bitterly, exclaiming that some-one had conveyed away her treasure; and the surprise occasioned by the intelligence was not less, when it became known that his bed was also missing. Some said that he had fled; others, that he was murdered.

Plebeus, however, continued his clamour at the gate. "Bring out your pilgrim; to-day I will present his head to the king."

Now, while all was bustle and inquiry in the palace, the fisherman made his way to the royal seat, and said, "Grieve not, my lord, for the loss of the pilgrim. Fishing last night in the sea, I observed him floating upon a bed. I took him on board my vessel, and he is now asleep at my house."

This news greatly cheered the king, and he immediately sent to him to prepare for a renewal of the contest. But Plebeus, terrified, and apprehensive of the consequence, besought a truce. This was denied, even for a single hour.

Both, therefore, re-entered the lists, and each struck twice;

but at the third blow Guido cut off his opponent's arm, and afterwards his head. He presented it to the king, who evinced himself well satisfied with the event; and hearing that the sons of Plebeus were instruments in the treachery, he caused them to be crucified.

The pilgrim was loaded with honours, and offered immense wealth if he would remain with the king, which he resolutely declined. Through him Tyrius was reinstated in his former dignity, and recompensed for his past suffering. He then bade the king farewell.

"Good friend," returned the monarch, "for the love of Heaven, leave me not ignorant of your name."

"My lord," answered he, "I am that Guido of whom you have often heard."

Overjoyed at this happy discovery, the king fell upon his neck, and promised him a large part of his dominions if he would remain. But he could not prevail; and the warrior, after returning his friendly salutation, departed.

Guido embarked for England, and hastened to his own castle. He found a great number of paupers standing about his gate; and amongst them, habited as a pilgrim, sat the countess, his wife. Every day did she thus minister to the poor, bestowing a penny upon each, with a request that he would pray for the safety of her husband Guido, that once more, before death, she might rejoice in his presence.

It happened, on the very day of his return, that his son, now seven years of age, sat with his mother among the mendicants, sumptuously apparelled. When he heard his mother address the person who experienced her bounty in the manner mentioned above, "Mother," said he, "is it not my father whom you recommend to the prayers of these poor people?"

"It is, my son," replied she; "the third night following our marriage he left me, and I have never seen him since."

Now, as the lady walked among her dependents, who were

ranged in order, she approached her own husband Guido, and gave him alms—but she knew not who he was. He bowed his head in acknowledgment, fearful lest his voice should disclose him. As the countess walked, her son followed; and Guido raising his eyes and seeing his offspring, whom he had not before seen, he could not contain himself. He caught him in his arms, and kissed him.

"My darling child," said he, "may the Lord give thee grace to do that which is pleasing in His eyes."

The damsels of the lady, observing the emotion and action of the pilgrim, called to him and bade him stand there no longer. He approached his wife's presence, and without making himself known, entreated of her permission to occupy some retired place in the neighbouring forest; and she, supposing that he was the pilgrim he appeared to be, for the love of God and of her husband built him a hermitage, and there he remained a long time. But being on the point of death, he called his attendant, and said, "Go quickly to the countess; give her that ring, and say that if she wishes to see me, she must come hither with all speed."

The messenger went accordingly, and delivered the ring. As soon as she had seen it, she exclaimed, "It is my lord's ring!" and with a fleet foot hurried into the forest. But Guido was dead.

She fell upon the corpse, and with a loud voice cried, "Woe is me! my hope is extinct!" and then with sighs and lamentations continued, "Where are now the alms I distributed in behalf of my lord? I beheld my husband receive my gifts with his own hands, and knew him not. And as for thee" (addressing the dead body), "thou sawest thy child, and touchedst him. Thou didst kiss him, and yet revealedst not thyself to me! What hast thou done? Oh, Guido! Guido! never shall I see thee more!"

She sumptuously interred his body; and bewailed his decease for many days.

Tale 173

ALLEGORY OF THE FAIR

A CERTAIN KING ONCE WENT TO A FAIR, AND TOOK WITH him a teacher and his scholar. Standing in the market-place, they perceived eight packages exposed for sale. The scholar questioned his teacher respecting the first of them. "Pray," said he, "what is the price of poverty—that is, of tribulation for the love of God?"

"The kingdom of heaven," answered the teacher.

"It is a great price indeed. Open the second package, and let us see what it contains."

"It contains meekness; blessed are the meek."

"Meekness, indeed, is a very illustrious thing, and worthy of divine majesty. What is its price?" asked the scholar.

"Gold shall not be given for it; nor shall silver be weighed against it. I demand earth for it; and nothing but earth will I receive."

"There is a spacious tract of uninhabited country between India and Britain. Take as much of it as you please," replied the scholar.

"No; this land is the land of the dying, the land which devours its inhabitants. Men die there. I demand the land of the living."

"I muse at what you say. All die, and would you alone be exempt? Would you live for ever? Behold, blessed are the meek, for they shall inherit the EARTH. What is there in the third package?"

"Hunger and thirst," answered the teacher.

"For how much may these be purchased?"

"For righteousness. Blessed are they who hunger and thirst after righteousness, for they shall be filled."

"Therefore you shall possess righteousness, provided there be no neglect. What does the fourth contain?"

"Tears, wailings, and woe; Moisture above, and moisture below," said the teacher.

"It is not customary to buy tears and wailings, yet I will buy it; because the saints desire it at this price. Blessed are they who mourn, for they shall be comforted. What is the fifth package?"

"It is a precious thing, and contains mercy, which I will weigh to please you. At a word, I will take mercy for mercy, eternity for time."

"You were a bad umpire to ask this, unless mercy should plead for you. Nevertheless, she shall become your surety. And blessed are the merciful for they shall obtain mercy. In this life we abound in poverty and wretchedness and hardship. Undo the sixth package; perhaps it may contain something better."

"It is clearly full; but it loves not, like a purple robe, to be exposed before the common eye; you shall see it in private, and there we will agree about the price."

"Very well; what is it?" inquired the scholar.

"Purity; which is extremely valuable. There are gold and silver vases, namely, piety, goodness, charity, and spiritual joy. Now, then, let us open these precious garments. Here are lectures, meditations, prayers, and contemplations. The judgments of the Lord are justified in themselves and more to be desired than gold and precious stones."

"There is a great reward in the possession. Ask, therefore, what ye will."

"To see God."

"Therefore, blessed are the pure in heart, for they shall see God. Open the seventh package."

"It contains *peace*," said the teacher.

"What! are you going to sell me your peace?"

"It does not accord with my poverty, nor would it with your justice and great wealth, to take anything of me for nothing. But your liberality will make me rich. What then? I am a mean country fellow, and made of clay; formed of the very dust of the earth. My want of nobility oppresses me, and I would no longer bear the reproach which says, 'You are earth, and to earth you shall go.' I would rather have it said to me, 'You are heaven, and to heaven you shall go.' I eagerly desire to fulfil the destiny of the sons of God; I would become a son of God."

"I have done: I confess the truth, and distrust you no longer," said the scholar. "Blessed are the peace-makers, for they shall be called the sons of God. If, therefore, you preserve the love of a son, you shall receive the paternal inheritance. Now, what is contained in the last package? Explain it."

"It contains only tribulation and persecution for the sake of righteousness."

"And what do you want for it?" asked the scholar.

"The kingdom of heaven."

"I gave you that as the price of poverty!"

"True; but month after month, week after week, man wanders in his wishes. You are mistaken; I ask this for the present week or month; as to the future I wait humbly," said the teacher.

"I marvel at your sagacity in making a bargain. Now hear, good and faithful servant! because thou hast been faithful over a few things, I will appoint thee lord over many: enter thou into the joy of thy lord."

Tale 174

THE KING, THE SERPENT, AND THE PHILOSOPHER

AN EMPEROR RODE OUT IN THE AFTERNOON TO HUNT. HAP-pening to pass a certain wood, he heard a serpent, which some shepherds had caught and bound firmly to a tree, making a most horrible clamour. Moved by pity, he loosed it, and warmed its frozen body in his own bosom. No sooner, how-ever, did the animal find itself recovered, than it began to bite its benefactor, and shot a flood of poison into the wound.

"What hast thou done?" said the emperor. "Wherefore have you rendered evil for good?"

The serpent, like the ass of Balaam, being suddenly en-dowed with voice, replied, "The tendencies which nature has implanted no one can destroy. You have done what you could; and I have only acted according to my nature. You exhibited towards me all the kindness in your power, and I have recompensed you as well as I might. I offered poison, be-cause, except poison, I had nothing to offer. Moreover, I am an enemy to man; for through him I became punished with a curse."

As they thus contended, they entreated a philosopher to judge between them, and to state which was in the wrong.

"I know these matters," answered the umpire, "only by your relation; but I should like to see the thing itself upon which I am to pronounce judgment. Let the serpent, there-fore, be bound to the tree, as he was in the first instance, and let my lord the emperor remain unbound; I shall then de-termine the matter between you." This was done accord-ingly.

"Now you are bound," said the philosopher, addressing the serpent, "loose yourself if you can."

"I cannot," said the serpent; "I am bound so fast that I can scarcely move."

"Then die," rejoined the philosopher, "by a just sentence. You were always ungrateful to man, and you always will be. My lord, you are now free; shake the venom from your bosom, and go your way: do not repeat your folly. Remember that the serpent is only influenced by his natural propensities."

The emperor thanked the philosopher for his assistance and advice, and departed.

Tale 175

OF THE WONDERS OF THE WORLD

PLINY SAYS THAT THERE ARE CERTAIN MEN WHO HAVE THE heads of dogs; who bark when they converse, and clothe themselves in the skins of animals. These represent preachers, who ought to be coarsely clad, as an example to others. Also in India there are men who possess a single eye, which is placed in the forehead. They live upon the flesh of animals. These are they who have the eye of reason.

In Africa there are women without heads, having eyes and mouth in their breasts. Such are like humble men. In the East, over against the terrestrial Paradise, are people who never eat, and whose mouth is so small that what they drink is conveyed into the stomach by means of a reed. They live upon the odour of apples and flowers; and a bad smell instantly destroys them. These are abstemious men; and to die of an ill odour is to die of sin. There are men without a nose, but otherwise with complete faces; and whatsoever they see they think good. Such are the foolish of the world. And there are some whose nose and lower lip is so long, that it covers all the face, while they sleep. These are just men.

In Scythia are men with ears that completely envelop their whole body. These represent such as listen to the word of God. Some men there are who walk like cattle, and these are they who honour neither God nor His saints. There are likewise people who are horned, having short noses and the feet of a goat. These are the proud.

In Ethiopia are men with but one leg, whose velocity nevertheless is such, that they run down the swiftest animal. These are the charitable. In India are pygmies two cubits long; they ride upon goats, and make war against the cranes. These are they who begin well, but cease before they are perfect. In India there are also men who possess six hands. They are without clothes, but are extremely hairy, and dwell in rivers. These are the zealous workers who labour and obtain eternal life. There, too, are men who have six fingers on each hand, and six toes on each foot; during the week they keep themselves pure, and on the seventh day sanctify themselves. Certain women there are bearded to the breast; but their heads are totally bare. These represent men who obey the Church, and are turned from that course neither by love nor by hatred.

In Ethiopia there are men with four eyes each. These are they who fear God, the world, the devil, and the flesh. They turn one eye to God, to live well; another to the world, to flee from it; a third to the devil, to resist him; and the last to the flesh, to chastise it. In Europe are very beautiful men; but they have a crane's head, and neck, and beak. These designate judges, who ought to have long necks and beaks, in order that what the heart thinks may be long before it reach the mouth. If all judges were thus we should have fewer injudicious awards.

Tale 176

THE DIVIDED CHILD AND THE POISONED TREE

THERE WAS A MALE CHILD BORN, DIVIDED FROM THE NAVEL upward. Thus he had two heads and breasts, and a proper number of sensitive faculties to each. While one slept or ate, the other did neither. After two years, one part of the boy died, and the other survived about three days.

Also, as Pliny records, there was a tree in India whose flowers had a sweet smell, and its fruit a delightful flavour. A serpent, called Jacorlus, which dwelt near, had a great aversion to the odour, and that he might destroy its productiveness poisoned the root of the tree.

The gardener, observing what was done, took an antidote of that country, and inserted it in a branch at the top of the tree, which presently drove the poison from the root. The tree, before barren, was now loaded with fruit.

Tale 177

QUEEN HESTER

KING ASUERUS MADE A GREAT FEAST TO ALL THE PRINCES of his kingdom. He commanded the queen, Vasti, to appear at the festival, that his people might behold the splendour of that beauty which he had raised to the throne. When she refused to come in, the king deprived her of her royalty, and raised Hester to the rank of queen in her stead.

After this the king promoted a certain Aman, and made all the princes of his empire pay him homage. They complied; but Mardocheus, the king's uncle, would not honour him. Enraged at this disregard of his authority, Aman delivered him to death, with all his family, and made an ordinance under the royal seal to exterminate every Jew in the kingdom; and constructing a high gibbet, he resolved that Mardocheus should be fastened upon it.

But, in the mean time, it was the fortune of the latter to discover two traitors who had conspired to kill the king; and immediately giving such information as led to their apprehension, he was clothed in a purple robe and crowned, and rode on a royal steed through the city, while Aman, with all his knights, were reduced to the necessity of extolling him.

When this was done, Mardocheus related to the queen that Aman intended to put all their nation to death; wherefore she proclaimed a fast, and afflicted herself with fasting and prayer. She then made a great feast, to which she invited the king and Aman. First imploring the life of her people, she explained how the latter had condemned all to death. Full of indignation, the king ordered him to be fixed upon the same gibbet which he had prepared for Mardocheus, who succeeded to all his honours.

Thus, by the disposing hand of Providence, the innocent people were freed, and the generation of the wicked utterly exterminated.

Tale 178

THE PAINTER INSTRUCTS HIS KING

A CERTAIN KING WAS DESIROUS OF ASCERTAINING THE BEST mode of governing himself and his empire. He therefore called to him one more excellent in wisdom than the rest, and required of him to impart some rule by which he might attain his wishes.

"Willingly, my lord," replied he; and immediately upon a wall he painted the king, crowned, sitting on a throne and habited in a purple robe. His left hand supported a globe, while his right held a sceptre; above his head was a light burning. On the left was the queen, crowned also, and clad in golden vesture. The other side was occupied by counsellors seated in chairs, and before them an open book. In front of these was an armed knight on horseback, having a helmet on his head, and a lance in his right hand. The shield covered him on the left, and a sword hung by his side. His body was cased in mail, having clasps upon the breast. Iron greaves protected his legs; spurs were upon his heels, and iron gauntlets on his hands. His horse, practised in war, was gorgeously trapped. Beneath the king were his deputies; one, as an equestrian knight, in cloak and cap of parti-coloured skins, bearing an extended rod in his right hand.

The people stood before the deputies in the form following:—One man carried a spade in his right hand, wherewith he was digging, and in his left a rod, with which he directed the motions of a herd. In his girdle hung a sickle, with which corn is cut and vines and other trees pruned. To the right of the king a carpenter was painted before a knight; one hand bore a mallet, and the other an axe; in his girdle was a trowel. Also, before the people stood a man having a pair of pincers in one hand, and in the other a huge sword; with a note-book and a bottle of ink in his girdle, a pen stuck in his right ear. Moreover, in the same part of the painting was a man bearing a balance and weights in his right hand, and an ell-wand in his left; a purse containing various kinds of money hung at his girdle.

Before the queen were physicians and colourmen under this form. A man was placed in a master's chair with a book in his right hand, and an urn and box in his left; an instrument for probing sores and wounds was in his girdle. Near him stood another, with his right hand elevated to invite the passengers to his inn; his left was full of exceedingly fair bread; and above stood a vessel full of wine; his girdle held a bunch of keys. Also on the left side, before a knight, was a man with large keys in his right hand, and an ell-wand in his left; at his girdle was a purse filled with pennies.

Before the king, also, was a man with rugged and disorderly hair; in his right hand was a little money, and three dice were in his left; his girdle held a box full of letters.

When the king had attentively considered this picture, he found it filled with wisdom.

Tale 179

OF THE EVILS ARISING FROM GLUTTONY AND DRUNKENNESS

CESARIUS, SPEAKING OF THE DETESTABLE VICES OF GLUTTONY and drunkenness, says that the throat is the most intemperate and seductive part of the whole body. Its daughters are uncleanness, buffoonery, foolish joy, babbling, and dulness.

It has five grades of sin. The first is, to inquire for high-seasoned and delicate food; the second, to dress it curiously; the third, to take it before there is occasion; the fourth, to take it too greedily; and the fifth, in too large a quantity.

The first man, Adam, was conquered by gluttony; and for this Esau gave away his birth-right. This excited the people of Sodom to sin, and overthrew the children of Israel in the wilderness.

So the Psalmist, "While the meat was yet in their mouths, the anger of God came upon them."

The iniquity of Sodom arose in its superabundance; and the man of God, who was sent to Bethel, was slain by a lion in consequence of indulging his appetite. Dives, of whom it is said in the Gospel that he feasted sumptuously every day, was buried in hell. Nabusardan, the prince of cooks, destroyed Jerusalem.

How great the danger of gluttony is, let the Scriptures testify. "Woe to the land," says Solomon, "whose princes eat in the morning." Again, "All the labour of man in the mouth will not fill his soul."

The daughter of gluttony is drunkenness; for that vice is the author of luxury—the worst of all plagues. What is there fouler than this? What more hurtful? What sooner wears away virtue? Glory laid asleep is converted to madness; and the strength of the mind, equally with the strength of the body, is destroyed.

Basilius says, "When we serve the belly and throat, we are cattle; and study to resemble brutes which are prone to this, and made by nature to look upon the earth and obey the belly." Boethius also, *De Consolatione*: "He who forsakes virtue ceases to be a man; and since he cannot pass to the divine nature, it remains that he must become a brute." And our Lord, in the Gospel: "Take heed lest your hearts be hardened with surfeiting and drunkenness."

Oh, how great had been the counsels of wisdom, if the heats of wine and greediness interposed not. Dangerous is it when the father of a family, or the governor of a state, is warm with wine, and inflamed with anger. Discretion is dimmed, luxury is excited, and lust, mixing itself with all kinds of wickedness, lulls prudence asleep.

Wherefore, said Ovidius, "Wine produces lust if taken too copiously." Oh, odious vice of drunkenness! by which virginity—the possession of all good things—the security of happiness—is lost for ever and ever.

Noah, heated with wine, exposed himself to his children. The most chaste Lot, thrown by wine into sleep, did that which was evil in the sight of the Lord.

We read of men, who were such firm friends that each would expose his life for the other, becoming so inflamed with wine that they slew one another. Herod Antipas had not decapitated the holy John, if he had kept from the feast of surfeiting and drunkenness. Balthasar, king of Babylon, had not been deprived of his life and throne, if he had been sober on the night in which Cyrus and Darius slew him, overpowered with wine. On which account the Apostle advises us to be "sober and watch."

Let us then pray to the Lord to preserve us in all sobriety, that we may hereafter be invited to a feast in heaven.

Tale 180

HOW THE KNIGHT SAVED HIS MASTER

PAULUS, THE HISTORIAN OF THE LONGOBARDS, MENTIONS a certain Onulphus, surnamed Papien, a knight who gave signal proofs of fidelity to his master, King Portaticus; insomuch that he exposed himself to death for his safety. For when Grimmoaldus, duke of Beneventum, forcibly entered the pavilion of Godobert, king of the Longobards, who had been treacherously slain by Geribaldus, duke of Ravenna, the first betrayer of a royal crown, Portaticus, the brother of the aforesaid king Godobert, flying to the Hungarians, was reconciled to Grimmoaldus by the knight Onulphus, so that without fear he might quit Hungary and solicit pardon at the king's feet.

Thus his life was secure, although he obtained not the

regal dignity which was his due. But a few days after this reconciliation, some malicious tongues disposed Grimmoaldus to put to death Portaticus.

To get rid of him the more easily, and prevent his seeking safety in flight, he commanded that wine should be served to him, that he might become intoxicated.

Onulphus hearing this, went, with his squire, to the house of Portaticus; and leaving his attendant in bed, concealed with the coverture, he led out Portaticus, disguised as his squire, threatening, and even striking him, the better to cover the deceit. Thus they passed through the watch or guard, placed before the house of Portaticus, till they reached the abode of the knight, which was built upon the city walls.

He then hastened to let him down by a rope; and catching certain horses from the pasture, Portaticus fled to the city of Astensis, and from thence to the king of France.

In the morning Onulphus and his squire were brought before the king, and examined as to the escape of their master. They answered exactly as the case was; and Grimmoaldus, turning to his counsellors, said, "What punishment do they deserve who have done this, contrary to our royal pleasure?" All agreed that it should be capital. Some protested that they should be flayed alive; and others, that they should be crucified.

"By Him that made me," replied the king, "they are deserving of honour, not death, for their unshaken fidelity."

Acting up to this feeling, Grimmoaldus loaded them with favours; but Geribaldus the traitor was miserable, though justly slain by the hand of Godobert's squire, the follower of him whom he had treacherously deprived of life and kingdom.

This happened on the solemn festivel of Saint John the Baptist.

Tale 181

THE UNFAITHFUL LIONESS

A CERTAIN KING HAD A LION, A LIONESS, AND A LEOPARD, whom he much delighted in. During the absence of the lion, the lioness was unfaithful, and colleagued with the leopard; and that she might prevent her mate's discovery of the crime, she used to wash herself in a fountain adjoining the king's castle.

Now, the king, having often perceived what was going forward, commanded the fountain to be closed. This done, the lioness was unable to cleanse herself; and the lion returning, and ascertaining the injury that had been done him, assumed the place of a judge—sentenced her to death, and immediately executed the sentence.

END